ONE G EASON

S

MILLS & BOON®

All the characters in this book have no existence outside the imagination of the author, and have no relation whatsoever to anyone bearing the same name or names. They are not even distantly inspired by any individual known or unknown to the author, and all the incidents are pure invention.

First published in Great Britain 2012
by Mills & Boon, an imprint of Harlequin (UK) Limited,
Eton House, 18-24 Paradise Road, Richmond, Surrey TW9 1SR

2in1 ISBN: 978 0 263 89423 3

23-0412

Harlequin (UK) policy is to use papers that are natural, renewable and recyclable products and made from wood grown in sustainable forests. The logging and manufacturing processes conform to the legal environmental regulations of the country of origin.

Printed and bound in Spain
by Blackprint CPI, Barcelona

Sarah Mayberry lives by the seaside in Melbourne, Australia. She has recently married her partner of eighteen years and is enjoying their new home and fabulous but exhausting garden. Her goal for the next year is to learn how to prune the thirty-two different fruit and nut trees on their property and to be more organized. When she's not writing, she loves to cook, sleep, shop, read and watch movies. She really wishes going to the gym made it onto the "loves" list, but she makes herself go anyway. Long live ice cream!

I have to thank my husband for his endless patience
with me while I was writing this book.

That deadline was some doozy, my darling, but you fed and watered me and mopped my fevered brow and I thank you from the bottom of my heart for your kindness and support.
Where would I be without you?
In my book, you are the ultimate hero.

I also want to thank Wanda for her endless faith in me—you said I could do it and I did. Phew!

PROLOGUE

January

JON ADAMSON WOKE WITH A START. Someone was in his room. A heartbeat later, he was on his feet, fists raised, every muscle tense as he squared up to the intruder.

"Mate." His brother held up his hands, took a step backward. "It's just me."

Jon dropped his fists. "You should have knocked."

"I did." Tyler's gaze flicked to the half-empty bottle of bourbon beside the bed. "Several times."

The light was hazy in the room. Jon tried to guess the time. Nine in the morning? Ten? He reached for the jeans he'd dumped at the end of the bed when he'd finally crashed last night.

"I was up pretty late."

He wasn't about to offer explanations for the bourbon or anything else. A man could have a few drinks at the end of the day. Besides, Tyler was the younger brother—it was Jon's job to be the heavy, not the other way around.

"What are you doing up this way?" he asked as he stepped into his jeans.

Jon had been back in Australia, living in their late father's house in the rural Victorian town of Woodend for eleven months now. Tyler lived an hour and a half away in Melbourne, so the two of them didn't cross paths very often. Not that that would have changed even if they were geographically closer. They'd never been the kind of brothers who lived in each other's pockets—witness the ten years Jon had spent in Canada.

"I hadn't heard from you for a while. Thought I'd better check in."

Jon pulled his T-shirt over his head, aware of the unspoken questions behind his brother's words.

Why didn't you return my phone messages? What's going on?

"I've been busy."

"Yeah, I saw that. When did you knock down the wall between the kitchen and living room?"

"Figured both rooms would benefit from the light. It's all about open plan these days."

"What happened to tidying up the yard and giving the place a lick of paint before we listed it?"

"If you're that desperate for the money, I can get a valuation done. Pay out your half."

"It's not about the money."

Jon walked toward the door. "Yeah? What's it about, then?"

Tyler followed him to the kitchen. Jon had pulled up the old linoleum tiles and the boards were rough beneath his feet. He sidestepped the hole where he'd removed a rotten plank and crossed to the sink. Turning on the tap, he sluiced handfuls of cold water onto his face.

Tyler was looking around, inspecting the gaping holes in the plaster where the kitchen cabinets had once hung. The only remaining features of the original kitchen was the sink unit, the freestanding stove and the fridge. And they'd be gone any day now, too.

"I suppose you've gutted the bathroom, too?"

"Everything except the toilet and shower recess."

Tyler's gaze was knowing. "Wouldn't it have been easier to knock the place down?"

"I'm fixing it up for resale. We both agreed it needed work before we put it on the market."

"Mate, you're demolishing it from the inside out."

"The kitchen needed updating. The bloody thing hadn't been touched since the fifties. And the bathroom was leaking into the subfloor. You can see the joists I had to replace if you want to."

Tyler didn't say anything, but he didn't look away, either.

Jon could feel his hackles rising. Tyler was making a big deal out of this, reading things into Jon's actions. Whatever Tyler thought was going on, he was wrong. Way wrong.

Jon crossed his arms over his chest, widened his stance. "I'm doing you and Ally a favor. You'll make a lot more with this place fixed up than you would have if we'd put it on the market as it was."

"Will you quit it with the money? I don't give a damn how much we make. I'm here because of you."

"I'm fine."

"Yeah? You looked in a mirror lately? When was the last time you shaved or had a haircut?"

Jon brushed a hand over his bristly jaw. "I've been busy."

"Too busy to eat? Because you look like a bag of bones."

"I'm *fine*."

"Which is why Ally got a call from Wendy in the middle of the night on Monday, telling her it sounded like you were holding a demolition derby."

Wendy was the next-door neighbor. Until this moment, Jon had thought she was all right. He'd even tried to talk her into bed a few times, but she was seeing some computer guy.

"I was taking the wall out," Jon said.

"At two in the morning?"

"If I woke her, I'll apologize."

"And what about all the bottles in the recycling bin?"

Jon's eyes narrowed. His brother was quite the amateur sleuth. "I'd say that gets filed under 'none of your business,' same as everything else."

"Doesn't work that way, sorry. I'm not going to stand by and watch you kill yourself over an old bastard who wasn't worth it."

"This has nothing to do with him." But he could barely get the words past the sudden tightness in his throat.

"You think if you change enough of this place it'll change what happened?"

"I think you've been living with an advice columnist for too long."

Tyler eyed him for a long beat. Then he tilted his head to one side and nodded slowly, a gesture which Jon read as conceding defeat.

Good. He didn't need a keeper.

As for the things Tyler had said… This had nothing to do with the old man. It had nothing to do with anything.

"I told Ally you wouldn't listen," Tyler said.

He crossed to the kitchen door and collected something from the hall.

An overnight bag.

It took a moment for the penny to drop.

"No," Jon said.

"I figure if we both pitch in, we can get this place

finished in a few weeks. Get it on the market. Then you can go back to Toronto or wherever. Get away from here."

Jon swore. "I don't want you here."

"Tough."

"I don't need a babysitter."

"Then stop acting like you do."

Jon breathed in slowly through his nose and out through his mouth. It didn't make much difference—he still wanted to smash a hole in something.

He strode across the room, picked up the overnight bag. Started for the door. Maybe once he'd tossed Tyler's gear into the street his brother would get the message that his intervention was neither welcome nor necessary.

Tyler blocked his path. Jon stopped short of barging into his brother's shoulder. He met Tyler's gaze. There was determination there. And something else.

Compassion.

It made Jon's hand curl into a fist.

"Get out of my way."

"I'm not leaving unless you come with me," Tyler said. "Come to Melbourne, move into the spare room. Get away from this place."

"Get out of my way."

Tyler didn't move. Jon reached to push his brother out of his path. Tyler resisted, grabbing a fistful of Jon's T-shirt as he attempted to hold him off. Years ago, Jon would have been able to shift his brother easily, but Tyler was a man now, and they'd both inherited their father's big build.

Jon braced his legs, shoving harder. Tyler shoved back. For long moments they struggled, locked together.

In any other fight, it would have come to blows by now, but Jon was not going to throw a punch at his brother.

Not in this house.

"Move," Jon demanded.

"He's dead. And even if he wasn't, he's not worth it. Not in a million years."

A surge of anger gave Jon new strength. He wrenched his brother to the side. Shoved past him and into the hall and out the door.

The air was cool on his face, the grass still damp from the morning dew. He dropped the bag on the ground and stood half-turned away from the house, chest heaving from the exertion, aware of his brother in the open doorway, watching him.

This wasn't about his father. Jon refused to let him hold that much power over him. He was simply making the most of the house. Fulfilling its potential. It was what he did—he was a builder. He made homes for people. Until recently he'd co-owned a construction company in Toronto. This was business as usual.

His gaze found the recycling bin, filled to overflowing with various liquor bottles.

Too many bottles for one person. Way too many.

He swore. Ran a hand through his hair, fisting his fingers in it and pulling so tightly that it hurt.

Why couldn't Tyler have left him here to rot, or whatever it was he was doing? Why couldn't Tyler have left him to battle it out on his own with the ghost of a dead man?

He laughed, a short, hard bark of bitter amusement.

If this really was a battle, according to the tide of bottles spilling onto the lawn, he was making a pretty poor showing. He was in full retreat, utterly routed, on his way to surrender.

Tyler's hand landed on his shoulder.

"Let's patch it up and sell it. Then never look back."

Jon knew his brother was right but he hated the understanding in his voice. He twisted from under his brother's grip. Moved away from him.

"We should focus on the kitchen, knock it off first. The bathroom won't need too much time if we stick to the original layout."

Carefully not looking at his brother, he strode toward the house.

CHAPTER ONE

March

Gabby Wade belted out the chorus to Sinéad O'Connor's classic "Nothing Compares 2 U" as she pulled into her usual parking spot in front of T.A. Furniture Designs, her voice echoing loudly in the small space. She waited until the final notes of the song had faded before turning off the ignition with a contented sigh.

There was nothing better than a really good angst-ridden ballad to kick off a Monday morning, and no one was better at it than Sinéad. Gabby grabbed her bag then twisted to collect the jumbo box of doughnuts from the backseat. The smell of chocolate and strawberry wafted to her as she walked toward the showroom door. It was barely eight o'clock, so the entrance was still locked, and she balanced the box on her knee as she struggled to get her key in the lock. The doughnuts nearly hit the dust before she got the door open, but she managed to keep her grip on them. Not that it would have made much difference to the guys—they would probably eat cardboard if it had chocolate frosting on it. A little gravel would hardly put them off.

She locked up behind her, then passed through the showroom, making a mental note to rearrange the display sometime this week. Even though she was officially only the office manager, she'd been stepping into sales a lot more lately and a static showroom wasn't doing anyone any favors.

Heaven knew, Tyler was too distracted these days to notice those kinds of things. It was just as well she had his back.

The sharp whine of a power saw hit her as she entered the workshop. Dino was ripping some red gum, and Paul was setting up the router to bevel the edge on a cherry dining table. Carl was marking up some wood, squinting like crazy because he still refused to admit he needed glasses.

"Morning, boys," Gabby hollered over the noise.

Dino grunted without looking up, while Carl ignored her altogether. Paul glanced up briefly, throwing her a token wave. She waited for his brain to register what she held in her hands.

One cat-dog, two cat-dog, three—

His head whipped up again and his mouth curled into a sweet smile. "Is that what I think it is?"

"Yes, my gallant prince, it is. Two dozen of Krispy Kreme's finest for the fairest gentlemen in all the land."

The saw stopped abruptly. Suddenly all eyes were on her.

Nothing like refined sugars and fats to get a man's attention.

"Gabby, you're a gem." Dino started toward her, dusting his hands together.

"What he said," Carl echoed, his eyes on the box as he followed in Dino's footsteps.

"Try to leave some for Tyler and Kelly," Gabby said.

Paul took the box from her hands. "Of course. We're not animals."

Dino had a doughnut in each hand.

"I'll take your word for it," she said.

Dino laughed sheepishly as she turned toward her office. Then, as though it had only just occurred to her, she swung around.

"I almost forgot—we really need to get that boardroom table out tomorrow. So anything you guys could do to finish it would be really appreciated."

Dino froze midbite. "So these are bribe doughnuts? Nice. How cheap do you think we are?"

"I got chocolate custard, your favorite."

Dino's aggrieved look faded a fraction. "Fine. We'll do what we can. But no promises."

Gabby hid her grin as she walked to her office. If she knew Dino—and after three years of being Tyler's office manager, she was pretty confident she did—the table would be ready for the afternoon's deliveries. And all it had cost her was a trip to Krispy Kreme.

United Nations, eat your heart out.

She pushed open her office door—and froze.

A complete stranger—a man—sat at her desk, his back to the door as he used her computer.

She stared at his broad shoulders, strong neck and close-cropped dark hair. What the hell was he doing in her office? Making himself at home in her chair?

"Um, excuse me…?" she finally said when she'd gotten over her initial surprise.

He held up an imperious hand, not even bothering to glance over his shoulder to see who it was. "Won't be a minute."

She stared, incredulous, as whoever-he-was continued to tap at the keyboard.

Was he for real?

"Of course. Make yourself at home. Maybe you'd like a coffee while you're at it?"

He did glance up and she found herself staring into a pair of dark gray eyes.

"Tyler said I could jump on to check a few things. I'll be out of your hair in a second."

His voice was low and deep, a subterranean rumble along her nerve endings. Between it and those eyes and the shape of his jaw and face, it wasn't hard to work out who he was: Jon Adamson, Tyler's brother.

He turned to the computer and Gabby found herself staring at his shoulders again. He was bigger than Tyler, broader. She knew he was older by a year or so, too, but apart from that, the only things she knew about Jon were that until recently he'd been living in Canada, that he'd missed Ally and Tyler's wedding because of some business commitment there, and that the past few months he'd been in Woodend while he renovated the family home prior to sale. Correction, she knew one other thing—he was rude. Because surely even the most insensitive person could guess that invading somebody's personal space then virtually ignoring them when they discovered you was not exactly the way to go about winning friends.

She crossed her arms over her chest and waited. And waited.

And waited.

After what felt like an age, Jon hit a key on her computer and pushed away from the desk.

"Thanks for that," he said as he stood.

He was a little taller than Tyler, and now that he was facing her she noted further similarities and differences between the brothers. His cheekbones were pronounced like Tyler's but sharper, and the lines around his eyes and mouth were deeper. His jaw was the same strong, sure arc, his chin as determined, but his eyes were a much darker gray, the color of storm clouds instead of Tyler's unusual quicksilver.

Her gaze swept his body, taking in his pristine white T-shirt and his equally crisp-looking jeans. Both new, unless she missed her guess. Only his boots looked well-worn. She refocused on his face, noting his clean-shaven jaw and the military neatness of his buzz cut.

He looked…newly minted somehow. But in a raw, spare kind of way.

She was aware of him checking her out, too, and for a crazy second wished she was wearing something other than a faded T-shirt and jeans and that she'd gone for a proper haircut instead of trimming her fringe with the nail scissors this morning.

She shook the thought off quickly—all signs pointed to the fact this man was an ass, and she didn't give two hoots what an ass thought of her.

Not even one hoot.

"You're Gabrielle, right? Jon Adamson." He offered his hand.

She let him hang for a moment before sliding her hand into his. It seemed only fair, since he'd kept her hanging.

"It's Gabby."

His palm swallowed hers, and she felt the roughness of calluses against her own soft skin.

"You all finished now?" she asked. "I don't want to cramp your style."

He gave her an assessing look. "Like I said, Tyler didn't seem to think you'd mind if I used your office for a few minutes. But if I've stepped on your toes, I apologize."

His tone was very even, very calm. As though she was the one who was out of line here. She felt herself bristling even more and was forced to admit that maybe she *was* overreacting a little. After all, he'd simply borrowed her computer, with her boss's permission. Nothing to get her panties in a twist over.

Except…

He was too big and too strangely familiar, and yet not, and she felt…invaded and a little overwhelmed by his unexpected presence.

She wanted him gone. Wanted her space back.

"I was a little thrown, that's all."

"Again, sorry if I stepped on your toes."

He moved out from behind her desk and she took a hasty step to the side to avoid brushing against him as he headed for the door.

She watched as he strode away, his broad shoulders dipping from side to side like a cowboy as he walked. Only when he was gone did she take a seat in her chair. It was warm from his body and she shifted, feeling invaded all over again.

Why he couldn't have used Tyler's computer, she didn't know. Or at least Tyler could have given her a heads-up, told her he'd loaned her office to his brother.

Can you hear yourself? Anyone would think you were eighty-two, not thirty-two. Next you'll be talking about young people today and how things were different in your day.

Gabby took a deep breath and let it out. She'd already acknowledged she'd overreacted. Yes, Jon could have handled the situation better, too, but she was blowing the whole incident out of proportion. It was a blip on the radar, nothing to get worked up over. He was probably only visiting the workshop for a few minutes, using the excuse of checking out his brother's business to abuse the facilities. The odds were good she'd never see him again.

Launching her email program, she started reading the latest batch of orders and enquiries, absently running her fingers through her short dark hair. She was about to respond to a complicated request from one of their corporate customers when Tyler appeared at her door, a mug of coffee in hand.

"You got a minute?" He propped a shoulder against the frame. As usual, he was dressed in faded jeans and a black T-shirt, the color a perfect foil for his silver eyes.

It was impossible to look at him and not think about his brother. The resemblance was that strong.

"As in a genuine sixty seconds? Absolutely. Anything more than that and you'll be paying me overtime tonight."

"Dream on," Tyler said with a snort of amusement.

He sat in her visitor's chair, his big body loose and relaxed. Gabby studied him for a beat, fascinated despite herself by the change in him over the past year.

The easy laughter, the softness in his eyes, even the way he moved—Tyler was a new man since he'd met and married Ally.

Happier. More content. Less single-minded and closed off.

It was good to see. No, it was better than good—it was great. Tyler deserved some peace and comfort in his life.

She frowned at the wistful note to her own thoughts. *That'll be enough of that, young lady.*

"Don't get too comfortable," she said. "I wasn't joking about being snowed."

"You can work through lunch."

"Your turn to dream on. You know nothing gets between me and my food. Come on, spill. Quit chewing up my valuable time."

"It's no biggy. I need you to add my brother to our insurance policy."

Gabby sat a little straighter. "What?"

"Jon. My brother. He's going to be helping out here at the workshop for a while."

"But—" There were so many objections crowding her throat she couldn't decide which one to voice first. "But he's not a cabinet-maker or a French polisher, is he?"

"He's a builder, and he's good. He'll pull his weight."

"So, is this a temporary thing? A couple of weeks? A month?" Gabby asked.

"It's for as long as it needs to be."

"What are you? Yoda? *As long as it needs to be?* What the hell does that mean?"

Tyler sighed. "Sometimes I forget what a pain in the ass you can be. Can't you just do what you're told for a change?"

It stung. Useless to pretend it didn't. She was only looking out for him. Worrying about his business. And he thought she was a pain in the ass.

"Fine. I'll add him on as a permanent employee." She picked up a pen and poised it over her notepad, ready to take down his instructions verbatim, since that was clearly the kind of employee he wanted her to be. "Anything else I can do for you?"

"Gabby. Come on. Don't go all cat's-bum-mouthed on me. You know I was only joking."

Nice to know he found her hurt feelings amusing.

"Way to smooth talk me, silver tongue."

"I'm sorry I called you a pain in the ass." He said it like a dutiful schoolboy reciting his times tables.

She raised her eyebrows.

"And the cat's bum comment was completely uncalled for," he added.

"No kidding. And good work with the sincerity there, too. It's really convincing."

Tyler grinned. "Are we friends again?"

Friends.

For three years, they had been a lot more than friends. He'd been her lover, had practically lived at her place. She'd built all kinds of white-picket dreams around him. Then she'd realized that he was never going to share himself with her in the way she needed, and she'd pulled the pin on their relationship. He'd been angry at first. Convinced that she was asking for something he didn't have to give. But after a while they'd settled into a friendship and she'd come to work for him.

Then he'd fallen in love with Ally and given all of himself to her freely and openly without a second's thought.

"Your minute's up," she said.

Tyler laughed. Despite the fact that she was still annoyed with him, she couldn't stop her mouth from twitching in response to the rich sound.

He pointed a finger at her. "I saw that."

"Stop pretending you're charming, because you're not. You can't ask for my opinion and advice one minute and then tell me to pull my head in the next."

Tyler must have picked up on the seriousness of her tone because his smile faded.

"I was only joking, Gab, okay?" He was sincere this time, his eyes very sober.

She nodded, feeling ridiculous for being so prickly. She blamed the stranger she'd found at her desk this morning—Tyler's brother had thrown her off her pace and she was still trying to regain her equilibrium.

"I'll get the paperwork sorted today. What do you want me to set up as far as payroll goes?"

The million-dollar question—exactly what was Tyler paying his underqualified, transient brother?

"I'll take care of that."

She frowned, but this time she didn't say anything. Before she'd joined the business, Tyler had handled the administration himself, so he was more than capable of adding an employee to the payroll. Why he suddenly chose to do so now when she'd been taking care of it for years was a whole other issue.

"Right. Then I guess we're sorted," she said.

"Good stuff." Tyler stood, lifting his coffee mug in a casual salute before heading out the door.

She focused on her work, pushing all the nagging voices in her head to one side. At the end of the day, the name on the sign was T.A. Furniture Design. He was the one taking the risk, therefore he got to make the decisions.

Meaning she was going to have to get used to having his brother around.

It was an unsettling thought. Which was stupid. She got along with all the guys; she'd always been the kind of woman who got on well with men. They ragged on each other, told jokes, had the occasional beer together after work. They were her mates. And despite their not-so-great start, there was no reason why she wouldn't rub along fine with Jon, too.

No reason at all.

JON TURNED OFF THE ORBITAL sander and ran his hand over the tabletop. In the very early days of his apprenticeship he'd dabbled in furniture making, but he hadn't had the patience for it then. Now, he felt the smoothness of the wood beneath his fingers and felt a definite sense of achievement and satisfaction.

He was about to switch the sander on again when someone touched his arm. He looked up to see his brother standing there.

Jon slid off his ear protectors. "What's up?"

"It's quitting time. In case you hadn't noticed."

He glanced around in surprise. He'd been so lost in his work that he hadn't registered that the rest of the guys had gone home for the day.

"Right. Well, I've still got a way to go with this." Jon indicated the tabletop.

"You can finish it tomorrow. We're ahead of deadline on that job."

"I told Dino I'd have it ready for him in the morning. I'm happy to lock up if you want to head home."

"Gabby usually does that. She's still working."

"Is that safe?"

Tyler raised his eyebrows. "You worried she doesn't know how to handle a lock and key?"

Jon ignored the joke. "What if someone was hanging around? She probably doesn't weigh more than a hundred pounds."

In fact, his brother's office manager was so slight it had taken him longer than it should have this morning to figure out that the slim woman glaring at him was an adult, let alone Tyler's right-hand woman. With her boyishly short hair and jeans and T-shirt, she'd looked more like a skinny teen than a woman who helped run a multimillion-dollar business.

"Don't ever let Gabby hear you say that," Tyler said. "She'll tear you a new one."

"It's the truth, isn't it? She'd be toast if someone tried to overpower her."

Tyler groaned. "Definitely don't say *that* to her."

Jon gave his brother a look. "You're serious?"

"Gabby prides herself on her independence. Hates it when people do things for her that she can do herself. If you'd met her mom, you'd understand. Really scary lady."

Jon shrugged. "Fine. She can lock up, if that's what floats her boat."

Tyler pulled his car keys from his pocket. "Swing by the house on your way home if you change your mind. I've got some of that German beer you like and Ally's cooking lasagna."

Jon gave a noncommittal shrug. He knew Tyler was being hospitable, but the last thing Jon wanted was to sit on the sidelines of his brother's life and play witness to his happiness. Not that he begrudged Tyler any of what he had—the business, his home, Ally. He simply didn't need the reminder of all the things he'd messed up in his own life.

Plus it would make it a hell of a lot harder to stick to his self-imposed sobriety if he had to sit around and watch his brother knock back beers all night. And his abstinence would make Tyler curious.

Jon simply didn't want to go there. Yes, he'd had a

wake-up call about his excessive drinking, but that didn't mean he wanted to talk about it or advertise it.

"I guess I'll see you tomorrow, then," Tyler said.

"Sure."

He didn't go immediately, and Jon sensed there was something else on his mind. Jon reached for the sander, checking the tension on the clamps. After a long beat, he heard the metallic clink of his brother's keys and when he glanced up Tyler was heading for the door.

Not for the first time, Jon wondered whether accepting his brother's offer of a temporary job had been a good idea. He didn't need the money—he'd sold out of his construction business and had a sizable chunk of change in his bank account—but he also didn't need to be sitting around staring at the walls while he worked out what to do next. Taking up Tyler's offer to work for him once they'd finished renovating the house had seemed like the best option—it was either that or continue the downward slide toward oblivion in the bottom of a bottle.

There was no denying that the notion held a certain appeal—the end of the struggle, all the crap cloaked in a warm, fuzzy haze of alcohol—but he could still hear his father's voice in his head, telling him over and over how worthless he was and how he'd never amount to anything.

He flat out refused to let the bastard be right.

He started the sander again. The vibrations traveled up his arms as he moved along the grain. Slowly, the tension banding his shoulders relaxed and he lost himself in the simplicity of the task.

He had no idea how much time had passed when the sander suddenly fell silent. Instinct made him look over his shoulder. Gabby was standing beside the outlet, her handbag on her shoulder. He pulled off his ear protectors.

"Sorry. I tried shouting and you didn't hear me."

She didn't sound sorry. Didn't look it, either, her arms crossed tightly over her chest.

"If you're ready to go, I already told Tyler I'm happy to lock up," he said.

"But you don't know the alarm code."

Purely out of habit, his gaze dipped below her neck. She was small on top, one of those petite women with tiny breasts and narrow hips. She probably didn't even need to wear a bra.

Basically the exact opposite of the kind of women he found attractive.

"I will if you tell me."

She frowned. He wasn't sure if it was because of what he'd said or if she'd caught him looking.

"What? You think I'm going to rip my own brother off?"

She stiffened. "It's a complicated system."

"I'll take notes."

She pushed her handbag strap higher on her shoulder. "All right. The keypad's in the showroom." She said it grudgingly. Reluctantly.

He followed her, aware of the tension radiating off her in waves. Man, she was one uptight chick. Tyler seemed to rate her highly, but personally Jon couldn't see the appeal. Humorless, defensive, prickly—she was the very definition of hard work, and he didn't do hard work when it came to women. Not that that would ever be an issue with Gabby—everything about her screamed not available, not interested, not ever.

She stopped in front of the alarm console beside the front door of the showroom.

"The code is Tyler's birth year—not superoriginal, I know, but he insisted."

Jon watched as she punched four figures into the alarm console and explained the system.

"Cool, got it," he said.

"The lock is a little sticky. Sometimes you have to really force it."

"Sure."

"And we usually leave the showroom light on."

"Okay."

"Maybe I should leave you my number, in case you run into trouble."

It was on the tip of his tongue to tell her he had it covered, but she was already rummaging in her bag. He studied the neat part in her straight hair.

"Big night on the cards?" he asked. Maybe if they got to know each other a little she'd loosen up.

She glanced at him. "Not really, just dinner with my girlfriend."

He narrowed his eyes as the penny dropped. The no-frills clothes, the short hair, the lack of makeup, the whole not-available vibe—clearly, Ms. Wade batted for the other team. And based on the way she looked down her nose at him, she was one of those man-hating lesbians. The kind who thought the world would be a better place if men were cut out of the food chain altogether and replaced by lab technicians with turkey basters.

"Finally." She pulled a dog-eared business card from the depths of her purse. "My number's on the bottom. Call if you have issues with anything."

He tucked the card into the front pocket of his jeans. "I'm pretty sure I won't be needing it, but thanks anyway."

The expression on her face told him she had her

doubts, but she didn't say anything. She moved toward the door and seemed surprised when he beat her there and held it open for her.

"Thanks," she muttered, giving him a distinctly ungrateful look.

He remembered what Tyler had said about her not liking people doing things for her that she could do for herself and suppressed a smile. Probably it made him a bad person, but for some reason he liked the idea of yanking her chain a little.

"See you tomorrow," she said, ducking past him into the warm night.

He waited until she'd reached her car and was safely inside. The moment he heard her engine start, he locked the door and returned to the workshop.

His footsteps echoed in the empty space. There was no one waiting for him at home—if you could call a serviced apartment home. He could work here until the wee hours if he wanted to, and no one would miss him or care.

That was the way he liked it. No strings, no obligations. Nothing hard or demanding or restricting.

Just him—and the dozen or so monkeys on his back, of course.

CHAPTER TWO

GUILT NAGGED AT GABBY ALL through dinner with her old school-friend Shona. Jon had tried to be friendly, and she'd blown him off. He'd asked about her evening, opened the door for her. Then he'd watched until she was safely in her car. Even though those kinds of old-fashioned courtesies made her want to grind her teeth, she could appreciate the good manners behind them.

He was trying to be nice. And she'd been nothing but prickly and short.

Brushing her teeth before bed, Gabby tried to work out why he made her so bristly.

Sure, they'd gotten off on a bum note with the whole him-being-in-her-office thing, but she wasn't the sort of person to hold a grudge. And yes, she was worried that Tyler was taking on a staff member who was going to hold back the team rather than help them grow. But none of that was enough to explain the way she turned into Mother Superior every time she spoke to him.

She thought about the moment when he'd faced her after she'd switched off the sander. She'd met his eyes and seen…nothing in their gray depths.

She paused, her mouth full of minty foam.

Maybe that was what it was. Jon was a whole lot of man—a commanding, demanding physical presence by sheer dint of the fact that he took up so much damned room—but when she looked at him she got…nothing.

No sense of how he was feeling or what he was thinking. No hint of his mood or attitude. Just a contained, polite calm.

So what? Big deal if the guy doesn't go around advertising his emotions for all and sundry. He's a guy. That's generally what they do. If that's your big beef with him, you need to get over it, princess.

Gabby spit, then rinsed her mouth. Tomorrow was a new day. There was no reason why she couldn't start fresh with him. She'd take the time to chat with him, ask how he was settling in. She'd even insist on him using her computer again if he needed to check anything on the internet. Before long they'd be laughing and joking around the way she did with the other guys.

He was Tyler's brother, after all. It was impossible for her not to like him.

GABBY'S GOOD INTENTIONS turned to dust the next day when Jon didn't turn up until close to eleven o'clock. She was busy with her own work but she was very aware of his absence because she'd come in with the specific intention of starting over with him.

Initially, she thought he was simply running a little late, which was fine, since he'd stayed to finish the table last night. As the morning wore on, however, and he still didn't appear, she began to wonder if he was going to make history as the shortest-lived employee the company had ever had.

Then, just shy of eleven, Jon sauntered in. She took one look at him and knew exactly why he was late. The heavy eyes, the paleness—he'd had a *big night,* to use his own terminology. Probably been out to all hours, drinking and God knows what else. Then he'd slept it off and rolled into work as though he owned the place and answered to no one.

Gabby watched from her office as he exchanged a word with Dino, who was the senior on the workshop floor and didn't suffer fools gladly. She waited for him to let Jon know in no uncertain terms that the working day had started two and a half hours ago.

Dino said something. Jon replied. Dino laughed, the sound audible even over the whine of the table saw. She watched incredulously as he clapped Jon on the shoulder as though they'd been buddies for years. Dino was still chuckling as he crossed to the drill press.

As though he sensed her watching, Jon glanced at her, a big, no-holds-barred grin still on his face.

She blinked. He looked like a different man when he was smiling. Younger. A little dangerous.

Their eyes met and his smile sobered as he gave her a small acknowledging nod. Her own face felt frozen, but she forced herself to nod in reply. Then she swung in her chair and made a big deal out of being busy with her computer.

She told herself it was none of her business as she punched figures into the accounting software. If Dino was prepared to let the boss's unreliable brother get away with murder, it was no skin off her nose.

At lunchtime she walked around the corner and grabbed a sandwich. As she returned, she could see Jon through the window of the showroom. He was talking to a woman. Gabby frowned, taking in his body language: the way he was slouching oh, so casually against the counter; the almost-there smile on his face as he listened to something the woman was saying; the way his gaze traveled over her body in a slow, appreciative scan.

If he were in a bar, Gabby wouldn't hesitate for a

second in assuming that he was hitting on the woman. But this was Tyler's showroom, and the woman was a customer. Jon was probably simply being friendly.

Gabby pushed the door open, stepping into the air-conditioned cool of the showroom.

"The thing about good design is that it's timeless. Ageless," Jon said. "It only gets better."

The woman was in her early forties, blonde and wearing a tight black dress. She flipped her hair over her shoulder as Jon gave her a loaded smile.

Gabby might not have had a date in a while, but she knew when a man was on the make—and he was definitely eyeing the blonde with carnal intent.

In his brother's showroom. At—she checked her watch—one thirty-five on a Tuesday afternoon.

Nice. Really classy.

Putting on her best professional smile, Gabby joined their cosy tête-á-tête.

"Hi. Hope you don't mind me interrupting. I'm Gabby." She offered the other woman her hand.

The blonde looked a little startled—no doubt she'd been so busy eating Jon up with her eyes she hadn't noticed Gabby approach.

"Hi. Fiona. Pleased to meet you."

Gabby turned to him, her smile still firmly in place. "Thanks, Jon. I'll take over from here."

For a moment she saw a flash of something in his eyes—annoyance? Defiance?—then he straightened and gave Fiona a rueful shrug.

"Back to the grindstone."

Fiona laughed and flipped her hair again. "I'll keep in mind what you said."

"You do that."

Without looking at Gabby, he left the showroom.

"So, how can I help you…?" Gabby asked the other woman brightly.

Ten minutes later, Fiona was on her way with a handful of brochures and some preliminary pricing for the dining-room suite she was looking for. Gabby took a moment to gather her thoughts before heading to her office. Everything in her wanted to hunt Jon down and read him the riot act for behaving so unprofessionally. But he was Tyler's brother, and it was Tyler's business. If anyone was going to deal with Jon, it should be Tyler.

She entered the workshop, veering to the kitchen before hitting her office. She was rinsing a mug when she heard the heavy tread of someone entering. Her spine stiffened. Somehow she knew that it was Jon, but she refused to look to confirm it.

"She was into it, if that's what you're worried about," a deep voice said.

She turned to face him. "Excuse me?"

"Fiona. The blonde."

Gabby blinked, then shook her head. "Let me get this straight. It's your second day on the job, you walk in nearly three hours late, then you try to pick up one of our customers. And none of it is your fault?"

"That's not what I said."

"So you're not making excuses for treating our showroom like a pick-up bar?"

"*A pick-up bar?* Are you serious? We were having a *conversation*."

"When it comes to your brother's company I'm usually pretty serious. I'm a little crazy like that, caring about him staying in business and whatnot."

He made a rude noise. "Lady, you need to lighten up."

"This isn't about me."

"Listen, I know you're all bent out of shape because I used your computer for a few seconds yesterday—"

"This isn't about you using my stupid computer. What do you think I am, a child or something?"

His gaze dropped to her chest for a telling beat. Never had she regretted being an A-cup so much in her life.

"I don't know. I can't think of another reason why you'd nearly blow a gasket because I was having a friendly chat with another consenting adult on my lunch break."

"She was a *customer.* She was looking for furniture, not a quickie in the parking lot."

"Personally I prefer a nice big bed and plenty of time, but don't let that get in the way of a good story."

To her everlasting chagrin, Gabby could feel heat stealing into her cheeks. "Stop trying to make this about me. You're the one who's taking advantage of Tyler, taking his job offer and then arriving late on your second day. How do you think it looks to the other guys, the boss's brother strolling in whenever he feels like it and—"

"I called Dino, told him I'd be in late and that I'd make up the time tonight."

Gabby was thrown for a second. "Well, good. At least someone knew where you were."

"What's wrong? Worried about me?"

"Hardly." She was fiercely hot now, her armpits prickling with self-conscious heat. It didn't help that he looked as cool as could be, as though he could barely bother to raise a sweat over her.

"You know what? Forget I said anything. Why I even felt the urge to explain is beyond me." He turned to go.

"Uh-uh. You don't get off that easy."

She raced around the table, barely making it to the doorway in time to block his exit. He stopped short of plowing into her and she caught a whiff of male skin and spicy deodorant before he took a step backward.

"I want a promise from you that you won't talk to any of the customers again."

"What?"

"You heard me."

"Sweetheart, you have got to be the most uptight chick I have ever met in my life."

"My name is Gabby, thanks. And I want your word that you'll stay out of the showroom. If Dino's prepared to put up with you stuffing him around in the workshop that's his business. But Tyler and I handle sales and I won't have you screwing with our clients. Literally or figuratively."

Something fiery and dangerous flashed in his dark gray eyes. He grabbed her by the upper arms, forcibly picking her up and moving her to one side as though she were a piece of furniture. Then he was gone, and she was left gaping at his audacity.

"How *dare* you!" she said to the empty kitchen.

Good lord, she sounded like a Victorian maiden. An hysterical, outraged Victorian maiden on the verge of the vapors. Any second now she'd be reaching for her smelling salts or calling for her maid to burn some feathers.

How on earth had he managed to turn the tables on her so effectively? He'd been utterly in the wrong, yet somehow she was left feeling like some uptight morals campaigner. He was the one who'd taken advantage of Tyler's generosity, not her. Jon was the one who should be feeling stupid and wrong and out of sorts.

You're an asshole, Jon Adamson.

Damn straight he was. That was why she'd been so

prickly and bristly around him right from the start—her instincts had simply been ahead of the game, recognizing his essential asshole-ness way before he'd shown his true colors.

Which was great, except for one thing—she worked with him now. For the foreseeable future, she had to face him every day from nine to five.

Relax. He's a screwup. He'll mess up again. And next time Tyler will notice and then it will only be a matter of time.

She took a deep breath, then let it out.

Tyler was a good guy and a generous employer, but he was also an astute and passionate businessman. Once he realized his brother was deadwood, Jon would be gone.

It couldn't happen soon enough.

JON DIDN'T CONSIDER HIMSELF A tough guy to get along with. Sure, he wasn't a cuddly, let-me-be-your-instant-best-friend kind of guy, but he usually rubbed along okay with most people. He had a handful of good mates. He managed to end most of his romantic liaisons without tears and recriminations.

So why had Gabby taken such an instant and steadfast dislike to him?

He punched the table saw on and lined up his first cut, feeding the timber slowly into the blade.

He'd apologized for using her computer. He'd bitten his tongue last night when she'd been all bent out of shape about him locking up. He'd even sought her out to explain that she hadn't seen what she'd thought she'd seen when she'd come into the showroom. And she'd still looked at him as though she'd scraped him off her shoe.

It had to be the lesbian thing. Maybe she saw him as competition. Maybe she'd had a bad experience with a man that had tainted her view of his gender for all time. Whatever, he was done with worrying about her prickly sensibilities. From now on, it was every man—or woman—for himself.

You're the one who's taking advantage of Tyler, taking his job offer and then arriving late on your second day.

He frowned, shaking his head in an attempt to dislodge her words. As he'd explained to her, he'd called Dino, let him know he was running late. He'd been up half the night, unable to sleep, pacing the floor of his apartment and staring at late-night TV like a zombie. And when he'd finally fallen asleep in the early hours he'd been so out of it he'd slept through the alarm. But it wasn't as though he hadn't put in the hours yesterday—it had been nearly midnight when he left the workshop, bone weary and covered in sawdust—and it wasn't as though he wouldn't make up for the time today. As for taking advantage of Tyler… Jon's conscience was clear on that one, too. He and Tyler had an understanding, and it was none of Miss Prissy's business.

Jon lined up his next cut. Sawdust and wood chips flew as he ripped the length of the wood.

How do you think it looks to the other guys, the boss's brother strolling in whenever he feels like it?

He told himself to concentrate on the matter at hand, but Gabby's words continued to eat at him. He could tell himself she knew nothing and that her words held no weight. But the truth was that if he had an employee who'd turned up late on the second day of work, he wouldn't be too impressed, either. Not that he was Gabby's employee…but he could see her point.

Considered objectively, it had probably looked bad. And it definitely didn't send a great message to the other staff members.

He swore under his breath, then hit the stop button. Pulling the ear protectors from his head, he faced the inevitable: Gabby was right. But only about the late thing. He'd go to his grave defending his conversation with Fiona-the-blonde in the showroom. They'd been flirting, for Pete's sake—hardly a crime against nature. It wasn't as though he'd been about to club her over the head and drag her to his cave. They'd had a few laughs, eyed each other approvingly. Maybe, if things had warmed up, he'd have gotten her number. That's it.

Miss Prissy needed to get a life.

He glanced toward her office. She was visible through the open doorway, her head bent over her work. A small frown wrinkled her forehead. She was so *serious*. Did she never let her hair down? He tried to imagine it and couldn't. She was too stiff and distant and uptight.

She glanced up and he looked away before she caught him staring. God knew what she'd make of that. Sexual harassment, probably.

He smiled faintly. The idea of him trying to get it on with her was too absurd. She would probably kick him in the nuts then take photos of him writhing on the floor to show the rest of the sisterhood.

Dino walked past and gave him a questioning look. "You all right there, mate?"

Jon realized he was standing in the middle of the workshop with a piece of wood in his hands, staring at nothing. And that he'd wasted the past half hour thinking about Gabby Wade.

"All good," he assured the other man.

Then he collected the other pieces of timber and took them to where Carl was waiting.

GABBY LEFT WORK BEFORE SIX o'clock that night for the first time in months. Tyler and Ally had invited her for dinner to celebrate her birthday. Technically, it wasn't until the weekend but Ally and Tyler were hosting the firm's delayed Christmas party on Saturday night—they'd been so busy in the lead-up to Christmas that everyone had voted to postpone the party until a time when things were less hectic. Gabby would have been happy to combine the two events—or, better yet, forget her birthday altogether—but Ally had insisted they have a separate dinner to mark Gabby's special day.

Normally Tyler forgot her birthday, then made up for it by buying her something expensive a month or so later. Times had changed. He had Ally to remind him now.

Gabby parked close to their double-fronted Victorian home and fumbled in her bag for her lipstick. She found a roll of mints and two tampons, but no lipstick. Damn. Maybe she should have made the time to swing home and freshen up.

Who are you trying to impress, anyway? It's just Ally and Tyler.

Her hand stilled in her bag. It was a good question. Who *was* she trying to impress? Not Tyler anymore. That horse had well and truly bolted. As for Ally, right from the start she'd embraced Gabby has a friend.

Yet there was no denying the fact that Gabby found herself playing the comparison game whenever she spent any significant time with Tyler's wife. It was hard not to, given the superficial similarities between the two of them. They were both on the petite side, and they both had short, dark hair. Sure, Ally was much curvier than Gabby, and her hair was curly instead of dead straight, but it wasn't as though Tyler had gone off and married a six-foot-six redhead. Then there was the fact that both she and Ally were not exactly shy, retiring types…

Enough in common, really, to seed a host of unanswerable questions in Gabby's mind. But as she reminded herself regularly, Tyler had made his choice, and she was happy for him. Anything else was a waste of energy.

Which meant she didn't need to worry about lipstick. She was having dinner with two of her good friends. End of story.

Before she could examine her navel any more, she got out of the car and made her way up the well-lit path to Tyler and Ally's porch. The door opened before she could knock and Ally greeted her with a hug. Dressed in an aqua dress with white embroidery around the hemline, she looked fresh and bright.

"I was beginning to think you were never going to show up," she said.

"Sorry. I got held up at work."

"As usual. Your boss is a slave driver."

"Don't look at me—it's the office manager who wields the whip," Tyler said as he joined them in the wide entrance hall. He kissed Gabby's cheek. "Happy early birthday."

Gabby laughed. "I can honestly say that's the first time I've heard those words pass your lips."

"What can I say? Forgetting dates is a guy thing."

Ally poked him in the ribs. "You're on increasingly thin ice with that one, mister. All the latest research is showing that there's precious little difference between the male and female brain."

Tyler captured her hand in one of his to save himself from further prodding.

"I kind of like the differences. Don't know about you," he said, smiling into his wife's face.

Gabby looked away. She could tell herself she was happy for Tyler until the cows came home, but there was no getting around the fact that seeing the way he looked at Ally made her chest ache.

Not once in three years had he ever looked at her in the same way. Not once.

Which is why he married her and not you, dufus.

"Something smells great," she said, sniffing appreciatively.

Ally hooked her arm through Gabby's. "I made us Moroccan meatballs with preserved lemons, pistachio couscous and orange-and-date salad."

"We're going through a Moroccan stage," he explained as they walked toward the open living space at the rear of the house.

"Well, you know me, anything that I didn't cook myself is manna from heaven," Gabby said.

"Good. Tyler was worried it might be too exotic for you."

Ally released Gabby's arm to pour wine into three of the four glasses on the counter.

"Here's to you," Ally said as she passed Gabby a glass.

"Yeah, happy birthday, Gab," Tyler said.

Gabby clinked glasses, distracted by the single flute still on the counter. It was possible, of course, that Tyler or Ally had simply put out one too many. She hoped like hell that was what had happened, because the alternative was that someone else was joining them for dinner. And since it was a small and cosy family affair, she had a horrible feeling she might know who that fourth person might be.

Right on cue, the doorbell rang. Gabby's stomach dipped with foreboding.

"I'll get it," Tyler said.

"We thought it might be nice to have Jon over, too," Ally explained as he disappeared to answer the door. "We've barely seen him since he's been back, because he was in Woodend so long. Now he's here, I've been bugging him to come for dinner every night, and finally he said yes."

Ally looked pleased. Gabby could only imagine how *she* looked. Constipated? Bilious? The last thing she wanted was to sit around a table making polite conversation with Tyler's knuckle-dragging brother.

"Wasn't sure what you guys were having, so I brought red and white," Jon said as he and Tyler appeared.

Jon's step faltered when he saw her standing there.

"Evening," she said, raising her glass.

For some reason his obvious discomfort made her feel better, made her feel less childish for being unhappy about *him* being here.

"Hi." Jon was frowning slightly as he put down the bottles of wine he'd brought.

"Finally I get you in my clutches. I'm determined to put some meat back on those bones, you know," Ally said, planting a kiss on his cheek and giving him a warm hug.

Jon hugged her as warmly, a faint smile on his face. Ally seemed very small in comparison to his big body. Gabby experienced an odd clench of…something as she watched them embrace.

Looking away, she swallowed a big mouthful of wine.

Everybody loved Ally, it seemed. Even the arrogant, standoffish brother.

"Have some wine. We're toasting Gabby," Tyler said.

Jon's expression was unreadable as he accepted a drink.

"Gab, you know I'd be a mess without you. You're my right-hand woman. Hope this makes up for all the other birthdays I've forgotten," Tyler said.

Out of the corner of her eye, Gabby saw Jon tense as he registered the occasion. As she'd suspected, Ally hadn't told him tonight was her birthday dinner. In fact, given that small giveaway hesitation when he'd first entered, Gabby was pretty damn sure he hadn't known she was going to be here. No doubt he would have come up with an ironclad excuse otherwise. Lord knew, she would have if she'd known.

"Happy birthday, Gabby," Ally echoed.

Some instinct made Gabby glance at Jon as she took a drink. She saw him lift his glass to his mouth, tilt it and wet his lips. But he didn't open his mouth. It was over in a split second, so fast she almost thought she'd imagined it, but she hadn't.

Jon had faked drinking a toast in her honor.

Wow. He must really dislike her.

She was surprised how much the realization stung. Then she gave herself a mental shake. She didn't care what he thought of her. The idea was laughable. Ludicrous. She'd met him only two days ago, and what she knew of him proclaimed him to be a screwup of the highest order—she should consider it a badge of honor that he didn't like her, not a slap in the face.

Tyler crossed to the sideboard to collect a small, neatly wrapped box. "From us."

Gabby took the box, very aware of the tall figure standing at the edge of her peripheral vision.

"This is awfully small for the company car I've been campaigning for."

"Next year," Tyler said.

Gabby tugged the pretty silver ribbon free and lifted the lid. Inside, a pair of stud earrings rested on a velvet cushion. Set with golden-brown gems, they sparkled in the overhead light.

"They're beautiful," Gabby breathed.

"They're golden beryls. I saw them and thought they were a match for your eyes," Ally said. "Tyler couldn't remember if your ears are pierced, but I was pretty sure you wore earrings to his birthday in August."

"My ears are pierced." Gabby touched one of the glittering stones, trying not to be hurt that Tyler couldn't remember. He'd been in her apartment, in her bedroom, hundreds of times. Had he really forgotten her messy jewelry box? And what about the time she'd freaked out over sucking up one of her favorite earrings in the vacuum cleaner? Had everything pre-Ally been consigned to the archives of his mind?

"If you don't like them, we won't be offended if you want to swap them for something else," Ally said.

Gabby realized she'd been silent for too long and she offered her hosts—her friends—a big smile.

"They're absolutely perfect. Gorgeous. In fact..."

She eased the earrings from the box. A few seconds later she let her hands fall to her sides and offered herself up to Ally and Tyler's scrutiny. "How do they look?"

"Just as I imagined," Ally said.

Gabby stepped forward to kiss her cheek in thanks. "Thanks for thinking of me."

Ally drew her into a hug, squeezing her tight. "It was my pleasure."

Gabby squeezed her back.

When Tyler had first introduced her to Ally, Gabby had been determined to like the woman who had made him so happy, even if it killed her. She'd been prepared to overlook anything, to be generous and accepting of any and all faults or shortcomings because Ally was Tyler's choice, the woman he loved.

The woman he wanted to spend the rest of his life with.

Then she'd met Ally and realized that it would be no hardship to like her. She was warm and generous, smart and funny. Easily one of the most thoughtful people Gabby knew—witness the beautiful earrings, chosen with care and consideration. Not too dangly or elaborate—because Gabby was not a fussy woman—and, apparently, a match for her eyes. Although Gabby was pretty sure it was a stretch to compare her ordinary brown eyes to the warm golden gems. It hadn't taken her long to understand why Tyler had fallen in love with Ally. She was very easy to love.

Tyler patted her on the shoulder fondly as she and Ally broke their embrace. Gabby gave him a wry look, then her gaze slid to where Jon was standing at a distance, watching them. Their eyes met for a moment before he glanced down at his still full wineglass.

"Okay, people. Make a beeline for the table, it's time for the feasting to begin," Ally said, waving them toward the dining table that occupied one corner of the room.

Gabby dutifully followed orders, but Jon lingered at the counter, arms crossed over his chest.

"That means you as well, my friend. The last thing I need is you hovering while I serve our meal," Ally said.

"Funny. I thought only men suffered from short person syndrome," Jon said.

"What's that supposed to mean?" Ally asked.

Jon looked at her, a smile quirking his mouth. "What do you think it means?"

"I think you're saying I'm bossy."

"Hey. If the shoe fits..." Jon said with a don't-blame-me shrug.

Ally laughed and gave him a shove. "Move, you big lug."

Gabby watched, fascinated, as Jon resisted Ally long enough to make her really work before finally deigning to shift from his position. There was a lazy, amused light in his eyes, not quite the same as the expression he'd had when he was chatting up the blonde in their showroom this afternoon, but certainly just as playful.

"Next to Gabby, please. Since I've already been labelled a dictator, I might as well have it the way I want it," Ally instructed.

Gabby gave a silent sigh. Great. Now she was going to have to rub shoulders with Captain Studly through three courses and coffee. Not exactly the birthday celebration she'd been hoping for. But there was precious little she could do about it.

Buckle up, it's going to be a bumpy night.

CHAPTER THREE

GABBY FIDDLED WITH THE STEM OF her wineglass as Jon hesitated for a telling second before pulling out the chair next to her.

Nice.

"Don't worry, I don't have cooties," she said as he sat.

"Good to know. Although I've never really been sure what they are."

"I think they're the equivalent of girl germs."

"Yeah? I've always been kind of partial to those."

Gabby flashed to the scene she'd witnessed this afternoon. "No kidding."

She realized immediately that he might take the comment the wrong way, but when she glanced at him askance he was smiling slightly.

Don't get too excited, but you may have had your first civil exchange with Jon Adamson.

Not quite a miracle, but close to it given their record. Which probably meant she should make an effort to extend the cease fire.

"So, um, how are you finding Melbourne after so long away?"

"Busy. The traffic is nuts. I don't remember it being this bad."

"You've been away ten years, haven't you? Melbourne's grown by about a million people in that time."

"That would explain it."

A small silence fell and they both glanced to where Ally and Tyler were serving the meal. To Gabby's admittedly inexpert eye, it looked as though they were still several minutes away from being rescued by their hosts.

Which meant more small talk was called for.

Over to you, buddy. I did my bit.

"So. It's your birthday, huh?" Jon finally said.

"Yep. Keeps coming around every year, whether I like it or not."

"Am I allowed to ask…?"

"Thirty-three. It's actually on Saturday, but since we're having the work Christmas party then, Ally wanted to do something tonight so I'd feel special."

"Sounds like Ally." There was a softness in his voice when he said the other woman's name.

"Yeah. She's pretty great."

Another silence.

My turn. Think of something. Anything.

But the only thought that popped into her head was that he would have a hell of a time buying a suit off the rack with his broad shoulders.

She took a breath to launch into a discussion about work, but he beat her to it.

"So, Dino was telling me you usually dress up for the Christmas party?"

She gave him a mental elephant stamp for coming up with such a nice, neutral topic. Even they couldn't go awry talking about this one.

"It's kind of become a tradition."

"What are you coming as this year?"

"I was thinking Rudolph. But I'm still toying with the idea of a Christmas tree."

"What about your girlfriend? Does she get into the whole dressing-up thing?"

Gabby frowned. "I'm sorry?"

She was vaguely aware of Tyler and Ally ferrying dishes to the table.

"Here we go," Ally said.

"Or aren't partners invited?" Jon asked, his questioning gaze going from Gabby to Ally to Tyler.

Partners. Girlfriend.

The words circled Gabby's brain like thought balloons. It took her a full five seconds to join the two together and jump to the only conclusion possible.

"I'm not a lesbian." It came out sounding a lot more high-pitched and defensive than she would have liked.

Ally's eyebrows rose as she stared at Jon. "You thought Gabby was gay?"

Tyler laughed. "Bloody hell. Where did you get that idea from?"

Jon's cheekbones were a dull red. "She mentioned her girlfriend, and I thought..." His gaze went to Gabby's hair, then dropped below her chin to her body. "I must have got the wrong end of the stick."

"*Girlfriend* as in a *friend* who happens to be a *girl*," Gabby said.

She didn't need a mirror to know she was bright red—she could feel the heat radiating off her skin. Although why she was embarrassed was beyond her—he was the one who had made a fool of himself.

"Sorry. My mistake," Jon said.

"No kidding," Gabby said. Talk about a lack of perception.

Tyler was still smiling.

"Tyler. It's not funny," Ally chided.

"I know. Sorry. It's just— Gabby as a lesbian… It boggles the mind."

"Can we let it drop?" Jon said. The glance he shot her was full of apology.

Great. First he outed her as a lesbian, now he felt sorry for her.

"This looks great, Ally," she said brightly, picking up her knife and fork. "You know, if you weren't married, I'd be tempted to nab you for myself."

Everyone laughed, including Jon. The knot in Gabby's stomach loosened a little.

"This reminds me of a letter I got last month for the column…" Ally said.

Gabby reached for her water glass as Ally launched into her story. Gabby nodded and laughed and made comments in all the right places, but all the while, behind her smile and her I-couldn't-care-less demeanor, her mind was whirring, obsessing over Jon's mistaken assumption.

She told herself that she didn't care what he thought, that being thought to be gay was not an insult, that some of her best friends were gay. She told herself that his lack of perception said a lot more about him than it did about her. She even got herself to the point where she half believed it—except she kept returning to that significant pause when he'd looked at her hair, then her body before apologizing for getting it wrong.

"Excuse me." She pushed back her chair and stood.

Hopefully enough time had passed that her leaving the table wouldn't be read as retreat. Right now she was beyond caring.

The bathroom door closed behind her with a soft click

and she crossed the tile floor to stand in front of the full-length mirror mounted beside the old-fashioned tub.

She stared at the woman she saw reflected there, determined to prove to herself once and for all that Jon had his head up his backside.

The woman staring back at her had short, straight dark hair, with a crooked fringe and a pale face utterly devoid of makeup.

Heaps of women have short hair, her inner voice scoffed. *Audrey Tatou has short hair, and no one is calling her a lesbian.*

As for the no-makeup thing, well, she'd simply gotten out of the habit of it over the past few months. Admittedly, she looked a little…nondescript without it, but, again, it didn't make her gay.

She dropped her gaze to her body. Her T-shirt was old and stretched out, the fabric swamping her small breasts and bunching unattractively around her waist. Her jeans were cut for comfort rather than style, their fit loose and utilitarian. Her sneakers were old and scuffed, again chosen for comfort over appearance.

Gabby blinked, but it didn't change what the mirror was telling her. The voice in her head was suspiciously silent.

She looked like a boy.

Was it any wonder that Jon had made assumptions? Really?

She sat on the rim of the tub, feeling shaky. As though someone had pulled a veil from her eyes and forced her to see an unpalatable truth.

When had she stopped caring how she looked?

When had she stopped wearing makeup and going to the hairdresser instead of trimming her own hair with nail scissors? When had she stopped buying sexy underwear and high heels and pretty clothes?

When had she ceased to think of herself as an attractive, sexual being and slipped into this sexless, safe disguise?

She didn't know the exact date, but she could guess: the moment she'd given up on Tyler. Nearly four years, give or take. Four years of seeing him every day, convincing herself they were better friends than they had ever been lovers and that she'd done the smart thing—the only thing—in breaking off their relationship.

She laughed suddenly as a bitter irony hit her: she'd broken up with Tyler to protect herself, but he was the one who had moved on. He'd found love, while Gabby, apparently, had been marking time.

A wellspring of emotion tightened the back of her throat. She pressed her fingers against her eyelids. If she started crying, she'd never stop. And there was no way she was going to hide in the bathroom and cry at her own birthday party while her ex and his new wife fretted about her on the other side of the door.

No. Freaking. Way.

She took an unsteady breath, then another. She stood and shook out her hands.

"Come on, princess. Get it together."

She tried out a smile in the mirror. It looked more like a grimace than a smile, but it would have to do.

Then she threw back her shoulders, straightened her spine and opened the bathroom door.

She had a birthday party to survive, after all.

JON SHOOK HIS HEAD AS TYLER offered to refill his wineglass, his brother only belatedly noticing that Jon hadn't finished his first glass yet.

"Driving," Jon said at Tyler's enquiring look.

Tyler didn't say anything, but Jon guessed from the dawning understanding in his brother's eyes that they would be having a conversation about his abstinence in the near future.

Great. Exactly what he wanted. Not.

He glanced toward the hall for the second time in as many minutes, very aware that Gabby had been gone for a long time. Judging by their casual demeanors, neither Tyler nor Ally seemed to find her extended absence unusual but they were still in the honeymoon phase of their marriage, totally wrapped up in one another. They probably wouldn't notice if Jon jumped on the table and started doing the chicken dance.

It was possible he wouldn't have noticed Gabby's absence, either, had he not been sitting next to her. He'd felt her tense when he'd asked about her girlfriend. And even though she'd brushed off his assumption and made a joke about it, he'd felt her continuing tension. She'd practically vibrated with it, like a plucked harp string.

He'd hurt her feelings. Unintentionally, but the result was the same. He might be a lot of things, and she might be a pain in the ass, but if he could take back the moment, he would.

He was about to suggest Ally go in search of her absent guest when Gabby returned. Jon studied her face as she sat. She was wearing a polite social smile but he could see the unhappiness behind her eyes.

Damn.

He was going to have to apologize. Not that he hadn't already done so, but clearly he was going to have to try again.

He reached for his glass, his fingers closing around the stem. Only when he was carrying the wine to his mouth did he register what he was doing. He reversed the action without drinking.

Two months. That was how long he'd sentenced himself to abstinence. Not because he truly believed he had a drinking problem, more to prove to himself that he could stop if he wanted to.

It occurred to him that a guy who didn't have a drinking problem should be finding it a hell of a lot easier to go without than he had the past few days. Certainly he probably shouldn't keep catching himself fantasizing about grabbing a six-pack on the way home from work, or imagining the warm creep of alcohol stealing over his body and numbing his mind.

"So, Jon, what's this mysterious apartment you're staying in like? Tyler tells me it's around the corner from the workshop," Ally said, drawing his thoughts back to the moment.

"It's a serviced apartment. Nothing mysterious about it that I can see," he said.

"Great. Then I guess the coast is clear for Tyler and I to come over for dinner one night soon." Ally had a mischievous twinkle in her eye.

He was well aware that his sister-in-law was quietly campaigning for a closer relationship between him and his brother. It was never going to happen, for a variety of reasons, but Ally would realize that soon enough on her own without him pointing it out to her.

"Sure. As long as you like take-out pizza."

"You're as bad as Gabby," Tyler said. "I swear I was never that pathetic when I was single."

"Isn't there a rule about not dissing a person on their birthday?" Gabby said.

"No. And even if there was, it's not until Saturday, so I'm in the clear," Tyler said.

"I can cook," Gabby said.

"Ditto," Jon said, because he figured he owed it to her to provide backup.

"Microwaving frozen meals doesn't count," Ally said.

"Toast does," Jon said. There was an echo, and he realized Gabby had said the same thing simultaneously.

She glanced at him, disconcerted. He offered her a faint smile. Not too big, since he didn't want to push his luck.

Her gaze became frosty.

He was still in her black books, then. It figured. She hadn't liked him much before he'd got her sexuality wrong—she would probably go home and burn an effigy of him in her yard after tonight's events.

Ally served lemon cheesecake for dessert—Gabby's favorite, apparently—and they all watched as Gabby dutifully blew out the single candle. They moved to the couches while Tyler prepared coffees with their shiny new espresso machine.

Jon's gaze kept drifting to the wall clock, trying to calculate when it would be acceptable for him to leave. Immediately after coffee? Or would that mark him as the crassest of social boors?

He jiggled his leg impatiently, willing Tyler to hurry. Once the coffee was ready, Jon gulped his down while it was still too hot and earned himself a burned tongue for his troubles. Finally he decided he must be in the clear and made his excuses.

It wasn't until he was on the porch, the door closed behind him that he remembered he'd planned to apologize to Gabby again.

He turned, raising his hand to knock, but lowered it without doing so. The least he could do was apologize in private, save Gabby a rehashing of what had obviously been an embarrassing moment.

He'd have to find a few minutes alone with her at work tomorrow. No doubt she'd find some way to give him a hard time. But he'd do the right thing because, contrary to what she obviously believed, he wasn't a bad guy.

IT WAS NEARLY MIDNIGHT BY THE time Gabby let herself into her apartment. She threw her bag onto the couch and checked her answering machine—nothing—then walked to her bedroom and into the ensuite.

Flicking on the light, she gave herself a moment to adjust to the sudden brightness before beginning her nightly ritual. First, she washed her face, then patted it dry and smoothed a lightly scented moisturizer onto her face, neck and shoulders. She switched to almond-scented body lotion for her arms, hands and legs, working it in with long, smooth strokes.

At least you didn't give up everything. Apparently, you still care if your skin is nice.

Her hands stilled on her calf. Somehow, she'd managed to keep a lid on her emotions. But now she was in the safety of her own home and it was time to come clean with herself.

More than time—about four years overdue, in fact.

She straightened, and for the second time that night she stared at her own image in the mirror, trying to understand herself.

Was she still in love with Tyler? Was that what all this was about? Had she been kidding herself for years when all along she'd been holding a candle, pining, hoping?

Dear God. Please don't let me be that woman. Please don't let me be that pathetic.

She didn't want it to be true. But the facts were pretty damned convincing. She'd gone on exactly one date since she'd broken up with Tyler. One date in four years. And it wasn't through lack of invitations, either. She'd had her share of admirers in those first few years of being single again. She couldn't remember what excuses she'd come up with for not accepting any of the offers to see a movie or go out for dinner. She simply hadn't been interested, and eventually the offers had dried up.

If she was being honest, she'd have to admit she hadn't really noticed or cared. She'd been too busy organizing Tyler's business—whipping it into shape when she first came on board then doing all she could to help lift him to the next level in subsequent years. Too busy recasting herself as Tyler's faithful sidekick, the sexless, tireless little buddy who never let him down.

What did you think was going to happen—that he'd admire your skill with a balance sheet so much that he'd finally fall all the way in love with you?

Because, of course, Tyler had never loved her the way she'd loved him.

It still hurt, even after all these years. She turned her back on her reflection, unwilling to play witness to her own unhappiness. Which pretty much answered the big question, didn't it?

She brushed her teeth, staring at the tile wall. Once she was finished, she walked into the bedroom and stripped to her underwear. Kicking her clothes into the corner, she crawled beneath the covers.

The sheets were cool against her skin and she shivered as she waited for them to warm, legs drawn up, arms pulled tightly to her chest.

On nights such as these, she used to make Tyler spoon her from behind, the heat of his body like a furnace against her back. She'd loved feeling his warm breath on the nape of her neck, loved having one of his strong arms wrapped around her. Tyler had always moved in his sleep, however—he'd liked to spread out, to have his own space. Nine times out of ten she'd woken to find their positions reversed, him curling away from her while she clung to his back, her body molded to his.

Chasing him, needing him, even in her sleep.

She made a distressed sound and burrowed deeper into the pillow. It didn't stop the tears from coming. Four years' worth, pushed down deep.

The truth was, she'd never allowed herself to grieve for Tyler. She'd been too busy being tough. Moving on. Assuring him there were no hard feelings and that they'd still be a part of each other's lives. She'd convinced herself that she'd done all her grieving beforehand, before she'd made the painful, wrenching decision to call things off between them. She'd been so sure she had it all together, that she was on top of it.

More fool her.

Her pillow was getting wet. She rolled onto her back. The sound of her sobs seemed very loud in her quiet bedroom. Tears streamed from the corners of her eyes down her temples into her hair. She pressed her palms to her sternum and pushed, willing the ache to go away.

She didn't want to still love Tyler. She didn't want to be this weak and tragic.

Dear God, if Mom could see me now, she'd kick my backside into the middle of next week.

The thought prompted a hiccuping laugh. Gabby sniffed noisily, then sat up and wiped at her eyes with the backs of her hands.

She'd been raised by a fiercely independent woman who'd prided herself on never needing anyone—men being at the very top of that list. Divorced from Gabby's father when Gabby was only two years old and her sister, Angela, barely one, Rachel Wade had thrown herself into single motherhood like an Amazonian warrior. She'd taught herself how to change fuses, tap washers and car tires and had hammered into her daughters from the moment they were old enough to understand that they always had to stand on their own two feet and that no one could ever make them unhappy unless they allowed it.

Nice in theory, but often not so great in practice, as Gabby and her sister had discovered many times over the years.

Fortunately for Gabby, her mother was halfway around the world at present, living her dream of working and traveling through Europe.

Still, the thought of her mother was enough to make Gabby reach for the box of tissues. She blew her nose, mopped her eyes dry. Then she switched pillows and lay down and tried to go to sleep.

There wasn't much else she could do, after all. She'd been in love before—Billy Harrison when she was seventeen, Gareth Devenish when she was in her early twenties. Neither of them had been as important in her life as Tyler was, but both experiences had taught her that there was no willing away a broken heart. She would simply have to wait the pain out.

It's been four years. How long do you freaking want?

A good question. A scary one, too, because she'd already wasted four years longing for something she could never have.

She fell asleep late and woke early. The first thing she did was walk to her wardrobe and throw the doors open. She had to dig deep to get past jeans and yet more jeans, but after a few minutes she pulled out her black leather miniskirt and her stiletto ankle boots. A rummage in her chest of drawers produced the tight orange tank that through some mysterious trick of design managed to give her cleavage. In the shower, she shaved her legs and her armpits, washed and conditioned and exfoliated. Then she smoothed on body lotion and pulled out her make-up bag. Twenty minutes later she inspected herself in the mirror on the back of her bedroom door.

She'd always had good legs, and her backside was a nice shape, neat and round and perky. The boots and the skirt she'd chosen made the most of her two best assets, while the tank and push-up bra worked their magic upstairs.

Jon was going to eat his words when he saw her this morning. He was going to take one look at her in this outfit and realize how wrong he'd been about her. He was going to—

Gabby froze in the act of spritzing on her most expensive perfume as it occurred to her that, as well as all those other things, he was going to know that she'd done all this—the legs, the hair, the makeup, the clothes—for him. To prove something to him. Because she cared what he thought.

"Damn it."

Annoyed with herself, Gabby stripped. Dressed only in her underwear, she pushed hangers out of the way until finally, at the back of the wardrobe, she found what she was looking for—a pair of shapeless cargo pants she kept for really dirty work. The top shelf yielded the box with her Doc Martens boots, a relic from her teen years. She was stumped for a moment with regard to the top, but then inspiration struck and she grinned. Throwing herself across the bed, she grabbed the phone from the nightstand and dialed.

"Jen, it's Gabby. Sorry it's so early, but I need to borrow something..."

No way was she going to let Jon think that she cared what he thought or said. No. Way.

JON WOKE BATHED IN SWEAT, HIS heart racing. It took a full five seconds to work out where he was and that he'd been dreaming.

He let out a sigh and lifted a hand to his face. His skin felt clammy and cold. Throwing back the covers, he stood and walked out of the bedroom and into the apartment's living space. He poured coffee into a fresh filter and turned on the coffee machine.

Hard to work out what was worse—suffering broken sleep from the nightmares that had become his almost nightly companions since he'd given up drinking or waking with a thundering hangover.

This morning's dream had been a doozy—his father storming up the hallway of their family home toward him, the thick leather belt he favored for beatings clutched in one hand. Tyler's whimpers of fear from behind him. No sign of his mother, although Jon knew she should be there, that she should be the one standing between them and the monster bearing down on them. The almost overwhelming urge to run had gripped him. The need to abandon Tyler and run, run, run to save himself. And then, finally, he'd been hit with the dawning, horrible knowledge that there was no escape, that there was nothing he could do to save himself or his brother.

Really restful stuff. The kind of stuff that made a guy

want to spring out of bed whistling a tune, ready to head out into the day to rub shoulders with his fellow man.

The carafe was full. He grabbed a cup, poured coffee, stirred in sugar. Mug in hand, he wandered over to the sliding doors that led out onto his tiny balcony. He glanced at the redbrick wall opposite, then changed his mind about going outside. The lack of view hadn't bothered him when he'd taken the place, but the looming wall that filled every window was starting to get on his nerves.

No one's forcing you to stay. Book a ticket, get on a plane. Go find someplace with no memories, no ties. No expectations.

It was what he'd wind up doing eventually, he was sure. But he wasn't ready to go. Not yet.

He wasn't sure what was holding him back. But soon enough he'd get over whatever it was, pack his meager belongings and head off to a new start somewhere.

Downing the last of his coffee, he dumped the mug in the sink and went to shower. It was early, but he might as well be at work as here.

Half an hour later, he pulled into the parking lot at T.A. Furniture Designs. Belatedly it occurred to him that he'd left the key in his jeans from yesterday—then he spotted the red car parked close to the building.

Gabby. It figured she'd be the first in. If there was an employee equivalent of teacher's pet, she was it.

Still, it would give him a chance to apologize to her again without the risk of the guys overhearing. He'd get it out of the way, then he and Gabby could go back to pistols at ten paces or whatever it was they did whenever they were in the same room.

He locked his truck and strode to the entrance. He pressed the doorbell that had been provided for after-hours visitors and waited. When no one came after a couple of minutes, he knocked and tried the bell again.

A few seconds later the workshop door swung open and Gabby walked through. The good-natured smile on her face faded when she recognized him through the glass. His gaze took in first her T-shirt, then her baggy combat fatigues and finally her chunky punk rocker boots as she strode toward him. Lastly, he focused on her hair, which had been parted to one side and gelled into a shiny brown helmet of asexual hair.

She unlocked the door and pulled it open. "Exactly how long do you think it takes to walk from the back room to the front door?"

His gaze dipped to the image of k.d. lang printed across her chest. "Nice T-shirt."

He wasn't stupid—he knew a challenge when he saw one—and he couldn't hide the smile curving his lips a moment longer.

"What's so funny?"

He patted her on the shoulder as he moved past her. "I'm flattered you went to so much trouble for me. I didn't realize you cared."

He heard her quick intake of breath.

"Please. I know you think you're the center of the universe and God's gift to women, but you're not the center of my world, Jon Adamson. Maybe it's time to get over yourself."

He waited while she finished her little speech. Then he grabbed the price tag that was still dangling from her collar, tugging it free.

"Must have been hard to find that T-shirt on such short notice. Like I said, it's nice to know you care."

He dropped the tag into her hand. He'd delivered the

perfect exit line and the script called for him to walk away now. But he couldn't resist hanging around to see her reaction. Maybe it made him a little twisted, but he was starting to enjoy these sparring sessions.

She looked at the tag in her hand, then slowly raised her gaze to his. He was all set to savor his victory, but she shifted slightly and a shaft of sunlight hit her face, catching her eyes and glinting off the earrings that Tyler and Ally had given her.

He blinked.

Ally was way off base—Gabby's eyes were far richer than the gemstones sparkling at her ears. He didn't even have a name for the warm golden tone of her irises. Cognac? Honey? Amber? None of them seemed adequate. Set off by long, dark lashes, they were hands down, no questions asked, the most arresting, beautiful eyes he'd ever gazed into. No mineral composite dug out of the ground was ever going to do them justice.

The silence stretched between them. Jon realized he was staring, but couldn't make himself stop.

"I suppose you think you're pretty clever," she said.

"No."

For the life of him he couldn't think of anything else to say. Then she stepped out of the sunlight and his brain came back online.

"I want to apologize," he said. "For last night. For the whole gay/lesbian thing."

Her mouth tightened. "You already said sorry. It was a misunderstanding. I get it."

He looked at k.d. lang again. "Do you?"

She pulled her keys from the lock and dropped them into the pocket of her baggy pants.

"You done? Because I've got work to do." She turned

on her heel. He grabbed her elbow. She stilled, then narrowed those incredible eyes.

How had he not noticed them before? He must have been blind.

"I really am sorry, Gabby. I know we didn't exactly get off on the right foot, but I didn't mean to embarrass or hurt you last night."

He felt her stiffen. She shook off his hand.

"I wasn't embarrassed. And you certainly didn't hurt me. I barely know you. Why would I care what you think of me?"

She was so damned prickly. He bet the word *gracious* wasn't even in her vocabulary.

"You know, I have no idea. Just like I have no idea why I even bothered to apologize again. You go ahead and enjoy your indignation. I'm sure it's very satisfying." He walked away from her.

"Fine. I accept your apology," she called after him.

"Good. Great." He pushed through the swinging door with more verve than strictly necessary.

The door swung sharply back, cutting off anything she might have been about to say. He stood in the silent workshop for a long beat, trying to rein in his temper.

What was it about her that pissed him off so much? Even when he tried to be nice they wound up fighting. She took everything he said the wrong way, even his apologies.

He simply didn't get it.

The door opened and Gabby entered. She didn't look at him as she marched toward her office. He watched her straight spine, then he shrugged.

So what if she didn't like him? He wasn't one of those people who had to have everyone love him. He was a big boy. He could live with her animosity. It wasn't as though it was forever, after all. A few months from now, he'd be somewhere else and she'd be nothing but a fading memory, notable only for her defensiveness and fantastic eyes.

He turned his back on her. He had work to do.

CHAPTER FOUR

GABBY FELT LIKE AN IDIOT. She'd been so determined to show Jon that she didn't give two hoots what he thought of her. Then she'd put so much time and energy into dressing to meet his mistaken assumptions that she'd done the exact opposite. She might as well have stuck with the miniskirt and stilettos.

She glanced at the k.d. lang T-shirt. She'd had to drive twenty minutes out of her way to pick it up this morning before coming to work. Just so she could thumb her nose at Tyler's brother.

God, she was dumb.

But that was fairly well established after last night's self-revelation.

What had she said to him? *I barely know you. Why would I care what you think of me?*

It should have been true. She wished it was. But she had only to look in the mirror to know what a big fat lie it was. She'd spent *hours* this morning caring about what Jon thought of her. And for the life of her she didn't understand why.

The beginning of a headache pulsed behind her left eyebrow. She pulled her in-tray close and grabbed a stack of invoices. She needed to stop gnawing on this stuff. It was doing her head in—literally.

It took some serious willpower, but gradually she lost herself in her work. The rest of the team straggled in, until finally she heard Tyler's deep voice as he called out a greeting to the crew.

Her stomach tensed and she put down her pen.

Any minute now he would stick his head through the door and say hello. A dart of panic raced up her spine.

Relax. It's a day like any other. He'll say hi, and you'll say hi back, and the world will keep spinning. The same as it did yesterday, the same as it will tomorrow.

The only difference was, yesterday she hadn't acknowledged that she was still in love with Tyler. Seeing him this morning, looking into his face with all those feelings of grief and rejection so close to the surface... It was going to be hard. Damned hard.

"Morning, Gab. Anything I need to know about?" Tyler asked from the doorway.

She took a moment to compose herself before facing him. Tyler must never know how she felt. Ever.

"All good here, chief," she said, a bright smile on her face.

"Bloody hell. What have you done to your hair?"

She blinked. "Excuse me?"

"It looks like a helmet. Or that snap-on plastic hair they have for Lego figurines," Tyler said, moving closer to get a better look.

For a moment she didn't know what he was talking about, then she remembered she'd pulled out all the stops for Jon this morning, including gluing her hair down with gel and creating a ruthlessly straight side part.

"Is that hair gel?" Tyler asked.

"I'm trying something different."

"Like what? Sculptural hair? I could carve this stuff." He tapped her hair experimentally.

Gabby pushed her chair back out of his reach. "I'm

going to go out on a limb here and guess you have no idea how rude you're being right now."

If this were truly a new look she was experimenting with, she would be utterly crushed by his reaction. As it was, she was mildly offended. It didn't look *that* bad. In fact, before she'd scrubbed off her makeup this morning she'd thought she looked a bit like one of the models in that Robert Palmer "Addicted to Love" video.

"Sorry. It's just— I guess you took me by surprise."

"Next time I try something different I'll make sure to run it past you in advance."

Tyler wisely shifted the subject to a work matter. They talked for a few more minutes, then he gave her hair one last bemused look before heading for the kitchen to make his coffee.

She kneaded her forehead with her fingers after he'd left, painfully aware that the conversation was the sort of exchange a brother might have with his kid sister. Vaguely insulting and comfortably familiar. If ever there had been any doubt in her mind about where she stood in his life—and there wasn't—that conversation would have killed it stone dead.

She was Tyler's friend. No doubt if Ally had come along sooner in his life that was all she would ever have been.

The phone rang, providing a welcome circuit breaker for her thoughts. It was only as she was reaching for the receiver that it hit her that despite having known her for only three days, Jon had taken one look at her this morning and understood exactly why she was dressed like a drag king. Not so Tyler, who had known her for years.

She wasn't sure what the realization meant, but like everything to do with Jon, it made her uneasy.

AFTER TYLER'S REACTION, SHE should have known the rest of the crew wouldn't be able to resist offering their unsolicited opinions on her new hairstyle. By midmorning she'd pretty much resigned herself to a day of taking it on the chin. Every time she passed through the shop they hit her with another question. Dino wanted to know when she'd joined the army. Paul asked if they should call her Gabe from now on. Kelly kept calling her Che and asking when the revolution would begin.

They were her friends and they were funny and she couldn't help but laugh, even though she was acutely aware of Jon taking it all in, his dark gray eyes not giving anything away as usual. She wondered idly if he'd had to practice to perfect that opaque, emotionless expression. Maybe he'd taken the Sphinx as his model. Or one of those impassive stone heads on Easter Island.

It was pie day at the local pub on Wednesdays—a favorite with the boys—and Dino ducked into her office before lunch to persuade her to join them.

"Can't this week, sorry. Gotta get this stuff into the mail or we'll miss another billing cycle," she said, gesturing toward the pile of invoices on her desk. Getting their clients to pay in a timely manner was the bane of her existence.

"I'll have two pies, in solidarity," Dino promised.

"You're a trouper. I'm touched."

The workshop was silent when she exited her office in search of a stray invoice a short while later. As usual, there were several pieces in production, each at various stages of completion. A still-rough dining table in spotted gum. A hall table in plantation mahogany. A sideboard in rich red gum. But it was the small, delicate drum table sitting in the corner that drew her eye. She veered off course to inspect it.

Made from aged French oak, it was one of Tyler's new designs, based on a client brief. The legs were curved and sensuous, the top simple but beautiful, the clean design allowing the grain of the wood to take center stage. She rested a hand on the smooth surface, unable to keep the smile from her face. She had zero creative ability herself, but she could appreciate it in others and she'd always admired Tyler's ability to coax the best from a piece of wood.

"Pretty sexy, isn't it?"

She glanced over her shoulder as Tyler approached. "It's beautiful. The Lintons are going to be over the moon."

"They should be. Jon's put in a lot of hours making this design work."

Gabby couldn't hide her surprise. "Jon did this? I thought he was just a builder?"

"Nothing *just* about any of Jon's stuff. He and his partner in Canada built artisan houses, one-offs for people who could afford to pay for the best. Some of their places would blow your mind."

Tyler crouched and inspected the legs more closely. "I thought I was going to have to go back to the drawing board on this one. Once Jon started on the legs he realized there was no support at the stress point. I was ready to scrap the whole thing and start again, but Jon was sure he could do something. He used three interlocking dowels here to support the join. Managed to hide it, too. Pretty clever, huh?"

Tyler touched the point where the three legs intertwined in a seamless join. Gabby found herself crouching beside him to inspect it. As Tyler had noted, it was smooth and flawless, the work of a master.

"Yeah. Clever."

Tyler pushed to his feet. "With a bit of luck he'll hang around for a while. I could use his help with all those designs we'll be prototyping for the new collection."

Gabby was slower getting to her feet. "I've been meaning to talk to you about that. I'm doing payroll this afternoon. You didn't mention how you want me to handle Jon's wages…?"

"Right."

She remembered his reticence on the subject when he'd first announced Jon was joining the business.

"Look, if you want to handle it yourself, that's fine. I'll email the payroll file to you."

Tyler rubbed the back of his neck. "Yeah. That's probably not necessary, since Jon is still refusing to take a wage."

"What?"

But she knew she'd heard correctly.

"I argued until I was blue in the face, but it was the only way he'd take the job."

Gabby flashed to the self-righteous little speech she'd delivered after the incident with the blonde in the showroom. *You're the one who's taking advantage of Tyler.*

She closed her eyes briefly. "I wish you'd told me this earlier."

"Jon's a private guy."

"You know he was here at seven-thirty this morning? And that he'll probably be the last to leave tonight?"

Tyler gestured impatiently. "What can I do? Shove the money down his throat? As far as I'm concerned, it's enough that he's here. The rest can wait."

There was an undercurrent to his words, a frustrated determination. He wanted his brother here, in Melbourne. Close.

It was on the tip of her tongue to ask what was really

going on, but she swallowed the question. It wasn't only because she suspected Tyler would be reluctant to answer. She'd seen the way Jon held himself apart, the way he watched the world from behind those eyes. It might seem odd given the tenor of their relationship, but it felt disrespectful to be digging into his personal business behind his back.

"It could get awkward if the other guys find out about this," she said.

"Let's worry about it when it happens."

Gabby studied Tyler a moment. "If he stays longer than a few weeks, you have to revisit this. You know that, right?"

"You sound like Ally."

"Which means we're both right."

"I wouldn't get too hot and bothered about it. He probably won't hang around long enough for it to be a problem."

Gabby was unsettled as she returned to her office. It had all been much simpler when she thought she knew exactly who and what Jon was—before she knew he had it in him to apologize and that he was working for free and that he could bring beauty into the world with his clever hands.

Much, much simpler.

JON STAYED PAST QUITTING TIME again that night. He was working on another prototype for Tyler, but Dino was also waiting on the drawers for a partners desk and he didn't want to let either man down. He had no idea what time it was when he decided he'd done enough for the day and switched off the sander. He brushed the sawdust from his forearms and pulled his phone from his back pocket to check the time. Nearly eight. Right on cue, his stomach rumbled.

He glanced toward Gabby's office. Sure enough, the light was still on. No surprises there—it probably would have killed her to leave without fully briefing him on the alarm system again and giving him a hard time of some description.

He swept the floor and put away tools, and only when he'd run out of things to do did he approach Gabby's office. She wasn't behind her desk, however, and he went in search of her. Light spilling from the open doorway of a room at the rear of the building drew his attention. He stopped when he reached the threshold, frowning at the sight of Gabby on a tall ladder, burrowing through an archive box that was balanced at the very top of a long metal shelving unit. The remaining walls in the small room were lined with similar shelves, all of them loaded with filing boxes and folders.

"That must be some pretty urgent paperwork you're after," he said.

She started, clutching the side of the ladder to prevent herself from falling.

He stepped forward. "Sorry. I didn't mean to scare you."

"I'm fine. And you didn't scare me. You just took me by surprise."

"There's a difference?" he asked, reaching out to brace the ladder.

She twisted to look down at him.

"Yes." She frowned. "What are you doing?"

"Steadying the ladder."

"It's not going anywhere."

"Now it isn't."

She sighed heavily. "This is one of those male chivalry things, right? Like opening car doors?"

"You have a problem with me making sure your ladder doesn't overbalance?"

"I've climbed this hundreds of times. It's not going to overbalance. So if you wouldn't mind…" She waved him away with an imperious shooing motion.

"You really have a problem with me holding the ladder steady for you?" he asked incredulously.

"I have a problem with what it represents. If I were Dino, would you be standing there worrying about me?"

"Dino probably wouldn't need the ladder to reach the top shelf."

"That doesn't answer my question."

"If he was up that high, I probably would," he lied.

"Liar."

"Fine. Have it your way." He took a step backward, holding his hands wide to show her she was on her own. "My humble apologies—again—for being courteous."

"Courteous. Right. How would you like it if I implied you were incapable of climbing something as simple as a ladder? Or opening a door? Or changing a lightbulb? Are you telling me you wouldn't find that even vaguely insulting?"

Was there no end to this woman's stubbornness?

"Try not to burn your bra while you're up there," he muttered. "It'll set off the smoke alarm."

"If you're trying to be derogatory, at least get your facts straight. Contrary to popular belief, no bras were ever burned as part of the feminist movement."

He rolled his eyes. "I stand corrected."

"What's wrong, afraid to really think about it? Afraid it will mess with your world order if you acknowledge that I'm perfectly capable of climbing a ladder on my own?"

He frowned. "I was being courteous. Considerate. It was what my mother taught me to do."

She'd taught him a bunch of other things, too, of course. That he'd deserved every blow his father aimed at him. That he was ungrateful, selfish, no good. That he was destined for failure, along with his brother. That he was a disappointment and the cause of so much of her unhappiness.

"I bet your mother told you pornography was bad, too, and that women belonged on a pedestal," she said.

She was right on the money, but he wasn't going to let her know that.

"You telling me you think pornography is *good?*"

"Not all of it. There's some good stuff around, but a lot it is frankly laughable. At the end of the day, it's all about taste. So basically as long as it's consensual, I don't have a problem with it. I've got bigger things to worry about than sex between consenting adults."

There was a long silence as he grappled with the idea of a porn-loving Gabby Wade.

"What's wrong, cat got your tongue?" She was enjoying herself, her eyes bright with challenge.

"I'm wondering what bigger things than sex between consenting adults you have on your mind."

"Touché."

"At last."

She was smiling as she started down the ladder. "I guess every dog has his day. If he waits long enough."

"I've always been a patient man."

She glanced over her shoulder to give him a dry look—which was probably why she fumbled the next rung. She wasn't far from the ground. She probably wouldn't have hurt herself if he'd stood back and let it happen. She might even have recovered her balance.

He didn't give her a chance. He reached up to support her lower back, his other hand making a grab for the side of the ladder. That hand gripped cool metal. The other grabbed a handful of feminine backside.

A minor miscalculation.

They both stilled. He knew he should let go and take a step backward, putting some distance between them. Knew he was about to get the feminist tongue-lashing of a lifetime. But he was too busy registering the warm resilient shape of her in the palm of his hand to do much more than stand there like a dodo.

Who knew that Gabby Wade had been hiding a sweet, tight little butt beneath all that baggy khaki? A truly perfect handful.

She cleared her throat. "Would you mind unhanding my ass?"

"Sure. Of course." But it took a real act of will to make himself uncurl his fingers and step away.

She finished descending the ladder and made a big show of dusting her hands down the front of her khakis before meeting his eye.

"Thank you. For the rescue, not the grope."

"It was an accident."

"I know. I just wanted to be clear."

She grabbed a sheaf of papers from one of the lower shelves and turned for the door. He waited till she was gone before mouthing an obscenity.

This morning, she'd been an irritant, a thorn in his side. Then she'd walked into a beam of sunlight and he'd discovered the depths in her eyes.

And now he knew she had a fantastic ass.

She's still got a mouth that won't quit and more attitude than a mall full of teenagers.

Both of which should have more than neutralized the power of those eyes and that ass. But today he'd also discovered that she had a sense of humor. The guys had ragged her mercilessly over her terrible hairstyle and her army boots and she'd copped it on the chin and laughed along.

All of which led him to an almost inescapable conclusion: she wasn't quite the unmitigated pain in the rear he'd first imagined her to be. Instead, she was shaping up to be almost…fascinating.

Dude, you need to get out more. When was the last time you got laid?

It was a good question. Well over two months ago, by his calculations, back when he'd been wrestling with the ghosts of childhoods past in Woodend. Clearly he was overdue for a little horizontal action if he was starting to eye his brother's scary office manager with carnal intent.

As for the idea of actually making a move on her…

He laughed out loud. As if that was ever going to happen. He might be horny, but he wasn't deluded. Gabby would shred him verbally then stomp all over him with her hobnailed boots if he even looked at her funny.

Shaking his head at the craziness of his own thoughts, he followed Gabby.

GABBY COULD HEAR HER HEARTBEAT thumping in her ears as she marched to her office. She wanted to pretend it was because she'd set such a brisk pace returning from the archive room, but she wasn't that good a liar.

Her heart was beating like a tom-tom because Jon

had touched her ass. Not just touched, *grasped*. In a very male, very possessive, very intent way. She could still feel the heat of his hand burning through the seat of her khakis. Worse, she could still feel the answering heat that had washed through her.

It had been a long time since a man had touched her intimately. Years, in fact, for reasons she'd spent the night sobbing over. And yet she'd gone up in flames the moment Jon's hand had curled around her.

It had taken every ounce of self-control she possessed to tell him oh, so coolly to unhand her then look him in the eye and chastise him for groping her. What she'd really wanted to do was grab him by his shirtfront and shake him and demand to know why, after all these years, he had to be the one who reminded her that sex had once been a very welcome and needful part of her life.

Because that was what he'd done with a single touch. A bare five seconds of contact. Long enough to tilt her world off its axis.

I don't even like him.

But she was wise enough in the ways of the world to understand that sometimes it wasn't about liking the other person. Sometimes it was about pure animal attraction. And apparently, whether she liked it or not, the animal in her was definitely attracted to the animal in him.

She could hear Jon's footsteps and she pulled her keyboard close and started typing. Just in case he thought she'd been sitting here brooding over what had happened between them.

She watched in her peripheral vision as he stopped in the doorway and crossed his arms over his chest, propping his hip against the frame. Waiting for her to acknowledge him.

She made him wait a long time before she glanced up. "Sorry. I didn't see you there. I thought maybe you'd gone home," she fibbed.

He let a beat pass. She had the distinct impression he could see through her, down to the fact that she was struggling to look him in the eye without blushing like a Catholic schoolgirl.

"How much longer do you think you'll be?"

"About another half hour. Why?"

"Just checking." He pushed himself away from the doorway and disappeared into the workshop.

She stared at the place he'd been standing, going over what he'd said in her mind. Then she went looking for him.

He'd pulled a stool up to the corner workbench he'd made his own over the past few days and was poring over a set of blueprints.

"Listen, Jon, you don't need to hang around because of me."

He raised his eyebrows and immediately she felt stupid.

"I mean, I lock up on my own all the time. So you don't need to feel obliged to escort me to my car or anything."

"Okay."

It was the sort of frustrating nonanswer she should have expected from him and it left her with exactly nowhere to go. She shifted her weight from one foot to the other.

"Well," she said.

Turning on her heel, she went to her office. She spent the next twenty minutes trying to concentrate and failing miserably. Despite what Jon had said, she couldn't get past the feeling that the only reason he was still hanging around was because of her. She hated the notion that he felt he had some misguided obligation to play bodyguard to her, but she suspected it was exactly the sort of Me-Tarzan-You-Jane value he subscribed to.

She'd been working late for years, ever since Tyler had first employed her. Not once in all that time had she required the services of a security escort—and she didn't want one now. But how was she supposed to get rid of a man who refused to admit he'd cast himself in the role of gallant knight?

When she'd typed the wrong figures into a spreadsheet three times in a row, Gabby realized she was both too tired and too distracted to keep working. She saved the file and shut down her computer, then switched on the answering machine and grabbed her bag.

Jon was still at his bench, his head propped on his hand as he studied the blueprints. It wasn't until she was only a few feet away that she saw his eyes were closed. She remembered that, like her, he'd started early this morning. She reached out a hand to rouse him, only to find herself hesitating.

He looked oddly boyish with his eyes closed. His dark lashes fanned across his cheeks, and there was something supremely innocent and unguarded in his expression. Perhaps it was the softness around his mouth, or maybe it was because he wasn't barricading himself away behind those impenetrable eyes of his. Whatever it was, it made her pause for a heartbeat before she finally rested her hand on his shoulder.

"Jon," she said softly.

His eyes snapped open.

"You were asleep."

"Man. I only closed my eyes for a second." He looked sheepish.

She realized her hand was still on his shoulder. She dropped it to her side and took a step backward. "I'm heading off now. Do you want me to go over the alarm for you again?"

"It's Tyler's birth year, right?"

"That's right."

"Then I'm good." He gave her a small smile and she could suddenly see how tired he was.

"You should go home, too," she said before she could stop herself. It was none of her business what he did. She wasn't his mother, or—God forbid—his wife.

"Yeah, I should." He stood and stretched. "I'll walk you out."

The hem of his T-shirt rode up as he arched his back and she caught a flash of hard male belly. She looked away, disconcerted. The last thing she needed was to know what Jon's belly looked like.

They walked to the showroom in silence. Gabby unlocked the door, remembering how she'd had to let him in this morning and how they'd squabbled like children after he'd apologized. She glanced at him and saw that he was watching her, a faint smile lurking around his mouth, and she knew exactly what he was thinking.

"One for the road?" she asked.

"What the hell. What do you want to argue about? Freedom of speech? Animal cruelty? Politics?"

"They're all pretty tempting."

"We could always skip straight to the insults."

"Now, that's really tempting."

His eyes glinted with appreciation. He crossed his arms over his chest. "Go for it. I'll give you a free shot."

She eyed him for a moment, then shook her head. "You know what? It's been a long day. I'm going to pass."

"Chicken."

"Maybe. Good night, Jon."

She slipped past him to the parking lot. As he had last time, he lingered until she was in her car and had started the engine. Then, and only then, did he lift his hand in farewell.

As she drove home, she wondered how much longer he intended to work. Then she remembered that she'd been convinced he'd hung around only because he didn't want her to lock up on her own.

That was the thing with Jon—she never could find her feet with him. She had no idea where the truth lay—if he was a misguided chivalrous knight determined to minister to a reluctant damsel who definitely wasn't in distress, or if he was simply a man who was in no rush to go home.

She flexed her hand on the steering wheel, remembering the firmness of his shoulder when she'd woken him.

It was the first time she'd touched him voluntarily. She wondered why that felt so significant. Then she shrugged it off. She was hungry and tired. She'd stopped thinking straight hours ago.

Her apartment smelled stuffy when she let herself in. The light on the answering machine stared at her like an unblinking eye, signaling that she had no messages. There was dust on the windowsills and a vase of dead flowers on the corner table.

She stared at them, wondering how long they'd been all wilted and shriveled and unnoticed. Two weeks? Three? She honestly couldn't remember.

She walked slowly into her bedroom and stared at the mess she'd left this morning. The scrunched up tissues from her crying jag, the discarded clothes, her abandoned towel.

It occurred to her that Jon wasn't the only person who wasn't rushing home at the end of the day.

"Gabriel Wade, you need to get a life."

Even though she was only talking to herself, her words had the ring of resounding truth.

CHAPTER FIVE

JON WORKED LATE THE FOLLOWING two nights. Both times he manufactured reasons to hang around after the work Dino had assigned him was completed while waiting for Gabby to finish for the day.

He was well aware that Gabby would spit nails if she learned he was staying because of her. But it was beyond him to walk away and leave her alone in a dark building in the middle of an industrial neighborhood. Tyler might be fine with it. Jon was not.

It wasn't as though he had anywhere better to be, and there was an odd sort of comfort in knowing another human being was only a few feet away. Even if he and Gabby barely exchanged half a dozen words once everyone else had gone home, hearing her at her computer and move papers around on her desk was far better company than sitting in his apartment staring at bad TV.

It probably said something about both his social skills and current mental state that finding a more attractive third option was beyond him.

Saturday brought a new challenge—his first full day in months with no work on hand to distract him. When he'd been in Woodend, there had always been something to do, no matter what the time of day or week. But he was a wage slave now—even if he wasn't technically taking a wage—which meant his weekends were his own.

Yippee.

He tried to sleep in, but by 7:30 he was wide awake, staring at the ceiling. He cleaned the apartment and did his laundry. It didn't take nearly long enough. The apartment was a shoebox, and after months of working on the house, most of the clothes he'd brought with him from Canada had been more or less trashed. His current wardrobe consisted of several pairs of new jeans and a handful of T-shirts in either black or white. One load of washing and he was done.

Which meant by 10:00 he was at loose ends again. He walked to the corner store to buy a newspaper, but by the time he'd read the damned thing from cover to cover he was ready to throw something off the balcony.

He needed to do something. Frame a wall or rip up a floor or sand a table. Without the distraction of hard labour, his thoughts inevitably drifted to the past. He didn't want to go there. But what he wanted didn't seem to be holding much sway with his psyche these days.

He'd thought he'd left it all behind when he'd left Australia. Thought he'd consigned all the beatings and abuse and fear to the dark corners, never to see the light of day. He'd made a life for himself in Toronto, built a business. No one had known the truth about him, where and what he'd come from. He'd been free to become whoever he wanted to be.

Then, out of the blue, Tyler had called to say their father had cancer and it had all come rushing back.

The pain. The shame. The failure and guilt and anger. All the crap Jon thought he'd walked away from. All the memories.

His chair scraped across the floor as he stood abruptly and grabbed his car keys. What he really wanted to do was drive to the liquor store and load up on beer and spirits. Instead, he drove to the local school and ran lap after lap around the football field. Anything to stop his churning thoughts.

He ran till he was dripping with sweat, till his muscles ached and his lungs burned. Then he stretched out on the grass and stared at the sky while the sweat cooled on his body and his heart rate returned to normal.

For the first time all week he felt calm, his body relaxed. And all he'd had to do to get here was almost kill himself.

After ten minutes, the sound of voices approaching made him sit up. Two women were circling the field, each with a small white dog straining on the end of a leash. One of the women was tall with red hair and legs up to her armpits. The other was small and petite with short dark hair.

His eyes narrowed as he honed in on the shorter woman. Surely it wasn't…? What were the odds, given all the football fields in all the suburbs of Melbourne?

He glanced at himself. His T-shirt was soaked with sweat, his shorts equally drenched. He ran a hand over his hair, smoothing it down. Then he caught himself. What the hell did he care how he looked, even if it was Gabby?

Especially if it was Gabby.

The women were getting closer with every second. The smaller woman threw back her head and laughed. He looked away.

It wasn't Gabby. Gabby's laugh was low and earthy. This woman's was high, a little nervous.

He waited until the women had passed him before pushing to his feet and dusting the grass off his backside.

He should have known it wasn't Gabby the moment he'd spotted the fluffy dog. No way would she be caught dead with a designer pooch. If she had a dog, it'd be something big and scary and substantial like a Rottweiler or a Doberman or an Irish wolfhound. A big dog to match her big attitude. It hit him suddenly that he was disappointed that it hadn't been her.

Which means you really are a perverse SOB.

He thought about it as he crossed the field. It wasn't about those eyes of hers or the cute little behind he'd inadvertently discovered. It was simply that when he was with her, he wasn't thinking about anything or anyone else. Including himself. She sharpened his focus, kept him on his toes.

So, yeah, he was a little disappointed it hadn't been her.

Not a big deal.

Palming his car keys, he got in his truck and headed home.

GABBY WINCED A LITTLE AS SHE pulled on her underwear that evening. She'd paid a visit to the salon today and had the works—pedicure, bikini wax, facial, haircut. It was her birthday, and she'd figured she deserved a little pampering. After that, she'd met her sister for a late lunch and some shopping. She pulled the red dress she'd bought as part of her birthday splash-out over her head and wriggled until she'd tugged it down her body. The hem hit her at midthigh. Looking at herself in the mirror in her bedroom without the encouraging salesgirl at her side and all the bright lights and loud music of the store to lull her into a false sense of wonderfulness, she couldn't help wondering if maybe, perhaps, the dress was on the short side. She was thirty-three, after all, not twenty-three.

After a long moment she shrugged. What the hell.

It was only the company Christmas party. While Tyler always invited a few suppliers and clients and some of the guys often brought friends, it was unlikely that there would be many hot prospects there tonight. Still, it would be a good way to dip her toe into the dating waters. She could polish up her rusty flirting skills and ease herself into things. Once she was feeling a little more solid, she would phone one of her party-loving friends—Shona, or maybe Dee, or maybe both—and hit the clubs. Or wherever it was that women went to meet men these days. She honestly had no idea, which was sad in and of itself given how long it had been since she broke up with Tyler.

She slipped her black ankle boots on. Then she did her makeup. A touch of blush to highlight her cheekbones. Two shades of golden-brown eye shadow, black kohl. A deep berry-colored lipstick to match her nails and toenails. She finished with a spray of her favorite Dolce & Gabbana perfume and stood back. Her shapeless helmet of hair had been transformed into a tousled, sexy gamine style thanks to the attentions of a very expensive hairdresser. Her eyes looked big and mysterious, her mouth shiny and red.

She reached for the Santa hat she'd bought, a token nod toward her usual practice of dressing up for the Christmas party, then decided against it. You didn't spend two hundred bucks on a cut and color only to hide it under a hat. The world would have to live with the fact that this year, Gabby Wade was going to be the life of the party in a different way.

Brave words.

She wasn't feeling quite as brave as she inched out of her car half an hour later. Amazing the things you could forget, such as how hard it was to get out of a car without disgracing yourself when you were wearing a short skirt. Finally, she managed to haul herself to her feet, tugging the hem of her skirt down and smoothing it over her hips. One of her heels sank into the lawn and she held on to the car door while she tugged herself free.

A very elegant start to the evening.

It's practice, remember? This is a trial run.

That didn't stop the butterflies from doing an aerial show in her stomach as she click-clacked her way up the garden path. There was no way people weren't going to notice her change of appearance. They were going to comment, and Dino and the crew were going to make jokes. And Jon was going to look at her and—

She stopped in the middle of climbing the porch stairs.

Jon was going to look at her and…what? Stare? Drool? Laugh?

She didn't want any of those reactions from him. She didn't want anything from him at all.

A car door slamming announced the arrival of more guests and she stepped onto the porch and hit the doorbell. Ally opened the door wearing a flowing white halter-neck dress.

"Gabby! Wow. You look fabulous. You're going to cause a riot in that dress." Ally gave Gabby a frank once over. "Turn around so I can check all of you out."

Gabby dutifully turned in a circle.

"Check out that little caboose of yours. I think I'm going to have to stand out of the way so I don't get crushed beneath the stampede when the guys see you."

"Hardly," Gabby said, half-grateful, half-embarrassed by her friend's assessment.

"I have a feeling this is going to be a good party."

They walked together into the open living space at the rear of the house. The room was already crowded. Dino, Kelly and Carl were hanging around the kitchen counter, helping themselves to the chips and dips. To Gabby's everlasting chagrin, they all stopped and stared the moment they saw her.

"Hubba hubba. Come and sit on Santa's knee, Gabby baby," Dino said with a comic leer.

"Could have given us a bit of warning, Gab. Heart's not what it used to be," Kelly said.

Carl simply stuck two fingers in his mouth and wolf-whistled so loudly Gabby was amazed the windows didn't shatter.

Ally laughed, delighted. "What did I tell you?"

Gabby made a disparaging noise but she could feel herself blushing as people looked over, clearly wondering what all the fuss was about.

This is what you wanted, wasn't it? To remind everyone that you're a woman?

"What would you like to drink? Champagne? Beer? White wine?" Ally asked.

"Um, champagne would be great."

Gabby let her gaze drift around the room, smiling as she caught the eye of one of their major clients and lifting a hand to wave to Dino's wife, Lucia. Then Lucia shifted and Gabby found herself locking gazes with Jon.

He stood near the window, a bottle of beer in hand. He gave her a leisurely head to toe. She fought the urge to suck in her tummy or jut out a hip or tug down her hem. When he'd finished his perusal, he lifted his beer and took a long, slow pull. As usual, his dark eyes gave nothing away.

Yet somehow she felt she knew exactly what he was thinking: that her skirt was too short, her shoes too high, her makeup too heavy.

Well, too bad, buddy, because I didn't dress like this for you. I dressed like this for me.

She turned her shoulder on him. Screw him. He was the last person she wanted to impress.

Ally returned with a glass of champagne and Gabby took a gulping swallow. Bubbles hit the back of her throat and a few seconds later she felt the warmth of alcohol spreading through her empty stomach.

Ally was right. This was going to be a great party.

Tilting her head, she drained the rest of her drink and went in search of another.

JON WATCHED GABBY CROSS THE room in her stiletto boots, her hips and ass swaying provocatively with every step.

He wasn't the only man watching, just as he was sure he wasn't the only man wondering if her slim, finely muscled legs were as smooth and firm as they looked.

So much for her dressing as either a reindeer or a Christmas tree.

He swallowed another mouthful of apple juice. He'd made a deal with himself that he'd endure the party for another hour. But maybe now he'd stick around a little longer.

In case Gabby had any other surprises up her sleeve.

Ally and Tyler had asked him to come early so he could help Tyler rearrange some furniture—Ally was redecorating for the fourth time since he'd known her—and he'd been left to kick his heels for half an hour while his hosts had slipped off to "shower" before the guests arrived. As Jon had expected, neither Ally nor Tyler had been ready in time to greet the first wave of guests and it had been left to Jon to play host, directing people to the bar on the patio and taking their coats and handbags into the guest room.

At least it had given him something to do. Once Tyler had emerged from the master suite looking both sheepish and a little smug, Jon had been demoted to the role of guest and the real torture had kicked in.

He wasn't a party person at the best of times, but the prospect of enduring several hours of polite chit chat with a group of people he barely knew without the benefit of a few beers under his belt seemed like a refined form of punishment.

He'd been sober for ten days. Ten long, hard days. By now, he'd figured the whole abstinence thing should have been getting easier. It was simply a matter of discipline, right? And yet he'd cruised past the bar more times than he cared to count this evening, his gaze lingering on the bottles of beer spilling out of the ice tubs, his mind handing him excuse after excuse to grab one of those icy-cold bottles.

It was a party, after all. A special occasion. He could start his cold turkey thing again tomorrow.

And everyone else was drinking. He'd be out of step with the social rhythm if he remained stone-cold sober.

And so on.

Each time he'd kept walking, helping himself instead to one of the sparkling apple juices Ally had bought for him.

"In case you're driving tonight," she'd said when he'd first arrived. "I figured they'd be a change from water."

No point pretending that he hadn't been offended by

her considerate gesture. He'd felt coddled, patronized. As though everybody was bending out of shape to accommodate his perceived weakness.

Careful with drink around Jon. He can't control himself.

Only the knowledge that the past ten days had been far, far harder than he'd imagined had stopped him from letting her know what she could do with her apple juice.

Now, he crossed the room to dump the empty bottle in the bin, then worked his way through the crowd until he was stepping out onto the patio.

Gabby was on the lawn, her red dress drawing his eye like a flare. She was talking with Ally and a bunch of young guys he didn't recognize. To a man they were all grinning like idiots, their chests puffed out as they checked her out with varying degrees of subtlety. As he watched, Gabby laughed at something one of them said, then gulped from her champagne glass.

She was really knocking back the drinks. If she didn't pace herself, she'd be messy drunk within the hour.

Check out Sir Drinkalot. Policing other people's consumption when he can barely get a grip on his own.

What Gabby did was none of his business. Just as it was none of his business that every man in the group with her was wondering what it was going to take to get her into bed tonight.

Common sense told him to go inside and forget about her. Instead, he crossed to the barbecue where Tyler was holding the fort. Jon remained there for the next half hour, ostensibly making small talk and trading jokes with his brother and a few of the other guys, but in reality keeping tabs on Gabby.

For a little person, she sure could drink. In the time

he watched her she threw back two glasses of champagne before moving onto beer. By the time Tyler was piling the buffet table high with burgers and sausages, she was well on her way to oblivion.

Jon reminded himself that he'd just met her, and that they were hardly bosom buddies—for all he knew, this might be a typical Saturday night for her. Still, he loaded up a plate with meat and salad and a couple pieces of bread, grabbed a knife and fork and napkin, and made his way to where she was still holding court.

"Gabby," he said from behind her.

She turned, her eyes widening when she saw him. He thrust the plate into her hands.

"Ally told me to bring this to you," he lied.

She blinked, frowned, then pursed her lips as though she was about to object.

He should have known—nothing to do with this woman was ever easy.

"By the way, happy birthday. It's tonight, right?" He surprised them both by leaning forward and planting a kiss on her cheek.

She smelled of something floral and fruity and she jerked a little away from him as he withdrew.

"That's right," she said warily.

"Have a good one," he said, raising his apple juice in toast.

Then he headed to the barbecue, his good deed done for the night.

He could feel her following him with her eyes and he kept his face carefully blank as he rejoined his brother.

"What was that all about?" Tyler asked.

"Just making sure she gets something to eat."

"Don't worry, Gabby never passes up a free feed. I

have no idea where she puts it, but she eats more than almost anyone I know."

"Except for the times she skips dinner because she's working late for you."

Tyler frowned, then glanced at her. "She's eased back a lot on the overtime."

"Mate, she worked late almost every night this week."

"I guess I need to talk to her again."

"Like that's going to make a difference."

Tyler gave him a sour look. "You got a better idea, have you?"

"Yeah—hire her an assistant. Or outsource some of the work. She's working from dawn to dusk, which means there's too much to do for one person. Talking to her isn't going to make a difference. She's the kind of person who works until the job is done."

"She won't like that, either, you know."

"Because she's a control freak. Tough. She's killing herself putting in so much time."

Tyler didn't look happy, but Jon figured it was more about the conversation he was going to have to have with Gabby in the near future than the money he'd spend to hire her an assistant. From what Jon had seen, the business could more than afford to take on extra administration staff, and Tyler didn't strike him as being the stingy type.

Ally joined them, encouraging them to abandon their post at the barbecue to come mingle with the guests more. Jon left Tyler in her clutches and filled a plate for himself at the buffet. He found a chair in a quiet corner of the garden and sat, balancing his plate on his knee.

Every time he glanced up he caught sight of Gabby. It was that red dress of hers. Plus she always seemed to be laughing. She had yet another beer and he watched her make short work of it as she flirted and talked with her circle of admirers. So much for trying to slow her down with some food.

She's hardly your responsibility, mate.

The thought was enough to get him on his feet. All his life he'd dodged relationships and held people at arm's length in order to remain unencumbered. He didn't want to have someone else's well-being on his conscience. Didn't want the burden of worrying about their happiness—he had enough trouble keeping his own head above water without worrying about anyone else.

Given he was such a seasoned expert at avoiding personal entanglements, it was more than mildly baffling to him that he seemed to be unable to stop himself from watching over the office manager. First he felt compelled to play bodyguard to her, now he'd appointed himself her moral guardian.

The irony was that she was the last person to welcome his concern. She had attitude to spare, and then some. He was willing to bet that she'd fight to the death rather than admit she needed anyone.

So why was he hovering like a fretful nanny?

He walked inside. Maybe he'd go home after all. There was nothing for him here except temptation and aggravation.

"Just the man I'm looking for. Come help me get the extra wineglasses out of the hall cupboard." It was Ally in full hostess mode.

He allowed himself to be hauled off. He'd go after he'd helped Ally out. Definitely.

GABBY LAUGHED AT SOMETHING ONE of the guys—Vaughn? Or maybe it was Dane?—had said, then lifted her beer to her mouth for a swig. She overestimated the distance between her hand and mouth, however, and the rim of the bottle hit her front teeth with an audible click.

"Oops!" she said, laughing even harder.

God, this was a good party. The best Christmas party Tyler had ever thrown, hands down. Probably that was Ally's touch. She made everything better. She was that kind of person. Warm and friendly and fun. That was probably why everyone was having such a good time.

Because of Ally.

Against her will, her gaze picked Tyler and Ally out of the crowd. They were standing near the bar, heads close together as they talked. He laughed at something she said, then lifted a hand and rested it on the nape of her neck. She kept talking, and all the while his thumb caressed her gently, lovingly.

The way he looked at her, the way he held her—as though she was the most precious thing in the world to him. As though she was a wonder. A miracle.

Envy and sadness twisted inside Gabby. She hated herself for coveting Ally's happiness, for being unable to look away. There was no point to it, only pain.

A swell of music washed over the yard. Gabby allowed it to distract her. A couple of women had claimed the space to the left of the French doors as an impromptu dance floor and cranked up the stereo. Already more people were joining them, moving with varying degrees of skill and grace.

"Dancing. I love dancing," she said to no one in particular.

Dumping her almost empty beer bottle, she turned to the nearest man and grabbed his hand. "Dane. Do you dance? Please tell me you dance."

"Vaughn. And yeah, I'll dance with you." He said it in a way that implied he'd be happy to do a lot more than dance, too.

She smiled at him, enjoying the attention. *This* was what she'd been denying herself for the past few years. Male admiration. The sense that she was desirable. The sense that she meant something to someone.

To anyone.

"Let's go dance, then." Hooking her finger into one of his belt loops, she led him to the dance floor.

A couple of the other guys joined them and pretty soon she was surrounded. She had no idea who half of these people were. Vaughn—Dane?—was one of Kelly's friends. At least, she thought so. Most of them were younger than her, in their early twenties.

"You rock, Gabby," Dane said as he danced close behind her. "You've got the moves."

His hand brushed her hip, then the side of her thigh, then his hips were pressing against her backside, moving with her in time to the beat.

She could go home with him tonight if she wanted to. He was attractive in a young sort of way—blond hair, blue eyes, surfer-guy good looks. His body was lean and boyish, not yet fully developed, but no doubt he'd be an enthusiastic lover.

She tried to imagine kissing him, letting him touch her, but the notion left her cold. She'd never really been into blonds. But that didn't mean she should rule him out all together. She'd decided it was time to get a life, hadn't she? And Dane—Vaughn?—seemed like a good way to kick-start her social life. Definitely he seemed like a good way to create new memories to replace the old ones she'd been picking over like Miss Havisham for the past four years. Even if it was for only one night.

She deserved a little fun, didn't she? A little passion. A little attention.

The song changed to a classic dance track. The area became even more crowded. Closing her eyes, Gabby gave herself over to the music for a few beats, letting the mindless joy of the moment wash over her.

She was alive. She felt good. She was sexy and desirable and fun.

She could do this. She really could. She could get over Tyler.

Then she opened her eyes and caught a glimpse of a severe, expressionless face through a gap in the crowd. For a split second her gaze locked with Jon's. He stood near the French doors, a bottle of beer in his hand as he watched.

A devil prompted her to slip through the crowd toward him.

"Come on, Stonehenge. Loosen up and dance with me."

She grabbed his arm and attempted to pull him toward the gyrating throng. His arm was hard with muscle, his skin very warm. It was like trying to move a mountain and he didn't budge an inch.

"I don't dance."

"Now, there's a big surprise." She released her grip. "Do you ever do anything fun?"

He looked at her silently for a long beat. "I have my moments."

"Whatever that means." Because she wanted to get a rise out of him, she plucked the beer from his hand

and took a swig. Sweet bubbles flooded her palate. She pulled a face.

"What is this?" She peered at the label. "Sparkling apple juice?"

What was he doing drinking apple juice?

"If you're thirsty, I can get you some water."

"You can get me some champagne."

He frowned. She crossed her arms over her chest and imitated both his stance and his frown.

"Should have known you'd be a difficult drunk," he said.

"I'm not drunk," she protested. "Yet."

She poked him in the chest with her finger to emphasize her point, then turned on her heel and sashayed to the dance floor. She knew without a doubt that he watched her backside the entire way and she put a little extra wiggle into it. Just to really annoy him.

She slipped into the middle of the action and only glanced at him when she was sure enough time had passed.

He was still standing there. Watching her. Disapproving.

He'd felt as solid as a rock when she'd poked him. A big, warm, hard rock.

"There you are. Thought I'd lost you," Dane said.

She shifted her attention to the younger, happier man grinning at her and wondered why she'd even bothered to talk to Jon. What did she care if he obviously didn't know how to have a good time? It was nothing to do with her.

She danced to song after song till she was damp with sweat and her calves and thighs ached. She danced with men and women, to hard rock and techno and a club beat. She drank the beers her newfound friends brought her and closed her eyes and raised her arms in the air and moved as though her life depended on it.

For all she knew, it might. Crazier things had happened, and this was the first day of the rest of her life, after all. No matter what happened, she was going to make it count.

GABBY WAS, AS JON'S YOUNGER self would have phrased it, off her face. Not quite falling-down drunk, but pretty damned close.

Someone should do something. Step in and force-feed her some bread or water. Or at least cut her off before she did something really stupid, such as go home with one of the guys who'd been sniffing around her all night.

Jon looked around, but as usual Tyler and Ally were lost in one another, cuddled close together on one of the garden seats. A nuclear bomb could detonate a foot away and they'd be blind to it.

The music switched abruptly to a heartfelt ballad. The dance floor thinned predictably as James Blunt crooned about how beautiful someone was. Gabby looked annoyed, he couldn't help noticing. Then the blond kid who had been practically humping her leg earlier pulled her close and started swaying with her. She looked as though she was about to protest, but she subsided as another couple joined them. Jon smiled at the chagrined, slightly self-conscious expression on his brother's face as Ally stepped into his arms. Like Jon, his brother had never been a big dancer. But clearly he was prepared to make certain sacrifices to please Ally.

If the expression on his brother's face was any

indication, there was little he wouldn't do for her. Leap tall buildings. Split the atom. Fly to the moon.

Jon almost felt embarrassed by the raw devotion in his brother's eyes as he looked into his new wife's face. A little bit of dignity wouldn't go astray. There was no need for the whole world to know how utterly besotted the poor bastard was.

And yet… It was hard to be truly condemning. Tyler looked happy. Happier than Jon had ever seen him. That could only be a good thing.

He was about to cruise the dessert offerings when he caught sight of Gabby again. She was still with the leg humper, her arms looped loosely around his neck. She was watching Tyler and Ally over his shoulder and the misery and desperation on her face was so palpable it stopped him cold.

He followed her sight line to his brother, then returned his gaze to her. Suddenly it him like a freight train.

The unhappiness he'd sensed in her at her birthday party on Tuesday night.

Her almost zealous dedication to Tyler's business.

The "not available" signal she broadcast.

The look in her eyes right now.

She was in love with Tyler.

Desperately in love, if her expression was anything to go by.

Jon looked away. He felt as though he'd seen something he shouldn't have. Something intensely private and personal.

A million questions crossed his mind. How long had this been going on? Did Tyler know? Did Ally?

He looked at Gabby again. Unless he missed his guess, she was seconds from tears.

He scanned the crowd uneasily. He wasn't the only one watching the dancers. Any minute now someone else would see what he had and make the same connection.

He acted before he could think it through. Gabby was a grown woman, more than capable of looking after herself in ordinary circumstances—but tonight was an exception. She'd consumed enough alcohol to fell a horse, and consequently her guard was down. He knew without a doubt that she would be humiliated if she knew her secret was out.

He was there in two strides. He slipped past another couple, then tapped Leg Humper on the shoulder. "My turn."

The guy looked as though he was going to argue the point, but Jon simply stepped between him and Gabby and pulled her into his arms.

"Hey!" she protested.

"Don't worry, this is hurting me more than it's hurting you."

He half danced, half walked her to the edge of the dance floor. Once they were clear of everyone, he let her go.

"You want to sit down? A glass of water?"

"I want to dance. Which was what I was doing until you came along."

"You looked like you needed a break to me," he said quietly.

She shot him a searching, disconcerted look. He held her gaze and she glanced away.

"I was fine. I was having a good time."

"Were you?"

Her chin came up. Some of the desolation had left

her eyes. "Yes, I was. I know you probably found the signs hard to recognize."

"Let me get you some water," he said again. He wasn't going to get any sense out of her tonight. She was too far gone.

"I can look after myself."

She walked away from him, weaving slightly. She made it to the bar where she said something to the bartender. Jon frowned as he watched her accept a glass of champagne. Sober, Gabby was a pain in the ass. Drunk, she was hell on wheels and the most stubborn person he'd ever had the misfortune to know.

Sighing, he headed her way. She was about to sip her drink when he plucked the flute from her hand. Her expression of comic astonishment would have made him laugh under any other circumstances.

"Give that back." She sounded exactly like a thwarted child.

"Time to take it easy."

Her eyes widened with outrage. "Excuse me? Who are you to tell me what to do?"

"I'm doing you a favor. Trust me."

"I don't want you to do me a favor. I don't want anything from you. Except my drink."

Her hand shot out so quickly she'd grabbed the champagne from his grasp before he had a chance to react. Tilting her head, she gulped the entire contents in one big swallow.

The look she gave him as she lowered the glass was pure triumphant defiance.

"That's your last one," he said, taking the glass and handing it to the eavesdropping barman. "No more for Ms. Wade, okay?"

Predictably, Gabby turned pink with outrage as she registered his words.

"Who the hell do you think you are? You're not the boss of me. You're not even close to being the boss of me. I'll do what I like when I like and—"

She paused, a peculiar look passing over her face. She pressed a hand to her stomach.

"Ugh. I don't feel so good."

She'd barely got the words out before she bent over and threw up.

All over his boots.

CHAPTER SIX

GABBY SCOOPED ANOTHER HANDFUL of water from the running tap and sluiced it over her face. Cold water ran down her neck and onto her chest. She blinked, then repeated the action.

The towel Ally had given Gabby was soft against her skin as she blotted her face dry. Her bra was wet from all the water she'd splashed around, and she blotted it with the towel, also, before reaching for the T-shirt Ally had loaned her. She was a little smaller, but it was a decent fit, as were the pair of gray track suit pants, although she had to roll the cuffs a couple of times to stop them dragging on the ground. She wondered vaguely if that meant she was shorter than Ally or if Ally had to roll the pants, too.

Gabby stood in the center of the bathroom for a moment, looking for something else to delay the moment when she had to exit and face her humiliation.

Her sexy red dress was in the corner, a sodden pool of damp, funky-smelling fabric. Tyler had taken her shoes someplace to clean them.

She closed her eyes. Much of the evening was still a blur but the moment where she'd thrown up all over herself and Jon was etched in her memory, like acid on stone.

Of all the men in all the parties in all the world,

why did it have to be his boots she'd tossed her cookies on?

At least the nausea was gone. She'd thrown up twice in front of the bar, then Jon had calmly manhandled her to a distant corner of the garden where she'd thrown up a third time. After it had become clear that the urge to purge had passed, Ally had taken over, leading her inside to clean up.

Even though she was feeling markedly less muzzy than she had been, Gabby was still drunk enough to have lost track of time. How long had she been locked in here? An hour? Twenty minutes? She honestly had no idea.

The only way to find out was to gird her loins, open the door and face the music.

The hall was silent when she emerged. She padded on bare feet into the living area. Empty.

Which meant what remained of the party was probably outside—if it wasn't over entirely. With the exception of high school parties, she couldn't remember a single event that had been enhanced by one of the guests heaving spectacularly in the middle of festivities. Was it any wonder that people had run for the hills?

Gabby shuffled on reluctant feet toward the French doors. Sure enough, Tyler and Ally were out there, talking quietly as they collected empty beer bottles and glasses.

"Hey," she said sheepishly.

They both turned to face her.

"Gabby. How are you feeling? I was about to come check on you," Ally said with a sympathetic smile.

"Better."

Tyler was trying to hide a grin, without much success.

"Don't start," Gabby said. "I'm already going to get it from the guys on Monday."

"I had to tip the barman, he was so traumatized."

Gabby winced. "I'm really sorry. I have no idea what happened."

Tyler laughed outright. "Don't you?"

Ally gave him a dark look. "Don't laugh at her when she's feeling sick."

"Do you want a hand cleaning up?" Gabby asked, because she figured it was better than telling more lies.

She knew exactly what had happened—she'd drunk like a fish because she was in love with a man she could never have.

"We're fine. It's mostly glasses," Ally said. "We'll do the rest tomorrow."

"Then I'll call a cab and get out of your hair." Making a hasty escape smacked of cowardice, but Gabby figured there would be plenty of time to dwell on her foolhardy behavior tomorrow. Then, of course, there was Monday, when the full repercussions would come home to roost.

She figured it would take her about a month to live this night down. Certainly Dino and the guys would give her hell for at least that long.

"Give me a sec to find my keys and I'll drive you," Tyler said.

"No." Gabby held up her hand.

Both Ally and Tyler stared at her and she realized she'd sounded a little too urgent. But the last thing she wanted was to be stuck in a car alone with Tyler when she was feeling this stupid and vulnerable and sorry for herself.

"I mean, you've already had to clean up after me.

Which, again, I'm really sorry for. I'll grab a cab, and you guys can go to bed. I'll be fine."

"It's not a problem," he said.

"I'd really prefer to get a cab."

"Gabby. Relax. I don't mind." He was like the Terminator, unstoppable. Determined to do his duty.

"I'll take her," a deep voice said.

As one, they turned to find Jon standing in the doorway. He was wearing a pair of faded jeans that she recognized as Tyler's instead of the newer pair he'd arrived in, and his boots looked damp.

Great. Apparently, she'd hurled on his jeans as well as his boots. This evening just kept getting better and better.

"Perfect," Ally said. "Gabby's place in Brunswick is pretty much on your way to Thornbury."

Gabby tried to find the words to protest, but Jon already had his keys in hand. Short of throwing a genuine tantrum, there was no way she could avoid having him drive her. Another good deed for him to rack up for the night.

"I'll grab a bag for your things," Ally said, scooting past her into the house.

A few minutes later, Gabby was walking toward a black truck, a shopping bag containing her ruined dress and shoes banging against her calves.

Jon opened the door for her. She hesitated before getting in.

"Look, I can call a cab. I'm sure you don't want—"

"Get in, Gabby." He sounded long-suffering. Like a worn-out parent.

Muttering under her breath, she climbed in.

"Where are your shoes?" Jon asked, apparently noticing her bare feet for the first time.

"They're ruined. And Ally's are a size too small."

He shut the door without commenting. She waited until he'd circled the truck and climbed in before speaking.

"I want you to know I appreciate this. It's kind of you to go out of your way when you must be tired." Not to mention pissed with her for yacking on his boots.

"You might want to hold off on the thanks."

She gave him a searching look. What on earth was that supposed to mean? It was on the tip of her tongue to ask, but at the last minute she decided against it. Almost every conversation she'd ever had with Jon had deteriorated into a fight and she was hardly in top form right now. Far better to let it slide and live to fight another day.

Jon put the truck in gear and pulled onto the road. She clutched her clammy bundle and willed time and space to fold so she could be home that much faster.

"Where am I going?"

"Um, Perry Street. It's off Barkly Street."

"Which side of Sydney Road?"

"The Carlton side."

He nodded and the ride passed in uncomfortable silence. Three times she started to apologize but never got past the point of forming the words in her mind. There was something about his expression that put her off. He looked…forbidding.

Not that she was scared of him or intimidated by him. He might be bigger than her, but she was more than his match.

"We need to take the next left," she said as they drove along the busy café section of Sydney Road. "Perry's the second street on the right."

He followed her instructions and within moments they stopped in front of her apartment block.

"This is me," she said, and she could hear the relief in her own voice. "I'm really sorry about your boots and your, um, jeans. I'll cover the dry cleaning if you let me know what I owe you." She hesitated, then forced herself to finish. "And thanks for looking out for me tonight. You know, the water and the food and whatnot. I guess if I'd listened to you I wouldn't be sitting here in Ally's clothes right now." She threw a self-deprecating smile his way and reached for the door handle.

"It's not going to go anywhere. You know that, right?" he said. "Tyler likes you, but he loves Ally."

Her fingers tightened around the door handle. She wanted to tell him that she had no idea what he was talking about, but she didn't think she could pull it off. All she could pull off, apparently, was a bunny-in-car-headlights stare.

"And he's not the type to cheat, even if he wasn't head over heels." Jon didn't sound condemning. He was simply stating a fact. Yet she was still offended.

"You think I would do that to Tyler? To Ally?"

He shrugged. "People do strange things when they think they're in love."

"Think? I only *think* I'm in love with Tyler, do I?"

"You can never really know someone from the outside looking in. Hell of a lot of crushes have died through familiarity."

From the outside looking in? Crushes?

He doesn't know. He has no idea Tyler used to be mine.

The realization hit her like a slap. But why would he know? He'd been in Canada for over a decade. And before their father's illness had changed things, she'd never known Tyler to contact his brother. They hadn't known the finer details of each other's life, and she couldn't imagine a circumstance where her history with Tyler would have come up in conversation between the two brothers in recent weeks. Men simply didn't talk that way, especially men like Jon and Tyler Adamson.

For some reason, the idea that Jon thought she was the kind of silly, shallow woman who convinced herself she was in love with a man without ever really understanding or knowing him made her blood boil. She wasn't a little kid—she was a woman, with a woman's understanding of the world. Which was why she had bloody well broken up with Tyler in the first place—because she understood herself and him too well to let things grind on any longer.

"You have no idea what you're talking about."

"I saw your face tonight."

She'd guessed as much. Most of the evening was an inchoate blur, but she could remember the ache she'd felt watching Ally and Tyler slow dance together. And Gabby could remember the way Jon had looked at her after he hauled her off the dance floor. Apparently, her poker face needed some serious work.

"You still don't know what you're talking about." She opened the door and swung her legs out of the car. Strong fingers wrapped around her forearm.

"I'm saying this as a friend. Don't waste your time chasing a fantasy."

"We're not friends, and you are so far off base it's not funny. Tyler and I went out for three years. We practically lived together," she said. "So maybe you should get your facts straight before you start handing out advice people didn't ask for."

She tugged her arm free and slid out of the truck.

She slammed the door, then marched up the path and into her apartment building. In some well-hidden, still-sober corner of her brain she noted that Jon didn't drive away until she'd let herself into the secure foyer of her building.

He was such a freaking Good Samaritan.

She stepped into the elevator, fuming at his presumption. Then she caught a glimpse of herself in the polished steel doors—panda eyes, wet hair, someone else's clothes—and her shoulders sagged as all her outrage drained away, leaving her with nothing but shame and embarrassment.

She'd made a fool of herself. She'd behaved like a silly adolescent, flirted with all the wrong people and ignored good advice when it was offered. Then she'd compounded all of the above by getting maudlin and pathetic over Tyler and been so obvious about it that his brother—of all people—had guessed her dirty, sad little secret.

So much for getting a life.

She let herself into her apartment and walked straight to the kitchen. She poured herself a big glass of water, then crossed to the living room. She sat on the couch, knees drawn to her chest, and forced herself to drink all the water, even though she didn't really want it.

Tomorrow was not going to be pretty, on many levels.

She let her head drop back. She was tired and her feet hurt and she felt like the biggest idiot alive. Worse, she was now hugely indebted to Jon, who was the keeper of her secret.

It occurred to her that she should probably be worried that a man she barely knew was privy to her most personal feelings. If he told Tyler or Ally, Gabby's friendship with them would never be the same.

But she wasn't worried. Not even a little bit. Embarrassed, yes. Mortified and angry with herself, too. But not worried.

She pondered the notion for a few minutes, her alcohol-soaked brain moving slowly. She couldn't come up with a solid answer. All she knew was that in some odd, crazy way, she trusted Jon. He was an honorable man, and she knew without asking that he would consider telling anyone her secret a huge breach of trust.

You're really, really drunk.

There was no denying that. Struggling to her feet, she made her way to her bedroom. Between flashbacks to the party and the conversation with Jon, it was a long time before she fell asleep.

GABBY AND TYLER HAD BEEN lovers. Not just lovers, they'd been in a long-term relationship. Three years, she had said.

It felt wrong. Really wrong. And for the life of him Jon couldn't work out why. Tyler had obviously had a life before Ally. Gabby was a grown woman. Big deal if they'd been together.

But Jon couldn't stop chewing it over as he drove home, to the point where he snatched up the phone and called his brother the moment he hit the apartment. It was late, but he was confident Tyler would still be up. And if he wasn't, tough. This was important.

"What's up?" Tyler asked the moment he answered the phone.

"You never told me you'd gone out with Gabby."

There was a small pause. "It never came up."

"You didn't think it was worth mentioning?" He sounded angry, Jon realized. He *was* angry.

"Actually, no. What's going on?"

"How long ago did you break up?"

"I guess it's coming up to four years now."

"Why did it end?"

"You want to tell me why I'm under the hot lights at one in the morning?"

"Why did you break up with her?"

"I didn't end it, she did."

Jon frowned at the wall. Gabby had ended things with Tyler? Yet she was still in love with him. It didn't make sense. "You must have done something."

"Thanks for the vote of confidence."

"Gabby wouldn't have broken up with you without a good reason."

There was a long pause. "What's going on? Did something happen between you two tonight?"

"No."

"Then I don't get it. Why the third degree?"

"She said something, that's all. I was surprised."

"It's not a big deal. It wasn't working between us, she pulled the pin. I met Ally and realized Gabby had been right."

He sounded so matter-of-fact. And yet Gabby was eating her heart out over him.

"Jon. Hello?"

"Yeah. I'm still here."

"Is something going on between you and Gabby? Ally mentioned that she thought there was a bit of a vibe between you two—"

"Nothing's going on. And there's definitely no vibe."

"Right. So why are we having this conversation?"

Jon rubbed the bridge of his nose. "Sorry. I couldn't sleep. I'll see you on Monday."

Tyler sighed heavily. "You know, the sky's not gonna fall if you talk to me. Life as we know it isn't going to end."

"There's nothing to talk about. I was curious, that's all."

"Sure. Whatever you say. See you Monday." Tyler sounded weary.

Jon put down the phone. Calling Tyler had been a mistake. In fact, Jon was beginning to think that coming to Melbourne and taking the job offer had been a mistake, too. Every time he hung out with Tyler, every time they talked, it set up unrealistic expectations. Tyler was so loved-up courtesy of Ally that he couldn't see that it was too late for them to be the kind of brothers who pulled together through the hard times. It had never been that way, and it was crazy to think it could be that way now.

All through their childhood they'd fought their own battles, kept their own counsel. Other brothers might have bonded over the shared experience of a brutal childhood. But not them. And they'd continued the pattern into adult life. The moment he'd been old enough to legally leave home, Jon had bailed and hadn't looked back. Even though he'd known his absence would mean Tyler would bear the brunt of their father's anger, Jon had saved his own skin first. Tyler had left a couple of years later, and after that the only time they had seen each other had been on Mother's Day when they'd both made the annual obligatory guilt visit to Woodend. He'd flown to Canada the day after their mother had been buried and had barely exchanged a handful of emails and phone calls with Tyler over the next decade.

The truth was, Jon knew his ex-business partner better than he knew his own brother. He'd spent more time with him, shared more jokes, shared more of himself than he'd ever shared with Tyler.

Despite the lateness of the hour, Jon flicked on the TV. He knew himself well enough to know he wasn't even close to being ready to sleep yet. His mind was too busy. Gabby, his brother, Gabby *with* his brother, the fact that even now he wanted a beer so badly his mouth watered…

You're a freakin' basket case, you know that?

He turned up the volume on the TV. Anything to drown out this thoughts.

GABBY MADE SURE SHE WAS THE first person in the office on Monday. At least that way she could spare herself the walk of shame past all the men in the workshop. It would be bad enough as it was.

A hot day had been forecast so she'd dressed accordingly in a black wrap skirt and yellow tank. Despite the fact that she'd had half a pack of aspirin and several liters of water yesterday, she was still feeling gritty-eyed and tired as she dropped into her chair and turned on her computer.

Apparently, she was really out of practice with being a party animal. Fancy that.

She'd been working for an hour when she heard the first arrival. She braced herself. If it was Jon, she would have to look into his eyes and know that he was the keeper of her most personal secret. If it was anyone else, she would have to live through the first of what was sure to be many recaps of her behavior Saturday night.

She saw Dino's balding head and relaxed a little. Of the two options, she definitely preferred teasing to self-conscious squirming. Dino sauntered over to her office, his jeans hitched too high as usual.

"Yo, Gabby. How are you doing?"

"Good, thanks. How 'bout you?"

He nodded, a cheerful smile on his middle-aged face. Innocent as the day he was born.

Gabby wasn't fooled for a minute.

"Yeah, I'm good, thanks. Except… Ooh. Wait a minute. I don't feel so good…" A full minute of wretching noises ensued before Dino finally bent forward and let a pizza-shaped piece of plastic vomit fall onto the floor.

He immediately collapsed, laughing. She waited until he'd calmed down a little before smiling benignly at him.

"You done?"

"For the moment. You mind if I take that back?" He pointed to the plastic vomit. "I want to do it again when the boys get in."

"Of course you do." She gestured gracefully toward the plastic vomit. "Help yourself."

Still chuckling, he stooped to collect his prop. "Oh, and Lucia said to remind you about our anniversary party. Not this Sunday but the next, at the Burvale, one o'clock."

"Got the invitation on my fridge," she assured him.

He gave her a thumbs-up and disappeared into the shop to work up more pranks.

By lunchtime she'd collected three fake vomits and a can of pea-and-ham soup. The guys had laughed until they'd cried and she'd listened to them describe her moment of glory many times—complete with sound effects, naturally. Everyone, it seemed, had something to say about her party trick—except Jon. He worked quietly on the latest prototype Tyler had given him to finesse and only looked up from his tools a couple of times when Paul and Kelly were being particularly boisterous. Even then Jon glanced at her briefly as though assessing how she was taking it before resuming his work.

Generally speaking, she loved working in a predominantly male environment, but it was a long day and a real test of her sense of humor. She was more than a little relieved when the shop emptied at five o'clock. Even Jon left on time, which meant she'd be able to work in peace this evening. It felt like a small blessing.

She celebrated by stretching her legs and making herself a cup of coffee. She was pouring in the water when she heard movement in the workshop. She walked to the door of the staffroom. Sure enough, it was Jon.

"I thought you'd gone," she said before she could stop herself.

"I was giving Carl a lift home. His son borrowed his car today."

"Right."

Damn. So much for her peace and quiet. She returned to her office. She could hear Jon moving around as she saved the sales report she'd been working on. Now that it was only the two of them, she couldn't stop thinking about what he'd said to her on Saturday night and the way he'd looked at her when he'd said it. For some reason, that moment in the archive room popped into her head. The warm, firm grip of his hand on her backside. That long, sticky pause between him grabbing her and her telling him to unhand her.

She shook her head to dislodge the memory. She was here to work, not to brood over Tyler's difficult brother. She wrote up another six invoices, then printed them off and folded them into envelopes. She was searching her desk for stamps when she glanced up and realized Jon was standing in the doorway.

"Hi," she said warily.

"I'm going to grab a pizza. You want anything?"

"I'm fine, thanks."

No way was she sitting through an awkward meal with him. Or even a nonawkward one. The less time she spent with him, the better.

He turned to go.

"I don't know if Tyler told you, but there's no rush on that campaign table you're working on," she said, before he could slip off. "So there's really no need for you to put in all these long hours."

Because, really, her life would be a lot easier if she could go back to the good old days when she'd had the place to herself after hours. This arrangement was way too…intimate for her peace of mind.

"Sure."

He left, and she mulled over what he'd said. Or, more accurately, what he hadn't said. Last week she'd been suspicious that he was hanging around at work out of some misguided notion that she needed protecting. She was getting that sense again tonight, by the bucketload. Sure, he'd denied it when she confronted him, but that didn't mean she hadn't been right.

By the time she heard Jon returning with the pizza she'd worked up a righteous head of steam on the subject. She was a grown woman. She lived her own life, made her own decisions. She didn't need or want some random man appointing himself her protector. In the back of her mind, a small part of her observed that it was almost a relief to have a reason to be angry with him again.

Throwing down her pen, she rounded the desk and

strode out to confront him. A wary look came over his face and his steps slowed.

"I want an honest answer," she said. "Do you have work you need to do tonight or not?"

He shrugged. "There's always work to do."

A beautiful nonanswer. He was a master of the art form.

"Okay. Let me ask this another way so we can both be absolutely clear. Are you hanging around on purpose out of some stupid idea that I need help locking up?"

He put the pizza on the workbench. "Does it matter?"

"Uh, yeah, it does. In one scenario, you're here for a legitimate reason. In the other, you're acting like a patronizing chauvinist."

His eyes narrowed. "So thinking it's dangerous for you to be here alone in the dark and walk across a badly lit parking lot makes me a chauvinist?"

"No, assuming I can't take care of myself makes you a chauvinist. I know you'll find it hard to believe, but I stayed here on my own for years—*years*—before you. I don't need you to babysit me."

"Did you see the glass in the street the other day? Someone's car was broken into."

"So?"

"So what if you were leaving when that was happening?"

"I'd call the cops."

"Great. They'd arrive in time to draw the chalk outline."

"I'm not stupid, Jon. I park my car as close to the door as possible. I always make sure I'm locked in. And I might be small, but I can look after myself."

She grabbed his pizza from the workbench and

shoved it at him. "Eat your pizza at home. Your services are not required here, Sir Galahad."

He took the box, but his eyes flashed dangerously. She'd seen that look in his eye one other time—when he'd picked her up and bodily moved her out of the way. A thrill of something that was almost fear raced down her spine. She swiveled on her heel and marched to her office. After a short pause, she heard Jon following her. She ignored him, even though all the little hairs on the back of her neck were standing on end. Only when she was safely on her own turf did she deign to turn and acknowledge his presence.

"Still here?" she asked coolly.

"Show me." He was all belligerent male, his eyes turbulent, his body tense as he moved toward her.

"I beg your pardon?"

"Prove it. Prove to me you can take care of yourself and you won't hear another peep out of me."

Her jaw dropped open. "You are unbelievable. I don't have to prove anything to you."

"You're the one with all the big talk. What have you done? A self-defense course? A bit of tai chi or something?"

She gave him a scathing look.

"Go home, Jon. Before you really piss me off."

"Lady, you have no idea."

He moved closer, crowding her. Every instinct screamed at her to back off, but she refused to play his game.

"I'm not scared of you."

"I'm not the one you need to worry about."

He was so close now she could feel his warmth. His chest brushed her folded arms. She had to tilt her head to maintain eye contact with him, he was so much taller than her.

"What next? Are we going to have a stare-off?" she asked. "Or maybe we could see who can hold their breath the longest?"

He responded by moving closer again, so close that his thighs were pressed against hers, his whole body looming over her. Even though she was determined not to be intimidated, she couldn't stop herself from arching away from him a little. She felt the desk against the back of her thighs and realized she really was cornered.

"Wow. Impressive." She hated the fact that her voice rose slightly on the final word. She flat-out refused to be intimidated by him. "You've proven you're bigger than me. I bet if we got a tape measure your dick would be bigger than mine, too. Is that enough superiority for you for one night?"

He planted a hand either side of her on the desk, effectively boxing her in.

"I know you've got a tongue in your head, but that's not going to stop someone who wants to hurt you. Show me how you can look after yourself, Gabby," he said, his voice low and dangerous.

Their faces were inches apart. She could see the individual whiskers of his five o'clock shadow, could smell his skin and his deodorant.

"I'm not playing games with you."

His body was hot and hard against hers, six foot plus of solid, angry male.

"Aren't you?"

There was something in his eyes that made her shiver all the way to the soles of her feet.

"Back off or I'll give you a head start on singing soprano."

Before he could respond, she ducked under his arm and darted to her left. She barely made it two steps before he was on her, slamming her into the wall. She struck out blindly with her right arm but he grabbed it before it contacted, pinning it to the wall beside her head. She used her knee, but he deflected it with his leg. She fisted her left hand and drove it into where she hoped his solar plexus was, keeping her thumb tucked on the outside the way she'd been taught. He grunted, then he had her left arm, too, and she was pinned by his body weight and his grip on her arms.

They were both panting, their chests heaving as they glared at each other.

"Is that it?" Jon demanded. "That all you've got?"

He released her left arm, sliding his hand boldly down her body to grab her backside. His hand spread wide, he hoisted her higher up the wall. His hips pressed into hers, and she could feel the hard length of his erection pressing against her stomach. Something primitive and utterly instinctual exploded inside her.

"Not even close." She fisted her hand in his T-shirt and leaned forward, sinking her teeth into the thick cord of muscle where his neck met his shoulder.

He stilled. She tasted salt and skin and her head was full of the smell and feel of him. So big and hard and strong. She pressed her tongue against him, tentatively at first, then more brazenly.

Slowly she relaxed her jaw. Lips replaced teeth as she explored his neck with hungry openmouthed kisses. The hand on her backside tensed, then relaxed, and then Jon's hips were grinding into hers and both of his hands were on her backside, as well, lifting and angling her, encouraging her to wrap her legs around his hips. She locked her ankles behind his back and moaned against his throat as she felt his erection pressing against her where she needed it most.

"Gabby," Jon said, his voice pure gravel.

His mouth found her ear, then the sensitive skin beneath it. She pulled him closer. He kissed his way across her cheekbone until finally their mouths met, a fiery clash of lips and teeth and tongues as they tried to devour each other.

She slid a hand down his chest to find the hem of his T-shirt. His belly muscles tensed as she smoothed her palm upward until she was cupping one smooth pec in her hand. Jon angled her head back, intensifying their kiss. She found his nipple with her thumb and rubbed it before pinching it firmly. He jerked against her, then suddenly the wall was gone from behind her. He dropped her on the desk, still kissing her, and she swept her arm blindly to clear the surface, pushing papers over the edge with reckless abandon.

He broke their kiss, stared at her. For the first time since she'd known him everything he was feeling was in his eyes for her to see—need and desire and demand. Maintaining the eye contact, she used her elbows to crawl backward until she was lying fully across the desk. She reached for the hem of her tank top and yanked it over her head. He did the same with his T-shirt. She eyed his chest and belly, excitement surging inside her. She snapped open the front closure on her bra and let it slide down her arms.

Jon's eyes roamed from one peak to the other before he put a knee on the desk and climbed on top of her. Her legs fell open in welcome. He ducked his head and pulled a nipple into his mouth, his tongue laving her roughly before sucking firmly. The pleasure was exquisite, sharp and sweet, and she arched, grabbing his head and hanging on for dear life.

He suckled her till it almost hurt, then soothed her with his tongue before switching his attention to her other breast and starting all over again. She moved restlessly, her hands running over his shoulders and back and belly, her hips rubbing against his. He was so big, so overwhelming, but she didn't feel overpowered. She felt powerful. Sexy. Desired.

He blazed a second trail across her body with his hand, cupping her breast, pinching her nipple, gliding down her rib cage to her belly. She trembled as his hand smoothed over her skirt then beneath it to her wide-spread thighs.

"Please," she pleaded brokenly.

She didn't even know what she was asking for, but Jon seemed to understand. He slid his hand onto her mound, cupping her quivering sex in his palm, exerting just the right amount of pressure. She started to pant, her fingers digging into him.

He replaced his hand with a single, knowing finger as he traced the seam of her sex through her underwear. She jerked against him when he found the right spot and she felt him smile against her breast. Then his thumb was rubbing her and she forgot to breath.

It was so good. So intense. She felt like a teenager again, as though she was discovering all of this for the first time. Her first kiss, her first caress, her first taste of true desire.

Except she was a women, not an inexperienced girl, and she knew exactly what she wanted.

Her frantic hands found the waistband of Jon's jeans and tugged at the stud there. He slipped a finger beneath the elastic on her underwear and made an approving sound when he felt how wet and ready she was. She almost came off the desk when he slid a finger inside her. She clenched her thighs around his hips and moaned as he stroked her again and again. Tension built inside her, an ache that demanded satisfaction. She renewed her assault on his jeans, tugging the zip down and reaching into his boxers for his erection. Her hand closed around him and she gave a little moan of approval. He was incredibly hard, and so long and thick she wanted to cry.

He slid a second finger into her, his thumb hitting her sweet spot every time he withdrew.

She shivered and twisted beneath him, craving so much more.

"You," she whispered. "I want you."

She pushed at the waistband of his jeans again, and he took the hint and pushed them the rest of the way down, his mouth never leaving her breasts. She levered her hips up and slid off her panties, tugging at the tie on her skirt to free herself. Jon lifted his head from her breasts to finish kicking off his jeans. She stared at his erection as he tore open the foil packet he took from his pocket. He was every bit as big and beautiful as she'd imagined. More so. Her gaze traveled hungrily over his powerful thighs and the defined ridges of his belly. She'd never seen a man like him.

He smoothed on the condom, his movements slow and very deliberate. He surveyed her when he'd finished, his gaze traveling over her breasts and belly before zeroing in on the heart of her. She bit her lip as he smoothed a hand up her thigh, using his thumb to tease her intimate folds, watching his own actions and her reaction with a focused, knowing intent.

His gaze found hers. Neither of them broke the

contact as, at last, he pushed forward, probing her entrance with his erection. Then he flexed his hips and she closed her eyes to savor the slow, thick slide as he came inside her for the first time.

She gripped him with her thighs, her hands, her inner muscles. He felt so good. So right.

He muttered something under his breath—possibly *unbelievable,* she wasn't sure—then he started to move with deep, controlled strokes.

She lost track of time. The world contracted to the feel of him inside her, to the suction of his mouth on her breasts, to the knowing caress of his thumb just above where they were joined. She smoothed her hands over his body, reveling in the sheer strength of his shoulders, squeezing his firm, round ass in her hands, digging her fingers into the muscles of his back, wrapping a leg around his hips to encourage him deeper.

Jon made a guttural noise and abandoned her breasts to kiss her, his hand framing her jaw as his tongue slid against hers, his teeth nipping at her lips before he plunged deep to claim her.

She tensed as her climax swept toward her, holding her breath. Her back arched and she closed her eyes tightly.

"Yes. Come for me, Gabby," he whispered near her ear. "Come for me."

Her climax seemed to last forever, a never ending wave of pleasure. He wrung every last drop from her with small, nudging thrusts, barely withdrawing before grinding himself into her again. Finally, the pleasure waned, and she opened her eyes to find Jon watching her, a triumphant glint in his eye.

He ducked his head to kiss her, then he began to move inside her once more, his thrusts increasingly urgent. His upper lip curled back from his teeth, his jaw clenched. His body tensed, every muscle solid. He drove himself deep inside her one last time, pressing his cheek against hers, his breath harsh in her ear as he shuddered out his own climax.

She felt the tremors in his body, felt him ride the wave of pleasure.

He let his weight rest on her for a moment afterward. She could feel his heart hammering, could feel the dampness of sweat where his body pressed against hers—chest, belly, thighs. Then he pushed himself up, withdrawing from her as he rolled to the side.

She blinked at the ceiling, feeling utterly drained and more than a little dazed. Her heart was pounding in her ears, her sex throbbing with the intensity of their lovemaking. Her brain was foggy, overwhelmed with sensation.

She'd never experienced anything like it. She felt… subsumed. As though she'd lost a piece of herself.

He stood and she watched as he stooped to put on his jeans. It wasn't until he looked at her that she came fully down to earth. He'd retreated behind his guard again, giving away nothing, and she was suddenly acutely aware that she was sprawled on her desk, naked, while he was mostly dressed.

"Won't be a moment," he said.

He left her office. She assumed it was to dispose of the condom. She slid off the desk. She didn't bother trying to pull her bra on, instead scooping her tank top from the floor and turned it right side out with not-quite-steady hands. She was knotting the tie on her wrap skirt when Jon returned.

Her gaze gravitated to the angry red mark on his left shoulder, a perfect imprint of her bite. Never in her life had she deliberately hurt anyone, and definitely not during sex.

She looked away from the evidence of her own out of control need. She crouched and began to collect the paperwork she'd pushed off her desk. After a few seconds he joined her.

"It's fine. I've got it," she said tightly.

He kept working and she clenched her jaw.

Five minutes. Five minutes and this will be over with, she promised herself.

Finally, they'd collected the last of the papers. She stood. Jon followed suit. He placed his pile of on her desk and she put hers beside it.

"Gabby."

He hadn't put on his T-shirt yet and she couldn't look at him, couldn't stand the sight of the mark she'd put on his shoulder.

"I don't want to talk about it," she said.

He was silent for a long moment and she could feel him looking at her.

"I need to know if you're okay. Did I hurt you?"

Her gaze flew to his face. "No. Of course not."

He was the one with the mark on his shoulder, not her.

He studied her face. "Okay."

He turned to collect his T-shirt from where he'd thrown it over her chair and her throat tightened when she saw his back. Welts criss-crossed his shoulders and lower back, more evidence of how crazy she'd been.

She glanced down at her hands. Her nails weren't even that long.

"I think you should go." She desperately needed to be alone. Any second now she was going to lose it, and the last thing she wanted was for Jon to witness it.

He took a long time to answer. "If that's what you want."

"It is."

He didn't say anything more, simply turned and left. She listened to the sound of him walking through the workshop. She heard the exterior door open, then close. Then and only then did she let out the breath she'd been holding.

She was in shock. There was no other way to phrase it. Never in her life had she experienced anything so intense, so all consuming. She had literally been beyond control. She'd goaded Jon, then she'd fought him and hurt him before she'd finally admitted what she really wanted from him.

And not once—not for a second—had she thought about Tyler. It had all been about Jon. His body. The way he looked at her. How much he infuriated her. The things he said to her. The way he challenged her.

She didn't understand herself. The night of her birthday dinner she'd been convinced she still loved Tyler. The pain in her chest had been real. Her grief had been real. Her tears had been real.

And yet less than a week later she'd had knock-down, drag-out sex with his brother. On her desk. At work.

She sank into her chair and pressed her hands to her face.

She was so confused. She felt as though she'd been careening from one disaster to the next since she'd met Jon. He'd thrown her off balance from that first day and she'd never recovered her equilibrium. He'd forced her to take an honest look at herself…at her life. She'd revealed her secrets to him. And now she'd had sex with him.

She remained there for long minutes, her thoughts

whirling, her stomach churning. The press of a growing headache finally forced her to move. She collected her bag, turned off the light. Feeling ridiculously fragile for a woman who had tried to take a chunk out of a man's shoulder, she did a circuit of the building, flicking off lights and checking that the machinery was all shut down. She punched the code into the keypad, then slipped out the door with the ease of long practice. It was only when she turned to walk to her car that she realized there was a second car in the parking lot.

Jon's black truck was in the far corner. The windows were dark, but she could feel him watching her. After a small hesitation she walked to her hatchback. She got in, started the engine. She turned her lights on, but didn't pull out. After a few seconds, Jon's lights came on and he drove away.

He'd waited for her. Even though she'd told him to go. Even though this whole thing had started over her refusing to allow him to take responsibility for her.

He'd sat in the dark to ensure she was safe.

She didn't know whether to laugh or cry, to be angry or touched. Apparently she was all about not knowing these days. Apparently that was her thing.

She drove home, thoughts still churning. She didn't bother turning any lights on when she let herself into her apartment, walking straight to her ensuite. She turned the shower on while she shed her clothes, then stepped beneath the spray.

Needles of hot water pricked her skin. She reached for the soap and washed her breasts and belly and finally between her legs, trying to ignore the residual sensation there. It wasn't until she stepped out and flicked on the overhead light to locate her toothbrush that she saw her body in the mirror. She gasped, her hands going to her chest.

A red suck mark marred her left breast, and another marked the skin beneath her ear on the right. Her face was pink from whisker burn, and when she turned she saw five small, distinct bruises across her backside where Jon had lifted her against him.

She should have been shocked, but she wasn't. Instead, something inside her relaxed. What had happened—whatever it was—had been mutual. They'd both been caught up and crazy.

She wasn't sure why it made her feel better, but it did. Which went to show how messed up she really was.

CHAPTER SEVEN

JON PICKED UP THE PHONE, THEN put it down. He paced to the balcony, then back to the kitchen counter. Picked up the phone. Looked at the keypad. Put it down again.

He'd been caught in the same loop since he'd arrived home. He couldn't call Gabby—she didn't want to talk to him—but he couldn't stop thinking about her, about what had happened.

Even if she did take his call, he had no idea what he would say to her.

Sorry for assaulting you and throwing you on your desk and having dirty, rough sex with you?

Yeah, that would fix everything.

He dragged his hand over his face.

He'd never treated a women that way in his life. Had never so much as lifted a finger in anger. The lessons of his childhood were far too deeply ingrained for him to ever want to watch someone weaker than himself cower in fear.

And yet he'd tried to intimidate Gabby. All five-foot-nothing of her. He'd been so angry—furious—at her refusal to be smart about her safety that he'd lost it. She was all lip and attitude—and she wouldn't stand a chance against anyone out to hurt her. Yet she stubbornly refused to believe it.

The thought of her trying to fend off some desperate junkie or opportunistic hood made his blood run cold.

He'd gone into her office with the intention of showing her how vulnerable she was, to prove to her that being feisty and mouthy was no defence against superior strength. But she hadn't backed down. She'd stood her ground, glaring defiance at him with those golden-brown eyes of hers and refusing to so much as flinch. He'd pushed and pushed until he was so close he could feel the adrenaline vibrating through her body—and the excitement.

Her pupils had been dilated, her breathing shallow. Her body had been hot against his as he'd pressed her against the desk.

Then she'd tried to slip away from him and things had gotten really crazy.

He grit his teeth as he remembered the way he'd slammed her against the wall and pinned her there with his body weight.

You're a real freaking hero, you know that?

He'd hurt her. He'd bullied her and manhandled her and then he'd rubbed his freaking erection against her and—

Jon punched the wall. Hard. The plaster cracked but didn't give. He shook his hand out. The anger drained away as abruptly as it had flooded him and he sank onto the couch.

He dropped his head into his hands.

Images flashed across his mind's eye, but the one that stuck was the look on her face when she'd told him to go. She hadn't even been able to look him in the eye, she'd wanted him gone so much.

And why wouldn't she? He'd behaved like an animal. Like Robert Adamson's son.

"Jesus."

He shot to his feet. He didn't want it to be true. Didn't want to be the man he'd undeniably been tonight.

Angry. Out of control. A slave to his passions.

He grabbed his keys and headed for the door. Everything in him wanted to drive over to Gabby's and beg her to forgive him. But there was nothing he could say that would take back what had happened and she'd copped enough of his crap for one night.

The lights were still on at Tyler and Ally's place. He strode up the path and waited tensely for someone to answer the door. He heard footsteps, then a short pause and the rattle of a door chain being disengaged. The door swung open.

It was Ally, dressed in bright pajamas, a pair of reading glasses on the end of her nose.

"Jon," she said. Her welcoming smile faded as she took in his tense posture. "Is everything okay?"

"Is Tyler around?"

Her brow wrinkled with concern. "I'm sorry, but he's helping a mate pick up a fridge or something. He should be back soon, though."

Damn.

He glanced toward his truck, trying to think. He didn't want to be in his apartment. And he was afraid to go to the pub.

"Come in," Ally said, her hand closing around his forearm. "Wait for him."

He didn't want to wait, but he didn't know what else to do so he let Ally lead him into the house.

"I'll make you a coffee." She didn't release his arm, almost as though she was afraid he'd run off if she did. "Or maybe you'd like a hot chocolate?"

"What I'd really like is a bottle of Scotch."

She smiled sympathetically. “Yeah. I know that feeling.”

She pushed him toward the couch and crossed to the kitchen to put the kettle on. He sat on the edge of the seat and looked at his hands. He had no idea why he'd come here. Gabby was like family to Tyler and Ally; the moment his brother heard what had happened he'd punch Jon's lights out.

Maybe that was why he was here—to cop to a little of what he'd dished out tonight. To get a little of what he deserved.

Ally returned and sat at the other end of the couch. “Have you eaten? Do you want some cheese and crackers? Or I could make you a sandwich?”

“I'm fine. Thanks.” He examined his hands, rubbing the thumb of his left hand over the newly bruised knuckles of his right.

“Listen, Jon, if you want to wait for Tyler in peace and quiet, I can disappear. I've got some edits to do on my column, it's not a problem.”

“I don't want to keep you from your work.”

“That's not what I was saying.” She sighed. “You Adamson men. I swear, it's like pulling teeth getting you to talk about anything.”

He glanced at her, then at his hands. He didn't want to talk to her about this. It was too ugly. *He* was too ugly.

“Something happened with Gabby tonight,” he said, surprising himself as well as Ally.

“What sort of something are we talking about? A conversation? A fight? The opposite of a fight?”

He shifted uncomfortably.

“Both,” he eventually said.

“A fight? And the opposite of a fight?”

He sighed, ran a hand over his head. He might as well get this over with. Cut to the part where she stared at him in horror.

"I've been working late so I can be around when Gabby locks up. I knew she wouldn't be too keen on anyone looking out for her, so I've been making up excuses. Well, apparently I suck as an actor because she called me on it tonight and sent me home."

"Sounds like Gabby," Ally said with a small smile. "But I'm willing to bet you didn't go home, right?"

He shot her a look. "Why do you say that?"

"Don't take this the wrong way, but stubbornness runs in the Adamson blood. And you've got that whole older-brother-protective-thing going on. A pretty deadly combination."

He frowned. Obviously Tyler hadn't told her how he'd bailed on him when they were in their teens. Hardly the actions of the protective older brother she was painting him as.

"You know what that neighborhood is like. Smashed glass in the gutters, syringes. Once all the factories close for the night, there's no one around. It's dangerous. I couldn't leave her there on her own."

"So you guys had it out, huh?"

"I told her I'd go if she could prove to me she could take care of herself."

"I bet that went down well."

"She told me to go to hell. So I decided I was going to show her why she was wrong. I backed her up against the desk—"

He shot to his feet. No way could he describe what had happened next. It was too personal. Too visceral. Too shameful.

Ally simply waited. He stood in front of the couch,

head lowered, one hand rubbing the back of his neck. He told himself he should go, but instead he found himself talking again.

"She wouldn't back down. We...we fought. Physically, I mean." It was hard to push the words past the tightness in his throat. "She tried to get away from me, I slammed her into the wall. Then we— Then things changed."

"This is the opposite of fighting bit, right?"

He looked at her. She didn't look even slightly appalled by what he'd told her. "Yeah."

"Well, then. Tyler owes me fifty bucks."

Jon stared at her. He'd confessed to throwing a ninety-pound woman against the wall, to fighting her physically, and Ally was pleased that she'd won a bet?

"I could have really hurt her."

"*Did* you hurt her?"

"I pushed her against the wall."

"I bet that would have really pissed Gabby off."

He thought about the way she'd bitten him. "It did."

Ally patted the couch. "Sit. You're giving me a crick in my neck."

He sat.

"You're giving yourself a hard time because things got physical with Gabby, right?"

Wasn't it obvious?

"I could have hurt her," he said again.

"But you didn't, Jon."

"Things were out of control."

"Right." Ally nodded. "That's important for you, isn't it? Being in control?"

Wasn't it to everyone? As far as he was concerned, taking responsibility for your own actions was the most basic requirement of adulthood.

"Typically the children of abusive parents go two ways," Ally said thoughtfully. "Some of them become abusers themselves, perpetuating the misery. And the others do everything in their power to break the cycle. It constantly amazes me that you and Tyler are the people you are, given what you came from. That even though you were given so little love and compassion, you're both good, good men."

He shifted uneasily. "This isn't anything to do with any of that."

Ally spoke very gently. "I think it is, Jon. I think it's everything to do with why you're upset tonight."

He checked his watch. "I should let you get to bed. It's getting late." He stood.

Ally looked up at him ruefully. "Pushed you too far, huh?"

"It's late."

Ally stood. "Can't tempt you with some ice cream?"

"Thanks, but I'm not really an ice cream fan."

"Huh. Interesting. Gabby's not mad about it, either."

Jon collected his keys and phone from the coffee table. "Don't turn this into some big romance, Ally. Gabby and I… Even if she doesn't hate my guts after tonight, there are a lot of reasons why nothing's ever going to happen between us."

Starting with the fact that Gabby still had feelings for his brother.

"What's your favorite thing about her?"

The question was so unexpected he responded without thinking. "She never quits fighting her corner, even when a smart person would stop. And she's mouthy."

Ally's smile was smug. "I like those things about her, too. Plus she has an awesome ass."

She shocked a laugh out of him. They walked to

the front door in an oddly companionable silence. He opened the door before pausing to say goodbye.

"Thanks. And sorry if I messed with your work schedule."

He leaned close and kissed her on the cheek. He was about to turn and exit when Ally's hand caught his wrist.

"Jon. You can come here anytime, okay? Day or night. Whatever. Tyler and I are both here for you. If you want to talk or not talk. Even if you just want to hang out. Okay?"

She stood on her toes and embraced him. He patted her back awkwardly. She sank onto her heels and gave him a wry look.

"One of these days you're going to hug me properly, you know."

He looked down at his car keys. "I do appreciate it, Ally," he said quietly.

"I know. Off you go. I won't make you any more uncomfortable."

He descended the steps and started up the path. Halfway to the gate, he pivoted on his heel.

"Don't forget to put the chain back on," he said.

"I won't, big brother."

He hesitated. He felt as though he was perpetuating a fraud, letting Ally assume he was the typical kind of big brother, the kind who took responsibility and looked out for his siblings. But tonight wasn't the night to straighten her out.

His brain was less busy as he drove home. Despite how quickly he'd bailed when Ally had brought up his father, the stuff she'd said about self-control being important to him had struck a chord. It was true that he'd always been careful to govern his passions. He never ate too much, never acted in the heat of anger, never let himself get too swept up with a woman. For many years his one vice had been cigarettes, but despite a short relapse recently he'd managed to kick the habit.

In fact, there were only two areas where he'd ever really lost control: with drink, and with Gabby. He was coming to grips with his drinking, but Gabby… No matter what he did, he didn't seem to be able to keep a lid on himself when she was around. She pushed him in so many ways. And tonight she'd pushed him to the edge and over.

Then stay away from her. It's that easy.

A pretty simple solution. He'd been making noises about moving on for a while now, but maybe it was time to put words into actions.

One thing was for sure, Gabby would be glad to see the back of him.

GABBY WOKE WITH A SINGLE IMAGE from the previous night etched in her mind: Jon's face when he'd returned to her office and she'd refused to talk to him. He'd looked…*shaken* was the only word she could come up with. Maybe even stricken.

At the time, she'd been so busy trying to protect herself that she hadn't thought about him. She'd let him inside her body, run her hands and mouth all over his, yet she hadn't considered his reaction.

There was an argument to be made that Jon had most likely been more than happy to escape so lightly from a potentially awkward situation. The fun bit was over; he'd had his thrills. What more could he want?

A lot of guys—most guys—would have been skipping all the way to their cars, thrilled to have avoided a postcoital debrief.

But Jon wasn't most guys. He had a fierce sense of duty and he always did the right thing. Always. He'd given in to Ally's cajoling and come to dinner, even though the whole deal had clearly not been his cup of tea. He'd apologized to Gabby about the whole lesbian thing—twice. He'd made up excuses so he could watch over her while she locked up. He'd tried to step in when she was heading for trouble at the Christmas party. He'd been painstaking in his attention to detail in the work he'd done for Tyler.

Jon was a good man. An honorable man. Overbearing at times. Arrogant in his own unique I-know-best way. But he had a good heart, and he'd been decent to her on numerous occasions. Some might even say he'd been kind.

She owed him an apology, and she owed him a conversation. She had no idea what that conversation would consist of. No doubt it would end with them disagreeing. So be it. It had to be done.

She lay in bed girding her loins for a full ten minutes after her alarm went off, then she rolled out of bed and marched into the bathroom.

She gasped when she saw the hickey on her neck in the cold light of day. Last night, the evidence that Jon had been as lost in their mutual passion as she'd been had been comforting. This morning, not so much.

The mark on her breast she could live with—no one was going to see that—but she'd already survived a solid day of being pilloried for her performance at the Christmas party. The thought of enduring another round of teasing and questions and innuendo over the scarlet mark on her neck was enough to make her want to write a letter of resignation on the spot.

Which meant the hickey had to go. The last time

she'd had to employ hickey camouflaging techniques had been the first year of high school. She had a vague memory of something to do with toothpaste, but she figured that a scarf tied in a jaunty little bow and some cover-up stick was probably the better bet.

She experimented for twenty minutes with the only summer-weight scarf she owned before she was satisfied she could hide the incriminating mark. Red with white dots, it made her look a little like Maryanne off *Gilligan's Island,* but it wasn't as though she had much choice. She was tweaking her scarf for the fourth time when she caught sight of her alarm clock and made a grab for her keys and headed for the door. She was almost certain that her office still needed a bit more work before it could pass as a place of business again instead of a makeshift bordello, which meant she needed to be the first one in.

Half an hour later, her office was back to its pre-desk-sex state and she was watching the clock, waiting for Jon to arrive for the day so she could do what had to be done.

Her foot jiggled beneath the desk and she glanced up every time she heard the showroom door open. Carl was in first, then Dino. Finally, the door to the showroom swung open and she was rewarded with the sight of Jon's broad shoulders and dark head. Nerves tightened her belly. Her palms got sweaty.

Time to woman up, princess.

She stood, twitching her scarf a little more to the right. In the workshop, Jon hung his jacket over the back of the stool at his workbench and began to set up for the day. She stared at his shoulders, impossibly wide under a white T-shirt, then let her gaze drop to his backside.

She'd never truly allowed herself to appreciate it before, but it was great. Really, really great.

A rush of sense-memories washed over her—the rasp of his beard on her breasts, the slide of his fingers between her legs, the resilient firmness of his muscles beneath her hands.

She plucked at the front of her T-shirt, trying to dissipate some of the heat. She was not approaching Jon the morning after their ill-advised liaison with glowing cheeks. That was not going to happen.

She fanned her top a few more times, then plunged into the fray.

Her legs felt shaky as she rounded her desk. She concentrated on putting one foot in front of the other. Through some malicious trick of psychological chicanery, the distance to her doorway seemed to stretch to eternity.

Get it done and over with, you big scaredy cat.

Jon was frowning at some brass cabinet fittings when she reached his side.

"Jon. Hi. Um, would you have a minute to spare?"

He put down the hinge he'd been examining and looked at her. A muscle twitched in his jaw. "Sure. When did you have in mind?"

"Now. If you're free, that is?"

"I'm free."

"Well, then." Feeling supremely uncomfortable, she turned to lead him back to her office and nearly tripped over her own feet. Out of the corner of her eye she saw him reach out a hand to steady her—only to hesitate at the last moment.

He didn't want to touch her.

Something small and sharp twisted in her chest.

"I'm fine," she said, even though he hadn't asked.

She waited until he'd entered her office before she shut the door behind her. Anyone passing would wonder why—she never closed her door—but she wasn't taking any chances with anyone overhearing what she had to say.

She faced him. He was standing in the center of the room, and she knew him well enough now to know that he was far from comfortable. Good. She'd gotten herself so worked up she felt sick—it was nice to know she wasn't alone.

"I wanted to apologize for last night."

Jon went very still. His gaze slid to the desk.

"Not for the sex," she clarified hastily. "For afterward. When you came back and I said I didn't want to talk. That's the part I'm sorry for. Not the other bit."

The other bit?

She winced mentally. She was such an idiot. And she'd even rehearsed this in bed less than an hour ago.

He shifted his weight. "Okay."

She took a breath. "Also, I wanted to ask how your shoulder is."

Impossible to stop herself from blushing now.

"It's fine."

"Are you sure? Because it looked pretty raw last night."

"It's fine."

She'd never seen him look more serious.

"Well, good." Her hands found each other at her waist and she clasped them together. "That was… That's not something that's ever happened for me before. I'm not really sure what happened—"

"I do. I pushed you. I backed you into a corner."

She could hear the self-condemnation in his voice, the judgment.

"You didn't push me anywhere. I gave as good as I got."

"No." His voice was very tight, utterly certain.

She studied him, noting the signs of tiredness in his face, the tension around his mouth.

He'd been giving himself a hard time over this, she realized. Convincing himself that he'd been responsible for what happened. In all her obsessive analyses of what had occurred last night—and there had been many as she lay awake into the small hours—the notion that he might think the sex had been anything but a meeting of equals had not even crossed her mind.

"There were two people in this office last night, Jon, not one. And you didn't do anything to me that I didn't do to you."

"Except one of us is six foot two."

"You're the one with the injuries, not me. And please don't even start to tell me that the sex was all your idea or something ridiculous like that. I wanted it. I enjoyed it. Okay?"

He frowned.

"If I'd wanted you to stop last night you would have stopped. At any point."

"How do you know that?"

She could hear the uncertainty in his voice.

"Because I wasn't scared. Not once. Not even a little bit. And you knew that. If I'd called a halt, if you'd seen I was scared, you would have stopped."

"You have a lot of faith in me."

"You've earned it."

His frown deepened. He looked so uneasy and unhappy. This was a really big deal for him.

"Okay. Fine," she said. "I get that you're a man of

action, that words aren't your thing. So if what it takes is a rematch, let's get down to it."

She reached for the hem of her T-shirt.

"Whoa," Jon said, taking a step forward, one hand extended. "Aren't you forgetting something?"

He glanced toward the glass panel in the door. He looked so scandalized she almost smiled. Given what they'd done on her desk, the prospect of the guys seeing her in her bra seemed pretty tame.

"Here's a deal for you—you stop blaming yourself for something we both took part in, and I'll keep my T-shirt on."

That got a small smile out of him. "Do you ever not play hardball?"

"Absolutely—when I figure my opponent isn't up to it. So, what's it going to be, Jon?" She tugged her T-shirt up a couple of inches, displaying her belly to him. "Am I going to traumatize the guys for life or are you going to admit it takes two to tango?"

That shocked a laugh out of him. She could tell he still didn't quite believe she'd go through with it. She arched an eyebrow.

"Well? What's your answer?" She lifted her T-shirt some more, exposing the lower half of her bra.

"Gabby. Come on." He shot a worried look toward the window, then took a step forward and grabbed the hem of her T-shirt, tugging it down and holding it there.

They were standing very close, his body almost brushing hers, his hand warm on her belly. She looked into his eyes.

"That fight was an excuse for us to both do what we wanted to do. You know that, right?" she said.

He looked at his feet, his lashes brushing his cheeks.

She was reminded of the night she'd caught him sleeping at his workbench. He'd looked so vulnerable then.

He was vulnerable now, too.

She had a sudden flash of insight, a moment of intuitive connection, as she studied his downturned face. Last year, she'd stood on the sidelines as Tyler struggled through his father's final days. He'd never said anything directly, but she'd understood that there had been a lot of unhappiness in his childhood. Violence, maybe, or some other form of abuse. It hit her now that a man who'd grown up in an angry, violent household might find it difficult to put last night into its proper perspective. In fact, such a man might find it almost impossible to forgive himself for letting his passions get away from him.

It was just a guess, but it felt right. A wave of compassion washed over her and the urge to comfort him was so strong she didn't even try to deny it. She wrapped her arms around him and lay her cheek against his chest.

"It's okay, Jon."

He tensed, his body as unyielding and unbending as concrete. She refused to let go. She knew he was stubborn—it took one to know one, after all—but he had to let go of the crazy idea that he was responsible. She felt his rib cage expand as he breathed in, then all of a sudden his arms came around her and he pulled her more tightly to his chest. She felt his cheek press against the top of her head, could hear the unsteady thump of his heart beneath her ear as he held her.

There was an intensity, almost a desperation to his embrace that touched something deep inside her. Maybe she was being fanciful, but she had the feeling that Jon had experienced precious few moments of compassion and acceptance in his life.

The thought brought the unexpected heat of tears to her eyes.

"You'd better get that," Jon murmured.

"What?"

His arms loosened and he stepped backward. She realized her phone was ringing.

"Right," she said. "The phone."

She moved to her desk and lifted the receiver.

"Gabby Wade speaking," she said.

"Gabby, it's Brandon Sinclair from Vibe Interiors," a voice said in her ear.

"Hi, Brandon, how are you?" She assumed her best professional voice.

Movement caught the corner of her eye and she turned to see Jon heading for the door. She stared at him as Brandon explained why he was calling. For the first time it struck her that being a big man, a powerful man, brought with it its own expectations and prejudices. It was all too easy to assume that a man who looked as solid and unassailable as Jon did never had any doubts or fears. But he was flesh and blood, with all the usual weaknesses and foibles that came with being human.

"So I was wondering if you guys thought you could meet those deadlines," Brandon was saying in her ear.

She blinked and dragged herself back to the here and now.

"Sorry, Brandon, I was just calling up your file on the computer," she fibbed. "What were those dates again?"

CHAPTER EIGHT

JON KEPT HIS HEAD DOWN FOR most of the morning, not participating in the chat between the guys, pretending an absorption in his work that, for once, he didn't feel.

Gabby had floored him with her apology. And that stunt with her T-shirt…

He'd told Ally that one of the things he most admired about Gabby was her willingness to fight her corner even when a smart person would concede defeat. She'd been pretty damned convincing, boldly telling him that he hadn't scared her, that she trusted him, that their fight had simply been an excuse they'd both used to get close.

But the thing he really couldn't get out of his head was the way she'd wrapped her arms around him, so easily and naturally and forgivingly. He'd always thought of her as a small woman, petite and delicate despite her large personality, but her arms had been strong and sure. When she'd rested her head on his chest he'd been powerless to stop himself from returning her embrace.

It was such a small, trusting gesture. More than anything she'd said it had proved to him that she wasn't afraid of him. That he hadn't stepped over the line with her last night.

He'd never been comfortable with physical affection. There hadn't been a lot of it in the Adamson household and as an adult, sex was the only time he felt comfortable getting physically close to another human being. It had always seemed to him that hugs and kisses and casual caresses came with strings attached, and he didn't want to be forced into the position of disappointing anyone's expectations.

Gabby's embrace hadn't felt as though it had strings attached to it. He hadn't felt as though she wanted anything from him; she'd simply offered him comfort.

It had scared him how much he'd wanted to accept it, how good she'd felt.

Letting her go had been one of the hardest things he'd done in a long time.

"Mate, Tyler wants you."

He looked up to find Paul by his workbench, gesturing to where Tyler was standing at the top of the stairs. It was evident from Tyler's bemused, slightly frustrated expression that he'd been trying to get Jon's attention for some time.

"Right. Thanks." Dusting off his hands, he started up the stairs to the mezzanine.

"You had your ears tested lately?" Tyler asked good-naturedly.

"I was concentrating." Jon could just imagine his brother's reaction if he told him that he'd been thinking about a hug, of all things.

Tyler gestured for him to precede him into his office and Jon dropped into the chair opposite the desk. To his surprise, Tyler sat beside him rather than behind the desk.

Jon was instantly wary, remembering the conversation with Ally last night. Only an idiot would expect spouses to keep secrets from one another.

"I wanted to talk to you about your salary."

His shoulders relaxed a notch. This wasn't about Gabby, then.

"I don't have one. Remember?"

"As if I could forget. I've had Gabby in my ear every five seconds telling me I need to pay you."

This was news to him. "I didn't realize she knew."

"Mate, there's not much she doesn't know about this business."

"Right."

"I know we talked about this being a temporary role while you worked out what you will do next. But I wanted to ask how you've been finding it."

"If you're asking if I like the work, the answer's yes."

"Does that mean you'd consider sticking around?"

Jon looked at his watch, fiddling with the strap as he tried to work out what to say. Last night, he'd more or less made the decision it was time to move on. He'd planned to ask Tyler for access to a computer to look for airfares. After his conversation with Gabby this morning, some of the urgency had gone out of the decision.

He figured he could give his brother a few more weeks, maybe a month, tops. Anything longer was only delaying the inevitable. As much as he admired what his brother had built up here, he didn't have it in him to be anyone's employee anymore, not after years of being his own boss. He might be floating at the moment, but long-term he wanted to be running his own business again.

"How long do you need me for?"

"How about thirty years, depending on when you want to retire?" Tyler asked.

Jon's first impulse was to laugh—then he saw the bound document in Tyler's hands.

"These are the company records for the past four years." Tyler leaned forward and collected another document from his desk. "These are our profit projections for the next five years."

Jon looked at the proffered documents but didn't take them from his brother's hands.

"I appreciate the offer. But like I told you in Woodend, I'm not looking to settle here. I'm happy to fill a gap or take up the slack for you till you find someone permanent, but I'm not interested in a long-term job."

"I'm not offering you a job. I want you to buy into the business. Become my partner."

Whoa.

Jon stared at his brother, his mind a complete blank.

"I know it's out of the blue. And you don't need to make a decision right now, but I want you to think about it," Tyler said. "I figure we could do a fifty-fifty split, because I know I wouldn't be interested in anything else if the shoe was on the other foot, but the details are negotiable."

He offered the paperwork to Jon again. He took it and stared down at the glossy cover.

He didn't know what to say. Not for a second had he imagined that his brother would be willing to share something that was obviously so close to his heart. Tyler had built this business from scratch, poured his sweat, blood and tears into it, and now he was riding what Jon suspected was the very beginning of a massive wave of success. And he was inviting Jon along for the ride.

It was incredibly generous. Especially given their long estrangement.

"I wasn't expecting this," he finally said.

"Yeah, I got that." Tyler leaned back in his chair,

apparently completely relaxed about the outcome of their discussion. Only the telltale jiggling of his foot gave away that this meant anything to him.

"How would you see this working?"

"Until recently, I've been splitting my time between design, production and sales. Gabby's been stepping into sales more, and doing a bloody good job of it, so I feel we're covered there. The workshop still needs a lot of my time. Dino's prepared to step up to a certain point, but he doesn't want more responsibility or hours than he already has, and none of the other guys has the initiative to make a good production manager. Every time there's a problem, I get dragged away from design work—and let's face it, nothing gets made if I don't design it first."

Jon could see his brother's problem. Essentially, there was only one of Tyler, but there were a number of areas where his skill, passion and commitment were required to keep the business driving forward.

"I'm a builder. I haven't done this kind of thing before."

"You've run a construction team. You've made some incredibly ambitious plans a reality. That place you built in the Laurentians was freaking amazing. The way you had to sink those concrete supports into the mountainside to support that cantilevered roof…"

Jon stared at his brother. He had no idea that Tyler was familiar with his Canadian builds. Then he thought about the times he'd looked Tyler up on the internet over the years. He'd told himself he was simply making sure Tyler was still alive, but he'd been pleased to see Tyler's growing success.

Tyler moved to the edge of his seat. "Look, I know the work won't be as challenging for you here, but there are still lots of areas for us to branch out into. High-end bespoke kitchens, for starters."

It was on the tip of Jon's tongue to assure his brother that he'd gotten a lot of satisfaction out of the pieces he'd built since he'd come on board, but he didn't want to mislead him or get his hopes up. It was a good offer—a great one—but that didn't mean it was an offer he would accept.

He flipped open the cover on the financial report, scanning a few lines while he tried to word the question in his mind. Finally he realized there was no polite way to say it.

"Why?" he asked, meeting and holding Tyler's gaze.

"I told you. I need a partner to make the next step forward."

"You could find a production manager if you looked hard enough. You could even offer him a smaller cut of the business if you wanted him to have an investment."

"It wouldn't be the same. You're my brother."

"So, what? Blood is thicker than water? We both know that's bullshit."

Tyler's gaze was steady. "I don't think it is."

Jon couldn't maintain the eye contact. He fought the urge to remind his brother of all the times he'd let him down in the past. But that would mean getting into a bunch of stuff he had no intention of exhuming. "Can I have some time to think about it?"

"Take all the time you need."

Jon stood, reports in hand. He turned to leave, then paused. "Does Gabby know about this?"

Had she known about this when she spoke to him

this morning? Was that little speech about keeping him around?

"I haven't spoken to her yet. I figured I should sound you out first."

He was relieved, and he realized it was because he'd wanted this morning to have been about him and Gabby alone.

"I'd better get back to it," he said.

He glanced at the reports in his hand on the way down the stairs. He still couldn't quite believe that his brother was prepared to put so much trust in him. To share his future.

Gabby was talking to Dino about a delivery. Jon studied her profile, wondering how she was going to feel when she learned about Tyler's offer.

Happy? Uncomfortable? Indifferent? He asked himself how he'd feel, being tied to a business that included her.

Gabby laughed at something Dino said then gave him a little encouraging punch on the arm. Smile firmly in place, she headed for her office and it hit him that he could think of worse fates than having to see Gabby every day.

GABBY WAITED NERVOUSLY TO SEE what would happen when quitting time came around that night. One by one the rest of the crew cleaned up their workstations and said their goodbyes, heading home to their partners and families. By five-thirty it was down to her and Tyler and Jon.

She eyed Jon's back as he bent over the campaign desk he'd been working on the past couple of days. She knew it was pointless to try to convince him that he didn't need to hang around for her. For whatever reason, he had a real thing about her being alone here at night. She didn't know any way of getting him to respect her wishes on the subject, short of seeing him off the premises at gunpoint—and even then he'd probably wait in his truck the way he had last night.

She was about to head to the archive room to get rid of some files when Ally breezed into the workshop. Gabby listened to her greet Jon with fond familiarity before she appeared in the doorway of Gabby's office, a big smile on her face.

"I've come to rescue you."

"I wasn't aware that I needed rescuing."

"I have it on good authority that you're being held captive by paperwork. I've got lighter fluid and a box of matches and I'm going to blow you out of this gulag."

Gabby laughed. "The spirit is willing, but the in-tray says otherwise."

Ally looked at the overflowing tray suspiciously.

"Is there anything in there that can't wait? A cure for baldness? A miracle weight loss treatment?"

"No, but—"

"Then you're coming out for dinner."

"Ally—"

"No buts. This is the one and only time I will ever exert my authority as wife of the boss. You deserve a break, Gabby. Plus I have a voucher from the newspaper for a meal for four at a swanky restaurant in North Fitzroy."

Gabby's gaze slid over Ally's shoulder to where Jon was packing up his things. He met her gaze and she knew without asking that he was the fourth member of their party.

Twenty-four hours ago she would have faked an appendicitis attack to avoid dinner with Jon.

Ally settled into her guest chair. "The table's booked for six-thirty."

Gabby checked her watch and saw it was nearly ten past six. It would take them at least fifteen minutes to get to North Fitzroy in rush hour traffic. Which meant she needed to hustle if she was going to make herself presentable.

"Pass me my bag," she said.

It took her a couple of minutes closeted in the ladies' room to put on some lipstick, tidy up her eye makeup and tweak her hickey camouflage. Once she was as presentable as she was going to get, she shouldered her handbag and left the bathroom.

Jon and Tyler had joined Ally in her office.

"Okay. I'm ready to go," Gabby said.

"Cool. Let's hit the road," Tyler said.

After a brief discussion in which Tyler and Ally suggested they all go in their car and Gabby insisted on driving herself, they started out for the restaurant in a two-car convoy. Traffic was predictably busy and Gabby spent most of the stop-start drive tailing Tyler's truck, staring at the back of Jon's head through the rear window.

She still couldn't quite believe that she was about to voluntarily have dinner with Jon. After what had happened between them last night, they should have been putting as much distance between them as possible. But the whole world had shifted after their conversation this morning. North was south, east was west, and she no longer knew which way was up or down. She felt as though she was seeing him for the first time. She'd made so many assumptions about him. She'd thought he was arrogant and distant, an overdeveloped knuckle-dragger. He wasn't any of those things. He was very private, and he held himself to a high standard, and he had a fierce sense of duty. He was also, she suspected, a pussycat under all those muscles.

To be fair, he'd made some screwy assumptions about her, too. Apparently neither of them had taken the time to stop and consider before judging and jumping to conclusions about the other.

Ahead of her, Tyler stuck a hand out the window and pointed toward the group of cafés they were approaching. She took this to mean that they'd arrived at their destination and started trawling for a parking spot. She found one ten car-lengths ahead of Tyler and fed change into the meter. The others were waiting for her in front of the restaurant as she approached, Tyler and Ally standing arm in arm, Jon a little off to one side. It struck her that he often stood to one side that way, slightly removed—as though he wasn't quite sure where he belonged. Or maybe it was more that he wasn't sure he'd be welcome.

"Okay, before we go in, I have some ground rules for the evening," Ally said. "No matter what, we all order three courses, and we all stuff ourselves. I get about one perk every five years from those cheapskates at the newspaper, and we are milking this sucker."

"Aye-aye, sir," Gabby said.

"Your word is our command," Jon said.

Their table was in front of a huge floor-to-ceiling window that had been softened with a sheer curtain in a hazy shade of bronze. The lighting was low, the tablecloth a crisp white, the chairs all upholstered in bright jewel tones. Not surprisingly, Gabby found herself sitting next to Jon. Equally not surprising, his arm brushed hers once they'd shoehorned themselves into their seats.

"Sorry. There's not a lot of room," Jon said.

"It's okay," she said.

"Right. Let's do this," Ally said after the waiter had left them with their menus. "Remember, three courses." She fixed them each with a stern eye. "No shirking."

"Are we allowed doggy bags?" Tyler asked.

"As if you'll have trouble fitting three courses in," his wife said.

"Gabby can help me if I struggle," Tyler said.

Gabby kicked him under the table.

"Hey!"

"Oh, I'm sorry. Was that your leg I kicked? I was aiming for something higher."

Out of the corner of her eye she saw Jon smile.

Ally was studying the menu with a small frown.

"Hmm. The ravioli looks nice. But I wonder if pecorino is classed as a soft white cheese."

Gabby shrugged. "Sorry. My expertise is limited to tasty versus cheddar."

"We can ask the waiter," Tyler said.

"It's all right. I'll have the crab cakes. Oh, damn." Ally frowned.

"What?" Gabby asked.

Ally darted a look at Tyler. He was watching her indulgently, a small smile on his face.

"Off you go," he said.

"You don't mind?"

"It's totally up to you."

Gabby exchanged a sideways glance with Jon. He quirked an eyebrow. Clearly, he had no idea what was going on, either.

Ally placed both hands flat on the table and took a deep breath. "I'm pregnant. About seven weeks, we think. Which means no seafood and no soft white cheeses and no sushi and no champagne—"

"Wow. That's fantastic news. Congratulations. I know my math should be better, but when are you due?" Gabby waited for the inevitable twinge of jealousy. After all, if she and Tyler had made it as a couple, she might be the one announcing a pregnancy.

But all she felt was genuine happiness for her friends.

Interesting.

"We think mid-October, but the doctor's going to confirm that at my twelve-week scan," Ally said.

"Great news," Jon said.

Ally looked so excited Gabby couldn't resist reaching across to squeeze her hand. "You guys are going to be great parents." She looked to Tyler, smiling.

He smiled back. She'd honestly never seen him look happier.

It wasn't until she released Ally's hand that she registered the tension in Jon's body. She glanced at him curiously. He was smiling, but one of his hands was busy fiddling with his wineglass, twisting it round and round on the table in endless circles on the tablecloth.

Gabby looked to Tyler to see if he noticed his brother's odd reaction, but he was focused on Ally.

"I guess that means you're going to be an uncle, then," Gabby said to Jon.

He glanced at her, and for a split second she saw a terrible bleakness in his eyes. Then he blinked and it was gone.

"Yeah. Better sharpen up my footy skills."

"I think I can teach my own kid how to kick a footy," Tyler said.

"Sure you can. But if you want him to be any good at it…" Jon trailed off suggestively.

Tyler laughed and gave his brother a challenging look. "Are you saying I can't play footy?"

Jon paused for the exact right amount of time before focusing on Ally. "I think pecorino is sheep's cheese, Ally. There's a glossary at the end of the menu."

Tyler grinned. "Too scared to say it, mate?"

"Not scared, no," Jon said. "But I figured you wouldn't want me to embarrass you in front of your wife by talking about the time you kicked a goal for the visiting team."

"I was seven!"

Gabby listened to the two men banter. She'd never seen Jon like this, relaxed and easy. Tyler seemed delighted by his brother's playfulness, too, and for a moment she could see the boys they'd once been as they battled for supremacy.

The waiter's arrival ended the football discussion—if it could be called that—and they all dutifully ordered three courses.

When it came time to order drinks, Tyler opened the wine list and glanced at Gabby.

"Red or white?"

"I don't care. What's everyone else feel like?" She glanced at Ally, then Jon.

"I can only have a sip or two, so I don't think my vote counts," Ally said.

Jon shook his head. "Nothing for me." He turned to the waiter. "I'll have some mineral water, thanks."

"Let's grab a bottle of red, Gab. That way we can kid ourselves it's good for us," Tyler said.

"Sure," she said distractedly.

She was too busy remembering the apple juice Jon

had been drinking at the party to pay much attention to what Tyler ordered. She didn't think it was a coincidence that Jon hadn't drunk then and that he wasn't drinking again tonight, especially since he wasn't driving.

She knew a couple of people who didn't drink. One had a parent who was an alcoholic. The other *was* an alcoholic. She glanced at Jon's profile. He was listening to Ally, but he turned his head slightly and met her gaze and she knew that he knew exactly what she was thinking. He waited until Ally had finished her story and Tyler was speaking before leaning toward Gabby.

"I'm taking it easy for a while," he said quietly.

"Okay."

He lifted an eyebrow. "That's it? Okay?"

"What else is there to say?"

He stared at her intently for a beat. "Just when I think I've got you pegged..." he murmured, almost to himself.

"Ditto, buddy. Ditto."

He smiled and she couldn't help smiling in response. When she tuned into what was happening on the other side of the table, she saw Ally was watching them with bright, curious eyes.

Gabby steeled herself for the inevitable inquisition. Ally wasn't the kind of person who pulled her punches or thought twice about asking embarrassing questions.

But Ally simply reached for her water glass and took a sip before commenting on the painting hanging on the far wall. Gabby slowly relaxed. She made a mental note to avoid going to the bathroom tonight if she possibly could. No way did she want to risk being cornered by Ally and being badgered into answering questions about Jon. Not when she had no clue what the answers were.

The rest of the meal passed smoothly. Jon talked

about a build he did in Canada where the client had wanted to incorporate a living tree into the design, and Ally shared the juiciest morsels from her latest round of letters. Tyler tried to get Gabby to fill him in on her mother's latest exploits, but Gabby staunchly refused.

"You want to laugh at her," she said.

"I would never laugh at your mother. She's way too scary," Tyler said.

"Gabby has a scary mother? Now, that surprises me," Jon said, deadpan.

Gabby gave him a look. "Careful."

"I said I was surprised," Jon said, playing innocent.

"My mother is simply very protective of her independence," Gabby said.

"Gabby. Come on. She hasn't had a boyfriend for thirty years. That's not protective, that's a declaration of war," Tyler said.

"I want to meet her," Ally said. "She sounds awesome."

"She is," Gabby said firmly.

Tyler made eye contact with Jon and mouthed the word *scary* again.

Only the arrival of their coffees prevented Gabby from kicking him for a second time. By the time they'd finished those and a plate of complimentary chocolates, it was nearly eleven.

"I'd better get going. Got to get in early to take care of all the paperwork I didn't do tonight," Gabby said, shooting Ally a smile.

"I've been meaning to talk to you about that. I think it's time we hired someone to help out with the admin," Tyler said.

"Not yet. We said we'd review it later in the year, remember?" she said dismissively.

"You need help now, Gabby," Tyler said.

"I don't think—"

She blinked in surprise as Jon pressed his fingers to her lips.

"Listen to the boss," he said. "You work too hard. You need help."

She blinked again, more than a little astonished by what he'd said and the way he'd said it. As though he cared. As though he liked her.

"Well. There's not much I can say to that, is there?" Flustered, she grabbed her bag. "Thank you for a great meal."

Jon started to stand. She pointed a finger at him.

"Don't even think about walking me to my car."

He met her determined gaze. She tilted her head to one side, silently daring him. He resumed his seat. Gabby was aware of Tyler and Ally exchanging amused glances.

"Thanks for sharing your perk with me, Ally. I'll see the rest of you tomorrow."

She gave them a little wave and headed for the door. She half expected Jon to follow her despite what she'd said and debated with herself whether she would make a scene or not. She glanced over her shoulder when she reached the front door, but he was still seated at the table.

Huh.

You are the world's biggest freaking hypocrite, Gabby Wade.

It was true, she was, because there was no denying she was a little disappointed Jon had given in so easily—not because she needed his self-appointed security services, but because she'd been looking forward to the tussle of wills with him.

Which officially made her a sick puppy.

She was so preoccupied with her own twisted thoughts that she didn't realize it had started raining until she stepped out into the night. The road was shiny-wet, the air full of the smell of rain on hot concrete. She glanced toward her car, then tucked her bag firmly under her arm and broke into a run.

She was only feet from her car, fumbling to activate the keyless entry, when she noticed her hatchback was listing to one side. Her steps slowed and she did a quick circuit of the car. She groaned when she saw that the passenger side rear tire was completely flat.

"Shit."

She stood in the rain for a moment, contemplating her bad luck. Then she opened the passenger door and tossed her purse inside before opening the trunk to haul out the spare.

Sometimes being an independent woman and her mother's daughter sucked, but someone had to do it.

CHAPTER NINE

JON WATCHED GABBY UNTIL SHE disappeared through the door. He told himself they were in a busy café area with good street lighting, and that her car was barely a minute's walk away.

And, as she had told him on more than one occasion, she could take care of herself.

He focused his attention on the table to find Ally and Tyler watching him with identical knowing smiles.

"Nothing's going on," he said instantly.

"We can tell," Tyler said as he pushed himself to his feet. "I'll go get the car."

Ally frowned. "Why on earth would you do that?"

"It's raining," Jon said.

"Well, then I guess we'll get wet." She stood.

"I'll get the car. You two wait here," Tyler said firmly, pressing her back into her seat.

"Tyler. Don't be ridiculous," Ally said.

Tyler kissed her firmly on the mouth. "Stay here."

Ally harrumphed with frustration and Jon hid a smile as his brother headed for the door.

"I'm pregnant, not water-soluble," Ally grumbled. "He is so not treating me like this through the whole pregnancy. I'll go nuts."

"Good luck with that."

She gave him an assessing look. "How are things with you and Gabby?"

"Okay." Jon should have known she wouldn't let it slide.

"I'm going to need a little more than that."

"We talked this morning." He figured he owed her something, since she'd listened last night.

"And?"

"She said she's fine. She said she was just as responsible for what happened as I was."

"That's my girl."

He checked his watch. Ally grinned.

"Enjoying being my captive audience?"

"What do you think?"

He frowned as he saw Tyler entering, a disgruntled expression on his face. His hair and the shoulders of his shirt were wet with rain.

"What's up?" Jon asked as Tyler strode to their table.

"Gabby's got a flat tire. She's being difficult about letting me change it, so I wanted to let you guys know I may be a few minutes with the car." He sounded supremely frustrated as he turned to go.

Jon was pushing back his chair to join him when Ally spoke.

"If she wants to change the tire, let her do it."

Jon turned to stare at her, aware that his brother was doing the same thing beside him.

"It's dark, it's raining," Tyler said.

"She's got to jack up the car, loosen the nuts. Then she has to lift the spare. You ever tried to lift a tire?" Jon said.

"Can she do it on her own? Is it physically possible?"

"Probably," Jon conceded. "But that's not the point."

Tyler looked to Jon. "She doesn't understand."

"No, you guys are the one's who don't understand," Ally said. She sounded pissed. "If we women let men do everything for us, what happens when you're not around? Huh?"

Tyler opened his mouth to respond, then shut it without saying anything.

"Exactly," Ally said.

"We can't drive off and leave her," Tyler said.

Jon stood. "You guys go. I'll take care of it."

Ally gave him a warning look. "Jon…"

"Thanks for dinner," he said.

He exited the restaurant. Hunching his shoulders against the rain, he crossed the road and strode to where he knew Gabby had parked.

He could hear her talking to herself as he approached. "Stupid…freaking…mechanic…"

She'd managed to undo three of the four nuts and was using all her body weight to bear down on the tire brace to try to budge the remaining one. He noted with approval that she hadn't jacked the car up yet.

"Hey," he said.

She sat back on her heels and wiped the rain out of her eyes.

"Jon, I swear, if you've come out here to try to change my tire for me—"

"You got an umbrella?"

She peered up at him suspiciously. "Yes. It's on the backseat. Why?"

He didn't bother responding. He pulled open the rear door and glanced around until he spotted the umbrella. It was one of those stupid little ones that women always favored, all folded in on itself. Still, it was better than nothing. He shut the door and hit the button to open the umbrella. Then he stepped closer to Gabby and angled the umbrella so that she would be sheltered while she worked.

She looked up at him in silence for a long moment. "Thank you."

She meant it, too, he could tell.

"You're welcome. I don't suppose you'd let me loosen that nut for you?"

She thought about it for a second. "Yes. Thank you. That would be very helpful."

He handed her the umbrella and she shuffled to one side as he gripped the tire brace. He pushed experimentally. The brace didn't budge.

"Next time you get your tires checked, tell them not to use the air gun to finish up the nuts. Makes them too tight to undo by hand," he said.

"Don't worry, I've already made a mental note."

He braced himself, flexed his shoulders and gave the brace a good turn. He was beginning to get worried when it finally gave.

He looked at her with new respect. "Man. How did you get the other three off?"

"Determination. And a lot of four-letter words."

She handed him the umbrella and he moved out of the way. Gabby squatted and felt along the bottom of the chassis for the jacking point, then placed her jack and started winding. After a few turns of the lever she swore and yanked at the scarf around her neck, stuffing it into her pocket.

"Driving me crazy," she explained as she went back to work.

Jon watched as she wound the jack until the rear wheel was off the ground, wishing like hell she'd let him take over. A couple walked past huddled under their own umbrella, both of them giving him a dirty look when they saw a woman was changing the tire.

"It's okay. I do all the work in bed," he said.

He heard a splutter of choked laughter at his feet. The couple quickened their pace without saying a word. When he looked down again Gabby was grinning.

"This is killing you, isn't it?"

"Someone's going to take a picture of me and I'm going to wind up on one of those email chain letters under the title Man of the Year or something."

She laughed outright. "If it's any consolation, I'm not having much fun, either. But you gotta do what you gotta do."

It took her another fifteen minutes to remove the old tire, replace it with the spare, tighten the nuts, let the jack down and tidy everything away. Since the spare was a doughnut tire, she would have to get the damaged one repaired or replaced as soon as possible.

"Done. Thank God," she said as she turned from dumping the ruined tire in the trunk.

Despite his best efforts with the umbrella, she was soaked to the skin, her T-shirt and arms streaked with dirt from lifting the tires.

"You've got something on your face." He used his thumb to brush a smear of mud from her cheekbone.

She looked at him uncertainly. "Thanks."

He spotted something on her neck. "What's that?"

She clapped her hand to her neck. "Nothing."

He tugged her hand away. Sure enough, she had a hickey. "I did that?" he asked, even though he knew.

"It'll fade."

She started to move away from him, but he slid his hand around the back of her neck to keep her still.

"Does it hurt?" he asked, smoothing his thumb over the angry-looking mark.

"No. Haven't you ever had a love bite?"

"No."

"Really?" She gave him a speculative look.

"I've led a sheltered life."

"Sure you have." He was still rubbing her neck and she swallowed and shifted nervously.

"Shouldn't we be fighting right about now?" she said, her voice low.

"Maybe we've got better things to do than fight."

Her gaze went to his mouth as he lowered his head. He pressed his lips against hers gently, tasting her lower lip with his tongue. Her lips moved against his, butterfly light. He cupped the back of her head with his palm and moved closer. She shivered and reached up to wrap her arms around his neck.

Heat grew within him, but he kept things light, wanting to show her that he had it in him to be gentle after the craziness of last night. She curled her fingers into his shoulders and followed his lead.

He lost track of time as he explored her mouth with his own. A passing car sounded its horn, its occupants calling for them to get a room. They broke apart. Gabby took a step backward.

"I should probably get you home," she said, not looking at him.

He let her hustle him into the passenger seat, mostly because he'd never seen Gabby shy before.

"I'll head back up Brunswick Street to St. Georges Road," she said as she started the car.

"Sure."

"Did you like your meal? I loved that smoky tomato

thing I had with my starter. But I love anything smoky. You could smoke a piece of cardboard and I'd eat it."

"Could I?"

She flashed a look at him before concentrating on the road. "Sorry. I'm a bit nervous."

"Why?"

"I don't know. Maybe because I only know how to handle you when we're disagreeing."

"You want me to pick a fight?"

She smiled. "It's not the same if you fake it."

"I know."

Her smile widened and he asked the question that had been on his mind all night.

"Are you really okay about Tyler and Ally having a baby?"

"I'm happy for them," she said firmly. He got the sense she'd given the issue some thought. "I think they'll make great parents. And that kid is going to score some awesome nursery furniture."

He couldn't doubt her sincerity. She really was pleased for them. Whatever sway Tyler still had over her heart wasn't that powerful, then. Something in his chest relaxed.

"What about you?" she asked.

"What about me?"

"Are you happy for them?"

"Of course. Why wouldn't I be? They both seem to want it. Like you said, they'll make good parents."

He wondered if she could hear the lack of conviction in his voice.

"I thought you seemed a little tense when they made the announcement." She took her eyes off the road to glance at him. She didn't miss much, then or now.

"Did I? I guess I was surprised."

That, at least, was true. The list of things he and his brother had never discussed was as long as his arm, but he'd always assumed that, like him, Tyler would never risk having his own kids. Just in case. As far as he was concerned, the cycle of misery stopped here, period.

"Something occurred to me," she said as she signaled to make a right turn. "At my birthday dinner, when you didn't drink a toast to me—that was because you weren't drinking. Right?"

"You saw that?"

"I thought you didn't drink because you didn't like me."

He frowned. "I never didn't like you."

She made a rude noise.

"I thought you were a pain in the ass, but I didn't dislike you." He realized with some surprise that it was true. Through all their ups and downs, a part of him had always sought her approval. Why else had he kept trying with her?

"So you don't think I'm a pain in the ass anymore?"

She stopped at the curb in front of his apartment building.

"I think you have a great ass," he said. "Want to come upstairs?"

She smiled at his joke but her eyes were uncertain. "Look, Jon—"

"You have a nice neck, too."

She blinked. As though no one had ever paid her a compliment in her life.

"I don't think—"

"And you have a very sexy mouth."

"Jon—"

He silenced her with a kiss, his hand on her jaw as he

slid his tongue along hers. She was breathless when he broke the contact. He could feel his own pulse thudding in his ears.

"Please don't tell me I have great breasts because I will know you're lying then."

"You have perfect breasts. They're like firm, ripe little plums. Juicy and delicious."

He ducked his head and kissed her through her damp T-shirt, smiling as he felt her nipple bead against his lips. He pulled it into his mouth, fabric and all, sucking gently. When he lifted his head she looked a little dazed, her pupils hugely dilated.

"Come upstairs."

"Okay."

JON LED HER THROUGH THE LIVING room and straight to his bedroom. Gabby caught her reflection in the mirror and pulled a face.

"God. I'm filthy," she said, looking at her dirt-streaked arms. Either she really did have perfect breasts or Jon was more hard up than she thought.

"You want a shower?"

"That might be a good idea."

He showed her the ensuite bathroom and handed her a clean towel. He started to leave the room then hesitated.

"You want me to wash your back?"

She flicked a glance at him through her lashes. The thought of him in the shower with her was enough to make her mouth go dry.

"Um, okay. If you like."

He gave her a slow, lazy smile. "I like."

She reached for her T-shirt and tugged it over her head. He yanked his T-shirt off. She toed off her sandals.

He bent and pulled his boots off. A little surge of nerves hit her as she undid the button on her trousers. Last night, she'd been so crazy with need she hadn't had time to think. This was a little different and she had plenty of time to think about how bright the fluorescent lights were and how exposed she was about to be. She glanced at him, her gaze sliding over the round mounds of his pecs and down his ripped belly.

Screw it. She wanted him. She was going to have to get naked to have him.

She stuck her thumbs into the waistband of her panties and shed them along with her trousers in one sweep of her hands. She flipped the catch of her bra open, then let it slide down her arms. And then she was standing naked in front of Jon, staring at his naked body and very nice erection.

He was looking at her breasts. He reached out to cup the one he'd marked last night.

"Tell me that didn't hurt," he said quietly.

"It didn't."

They both watched as he ran his thumb gently over the bruise. Her nipple puckered and he shifted his attention to it, brushing his thumb back and forth over it until her knees started to shake. He shot her a knowing glance before moving closer. He placed both hands around her waist and smoothed them upward until her breasts were plumped by his hands. He looked at one, then the other, then made an approving noise in the back of his throat before bending his head to take her left nipple into his mouth. She braced herself against the tiled wall behind her as her body went up in flames. He nuzzled and sucked and kissed and bit and played with her breasts until she was panting and ready to fall over.

"Jon…" Her voice was a ragged whisper.

He lifted his head, a far-off look in his eyes. "Sorry. Got a little carried away."

"I'm not objecting. I just might not be able to stand up much longer."

He laughed, a low sound that made her clench her thighs.

"Let's get you clean so I can make you all dirty again."

He turned on the water and followed her into the shower. For the next ten minutes he slicked soapy hands over her body, exploring every dip and hollow. She returned the favor, chasing her hands across his body with kisses, tasting his skin, savoring the feel of warm skin over firm, hard muscle.

"Okay, we're done," Jon said as she slid her tongue into his ear while simultaneously stroking her hand up and down his shaft.

"Having trouble standing?"

He turned off the water and kissed her. "Having trouble being patient."

They fell onto the bed in a tangle of limbs. He rolled her till she was on her back and looked over her body with a hungry, approving eye.

"You drive me crazy," he murmured, then he started kissing her breasts again.

She kneaded her fingers into his shoulder muscles and arched her back as he began to trail kisses down her belly. She made a small excited noise and he shot her a deeply amused look as he slid between her wide-spread thighs. She didn't look away even as he lowered his head to take the first taste of her. She watched as he closed his eyes, savoring her, then she was utterly lost for endless, torturous minutes as he licked and lapped at her until the tension inside her reached a crescendo and she cried out her climax, her hands clutching his shoulders.

She collapsed onto the mattress, panting, while Jon kissed her thighs and her belly and worked his way up her body.

"Ask me how I feel about your—"

She pressed her fingers to his clever lips. "Trust me. I know."

He grinned. She pushed him onto his back.

"Condom?" she asked.

He started to sit up. "Back pocket of my jeans."

She liked that he didn't have a bulk pack in his bedroom. Not that she thought he was a saint, but still.

She found the condom and straddled him as she tore the packet open with her teeth. He was hot in her hands as she smoothed the latex on.

Taking him in hand, she raised her hips and slowly eased onto him. He closed his eyes, the muscles of his neck and shoulders tensing, his fingers tightening on her hips.

"Nice?" she whispered.

"Oh, yeah."

She started to move, riding him with smooth, sure strokes. He teased her nipples and watched her through slitted eyes. She tried to make it last but she could feel herself tightening again.

"Jon," she said, leaning forward to kiss him.

He gripped her tightly and rolled, never leaving her, and suddenly she was on her back, legs spread wide, as he stroked into her.

She forgot to breathe as he pushed her over the edge a second time. She was still shuddering around him when he plunged deep and stayed there.

"Gabby," he grated, his jaw tight. She held the back of his head as he pressed his face against her shoulder and came and came.

She closed her eyes afterward, basking in the warm sensation of complete satisfaction. His body was heavy on hers, his heart thumping against her breast bone, his breath in her ear. She ran her hands lightly over his back, enjoying the bold valleys and planes of his body.

He rolled to one side and got out of bed. Thirty seconds later he was back, tugging the sheet over both of them and pulling her tightly against his side.

"Give me twenty minutes and I'll make it hard for you to stand again," he said, closing his eyes.

She smiled sleepily. "You're on."

She woke two hours later to find Jon's arm wrapped possessively around her waist, his body curled around hers. She lay in the dark enjoying the purely physical pleasure of lying skin to skin with another human being again.

She'd missed this so much.

Not that it had ever been like this before.

She'd always enjoyed sex, but it had never been so intense, so consuming, so demanding as it was with Jon. Not even with Tyler.

Staring at the faint outline of the moon through the blinds on his window, she reflected that he was probably going to cast a long shadow over her future lovers.

Now there's a cheery thought.

Moving slowly, she eased out from under Jon's arm. She used the bathroom, then went to the kitchen for a glass of water.

Her thoughts shifted to the conversation they'd had on the way here. When Jon had asked her if she was okay with Tyler and Ally's pregnancy news, she'd honestly had to take a moment to understand what he meant.

She sipped the water. For someone who was supposed to still be in love with her ex, she was spending a lot of time naked with another man. A lot of time thinking about him, too. Just last week she'd been drunk and maudlin and ready to cry as she watched Tyler and Ally dance together, gazing into each other's eyes, talking quietly, communing with one another. Even now, she could still feel an echo of that pain. She envied their happiness. She missed the closeness of having someone to share her life with. She was lonely, and scared that it would always be that way because she'd put all her eggs in Tyler's basket and he'd turned out to be the wrong man.

It occurred to her that what she'd described didn't sound like love. It sounded like yearning, and maybe a little like grief.

All of which would explain why she was currently standing naked in Jon's kitchen, and why he'd been the starring attraction in her thoughts for quite some time.

Maybe she'd been a lot more ready to move on than she'd understood. Maybe she'd already moved on, in fact, on some unconscious level, and the rest of her was only now catching up. Maybe the angst and emotion she'd been experiencing in the past weeks was the curtain coming down on one phase in her life and rising on another.

She walked to the bedroom doorway. Jon was sprawled across the bed on his back, the sheets barely preserving his modesty. He looked ridiculously beautiful, his naked body stretched out, his sleek, powerful muscles loose and relaxed. It was impossible to see all that potent, undeniable masculinity and not feel a thrill of desire—not so long ago, this man had been inside her. They'd loved each other with hands and mouths and trusted each other with their pleasure. But it wasn't only desire she felt when she looked at him. Mixed in with all the earthy stuff was a fond sort of admiration for his pigheadedness, along with an appreciation of the care and skill he brought to his work and a grudging, growing understanding that his need to look out for others was the expression of a caring, nurturing instinct and not an attempt to control her or anyone else.

She liked him. She liked him a lot. The realization made her smile.

She returned to the kitchen to rinse her glass. She was placing it on the drain board to dry when she heard a noise. Thinking Jon had woken and was wondering where she was, she went to the bedroom. She saw that he was still asleep, his eyes closed. As she watched, his face creased into a frown and he moved his feet restlessly.

"No! Stop!" He moved his head, his body tensing.

She took a step toward the bed. He was obviously having some kind of bad dream.

"Stop. Don't. *Please*." His voice was low and anguished. He thrashed his legs, one of his hands opening and closing on the pillow. "I'll be good. Promise I'll be good."

Her chest tightened. He sounded so frightened. So scared. She climbed onto the bed and crawled to his side. "Jon," she said quietly, placing her hand on his shoulder.

"Leave him. Leave him. Please." His jaw was tight, his face distorted with fear.

She gripped him more firmly and shook his shoulder. "Jon. It's just a dream. It's not real."

His eyes opened with a snap and he jerked away

from her touch. They stared at each other, then the lost, hunted look left his eyes and he lifted a hand to drag it over his face, effectively masking his expression from her.

She didn't say anything, giving him a chance to find his feet. His breathing sounded very loud in the quiet room.

"Would you like a glass of water?"

"I'm fine. Thanks." He slid off the bed without looking at her, walking to the bathroom and closing the door.

She sat in the dark, listening to the tap running. Thinking.

Tyler used to have nightmares. Not very often, not as violent as this, but still. Something bad had happened to the Adamson boys. Something ugly and sad. But she had already guessed that, hadn't she?

She looked at the bathroom door. She guessed that Jon standing on the other side trying to work out how to handle her. Maybe even how to get rid of her.

The more she thought about it, the more certain she was that the moment he exited the bathroom he was going to either ask her or force her to leave in some way. He was too much of a man to enjoy having exposed himself so fully. And he was too much of a man to ask for comfort.

She moved quickly, fixing the bed and smoothing the pillows before finally crawling beneath the sheet. When the bathroom door opened a few minutes later she was lying on her side, facing away and feigning sleep.

She could feel Jon hesitate, could feel him trying to work out what to do. After a long beat the bed dipped as he climbed in beside her. She stirred.

"What time is it?" she murmured.

"Nearly one."

"Mmm."

She didn't try to embrace him directly. Instead, she shifted so that the curve of her back pressed along his side. Offering him the warmth of human contact with no strings. She kept her eyes closed, and after a few minutes she felt the tension leach out of his body. He rolled toward her, wrapping his arm around her. She felt his lips on the back of her neck as he kissed her. She murmured her approval, and when he began to play with her breasts she rubbed her backside against him.

She let him take the lead, let him take what he needed, and they made slow love in the dark, a long, intense ride.

Afterward, he fell asleep with his head on her chest. She waited until he was well and truly out of it before she slid from the bed.

She would have liked to stay, for him as well as herself, but her survival instinct had finally kicked in. It had been a big couple of days, and Jon was a complicated man. It wouldn't be a bad thing to put a little distance between them. At least until she could get a grip on things.

She gathered her clothes and shoes and took them to the living room so she could dress without disturbing him. She glanced around as she fastened her bra. The couch was gray and square and cheap-looking, the coffee table made from frosted glass. A TV sat on a nondescript unit. Near the window there was a small dining table with two modern plastic chairs with thin metal legs, the kind that cafés favored.

There was no color, no flowers, no cushions. She glanced toward the kitchen, but even the counters were bare. A pair of sneakers sat outside the bedroom door, but apart from that there was not a single sign that anyone lived in the space. It made her feel sad to think of Jon living inside this sterile little box.

No wonder he doesn't mind playing bodyguard if this is what he's got to come home to each night.

For a moment she was tempted to return to bed with him. To hell with caution. To hell with what was bound to be an awkward morning after. This man needed a little warmth and comfort and softness in his life.

Go home, idiot. Before you do something really stupid. Before you get so far ahead of yourself you'll never be able to pull back.

She slipped on her shoes, then tiptoed to the bedroom and made her way to the side of the bed. He was still sleeping deeply and she stooped to press a kiss to his cheekbone. Then she ran a hand over his hair in a gentle caress.

"I have to be up early. I'll see you tomorrow," she said quietly.

He stirred. "Gabby. Where are you going?" He made a groggy grab for her hand.

"I've got an early start. Go back to sleep, I'll see you tomorrow."

She kissed his cheek again and eased from his grasp. She picked up her handbag and slipped out the door, telling herself she was doing the right thing, the smart thing, to put some distance between them.

Even if it felt wrong.

CHAPTER TEN

GABBY WAS BUSY AT HER COMPUTER when Jon arrived for work the next day. She looked up to find him standing in her doorway. His eyes were wary, as though he wasn't quite sure of his reception. She didn't need to be a mind reader to know he was embarrassed about his nightmare, now that he'd had time to review their night together in the cold light of day. No doubt he'd been squirming ever since he'd woken and remembered what had happened.

"Hey." She smiled.

"Hey. Sorry I was a bit out of it when you left."

He looked so uncomfortable, so uneasy.

"I understand. I wore you out. You're not as young as you used to be..."

As she'd hoped, his shoulders lost some of their tension and his mouth kicked up at the corner. "Just how old do you think I am?"

She knew exactly how old he was; she'd filled out his insurance forms.

"I don't know. Forty-five? Fifty?"

He came fully into her office, a playful glint in his eyes. "You're pretty funny."

"There's no need to be embarrassed. You put in a good showing for a man who's no longer in his prime."

"Is that so?" He started rounding her desk.

"Morning, Jon, Gabby," Dino called as he walked past her door.

Jon stopped in his tracks. "*Today* he comes in early."

"Dino's always had great timing."

He gave her a long look. "I'll see you later, okay?"

He exited and she let her breath out.

So much for keeping her distance and taking it easy. But it was hard to be sensible when she was busy remembering the way he'd washed her in the shower, and the way he'd made love to her with his mouth, and the way he'd curled his body around hers afterward….

"For God's sake," she muttered under her breath.

Anyone would think she'd never had sex before.

Not like that, you haven't.

"Morning, Gabby. You got the details on the Montgomery quote? I need to check their specs again."

It was Tyler, a take-out coffee in hand. She tidied the already tidy pile of paperwork in front of her, trying to look as though she hadn't been sitting here, staring off into space daydreaming about having sex with his brother.

"Sure. Sure. Give me a second and I'll print it off for you."

"Did you get that tire sorted okay?" Tyler asked as she called up the file and hit the print icon.

"I did. Thanks."

"Did you let Jon do it?"

"I did not."

"You never cease to amaze me."

She knew he was laughing at her but she didn't care. "I let him hold the umbrella."

"Jon would have loved that."

"Oh, he did."

She collected the page from the printer and passed it over. Tyler scanned it briefly.

"Thanks." He folded it and tucked it into his back pocket. "I wanted to talk to you about something else, too."

To her surprise, he pushed the door closed before facing her. Gabby felt a little plunge of nerves in her belly. She couldn't remember Tyler *ever* wanting a closed-door meeting with her.

"Should I be bracing myself for bad news?"

"No bad news. I had a chat to Jon yesterday, and I haven't heard from him yet but I thought you should probably know what's going on. I've asked him to be become a partner in the business. Fifty-fifty."

Gabby blinked. "Wow. That's…not what I was expecting."

"We need someone to take charge of production. I figure with you on sales and admin, Jon on production and me on design, we're in good shape to meet our growth forecasts."

She nodded. Shock was starting to give way to the sting of hurt.

Why hadn't Jon mentioned this to her? Granted, there hadn't exactly been a huge amount of chat going on last night, but they were talking about a pretty significant offer here. A life-changing offer.

Maybe he didn't think it was any of your business.

It was a sobering thought.

"So, did he say when he might get back to you?" She hated herself for fishing.

"We left it open. To be honest, I think I kind of blindsided him. I've had the feeling the past couple of days that maybe he was thinking of taking off."

"Have you? Huh." She reached blindly for a paperclip and started playing with it.

"Shit. Sorry, Gabby. I know you and Jon are—"

"No, we're not. We're just…friends. Work colleagues, really." She could practically feel her nose growing longer with every lie.

"Well, so long as you know that was just me talking. Not Jon. I have no idea what he's thinking, to be honest. He plays things pretty close to his chest."

No kidding.

"It's cool. No worries," she said. She even threw in a smile to prove she was fine with everything she'd learned. "For what it's worth, I think it's a good idea. You guys complement each other."

"Glad you think so." He turned toward the door, patting his back pocket. "Thanks for the quote."

"Sure."

Gabby pretended to be absorbed in her work until she was sure Tyler was well and truly gone.

Maybe she was overreacting, but she felt as though she'd been slapped. A few hours ago, she'd been naked in Jon's kitchen, fretting about his depressing accommodation. She'd done her damnedest to offer him the comfort he didn't even know how to ask for after his nightmare, and she'd lain in his arms afterward, trying to be sensible about the growing sense of connection she felt to him.

And he hadn't bothered to mention the fact that his brother had offered him half of his very profitable business.

Her survival instincts had kicked in none too soon. Obviously, she and Jon had very different ideas of where this…thing between them was going. Which was fine. Neither of them had made any promises or representations to the other. Hell, a couple of days ago they could barely stand to be in the same room with each other without squabbling. Realistically, Jon was probably right to treat what had happened between them as a casual, inconsequential liaison.

It had felt like a lot more than that to her. All that anger and frustration they'd generated between them… the way he'd looked at her last night when they were standing in the rain…the way he'd curled his body around hers and held her so fiercely to his chest… None of that had felt inconsequential to her. It had felt real and meaningful and important.

But as she'd said to him only recently, it took two to tango, and it seemed as though the only tangoing Jon was interested in was the horizontal and not the emotional kind.

At least the way forward was clear now: keep her distance, keep her head, keep things light.

Be sensible.

JON TRIED TO CONCENTRATE ON adjusting the guide on the router but his mind kept circling to the events of last night like a dog chasing its tail. He was more than happy to review the good bits, but that wasn't the part his brain obsessed over. All he could picture was the moment he'd woken and found Gabby leaning over him, concern and pity in her face.

Pity. Because he'd had a big bad scary dream, like a little kid. And like a little kid he'd cried out and thrashed around and obviously woken her up.

He put down the router with more force than strictly necessary.

He'd thought he was getting a grip on the nightmares. He hadn't had one for nearly a week. He'd hoped that maybe the dreams had been a reaction to the fact that he'd stopped drinking, that he was finally breaking free from the quicksand that had enveloped him since his father's death.

Apparently not. Apparently he'd been waiting till he had an audience before he put on his next grand performance.

The only saving grace had been that she hadn't made a big deal out of it. He'd expected hand-wringing and amateur counseling when he'd exited the bathroom—instead, she'd been asleep. She hadn't said anything in her office, either. Which probably meant she wasn't going to. This was Gabby, after all. She wasn't exactly the queen of subtlety. If she wanted to know something, she asked.

The realization allowed him to move past his nightmare to think instead about the good parts of last night. Gabby's laughter. The look in her eyes when he'd started kissing his way down her belly.

Man…

Some women acted coy when it came to accepting pleasure in bed. They closed their legs and protested halfheartedly, even though they were quivering with need. Gabby had simply watched him with knowing, wicked eyes and sighed her appreciation. It had been that way every time with her—she knew what she wanted, and she wasn't ashamed of it, and she was hands down the sexiest, most responsive lover he'd ever had. Tyler must have been nuts to let her slip away.

Jon ground his teeth. He wasn't sure from which dark, reptilian part of his brain that thought had popped up, but he didn't want to hear from it again. The fact that Tyler knew Gabby intimately had always lurked in there somewhere, niggling at him, but he had refused to acknowledge it. He didn't want to think about his brother with her. Didn't want to imagine her undressing for him, moaning for him—

He shoved the piece of wood he'd been measuring along the workbench, sending a chisel flying into the wall.

He'd never been jealous of his brother, not even when they were kids. They'd had bigger fish to fry growing up, and as adults they hadn't seen each other enough to drum up any rivalry. Truth be told, he wasn't a jealous man. A perfectionist in his work, yes. A tough but fair boss, hopefully. But he'd never coveted another man's woman before, and this seemed like a particularly shitty time to start.

Gabby's not Tyler's woman. Not anymore.

He let the truth of the thought sink in for a beat. Then he returned the chisel to its place on the rack and took his marked-up timber to the bench saw along the far wall.

It struck him that it had been a long time since any woman had gotten him so worked up on so many levels. In the time he'd known her, Gabby had irritated him, infuriated him, engaged him and aroused him to the point where he'd lost control. Now, apparently, he was getting all dog-in-manger about her, too.

It was more than a little unsettling. His romantic history was littered with short-term relationships with women who had demanded little and received even less. He'd worked damned hard to keep them at arm's length, to make sure that no one expected anything from him apart from pleasure in bed and casual companionship. Yet here he was, knee deep in angst over Gabby without even trying.

At any other time, with any other woman, the realization would send him packing. The thing was, he really liked her. It seemed an obvious observation given all that had taken place between them. But it wasn't something he could say about all of the women he'd slept with over the years. He couldn't stop thinking about Gabby's sexy little body, and he enjoyed her mouthiness and straight-from-the-hip frankness. When he was with her he couldn't imagine being anywhere else—or wanting to be anywhere else, for that matter.

He thought about Tyler's offer. If Jon hung around, bought into the business…

He shied away from completing the thought. He was still on the fence about the offer. About a lot of things. Once he committed, there would be a lot of expectations, from all quarters.

He wasn't sure he was ready for them. The thing was, Gabby wasn't the kind of woman who screwed around. Every encounter they had bound them more tightly together. If he wasn't prepared to welcome those ties, he had no business sleeping with her again.

DESPITE HIS WARNING TO HIMSELF, Jon felt a definite thud of satisfaction when he entered the kitchen shortly after 5:00 and overheard Gabby talking on the phone with her mechanic. He was aware that she'd dropped her car off to have her tire repaired, but judging from her side of the conversation, it wouldn't be ready until tomorrow.

She ended the call and slid her phone into her pocket, clearly annoyed. "They promised me they'd have it done this afternoon. I should bill them for the taxi home," she said. "Why don't people ever do what they say they'll do?"

"I'll give you a lift," he offered before his brain had a chance to engage.

There was a long pause before she spoke. "That would be great, thanks."

"Let me know when you want to leave."

"Actually, I was going to have an early night tonight. So I'm ready when you are."

"I'll grab my gear." He walked to his workbench to collect his jacket, wallet and keys.

Given the kind of thoughts he'd been brooding over all day, he had no right to feel pissed that she'd had to think twice about accepting his offer. He should be glad she hadn't been jumping up and down, leaping at the opportunity to spend more time with him.

Except he wasn't.

He turned from pocketing his keys to find her standing outside her office, her purse in hand.

"Let's go," he said.

The afternoon sun was beating down on the parking lot and the truck was warm when he opened it.

"Give it a second to air out," he said when Gabby started to climb in.

She dutifully waited. He watched her through the cab. He studied the elegant slimness of her neck before letting his gaze drop to her breasts.

In deference to the hot weather, she was wearing a green tank top with spaghetti straps, with a pink and green silk scarf around her neck. Unless he was wildly mistaken, she wasn't wearing a bra. If anyone had ever told him that he could get hard in an instant over breasts that barely filled his palm, he would have laughed. He'd always been a breast man, and he'd always been attracted to women with generous cleavages. Yet Gabby's handfuls were fast becoming an obsession for him. The delicate color of her nipples—the palest of peachy-pinks. The way they sat so high and firm on her chest, almost as though they were offering themselves up to him. The silkiness of her skin, so pale he was sure it had never felt the kiss of the sun.

He lifted his gaze and realized that he'd been well and truly busted. Last night when he'd admired her breasts, she'd been aroused. Today, she glanced at her feet, fiddling with the strap on her handbag. He remembered that pause before she'd accepted his offer of a lift.

"We're probably fine now." He climbed in and waited until she was settled, her seat belt on, before reversing. For the first few minutes the only sound was the hum of the engine and the sound of the air-conditioning blowing. Out of the corner of his eye he could see her hand moving restlessly on her thigh.

She was nervous. Maybe even worried about something. He hated the thought that the something might be him—and not only because he wanted to sleep with her again. He reached out and caught her hand in his. Her hand tensed, her fingers flexing. He glanced at her but didn't let go. Her wary golden eyes met his, and when she realized he wasn't going anywhere, her hand slowly relaxed in his.

By the time they stopped in front of her place, he'd only released her hand twice—once to make a turn, the other to change lanes—and both times her hand had tightened around his when he took it up again.

"Would you like to come up?"

He did. A lot. But he needed to know something first. "You hesitated before, when I offered you a lift home. But now you want me to come up?"

"I wasn't sure if it was a good idea."

"Right."

She twisted to face him more fully, her eyes scanning his face. "What do you think?"

He almost smiled. Almost. Typical of Gabby to lob the hand grenade back his way.

"I don't know if it's a good idea, either."

Her lips twisted into a wry smile. "Anyone ever told you you're the master of the nonanswer?"

"Anyone ever told you you're great at answering a question with a question?"

Her eyes crinkled attractively. He wondered how he'd ever managed to overlook her innate beauty.

"We could go on all night like this," he said.

"We could." She eyed him seriously for a second, her gaze searching. Then she leaned over the hand brake and kissed him. Her tongue traced the seam of his lips before he let her inside, then she slipped in deeper to tease him some more. He cradled her jaw in his palm and let his thumb sweep across her cheek. When she pulled back, she was flushed and her nipples were tight beneath the fabric of her top.

"Come upstairs," she said.

He switched off the engine. She took his hand when he joined her on the sidewalk. The foyer to her building had a security keypad, he was happy to see, and he waited as she punched in her code.

They took the elevator to the third floor. She searched for her keys in her bag. He stepped close and bent to kiss the vulnerable hollow at the nape of her neck. She shivered and offered him a small smile before unlocking the door. She led him into her apartment and waved an arm to her right.

"Living room."

There were two couches placed either side of a fireplace, a two-seater in cream and a three-seater in charcoal. Bright cushions were scattered over both, a mixture of florals and stripes and polka dots. A deep green throw was folded over the arm of the charcoal couch, and a floor lamp that looked as though it had been made from a surveyor's tripod filled one corner. Sunlight streamed through wide-slatted white blinds, crisscrossing a bookshelf full of paperbacks and knick-knacks with golden light.

Gabby pushed open a door on the right wall.

"Dining room in here. It's pretty pokey."

He glanced in to see a table with four mismatched antique chairs and a wall covered with an eclectic mix of photo frames. She retraced her steps before he had a chance to inspect her photos and waved toward another door.

"Kitchen. Bedroom is at the end of the hall, and the bathroom."

She was nervous again, her hands fidgeting at her waist. "Do you want a drink? Juice? Water?"

"Juice would be good."

"Do you want to stay for dinner? There's a decent Chinese place around the corner. We'll have to go pick it up, but it's walking distance..."

"Sounds good."

She disappeared into the kitchen to take care of the drinks. He used the opportunity to inspect her bookcase. Crime novels, a whole collection of vintage Nancy Drew hardcovers and a number of glossy coffee table books on interior design. As well as those, each shelf boasted a handful of trinkets—a glass paperweight with swirls of color trapped within it, two small but perfect teacups carved from what he assumed was jade, an old pipe made from burnished wood. It was the contents of the second top shelf that intrigued him the most, however—a collection of tin windup toys. A robot, a monkey, an elephant, a whale...

He picked up the monkey and wound the spring and watched as it marched across the shelf.

"Here you go." Gabby's gaze went to the marching monkey as she handed his drink over. "I used to collect them when I was a kid. I keep telling myself to throw them out but I guess I'm too sentimental…"

He didn't have a single memento from his childhood—unless he counted the small bump on his nose from when his father had broken it. Robert had been careful to rarely punish his sons to the point where they needed medical attention, but that one time he'd lost it completely and backhanded Jon across the face with all his strength.

The monkey had hit the end of the shelf and Jon turned it around to let it walk the other way.

"I like them. Especially this monkey," he said.

She passed him a folded menu but he handed it straight back to her.

"You choose. I'll eat anything."

"That's pretty much a challenge for me to order something really weird, like chicken feet with congee, you know that, right?"

"I dare you."

He wandered to the dining room while Gabby pondered the menu. He'd never paid much attention to the way people lived before but for some reason her apartment fascinated him. It was warm and eclectic and interesting and welcoming, full of little clues to her personality, like those whimsical windup toys.

"When I bought this place I had big plans to knock that wall down, open this up," she said, noting his interest in the smaller space.

"What happened?" He surveyed the offending wall with a professional eye.

"Oh, you know. Big plans, not enough money, not enough time." She punched in a number and began to relay their order.

He inspected the dividing wall from both sides, considered the ceiling and the layout, tapped on the plaster. "This isn't load-bearing, so it wouldn't cost you a lot to knock it down," he said when she'd finished her call. "If you ran a lintel across here, you wouldn't even have to get the ceiling replastered, which is good because period cornicing is hard to match."

She came to stand beside him, tilting her head to look at the ceiling then at him.

"What are the odds, do you think, of it ever really happening?"

There was so much wry self-knowledge in her comment and her expression. When he'd first met her, he'd thought she was uptight, that she didn't have a sense of humor or know how to have fun. The truth was that she was funny and smart and she was more than up for a good time. As he knew only too well.

He stepped closer, sliding his arms around her. Her eyes widened as he smoothed his hands onto her backside, cupping her cheeks and squeezing them lightly. He encouraged her closer, until his hips were pressing against hers. He watched her gaze grow smoky as she registered his erection.

He kissed her, massaging her bottom, taking his time.

"What about dinner?" she said as he started peeling her top over her head. "They said it would be ready in ten minutes..."

He surveyed her breasts hungrily. "There's this thing called a microwave." He filled his hands with her breasts. His thumbs brushed over her nipples and he watched as they hardened. "You put the food in and push some buttons, and like magic the food gets—"

She cut him off with a kiss. "You had me at microwave." Then she took him by the hand and led him into her bedroom.

THE SMELL OF LEMON DETERGENT was sharp. He was at the kitchen sink, washing the dishes with Tyler. He could hear the television in the other room but nothing else. A good sign—his parents weren't fighting, which meant he and Tyler had a chance tonight.

He was too small to reach the sink and had to stand on an old soft-drink crate to wash properly. Tyler was on drying duty, carefully returning each piece of crockery or cutlery to its rightful place. Jon wasn't sure how the game started, whether he splashed Tyler first or the other way round. They stifled their laughter, not wanting to draw attention to themselves, splashing soap suds and water back and forth. Then Tyler upped the ante by twisting his wet tea towel and flicking it at Jon's legs. Jon waited until Tyler was busy drying a cup before grabbing the other tea towel and returning fire.

Tyler tried to dodge. His foot skidded on the soap-slicked floor. He flung out an arm to save himself and the cup in his hand hit the floor with a crack.

It shattered instantly and he and Tyler skidded to a halt, staring at what Jon now recognized as one of his mother's treasured Royal Doulton cups.

Footsteps sounded in the living room. His tummy dipped with fear. He knew what was coming now.

"*Oh!* What have you done?"

It was his mother, hands pressed to her chest as she stared, aghast, at her precious teacup. Behind her, their father filled the doorway, his face already darkening with rage.

"What's going on? What have you been up to?"

His gaze went from the china to their mother's face to Tyler, still standing frozen above the mess.

Jon opened his mouth to explain that it had been an accident, that it was his fault as well and that they hadn't meant it, but their father was already reaching for his belt, pulling the thick leather clear of his trouser loops. Jon kept trying to get the words out—if only he could explain, make them see that he and Tyler hadn't meant to be naughty, they'd only been playing—yet no sound came out.

Time slowed as his father wrapped the thick leather around his fist. Once, twice, three times, leaving the buckle end free. Then he stepped toward Tyler, grabbing him by the hair. Tyler's face twisted with terror, his mouth opening wide, tears sliding down his cheeks. His eyes begged Jon to do something, anything, to stop the pain.

Again Jon tried to speak, to make his heavy, leaden feet move but he was stuck to the floor, his tongue thick in his mouth, his throat tight.

"Please. I didn't mean it. I didn't mean it," Tyler pleaded as their father bent him over and raised his arm for the first blow.

Again those pleading eyes burned into Jon's, begging for help. For a way out. For safety.

Suddenly it was Gabby's face he was staring into and she was the one pleading with him with her big golden eyes and it was her terror he was standing by and witnessing and not doing a goddamned thing about as the leather whistled through the air—

"Jon. It's a dream. You need to wake up."

Jon clawed his way to consciousness. It was dark and he was in an unfamiliar bed, Gabby leaning over him. His heart was racing, pounding against his breastbone, and his body was damp with sweat.

"You're okay," Gabby soothed, her hand gentling his shoulder. "It was just a dream."

Shit.

Shame prickled through his body. Two nights in a row. Gabby must think he was a complete freaking head case.

"Are you okay? Do you need anything?"

She flicked the bedside lamp on and he blinked in the light. Her eyes were twin pools of concern as she watched him, her face tight with worry.

"I'm fine." He rolled out of the bed and looked around, disoriented.

"That door," she said quietly.

He shut himself in her black-and-white-tiled bathroom. His face in the mirror was haggard, the echo of old terror still sitting in the back of his eyes. He ran the tap and scooped water to his mouth, drinking deeply. He washed his face, then sat on the edge of the tub and braced his elbows on his legs and stared at the floor.

He couldn't take much more of this. Something had to give.

An image from his dream flashed across his mind's eye—Gabby, pleading with him to save her.

"Bloody hell." He shut his eyes but it didn't stop the tears from leaking from beneath his eyelids.

He wanted it to stop. He wasn't a saint, but he wasn't an evil man, either. He'd never gone out of his way to hurt anyone, physically or emotionally. He gave to charities, wasn't afraid to work hard, always did his part to chip in. He'd survived his childhood, made his own life, buried his father. And *still* it was with him. The guilt. The shame. The fear. And he just wanted it to stop.

His breathing was choppy with suppressed emotion and he forced himself to breathe past the constriction in his throat until he felt his heart rate normalizing. Big belly breaths, sitting naked in Gabby's bathroom while she worried about him on the other side of the door.

After a few minutes he stood and opened the door. The last thing he wanted to do was face Gabby, but he knew he had to. He walked out. She was sitting in the middle of the bed, knees pulled to her chest, arms wrapped around her legs.

"You okay?" She unfolded her legs and moved toward him. She was going to hug him, he knew. To offer him comfort.

He turned away and made a grab for his jeans. Out of the corner of his eye he saw Gabby pause, undecided. He dragged his jeans on, then pulled his T-shirt over his head and grabbed his boots.

"I'm going to go," he said, not quite looking at her.

"All right."

She pulled on a blue silk dressing gown and they walked to the door in silence.

He paused on the threshold, trying to find something to say that would make any of this okay. He couldn't think of a single freaking thing.

"Thanks for dinner," he said.

He leaned close and kissed her cheek, then ducked out the door. He stuffed his socks into his pocket and pulled his boots on in the elevator.

Once he was in the safety of his truck he leaned against the seat and let his head fall back.

Over the years, he'd called his father every name under the sun. He'd lain awake at night thinking of the things he wished he'd said and done to force his father to recognize his crimes against his own children. Jon had cursed the man, demonized him, tried to forget him—and even though he was dead and rotting in the ground, he'd never hated his father more than he did at this moment.

He had something good here. He could *feel* it. The business with Tyler. Gabby. But he couldn't get beyond this bullshit to let it happen because the past still owned him.

And for the life of him he didn't know how to break free.

Bone weary, he started his truck and drove to his empty box. He would make it up to Gabby tomorrow. If she'd let him.

GABBY STOOD AT THE WINDOW, watching Jon drive away. Everything in her had wanted to go down there and throw her arms around him and tell him it was going to be all right. But Jon didn't want her comfort. He'd made that more than clear. He held himself as tightly as a fist and while he might let her in for sex, he wasn't about to share the other parts of himself with her.

Remind you of anyone?

She'd already played this game with one Adamson. She didn't think she had it in her to try again.

And yet she remained at the window until Jon's tail-lights disappeared into the night. Eyes gritty, she let the curtain fall. She made herself a cup of tea, working on autopilot.

She understood now why Tyler had been so keen to have his brother on board that he'd agreed to Jon's no salary stipulation. Jon was in crisis. The drinking, the not drinking, the weight loss, the nightmares… He put up a good front, standing around joking with the guys, arguing with her, sleeping with her, but he was in so much pain it was a wonder he could function.

She listened to the kettle boil and wondered if she should call Tyler. Jon had been so distressed. Surely someone should be with him? Then she remembered what Tyler had said that morning. *I have no idea what he's thinking. He plays things pretty close to his chest.* Clearly, Jon wasn't talking to his brother, either.

She took her tea to the bedroom and sat against the pillows. Her chin started to wobble and she realized she was close to tears. She took a sip of her tea, then another. Slowly, the urge to cry passed.

She grasped the cup in both hands and stared at the amber fluid, trying to decide what to do. Keep trying to get through? Take what he was offering and ask no questions? Try to find some middle ground?

There was really only one thing she could do, and in her heart she knew it. She'd tried for years to get Tyler to open up to her, to no avail. His many small rejections had meant the death of a thousand cuts for their relationship. She couldn't do it again. She already felt too deeply for Jon. She already wanted to swoop in and save him and take away his hurts.

She needed to take a step back. She needed to protect herself. No more fabulous sex. No more letting her heart get ahead of reality. If Jon wanted to talk, if he needed a friend, she would be there for him. But she was not going to sacrifice herself to his cause. Maybe that meant she was selfish, but she couldn't keep taking body blows only to get up and let it happen all over again. She only had so many recoveries in her, and the way she felt when she was with Jon… She couldn't do it.

She fell asleep with the light on and woke with a

start when the alarm went off at six. For the first time in months, she pressed the snooze button and rolled over. She didn't fall back into true sleep and when she resurfaced she felt worse instead of better. And she was late for work.

It was only when she was ready to head out the door that she remembered her car was in the shop. She called a taxi and went to the window to wait. It took her a moment to register the black truck parked out front.

She stared at Jon's familiar silhouette in the driver's seat, then dialed the cab company again and canceled her taxi. She locked up the apartment, then took the elevator to the foyer. Jon got out of the truck when he saw her approaching.

"I thought you'd need a lift. With your car in the shop…"

"I do. Thanks."

He looked terrible, drawn and tired. For a moment her resolve wavered. She stopped in her tracks, willing him to say something, anything, about last night. Willing him to give her some sign that she should hang in there despite her best instincts.

"Did they say when your car would be ready? I can take you to pick it up this afternoon if you like."

She pressed her lips together. Not quite what she'd been hoping for.

"Thanks, but they said they'd drop it off." She got into his truck. He started the engine and pulled into traffic.

"I was thinking we could go out somewhere nice on the weekend if you'd like. One of the guys was talking about the new seafood place at the Docklands. Or maybe you've got some place you want to try out?"

Her heart sank as she listened to the careful casualness

in his voice. A nice dinner out was his way of making it up to her, of course, without actually acknowledging there was anything to make up for.

"I can't go out with you on the weekend, Jon."

"Okay. Maybe next week sometime, then?"

"Maybe I should rephrase. I can't go out with you, Jon. Full stop."

His hands tightened on the steering wheel. "Look, if this is about last night, I'm sorry. This not drinking thing has really messed with my sleeping patterns. I'm thinking about seeing the doctor for some sleeping tablets."

She wondered how long he'd worked on his explanation. All night, by the look of him.

"You never asked me why Tyler and I broke up."

He glanced at her, clearly surprised by the change of topic. "I figured it was none of my business."

Normally, she would agree, but this was a pretty unique situation and Jon deserved to know why she was drawing a line under what had happened between them.

"We saw each other for three years. At one point we were practically living together. But I never felt as though he'd really bought into the relationship." She glanced at Jon, but his gaze was fixed on the road ahead.

"You know those old fifties movies where if they showed a married couple in bed one of them always had to have their foot on the floor to get past the censors? That was how I felt Tyler was through our whole relationship—one foot on the floor all the time, never quite in the bed. There were all these no-go areas. His childhood, his parents, the nightmares he had sometimes."

Jon shot her a quick, searching look. She wondered if

he knew these things about his own brother, if they'd ever talked at all. Knowing them both, she suspected not.

"I tried so many times to get him to talk to me about it. I waited. I begged. I got angry. And eventually I realized it just wasn't going to happen. That maybe he couldn't open up about it, and either I had to be prepared to accept a relationship that was based on sex and a few laughs and a bunch of other superficial stuff, or I had to walk away. So I walked away. Then a few years later, Tyler met Ally and the rest is history."

She fell silent for a moment, gathering her thoughts. "Some people might think I'm stupid for giving up someone I loved. But you've seen what he's like with Ally. There are no secrets between them. He let her in."

They arrived at the workshop and he pulled into a parking spot. She twisted to face him more fully.

"I want that, too, Jon. I want the man I love to let me in. I want to really be a part of his life. I want the highs and the lows. And I know I probably sound like some kind of crazy stalker, having this conversation with you after only a few days, but whatever is going on between us has felt like a lot more than sex to me right from the start."

He was studying the dash and she willed him to look at her. Finally, he did, and she could see how wary he was, how threatened he felt.

"I don't know what to tell you," he said.

She felt incredibly sad. "I know you don't. I guess that's what I was saying in a really roundabout way. We obviously want different things. That's why I'm making it easier on both of us, Jon. Thank you for the past few days. And thanks for the lift."

She leaned across and kissed his cheek.

"For what it's worth, you're a great guy and I hope that one day you meet your Ally. When you're ready for her."

She slipped from the truck and strode quickly toward the building, blinking away tears. She told herself she'd done the right thing every step of the way. By the time she got to the showroom door, she still didn't believe it.

CHAPTER ELEVEN

JON WATCHED GABBY WALK AWAY from him. Everything in him wanted to call her back, to tell her that he didn't want to meet anyone else, that he hadn't even thought about another woman since she'd walked into her office and started giving him a hard time for using her computer.

He didn't move, didn't so much as lift a finger.

He hadn't been lying when he said he didn't know what to tell her. She'd been very clear about what she wanted in a relationship, but he had no idea if he had it in him to give.

A lovely ironic twist—after years of sidestepping commitment and keeping women at arm's length, he'd finally found someone he wanted to get close to, and he didn't know how.

So, that's it? You're going to let her go? The best thing that's ever happened to you?

Because that was one thing he knew without a doubt—he would never meet another Gabby Wade in his lifetime. She was unique, a small, fiery, feisty gem. She'd predicted he'd meet his own Ally one day. He didn't want an Ally. He wanted Gabby. Only Gabby.

The realization crystallized things for him. He had to act or he was going to lose her. He had to do something to show her that he wasn't interested in only sex and laughs. He was interested in her. In the life they could have together.

Galvanized, he got out of the truck and headed for the building. He strode straight through the showroom and into the workshop and started up the stairs to Tyler's office.

His brother was seated at the drafting board positioned to the left of his desk, poring over a blueprint.

"I'll do it. I'll buy in," Jon said without any preamble.

For a long moment Tyler simply stared at him. Then his lips curved into a big smile and he put down his pen. "Hey. That's great."

Jon walked to the visitor's chair and sat. "What happens next?"

Tyler used his legs to push his office chair to his desk and reached for a folder. "It's not rocket science, so it shouldn't take too long to work out a deal. But you'll need to get your own lawyer to go over it, and I think we should get an outside valuation."

"Sure. Whatever you think."

Tyler grinned at him. "I gotta tell you, you've surprised me. I was pretty sure you were going to turn me down."

"You and me both."

His brother eyed him shrewdly. "Is this about Gabby?"

Jon hesitated a moment. But there was no reason to hide his intentions. He wanted Gabby to be a part of his life. "Yeah. It is."

"Good."

Jon waited for him to say more, but Tyler simply turned to his computer.

"Did you get a chance to go over all the figures in the five-year plan?"

They talked business for a few minutes. Jon felt his shoulders loosening more with each second that passed. Now that he'd jumped, he felt free. Crazy, when he'd effectively tied himself to his brother for life.

"One of the things I want you to know up front is that I'll want some time off when the baby's born," Tyler said. "I figure I might as well take advantage of being my own boss, and I want to be with Ally in those early weeks as much as possible."

"But you'd still be available for design work?"

"Of course. But I'll leave it to you and Gabby to handle client meetings and that end of things. I've been mucking around with some designs for nursery furniture. I was thinking it might be worth adding some pieces to the catalogue." Tyler talked about his and Ally's plans for the nursery for a few minutes.

Jon marveled at his brother's unwavering enthusiasm. Tyler was practically skipping and singing and clicking his heels he was so happy about Ally's pregnancy. He didn't seem to have a single doubt. Jon couldn't comprehend it.

"Aren't you worried?" The question slipped out before he could stop it.

"About all the stuff that could go wrong?" Tyler asked. "Sure. But Ally's got a great doctor and we're doing lots of research. It's a leap of faith. But I'd rather take the risk than not."

"I meant you. Aren't you worried about you?" Jon had started this, he figured he might as well finish it. "Aren't you worried you might be like him?"

Jon shifted in his chair, frustrated with his ability to articulate his feelings. It wasn't that he thought Tyler was in any way like his father. His brother was even-tempered and good-natured and there was no doubting his love for Ally. The odds were high that he'd be a great father. But there was no denying that their father's blood ran in their veins. For many years their only model of manhood—of fatherhood—had been a bullying, violent monster. That had to come from somewhere, and who was to say that it wasn't waiting inside either of them, waiting to be expressed?

Tyler put his pen down on the desk. "I know what you mean. Sometimes I hear myself say something, or catch sight of myself in the mirror and I see shades of him. That ever happen to you?"

"Every time I shave."

They both had their father's strong jawline.

"Yeah. When I was younger, every time I lost my temper, every time I wanted to rip someone's head off it would freak me out."

"I caught myself calling someone a bloody mongrel once. Made my blood run cold," Jon said. "Never said it again."

It had been their father's favorite epithet, usually spat in fury.

Tyler nodded grimly. "The thing is, we're not like him. He was like a little kid, needing to get his own way the whole time. He had no concept of self-control. You remember how he used to get when he was angry, smashing stuff, laying into us. I never once heard him take responsibility for his mistakes or failings. Not once. It was always about other people. I'm not perfect. Far from it. But I'm not like that. And neither are you, mate."

Tyler was so certain. So sure. For the second time in as many days Jon felt a twist of envy. His brother had his shit all worked out, while Jon was still flailing around. Tyler had Ally, a baby on the way, a house that was a home, not just a roof over his head…

You've got Gabby.

Except he didn't. Not yet, because he'd let her walk away this morning without offering her any of the things she needed to hear.

But that was why he was sitting here right now, talking to his brother, right? Buying into the business, letting her know that he wasn't going anywhere.

That he was serious about her, about them.

It had taken guts for Gabby to put herself on the line this morning. The least he could do was try to match her courage.

But he didn't want to offer Gabby the least. He wanted to offer her the most. The best. Which meant he had some serious work to do.

THE DAY DRAGGED FOR GABBY. For the first time in her life she failed to find solace and distraction in her work. Her mind kept drifting to Jon, or she'd catch sight of him in the workshop or hear him talking and laughing with the guys.

In her gut, she knew she'd made the only decision she could. Everything had happened so quickly between them. She felt as though she'd been running downhill, arms flailing, out of control—and it wasn't until the last minute that she'd recognized that there was nothing but disaster waiting for her at the bottom of the slope.

She assured herself she'd stopped in time so often during the day that it almost became a mantra.

At five o'clock on the dot she packed up for the day. She wanted to be alone. Or at least somewhere Jon wasn't. Dino pretended to faint when she offered a general goodbye to the team and headed for the door, carefully avoiding looking directly at Jon.

Last night they'd left together and she'd shown him her apartment and they'd eaten beef in black bean sauce and fried rice and made love once on the couch and once in her bed.

Tonight she microwaved a frozen meal and watched six episodes of *Friends* back to back in an effort to short-circuit her circling thoughts.

The next two days ground by. On Thursday Jon made a point of coming into her office and chatting for twenty minutes as though they were old friends and she had to go into the bathroom afterward so no one could see her chin wobbling.

She didn't want to be his friend. She was sick of being the friend.

By the time she crawled into bed on Friday night she was feeling flat and teary. She missed Jon. In a single visit he'd marked her apartment indelibly with his presence. She looked at her bookcase and remembered him playing with her windup toys, and she went into the kitchen and saw him spooning Chinese takeout into bowls and laughing at her insistence that they eat with chopsticks, and in her bedroom she remembered how he'd pinned her against her pillows while he tortured her with his roving mouth.

Lying in bed, staring at the ceiling, she told herself it would get better. It wasn't as though she'd fallen in love with him, after all. She'd caught herself, just in time.

She woke to the sound of loud knocking. She prized an eye open and looked at her alarm clock. Barely eight. On a Saturday morning.

"This had better be good," she muttered as she rolled out of bed and grabbed her robe.

If it was her downstairs neighbor asking whether Gabby had seen her cat again, she was going to be seriously hard-pressed not to reach for the nearest blunt object. It had taken her hours to fall asleep, and even if it hadn't been exactly restful it had at least been better than being awake, mooching around pretending she wasn't the next best thing to heartbroken.

She shuffled toward the foyer, tying the sash on her robe as she went. Yawning hugely, she opened the door.

Jon stood on the other side looking better than anyone had a right to when she was feeling so low and he was the culprit.

"Did I wake you? Sorry. I assumed you'd be up."

"It's Saturday. I sleep in on Saturdays."

"Ah. Well, I'm here now."

He bent to collect a large black box, angled his shoulder and stepped forward, forcing her to fall back. Before she knew it he'd pushed past her and into her apartment and was placing what she now recognized as a toolbox down in her living room.

"I've got some wood I need to bring up from the truck, and some tools. Might be a few trips."

"Jon. Wait!" she said, but he was already disappearing out the door.

She scurried into her bedroom to pull on some clothes and tried to ignore the slow bubble of happiness rising inside her. She reminded herself that Jon was a closed book, that she was already dangerously close to being beyond help where he was concerned, that she had to remain strong no matter what he said to her when he came back. With his tools and his wood.

She'd pulled on a pair of jeans and a tank top and

was standing at the door arms crossed over her chest by the time he returned.

"One more trip," he said as he entered with a large piece of timber over his shoulder and a circular saw in one hand.

"Jon. Stop."

"I figure if I go at it hard, I can get everything but the painting done today."

He was about to step out the door again but she stood in his path.

"Jon. What are you doing here?"

"I'm knocking down your wall."

"Why?"

"Because you said you wanted it knocked down."

He was laughing at her with his eyes.

"I don't think that's a good idea."

He hadn't said a word when she told him where she stood the other day in his car. He'd let her walk away. She needed to hang on to that, even though he was standing in front of her looking beautiful, his hair still damp from the shower.

"Don't you?" He hooked a finger into the waistband of her jeans and pulled her toward him.

She tried to resist, but he was strong and she wound up pressed thigh to thigh with him, her neck crooked to maintain eye contact. Jon looked at her and the smile slowly faded from his mouth.

"A couple of days ago, Tyler asked me if I wanted to be his business partner."

Suddenly she was afraid to breathe. "I know. He told me."

"I signed the papers yesterday afternoon." He brushed his fingertip across her cheek. "I want this to work between us, Gabby. All those things you said the other day… I want that, too."

She'd indulged in a few pathetic fantasies over the past few days, but this was better than all of them. Jon was staying. He was going to be part of the business. And he wanted to make things work with her.

In case all of that wasn't enough, he was going to renovate her living room.

But still she didn't say anything. It was too perfect. She wanted it too much.

The smile faded from Jon's lips. "If things have changed for you, Gabby, I understand. But I'd still really like to fix your wall for you."

"Things haven't changed for me." She was more than a little afraid she was going to disgrace herself with tears. "I missed you."

"I missed you, too, Gabby. You wouldn't believe how much."

They kissed. She closed her eyes and rubbed her cheek against his. Jon's hands found her backside and she slid her hands beneath his T-shirt to run her hands over his belly and back.

She'd thought she'd never get to do this again. She'd thought they were over. She moved closer, seeking physical reassurance that he was real, that this was real.

"Hold that thought," he said.

She opened her eyes in surprise as he slipped away from her and moved toward the door.

"Where are you going?"

It had been three days—three very long days—since they'd had sex.

"I'm double parked, and I've got more tools I need to off-load," he said apologetically. "If we keep going,

I'm going to need a cold shower before I can be seen in public."

"You're serious, aren't you?"

He closed the distance and dropped a quick kiss on her mouth. "Five minutes, tops."

He kissed her again and disappeared out the door. She stood staring blankly at the spot he'd been for a full ten seconds. Then her brain caught up and she closed her eyes and took a moment to simply savor the realization that Jon was here, and he was staying, and this was happening.

Against the odds. Against her expectations. He wanted her the way she wanted him.

Her eyes snapped open and she spun on her heel and raced to the bathroom to turn on the shower. By the time she heard the door close she'd showered and was brushing her teeth.

She spat and rinsed, then walked naked into the hallway. Jon was crouching beside his toolbox, sorting through the top tray.

"What are you doing?"

He looked up and his gaze instantly became very focused. "I thought you were still in the shower."

"What are you doing?" she repeated.

A slow smile curled his mouth. "I'm taking my clothes off," he said, standing and whipping his T-shirt over his head.

"That's more like it."

She turned and sashayed into the bedroom.

"Have I mentioned you have a great ass?" Jon called after her.

"Come tell me again."

"I'll do better than that," he said as he appeared in her bedroom doorway.

He was naked, hard and pretty damned amazing.

And he was here. With her.

"What do you have in mind?"

An hour later—a very steamy, toe-curling hour later—Jon pushed her out of bed.

"The clock's ticking," he said.

"Couldn't the clock tick while we're in bed?"

"Do you have any idea how hard it is to get a tradesman to turn up on a weekend?" he asked her as he pulled on his jeans.

"I'm trying to think of an appropriate comment that involves the lewd use of the word *tool,* but I'm drawing a blank."

She pulled on a tank top. Jon glanced at her. "Maybe you should wear a bra."

"Why?" She glanced down. Really, a bra was more of a matter of decoration for her than a necessity.

"Because I find it distracting when you don't."

She arched an eyebrow. "Do you now?"

He laughed. "I've handed you a secret weapon, haven't I?"

She eyed his big, broad chest. "You're doing all right over there with your nuclear warheads and whatnot, don't you worry."

The back and forth continued as they finished dressing and went to tackle her dining room wall. Jon had brought half a dozen disposable drop cloths and they covered her couches and dining set to minimize the clean-up. Every few minutes she stopped what she was doing to kiss him. Her heart felt full to overflowing.

He was here. This was happening.

Once they'd protected her furniture Jon picked up a big sledgehammer and adopted a wide stance.

"It's about to get noisy," he warned. He flexed his arms and the sledgehammer swung in a powerful arc, smashing a very satisfying hole in the wall.

"Cool," she said, inspecting the hole. "Can I have a go?"

Jon grinned. "Why did I know you were going to ask that?"

She held out a hand and he passed the sledgehammer over. She hefted it, assessing the weight. Heavy, but not too heavy. Copying his stance, she swung the hammer over her shoulder before slamming it into the wall with everything she had. A big chunk of plaster fell away, revealing the frame behind it.

"You have a talent for destruction."

She smashed another hole. "This is very therapeutic. People would pay to do this."

"I'd pay to watch you do this."

She looked over her shoulder to find him eyeing her backside.

It took an hour to break up the plaster and cut away everything but the top two feet of the stud frame. Jon got busy marking up the wood and by midday she had the bare bones of a lintel installed and a sense of how the larger space would feel.

"This looks so good!" she said, walking around and viewing the room from all angles. "I should have done this years ago."

"We're not finished yet, sweet cheeks," Jon said. "Gotta get the new plasterboard up, tape the joins, finish them with skim coat. Then we'll have to do something about the floorboards."

She wrinkled her nose at him. "*Sweet cheeks?* Really? You think that's me?"

"I thought we'd already covered my obsession with your butt."

"You're right, I almost forgot about that, sugar dick."

He burst out laughing. Gabby joined in and for a while they did nothing but laugh like idiots and lean against each other.

Finally, she wiped her eyes and looked at him.

"So that's a no on the nicknames, yeah?"

"Oh, yeah."

He crouched to mark up the plasterboard, and she lay a hand on his shoulder, just because she could. He looked at her, the laughter still in his eyes. Something big and warm and full expanded in her chest. He looked so happy, and she'd helped make him that way. He'd made her happy, too. In fact, she felt a little drunk with it.

It was three o'clock by the time they'd installed the plaster over the lintel frame, finished the joins and tidied up. After they'd packed everything back into Jon's truck, Gabby insisted on him taking her undercover spot beneath the building so that they could be assured his tools would be safe overnight, then they showered and made love again.

Gabby woke from a light doze several hours later to realize it was dark outside. Her stomach rumbled and she checked the clock.

"What time is it?" Jon asked, his voice gravelly with sleep. His arm slipped around her waist, pulling her back against his chest.

"Nearly seven. I'm starving. Pizza or Chinese again?"

"Pizza."

They walked around the corner to collect it, picking up a DVD from the rental place on the way.

"I hope you like it," Gabby said as they rode the elevator back up to the apartment. "*So I Married an Axe Murderer* is one of my favorite movies ever. It's funny and cute and smart—"

"I am prepared to love it, even if there is dancing and singing in it," Jon said solemnly.

She got an action replay of the expanding-warm-chest moment as he pulled her close and kissed her. She was going to reserve judgment until they hit midnight, to be safe, but she suspected this was pretty much the happiest day of her life. She'd gotten to smash stuff, she'd scored a new open living-dining space and she'd fallen the rest of the way into sloppy, profound, death-do-us-part love with a beautiful, kind, sweet man. Hard to beat that.

Her step faltered as they exited the lift.

"You okay?" Jon asked.

"Yeah. I'm good."

She smiled a reassurance at him and handed over the key so he could let them into her apartment.

Love. She was in love with Jon. It felt a little scary admitting it to herself, even though she'd been catching glimpses of it out of the corners of her eyes for the last few days. She'd fallen so hard and fast. Like a rock.

Admit it. You were gone the moment he showed up on the doorstep this morning.

Although Gabby was beginning to suspect she'd been gone the moment she looked into his eyes that very first day and that she'd been fighting a desperate rearguard action ever since. To absolutely no avail.

"Plates or out of the box?" he asked as they walked into the living room.

"People don't eat pizza off plates. That's an urban myth."

Jon grinned at her. "*I* never would. But people get strange ideas sometimes."

She felt a terrible urge to sit in his lap and wrap her arms around him and tell him all the different reasons she loved him. Because he was honorable and because he was kind and because he was funny and because he cared and because he was tender and generous…

She took one step toward him, then caught herself.

It was too early. They were on Day One. She could hold her horses for another day or two. She might even hold out for three days before she lay herself utterly at his feet.

They ate their pizza in front of the TV, Gabby pointing out all her favorite parts of the movie to him and reciting key pieces of dialogue along with the characters. The third time she did it, he pulled her close and kissed her thoroughly.

"What was that for?" she asked dazedly.

"You're adorable."

They stretched out along the sofa, Gabby's back pressed to his chest, one of his arms snugged around her body. She pretended to watch the screen while inside she was swooning.

She was adorable. Which implied that he adored her. Definitely this was the happiest day of her life.

Jon's hand slid from her hip to her belly, his palm warm through her tank top. She wriggled against him a little more and realized he was hard. She glanced over her shoulder at him.

"Do you want to—"

"Let's finish the movie first."

The hand on her belly began to move in small, teasing circles, slipping beneath the waistband of her shorts and getting closer and closer to the top of her panties but never quite close enough. Desire mounted inside her and she found it difficult to concentrate.

"Jon..." she said, moving restlessly.

"Watch your movie," he whispered in her ear.

He slid his hand into her underwear. He started to stroke her, and she gave up any pretense of watching the screen and spread her legs for him. He made an approving noise as he slicked his fingers along her sex.

She moaned as he slid a finger inside her. He stroked her gently, steadily, lovingly, and it wasn't long before she was quivering on the edge of climax. He nuzzled her ear and whispered dirty beautiful things to her as he pushed her over the edge. She fell back against him afterward, limp and exhausted. After a few minutes she opened her eyes and realized the film had finished.

"I missed the end. Did you like it?" She twisted around so she could look at him.

"It was the best movie I've ever seen."

She laughed.

"Come to bed, Gabby."

He made love with her again, then turned her on her side and curled his body around her and held her close. They talked quietly about what they might do tomorrow—drive to the beach, maybe eat fish and chips on the sand—and she slowly drifted off to sleep feeling warm and sated and precious.

Best. Day. Ever.

THE FOLLOWING WEEK PASSED IN A blur of great sex and laughter. Gabby couldn't remember when she'd been so happy. Jon stayed at her place every night. They worked their way through her favorite take-out places and decided that Thai was the best so they had it two nights in a row. She made him watch more of her favorite movies and he retaliated by taking her to the motor show at the exhibition buildings in the city.

When Saturday rolled around again, she felt as though she was living in a bubble of happiness. Having Jon in her life was like upgrading from a cathode tube TV to a plasma screen—everything was brighter, sharper, crisper. Every day brought new discoveries. The fact that he was incredibly ticklish behind his knees and would literally howl for mercy if she attacked him there. The knowledge that he wouldn't eat brussels sprouts no matter what the inducement. The growing realization that despite his size and controlled demeanor, inside he was incredibly sensitive and gentle and kind.

They spent Saturday putting the finishing touches on the living room, sanding and painting the walls and patching the floor. Jon came up with the clever idea of stealing floorboards from her closet to fill the holes created by the removal of the wall, claiming that a patch in the closet would be less noticeable than new floorboards in the main room. The result was a near perfect match and they celebrated with dinner at a small but expensive Italian restaurant.

"One of us should really learn to cook," she said as they scooped up the last of their shared dessert, a mouthwatering tiramisu.

"I'd hate to force you into such a traditionally feminine role," Jon said, deadpan.

"Funny. I was thinking exactly the opposite thing about you."

They went home and shared her bathtub before making love and falling asleep in each other's arms.

Gabby woke with a start in the early hours. For a moment she didn't know what had disturbed her, then Jon moved restlessly beside her.

"No. Please. *Please*."

Dread thumped in her belly. Another nightmare.

"Jon. Wake up," she said, shaking his shoulder firmly. His skin was damp with sweat, the muscles beneath his skin tense.

Jon's eyes snapped open. She could see the exact moment reality descended on him. *It was a dream. I'm in bed. Gabby's here.*

He closed his eyes for a beat. Then, without looking at her, he stood and left the bedroom.

Dread thumped in her belly again, but she shook it off. This was hard for him. She had to be patient. Whatever issues Jon was battling, they weren't going to go away overnight, and his attitude was not going to do a one-eighty shift so quickly, either. But he wasn't in this alone now.

She was no expert, but he was clearly dealing with the aftereffects of trauma. It was likely he needed help, to talk to someone who understood these things. Knowing him, it would be an uphill battle to convince him to seek professional help, but she was determined. For both of their sakes.

And the first skirmish in that battle was to get Jon to stop closing doors between them so she could, at the very least, offer him the comfort he so desperately needed.

She pulled on her robe then tapped on the bathroom door.

"Jon?"

There was a long silence. "I'll be out in a minute."

She stood, undecided. He had a right to privacy, but her gut told her that nothing good or productive was happening in there.

"I'm coming in." She opened the door.

Jon sat on the edge of the tub, his muscles tight, his legs braced wide, his back bowed. Atlas, shouldering an impossible burden.

Her heart swelled with compassion. He glanced at her briefly before looking away. She knelt beside him on the cold tile and put her hand on his knee.

"Tell me what's going on," she said softly.

"It's nothing you can do anything about." He kept his gaze fixed on a spot on the floor. His leg felt like granite and he was vibrating with suppressed emotion. She had the sense that if he could, he'd fling her hand off and push her away.

Well. As she'd already acknowledged, this wasn't going to be easy."You can't keep going on like this. And please don't tell me it's because you've stopped drinking. I know there's more to it than that." She kept her voice gentle but firm.

She had to get through to him somehow.

"It'll go away. It did last time."

"Last time? You've had nightmares before?"

He nodded, the barest dip of his head.

"When?"

"When I first went to Canada."

"Tell me about them. What are they about?"

His shoulder jerked impatiently. "They're not worth talking about."

"They obviously upset you. That must mean something."

He remained silent.

"Jon. Please talk to me. I'm worried about you. I care for you. I hate the thought of you dealing with all this on your own."

"Talking won't change anything."

"It might make it less powerful. Like opening the closet and shining a light on the bogeyman."

He shook his head. She knew what he was thinking: that she didn't understand.

"Okay. What about Tyler, then? I'm guessing this is about your childhood. Tyler must know what you're going through—"

"No."

"You need to talk to someone. You can't just let this eat away at you. And I mean that literally. How much weight have you lost lately?"

"I'm fine."

"No, you're not. You've had three nightmares in the past two weeks. Please tell me you don't think that's normal or acceptable. I can only imagine how hard it must be to put your head on the pillow every night, knowing what might be waiting for you."

"It'll get better."

"Will it?"

He still refused to look at her. She shuffled forward on her knees so she was in his direct line of sight, forcing him to engage. She knew he wanted her to leave him the hell alone, but even if she didn't love him, she didn't have it in her to walk away from someone who was in so much pain.

"What about a counselor? Someone who specializes in abused children?"

"Gabby… Just leave it, will you?" His face was set in stone.

"Or maybe there's a survivors' group. Somewhere you can go and talk to other people like you—"

He surged to his feet in an explosive burst. *"Will you freaking drop it?"* His voice echoed loudly in the small space.

She looked up at him, towering over her, naked and angry and scared. She stood.

"Jon—"

"No. You don't know what you're talking about. I appreciate the thought, I really do, but you've got no idea and talking or whatever isn't going to change anything. So leave it. Okay?"

"Do you think this makes you weak? Is that it? Because—"

"For God's sake, Gabby, get out of my head. I don't want you in there, I didn't invite you and it's *none of your freaking business!*"

He said it so forcefully she actually took a step backward. She blinked a few times. She felt as though she'd been standing in a wind tunnel, as though she'd been battered and bruised by his vehement, angry rejection.

Without saying another word, she left the room. She collected Jon's clothes, then she took them to the bathroom and left them on the floor. She retreated to her bedroom doorway and stood there, arms wrapped tightly around herself, holding herself together. Just.

She could hear him dressing. The hiss of his zipper. The metallic clink of his belt buckle. The thud of his boots. Then there was a small silence and he stepped out.

They looked at each other in silence for a stretched moment.

"Gabby—"

"It's okay. I get it. I've been here before. I know the drill."

She walked to the front door and held it open for him. She stared at the wall, waiting for him to leave. After a moment he moved past her. She didn't give him a chance to say anything, swinging the door shut between them and turning the bolt. She waited to hear the sounds of his departure. It seemed to take a long time for them to come.

Why does happiness speed by so fast while pain seems to last forever?

Numb and shaken, she sat on the couch. Mere hours ago, she and Jon had shared dessert and talked about what they'd do after Dino's anniversary party the following day. He'd held her close and made her body ache with his clever hands. He'd made her feel so damned precious and loved.

She pressed her fingers to her lips, but her chin started wobbling without her permission. She could feel the pain cracking open inside her.

So much hope. She'd really thought they had a chance. How stupid was she? He might have knocked down her dining-room wall, but he'd kept his own walls firmly intact. He was prepared to sleep with her, to laugh with her, to whisper sweet, dirty nothings in her ear. He was prepared to put down roots, to buy into Tyler's business. But he wasn't prepared to share his pain or weakness or fear. He wasn't prepared to tell her about his past.

He didn't trust her. For whatever reason. Maybe he didn't think she was up to it. Maybe he thought she wouldn't understand or that she'd judge him. She didn't know.

All she knew was that she had been in exactly this spot before and she knew it was impossible to share a life with someone who didn't trust you. Impossible to put your trust in their hands when they kept themselves guarded. There was no true intimacy, no connection.

I can't do, I can't do it, I can't do it.

The first tear slid down her cheek. She closed her eyes.

Jon needed her so badly. He needed her more than he

needed air. She knew it in her bones. But she couldn't do this again. She couldn't give him all of her and get carefully rationed parts of him in return. It would kill her. It would curdle her love into resentment and anger and it would destroy anything good between them. Worst of all, it would leave her with nothing but pain or loss.

Not that she wasn't dealing with that now. But it could have been worse.

How could it have been worse? Tell me how this moment, right now, could hurt more? Tell me how I could love him more and feel his loss more?

A distressed sound escaped her throat. She bowed her head as her grief overflowed. Her hands gripped her thighs and she held on for dear life as the tears came in earnest.

Her chest ached with hollowness. She felt so empty. So lost. So alone. The night, the weekend, the coming week, the rest of her life stretched ahead, bleak and unimaginable.

She reached for the phone. There was only one person who might come even close to understanding.

"Hello?" Tyler answered on the third ring, his voice thick from sleep.

"I need you," she said brokenly.

"Gabby? What's wrong? Are you okay?"

"No. Jon just left. Can you come over?"

"I'll be there as soon as I can. Hold tight."

She loved that he didn't hesitate. He'd always been a good friend to her. The best of friends.

She huddled on the couch, waiting for the buzz of the intercom to announce Tyler's arrival. Instead, there was a knock on her door. She opened it to find him standing there, hair mussed, T-shirt inside out.

"How did you get in?" she asked, even though she wanted to throw herself into his arms.

"I know the code. Remember?"

He opened his arms and she walked into his embrace. His arms closed around her, warm and strong. She tried to give herself over to the comfort of familiarity but after a couple of seconds she pushed herself from him and took a few steps backward, shaking her head. Tyler looked at her quizzically.

"Sorry," she said, feeling sad and helpless. "You're close, but you're not the one I want."

She knew he understood what she meant.

"Come on."

He led her into the living room and they sat on the couch. She pulled her knees tight to her chest and he watched her, compassion on his face.

"Jon and I have been seeing each other. In case you hadn't noticed."

"I noticed."

"He's been practically living here. We've spent every night together. He fixed my living room—" She hiccupped as more emotion welled up.

He waited patiently.

"We had a great day today," she said, trying again. "Really, really lovely. Then Jon had one of his nightmares."

"Jon has nightmares?"

"Three in the past two weeks that I know of. He's under siege, Tyler. God knows how many hours of sleep he gets a night. Each time he's had one, he's bailed in some way. This time, I thought he'd stay, that we would talk."

She took a deep, shuddering breath.

"But he didn't want to talk. He didn't want me to

touch him. And when I tried he told me it was none of my business. That he didn't want me in his head."

She started to cry again, remembering the utter, harsh rejection of the moment. Tyler moved closer and put his hand on her back.

"It's okay, Gab. It's okay."

"No, it's not, because I love him. I love him so much and now I have to try to get over him and I don't think it's going to happen. He's a part of the business and I'll see him every day. *Every day.*"

The full horror of it hit her as she contemplated the future. Jon in her life, in her workplace. Sexy and funny and kind—and completely, profoundly off-limits to her.

"I'm going to make you a cup of tea. You got a box of tissues somewhere?"

She swiped at her wet face with the back of her hand. "In the bathroom."

Tyler brought her tissues then disappeared into the kitchen. She blew her nose and mopped at her face. When he returned with a mug she was feeling moderately calmer.

He sat opposite her. "I know I'm supposed to say something profound here, but this isn't really my area of expertise. I do know he cares for you. Ally and I have both seen the way he is with you."

She sniffed and fiddled with the scrunched-up tissues in her hand.

"Maybe it's a matter of time. Of waiting him out. You've got to understand, the way we were brought up… We got really good at surviving on our own, you know? From a young age. We never had anyone we could trust, anyone who was there for us."

Gabby knew all this.

"But you trusted Ally."

"Yeah. I did."

"And you never trusted me." She said it without accusation. It was simply a fact.

He shook his head. "It's not as black-and-white as that. Ally and I… There was this connection, right from the start."

She nodded, smiling sadly. He was making her point for her. "I get it. I do."

"Give it time, Gab."

"How long? A year? Two years? I waited three years for you to trust me, Tyler, and you never did. It's taken me nearly four years to get over you. I've known Jon for two weeks and I'm so in love with him I feel like my chest is going to cave in. So how long should I sit around and hope?"

Tyler shrugged helplessly. "You know I can't answer that."

"I know. No one can."

She fiddled with the tissues some more.

"Why don't you drink some tea?"

She looked at him. "I need to resign."

The decision had been sitting in the back of her mind since Jon walked out the door and she'd understood exactly how deeply she'd invested in the dream of him.

"Come on. You're upset. This is not the time to make big decisions."

"It's exactly the time, because otherwise I'll let myself get sucked into sitting around in perpetual hope. I can't do it again, Tyler. I…can't. I love him too much to see him every day, knowing he's in pain, knowing he won't let anyone close to do anything about it."

"We can't run that place without you, Gabby. And,

frankly, I don't want to. You're as much a part of T.A. Furniture as I am."

"You'll find someone else."

"I don't want to."

"I need to do this, Tyler. For me. You don't know what it's like loving someone who doesn't love you in the same way. It kills a part of you. Makes you feel like maybe there's something wrong with you, something that's stopping them from fully committing."

Tyler looked anguished. "Look, I know I hurt you. If I could take it back, I would. That was about me. Or maybe it was about us, about us together not being right. But there is nothing wrong with you."

She nodded her understanding of what he was saying, but it didn't change anything.

"I'm not accepting your resignation. Not tonight. Not until you've had time to think about this. Really think about it."

"Fine. But I'll feel the same way tomorrow."

A half-amused, half-worried look crossed his face. "Jesus, you're stubborn."

Tears welled as she thought about all the times Jon had accused her of the same thing. How pathetic to think she would even miss their fights.

She did a mental calculation of how long it would take to find someone and train them to replace her. Probably six weeks, possibly eight. It seemed like a long time, but she couldn't simply walk out. And it was better than the alternative: staying. Waiting. Dying a little every day. Or, worse, giving in and embarking on the kind of relationship Jon was open to. Giving him all of herself while she accepted the crumbs from his table.

I deserve better. And so does he. He just doesn't realize it.

Sitting up straighter, she wiped her tears away. She was strong, her mother's daughter. She could do this.

JON HAD TO DRIVE INTO THE CITY to find a bar that was open. He ordered a beer with a whiskey shot and knocked them both back in a matter of seconds. He ordered another round and waited for the alcohol to make the world a better place.

Five beers and five shots later, he still couldn't get the scene in Gabby's bathroom out of his mind. He'd never spoken to a woman that way, just as he'd never manhandled anyone the way he'd manhandled Gabby that night in her office. She'd seen the worst of him, that was for sure.

Don't worry. She won't be coming back for a third helping.

He'd blown it. He'd seen the look in her eyes—he'd hurt her viscerally tonight. Really got at her. He'd meant to, too. Anything to stop her poking and prodding at him.

God forbid she learned how freakin' weak he really was. Far better for her to think he was a bully who only wanted her for sex and good times.

He signaled for another round. Maybe if he drank enough, he could fill the gaping hole in his chest.

The rest of the night melted into a blur. He had no real recollection of leaving the bar or getting home. He'd been with it enough to get a cab instead of attempting to drive. When he woke it was full daylight and his mouth tasted and felt as though something had died in it. He peered at the clock and groaned.

It was nearly twelve. His stomach lurched and he took a few deep breaths to get his nausea under control.

He moved to the edge of the bed and sat up in stages, giving his woozy head a chance to equalize. Finally he was ready to contemplate standing. He didn't move, however. There didn't seem much point in diving into the day. He'd planned to spend it with Gabby. Go to Dino's anniversary party together, head to a movie afterward. Obviously, that wasn't going to happen. He'd be lucky if she so much as smiled at him again.

If only he hadn't had another nightmare.

If only she hadn't pushed.

If only he wasn't complete screwed in the head.

She'd been trying to help him, and he'd sent her away. He'd seen the sympathy and concern in her eyes and rejected it unequivocally.

A pathetic voice in the back of his head piped up with an offer of hope. Maybe if he went to her place and tried to explain…

What would he explain? About his childhood? About the fact that, for the life of him, he didn't know how to move beyond the rage and hurt that was his father's legacy? About the fact that he couldn't look at his brother without feeling profound, bone-deep guilt at his failure to protect him?

Yeah, that was really going to win her over. That was really going to bring the light of love back to her eyes. What woman could resist the lure of a man who had abandoned his younger brother to brutality? No doubt Gabby would jump him on the spot, she'd be so turned on and touched by his confession.

You didn't deserve her anyway.

A knock at the door brought his head up. His first ridiculously hopeful thought was that it was Gabby, but he quickly dismissed it. There was no reason for her to seek him out after what he'd done.

He walked to the door and opened it to find Tyler. His brother gave him a once over.

"Big night?" He didn't sound surprised.

"What's up?"

"I wanted to talk to you. Can I come in?"

Jon stepped aside and waved him in. Tyler strode in and surveyed the small space.

"Cosy," he said.

"You want a coffee?"

"You look like you could do with one."

"I'll take that as a yes." Jon grabbed a fresh filter and spooned coffee into it.

"I wanted to talk to you about Gabby."

"What about her?"

"I want to know if this thing between you is serious. Are you in love with her?"

He gave Tyler a cool look. "Are you here in your capacity as Gabby's ex or as her employer?"

"I'm here as her friend. And yours, if you'll ever let your guard down enough to let me in."

Jon busied himself organizing mugs and milk.

"And there it is—the patented Jon Adamson silent treatment. Great. A cure for every evil, a solution to every discussion."

Jon banged the mugs onto the counter, temper rising. "What do you want me to say? If you've spoken to Gabby, you already know I screwed up. You want me to bleed on the rug for you? Fine. I think she's amazing. I think you were nuts to ever let her slip through your fingers. I feel privileged to have known her, even for a little while. She's smart and tough and funny and unbelievably hot and for a while I deluded myself into thinking we could have a future together. But the delusion is over."

He glared at his brother. "That enough for you, or do you want more?"

Tyler stared at him, a long, searching look that bored down into Jon's soul. "What's going on with you? You think you don't know how to be happy because we had a shit childhood? You think you're like the old man, that you'll turn into some kind of sadistic asshole if you let yourself get close to someone?"

"I know how to be happy. Gabby made me happy."

That shut Tyler up for a moment. Coffee was dripping into the carafe. Jon ran a hand over his bristly chin.

"She said you've been having nightmares."

Jon sighed. "Yeah."

"What are they about?"

He shook his head.

"Mate, you think you've got something special going on in your head that I don't know about? You think I haven't been there?"

Jon met his brother's eye. "It's different."

And it was. He'd been the older brother, the big one, the tough one. The one who was supposed to protect. Tyler didn't remember, or maybe he did but was prepared to forgive. But Jon wasn't.

"You're like a frickin' bank vault, you know that?" Tyler said. "Like a brick wall. No wonder she'd rather quit and walk away than try and get through."

Jon's head whipped around. "What?"

"Yeah, exactly. Gabby's resigned."

"You didn't accept it? She loves that place. It will fall apart without her."

"She doesn't want to have to see you every day."

The pain in his chest was so real he almost lifted his hands to check for a wound.

"Then I'll bow out of the partnership," he said after a long moment.

"As if she's going to let you do that."

"You can't let her go."

"She's not my indentured servant, she's my friend. I don't want her to go, but if this is what she needs to do, then I won't try to stop her."

"You're nuts. She's upset, she's not thinking straight."

Tyler shrugged. Jon looked around for his car keys. Tyler might not be prepared to talk sense to Gabby, but he was. She might not want him in her life but she'd damned well listen if it killed him.

Too late he remembered he'd left his car in the city. With a bit of luck it would have been towed by now.

"Can you drive me over to Gabby's place?"

"She's not there. Dino's anniversary party, remember?"

"Fine. Take me there."

Tyler gave him a critical head to toe. "No offense, but you might have a better shot if you didn't stink like a brewery."

Jon looked down at his sleep-crumpled clothes.

"Give me five minutes."

He strode into the bathroom and ripped his clothes off. Two minutes under the shower, deodorant, toothpaste, mouthwash.

He reappeared in the living room, glancing at his brother as he strode to the door.

"I'm driving," he said.

THE VERY LAST THING GABBY wanted to do was attend a party celebrating the tenth anniversary of someone else's happy marriage. But Dino and Lucia were her friends, and she had contributed to the weekend for two in Sydney that the company had bought as their gift. She had to go.

Her eyes were still red-rimmed from crying, but she did her best with mascara and eyeliner. She dressed in the skinny black jeans and flowery sleeveless shirt her sister had bought her for her birthday. She added a beaded necklace. There. She looked exactly like a heartbroken thirty-three-year-old woman who had been weeping all night and who was now trying to put on a brave face. Bully for her.

She gathered her phone, purse and keys. Ever since Tyler had left she'd felt numb. Simply…empty. She'd cried and wailed, she'd whined and complained. There was nothing left to do but take action.

In the cold light of the morning after, her decision to leave seemed even more smart and necessary than it had during the heightened angst of the small hours. She could not see Jon every day and not keep loving him. And she refused to flush more of her life away loving a man who was incapable of letting her in.

A pretty simple equation. With only one solution.

She drove to the suburban bistro hosting the party with the intention of staying the absolute bare minimum of time. An hour or two, tops. A noisy restaurant with a highly patronized children's playground attached was not her idea of joy right now.

She parked near the entrance so she could make a quick getaway and got out of her car. She was collecting her bag from the passenger seat when Tyler's truck drove past. She lifted her hand in greeting then froze when she saw Jon was behind the wheel, his face like thunder.

A little clutch of panic gripped her. She guessed Tyler had told him about her resignation. She squared her shoulders. So what if Jon didn't like it? It was nothing to do with him.

She started walking toward the entrance.

"Gabby."

She considered ignoring him, but figured it was better to get whatever it was he wanted to say out of the way before they went inside. This was a happy occasion after all.

She swiveled to face him as he approached. He stopped a few feet away from her. She was vaguely aware of Tyler hovering, but all her attention was on the angry man looming over her.

"Tyler said you've quit. Are you nuts?"

She pretended to think about it. "Don't think so, no."

"You love that place."

"It doesn't matter."

"Yeah, it does. If you're leaving because of me, don't. I've already spoken to Tyler. I'm backing out of the partnership deal."

"No."

"No?"

"I won't let you do that. You're good for the business and Tyler needs you." She eyed him steadily. "And you need it. You need it more than anyone."

She could see she'd thrown him. All the anger left his face and his shoulders softened.

"Don't do this."

"I have to. There's nothing there for me anymore."

He looked pained. He took a step toward her. "That's not true. You know how I feel about you."

Her treacherous, weak heart ached for the pain in his

voice and face. "I thought I did yesterday. But I realized I was wrong."

"You weren't wrong. I've never felt like this before, Gabby. Believe me. And I'm trying my best to give you what you want but this stuff doesn't come easily to me."

"I know. But I don't want to be some sort of penance you have to endure, Jon. I want you to love me as freely and openly as I love you."

She smiled as she saw the ripple of reaction across his face. "See? You're not even comfortable with me saying it, are you? You let me in only so far but no more. You're so busy protecting yourself there's no place for me in your life. You don't trust me with your secrets or your pain or whatever it is, and you don't trust me with your heart."

She blinked away tears. Surely she'd cried enough last night. Surely her bloody tear ducts could give her a break for five freaking minutes.

"None of that is true."

"Isn't it? Then what happened last night, Jon?"

He looked away.

She gripped the strap on her handbag. "I need to go. Dino and Lucia are expecting me."

Jon caught her arm. "Don't go."

She put her hand on his and squeezed it, looking into his eyes, willing him to understand. "Give me one good reason to stay. Tell me what your dream was about last night."

His expression immediately became shuttered. "None of that stuff matters."

Everything in her went cold as she watched him retreat. This man was so precious to her, but what kind of a life would they have without trust?

"It matters to me. And I think it means everything to you."

She pushed his hand from her arm and turned toward the entrance.

"Gabby."

But he didn't try to stop her this time. Her legs were shaking and she felt as though she was going to be sick as she entered the foyer. Ally popped up from a chair near the coat check, her face showing concern. Gabby guessed she'd been waiting for Tyler, since Tyler had come with Jon.

"Gabby. Are you all right?"

"N-no." She was doing her damnedest not to cry, but tears were still leaking out of her eyes.

Ally looked around. "Come on, in here."

The coatroom was unattended and Ally pulled Gabby inside and shut the door.

"This is about Jon."

"Yes."

"And your resignation."

"Yes."

"You know that Tyler and I love you too much to let you go, don't you?"

Gabby gave up the fight to stop the tears. "I have to go, Ally, I have to. I can't love another man who can't love me back."

Ally's face was creased with sympathetic understanding. "Jon isn't Tyler."

"Oh, I know. It never hurt this much with Tyler. Not even close. I guess that should have told me something, huh?"

"Jon cares for you a lot."

"I know. But how am I supposed to build a life with someone who quarantines parts of himself away from me, Ally? What if we had children? How would we ever discuss anything real?" Gabby threw her hands in the air. "Listen to me, talking as though any of that was ever really a possibility. As if Jon would ever have let me get close enough for any of that to happen."

Ally reached out and captured both of Gabby's hands in hers, squeezing them earnestly. "I think you're wrong. I love you and Jon too much to give up on this. Give him a chance, Gabby. I know you want to protect yourself—I know how powerful that instinct is. But you don't get the good stuff without risking the bad. And he is worth it. When you first meet him he seems so closed off and unapproachable, but inside he's sweet and so incredibly fiercely protective of people he cares about—"

"You don't have to sell him to me. I love him."

"Did you know he hassled Tyler about hiring an assistant for you? And that he came over to our place the other night beside himself because he thought he'd hurt you?"

Gabby shook her head.

"Stay. Take back that stupid resignation, and fight for him."

Ally made it sound so easy.

"You're worth it. He's worth it, too," Ally said.

She pulled Gabby into a hug. Gabby let her head rest on her friend's shoulder for long moments.

"You know, when Tyler first told me about you I thought I'd hate you," she said, sniffing.

Ally laughed. "I know. I should probably have hated you, too—the gorgeous, sexy ex still working with my man. But I didn't."

"Me, either."

Ally kissed her cheek. "I'm going to back off now,

put away my Dear Gertrude hat and leave you to it. But think about what I said, okay?"

Gabby nodded. "I will."

"You might want to hit the bathroom before you join the rest of the gang," Ally advised with a small smile.

"Mascara?"

"Oh, yeah."

They exchanged one last hug before Ally slipped out of the room. Gabby took a couple of deep breaths and tried to work out what to do. She wanted so much to believe what Ally was saying. But the memory of Jon's rejection was lodged like a splinter in her mind. And minutes ago she'd given him a second chance to offer her something—anything—she could latch on to, and he still hadn't been able to get past his own defenses.

And yet…

She loved him. She wanted this so badly.

Her head spinning, she decided that maybe a cloakroom wasn't the best place to make the most important decision of her life. Certainly she couldn't make it alone. She owed Jon and herself at least that much: a conversation that wasn't muddled by fear in the middle of the night or conducted publicly in a parking lot.

First, she needed to fix her face. She went in search of the bathroom.

JON STARED AT THE BEER SOMEONE had put in front of him. Last night he couldn't get enough of the stuff and now he couldn't even muster enough interest to lift the glass to his mouth. Carl and Kelly were swapping jokes next to him, cracking each other up as usual. Jon didn't have it in him to pretend to be anything other than what he was right now, which was shattered.

He was more messed-up than he knew. Gabby had

offered him a second chance—a third chance, really—and he still couldn't come to the party.

I want you to love me as freely and openly as I love you.

That was what she'd said. She'd boldly told him that she loved him—and he hadn't been able to come even close to articulating his own feelings for her.

She should run a mile. She should run and keep on running from a screw-up like you.

But she wasn't. He'd thought he'd blown it last night but he'd realized he still had a chance with Gabby. If he was man enough to take it.

She wanted the truth? He'd give it to her. Tell her about all the times he'd cowered to one side and let his father beat the living crap out of Tyler. How he'd said nothing while his little brother got kicked or whipped or punched. How he'd abandoned his brother the second it was legal for him to bail on school and leave home and make his own way in the world, never once looking back. How he hated himself for being such a coward, for never standing up to the old man. And how even at the very end he hadn't been able to stand up to him. Because that was why he'd left it so late—too late—to come home. Because he didn't know how to face Robert. Because he'd been afraid his father would take one look at him and know how much of a hold he still had over Jon's life.

Sweat prickled beneath his arms as he thought about sharing any of his shame with Gabby. She was so straight and strong and brave. He could only imagine what she would think of him, a woman who thought she could take on the world. She thought he was her match, but he wasn't even close.

Kelly gave him a nudge and gestured toward the outside part of the restaurant with his chin.

"Going outside for a smoke," he said.

Suddenly a cigarette seemed like a great idea. Jon had taken up smoking again when he'd first learned about his father's illness and while he'd managed to kick the habit before Christmas, right now he figured he could do with something to calm his nerves while he thought about how to tell Gabby what she wanted to know.

"Mind if I have one?" he asked.

"Yeah. Sure. Didn't realize you smoked." Kelly shot him a curious look.

Jon went outside with the guys and made small talk while he sucked nicotine into his lungs. They'd chosen a spot near the playground and he watched the kids run around while he pretended to listen to Carl talk about the weekend's cricket score.

He would find Gabby, and he would take her out to Tyler's car and he'd tell her. Lay it all in front of her. If she wanted to walk after she heard what he had to say… well, so be it. He wasn't going to beg. She had to know what kind of a bargain she was getting.

A little kid dodged around the table near them and tripped over a dip in the concrete. He sprawled at Jon's feet, his hands stretched out to break the fall. Jon instinctively crouched to check on him.

"Ow, that had to hurt. You okay, little guy?"

The kid scrambled away from him, shooting him a fearful look. Small and scrawny, Jon guessed he was seven, maybe eight.

"You all right there?" Kelly asked. He had two kids of his own, Jon remembered. "Your hands okay?"

The kid nodded, not making eye contact, smoothing his palms down the sides of his jeans. Jon guessed they hurt like hell, but he wasn't going to admit it. Ducking his head, the kid sidled away from them before breaking into a run again.

Jon stood, staring after him. "You think he's all right?" he asked the other guys.

Carl shrugged. "You know what kids are like. Made of rubber. You saw the way he bounced back. They don't know what fear is at that age."

Jon nodded, even though it had seemed to him that the boy knew plenty about fear. The way he'd looked at Jon…

"Another brewski?" Kelly asked, and Jon saw they were ready to go inside.

"Might stay out here a bit longer." He wanted to get his head sorted before he saw Gabby again. Wanted to make sure that he had all the things he wanted to say ready to roll. Because she was too important for him to screw this up.

"You want another one?" Kelly offered Jon his cigarette pack.

"I'm good, thanks."

The guys left. Jon propped his back against the fence around the playground. He closed his eyes and lifted his face to the sun, thinking. Maybe he should simply start at the beginning.

My father was an unhappy man who should never have had children.

The sound of a low, angry voice broke his concentration. He looked toward the noise. At the other end of the area, a burly guy with receding hair was talking to the little boy who had performed the face-plant in front of Jon. The kid stood, head lowered, as his father laid into him.

"I told you not to run off. You think it's not enough that I have to work all week to put food on the table and clothes on your back without having to run around after you all weekend, too? When I tell you to stay put, you stay put. You hear me?"

The kid said something that Jon couldn't hear.

"Don't you lie to me, you little mongrel. You think your old man's stupid? Huh? You think I don't know when a runt is trying to pull the wool over my eyes?"

Jon looked around, waiting for someone—security, staff, *someone*—to step in and tell the guy he couldn't talk to his kid that way. A couple of other parents were supervising their children. Jon watched as, one by one, they all looked away while the man continued to abuse his child. *Nothing to see here, la, la, la.* Nobody wanting to make a fuss, make things uncomfortable or awkward.

"Look at me when I'm talking to you. Always sneaking around, hiding in corners. You think I don't know what you're up to? Huh?" The man grabbed his son by the arm, gave him a shake. The kid's head rocked on his neck.

A woman lifted her little girl from a nearby swing and headed for the exit. Jon's gut was hard with tension, his shoulders cracking with it. Someone needed to intervene. Couldn't they all see that the kid was in danger? He couldn't understand why no one was saying anything.

"You know what? That's it. You've ruined it. We're going home." The man hustled his son toward the gate. When he tripped his father gave him another hard shake, nearly pulling him off his feet.

"You're more trouble than you're worth, you know

that?" He started across the parking lot, heading for a late-model sedan, almost dragging the boy.

Everything in Jon went hot, then cold.

He knew what would happen when they got home. He knew exactly what kind of pain was waiting at the end of that drive.

He was moving before he could think twice about it. His stride long, he closed the distance between them.

"Hey!" he bellowed.

The guy looked across at him, scowling. "What's your problem?"

"You think it's okay to talk to your kid like that? Drag him around like that?"

The father's eyes grew hard. "He's my kid, so why don't you mind your own business?"

"So you can take him home and beat the shit out of him? I don't think so."

"You are way out of line, asshole."

Jon moved closer, his hand curling into a fist. "I know exactly who and what you are, you pathetic weak-assed coward. I bet you've never picked on someone your own size in your life. I bet you specialize in women and children. I bet you get your rocks off proving what a big guy you are, smacking your kid around the house."

The other man's face was mottled with fury. He dropped his son's arm and pushed him away, squaring up to Jon, his fists raised.

Jon made eye contact with the boy. "Go back to the playground where it's safe."

The other man took his shot while Jon was distracted. The blow sent his head back on his neck. Pain blossomed along his jaw. He tasted blood in his mouth.

He grinned at the other man. "Thanks. I was really hoping you were going to do that."

Then he moved in for the kill.

AFTER FIXING HER MAKEUP, GABBY joined the group and did her best to look happy for Dino and Lucia. She watched Jon go outside with a couple of the guys and decided she wasn't ready to talk to him yet. She needed to be clear about what she wanted, what she was prepared to accept. She was sitting with Lucia's aunt and uncle when people started surging toward the exit. Gabby looked around, bemused, and spotted Lucia standing near the bar, her hand pressed to her mouth.

Gabby crossed to her side. "Are you okay?"

Lucia grabbed her arm. "Do you know where Tyler is? There's a fight out there. Someone said something about it being one of our guys…"

Gabby whirled on her heel and tried to see what was happening outside, but there were too many people gathered on the edge of the parking lot. A chill of prescience ran down her spine as she looked for Jon's dark head and broad shoulders among them.

She couldn't see him.

She thought about how angry and bleak he'd looked when she left him. Surely he wouldn't have picked a fight with someone?

She headed for the exit, her steps urgent as she made her way through the voyeurs hovering near the windows. Her high heels skidded on the stones outside and she took a second to catch her balance before pushing her way through the crowd.

"Excuse me. Excuse me. *Move!*"

She spotted a familiar back in the crowd and sidled up to Dino. "What's happening?"

He turned to her, his olive skin unusually pale. "Where's Tyler? We need Tyler. Carl and Paul tried to get him off but he's lost it—"

Time seemed to slow as Gabby looked past his shoulder and saw that Jon had another man pressed against the side of a car, one big hand gripping the neck of his T-shirt while he pulled back his other arm for a punch. Kelly and Paul stood nearby looking helpless, while a small, brown-haired boy watched the fight with tears running down his face.

"Jon!" she screamed.

Jon punched the man, sending blood spraying across the car. The other man's body flopped loosely and she had the sense that the only thing keeping him upright was Jon's grip on his T-shirt.

"Careful, Gabby!" Paul warned as she darted past.

Gabby ignored him, her focus on Jon, on the arm he was positioning for another punishing blow. She lunged forward, grabbing his arm with both hands, her body slamming into his. She could feel the anger and adrenaline vibrating through him, could feel how hot his skin was, how tense his muscles.

"Stop, Jon. Stop!"

He stilled the moment he felt her touch, his head jerking around toward her. It took a moment for him to return from whatever dark, angry place he'd been lost in to focus on her face.

"Let him go."

Sirens wailed in the distance. Jon hesitated, then dropped his arm, released the guy and stepped back.

His opponent's face was shiny with blood, his bottom lip split open, his nose possibly broken. He slid along the side of the car a few feet before he caught himself and lowered himself more slowly to the ground. A couple of people stepped forward to help him, but Gabby was too busy inspecting Jon to pay much attention.

"Are you okay?" Her heart was pounding out of control as she scanned his face and body for injuries.

"I'm fine." Jon searched the crowd.

Her hands trembled as she caught his chin so she could inspect the cut at the corner of his mouth and what she suspected was going to be a bruise on his right cheekbone. If anything had happened to him…

He tried to pull away from her.

"I can't see him. Where is he?" At first she didn't understand who he was talking about, then she remembered the little boy. She searched the crowd and spotted him talking with Lucia. The other woman crouched beside him, her arm around his thin shoulders.

"Lucia's got him. Dino's wife. See? Over there. He's okay, Jon."

He followed her pointing finger. "Someone needs to look after him. Make sure he's okay."

He seemed disoriented. As though he was only just coming back down to earth.

"Lucia's got him. She'll take care of him," she repeated.

A police cruiser flashed into the parking lot, stopping a few feet away. "He can't go back there, Gabby." Jon caught her hand and she saw that his knuckles were swollen and bleeding. "They can't send him back there. Someone has to protect him."

She wrapped both her hands around his injured one. She didn't understand why he was so concerned about the boy, but his distress was very real—she could feel him trembling with it.

"He's okay now."

Jon shook his head. "No, he's not, you don't understand. His father hits him. They can't send him home with the man."

Understanding dawned on her.

This wasn't a random fight, some belligerent guy Jon had somehow tangled with.

This was a rescue.

She searched his face urgently. "How do you know that, Jon? How could you possibly know that?"

"I know."

There was so much bleak knowledge in his eyes that she believed him, without a question of a doubt.

"I'll make sure the police know. I'll call Child Protection myself. Whatever it takes." She held his eye so he knew it was a promise.

"Thank you." His smile was relieved, grateful, infinitely sweet. "Thank you, Gabby. You're so good and strong. I love you."

Tears filled her eyes. On what planet, in which lifetime had she thought she could walk away from this man? This amazing, amazing man who had put his body, his freedom, his future on the line in order to protect a little boy he didn't even know?

"I love you, too, Jon. So much."

He lifted a hand to touch her cheek, then he kissed her. She could see the police approaching out of the corner of her eye. She blinked away tears and lifted his hand and kissed his knuckles gently.

"The police are here."

Jon took a deep breath, nodded. She squeezed his hand reassuringly.

"You want to tell us what happened here, sir?" one of the policemen asked.

Gabby kept a grip on Jon's hand as he turned to face the music. They were in this together now.

No matter what.

THE NEXT FOUR HOURS PASSED IN a blur of anxiety and frustration. Both Jon and the other man, Ian Patterson, were taken into custody and driven away in separate police cars. Gabby followed Tyler and Ally to the local station, but by the time they'd arrived Jon had disappeared into the depths of the building and no one was willing or able to tell them what was going on.

Tyler busied himself organizing a lawyer for his brother while Gabby called Child Protection to talk to them about Campbell Patterson, Ian's son. She'd made a promise to Jon that Campbell would be taken care of, but even if she hadn't there was no way she could turn her back on a child who was so obviously at risk.

She learned that the best way forward was for her to make a notification of abuse, which would be anonymous in order to protect her from repercussions. She was assured that a team from the organization would visit Campbell at home, either today or tomorrow, to investigate the situation. Dependent upon what the team found, charges could be laid, or Campbell might be removed from the house and taken to a close relative—kinship care—or into temporary foster accommodation. There would be a court hearing to sanction any decisions the team made, and if alcohol or drug abuse were suspected, Ian might be ordered to attend detox services or take anger management sessions.

Gabby's throat was hoarse by the time she'd finished talking with the social worker. She ended the call and rubbed her temples, hoping against hope that she'd done enough to ensure that Jon's act of bravery had not been in vain.

Ally passed her a bottle of water. "He's in the system. He's not an isolated little kid anymore."

"Plenty of kids still slip through the cracks, even if social services are looking out for them," Gabby said.

"So we follow up. We do whatever it takes."

Gabby nodded. Ally was right. This was the beginning of the fight, not the end.

It was another hour before Jon was brought to the front desk. He looked tired, and the bruise on his cheekbone had turned an ugly purple-gray. Gabby shot to her feet the moment she saw him. She gripped her hands tightly together and waited impatiently while Jon signed his bail papers, the lawyer by his side. The moment he was finished, she crossed the waiting room and threw her arms around him. He hugged her tightly, his big hands splayed across her back, his head lowered so he could press his cheek to hers.

"Are you okay?" he asked, his voice low.

He was the one who had spent the past five hours in police custody and he was concerned about *her* feelings?

"I love you," she fiercely. "I love you, Jon Adamson."

His hold tightened and he turned his head to press a kiss to her cheek, then her lips. Finally, they broke apart. She could see the question in his eyes and she touched his arm reassuringly.

"I've spoken to Child Protection. They'll be investigating either today or tomorrow."

Some of the tightness left his face. "Okay."

Tyler and Ally were hovering toward the rear of the waiting area. Tyler came forward when Jon caught his eye.

"Next time you want to be a hero, give me a call. I'd be happy to ride shotgun," Tyler said.

"You mean be charged as an accessory," Jon said drily.

"That, too."

Tyler clapped Jon on the back, but Gabby sensed that what he really wanted was to hug his brother. Their restraint and uncertainty with each other made her chest ache. She saw Ally blinking away tears, as well.

She wasn't the only one who wished things could be different between these two men.

They discussed Jon's police interview briefly and the lawyer informed them that based on his clean record and the mitigating circumstances, Jon would probably receive a good behavior bond. The lawyer promised to be in touch the moment he had further details.

Together they walked out into the parking lot. Jon shook his head.

"I can't believe it's still light out. I feel like a week has passed."

"I know," Gabby said, reaching for his hand. She wove her fingers with his.

"We should get something to eat," Tyler said. "Why don't you guys come to our place and we'll grab some take-out?"

Ally put her hand on her husband's arm. "I think Jon and Gabby might want a bit of time alone."

Tyler looked nonplussed, as though the notion had never even occurred to him. "Right. Sure."

Gabby smiled. "We'll see you tomorrow," she said as she pulled her keys from her bag.

During the drive home she filled Jon in on everything the Child Protection people had told her. Jon asked a few questions and she knew that he would be on to

Child Protection first thing tomorrow, following up the situation.

She and Jon were both silent as they rode the elevator to her floor. She glanced at him as they approached her door.

"Are you hungry? I can manage an egg on toast. Or there's breakfast cereal."

"They gave me a sandwich in lock-up."

"Very civilized of them."

"They were just doing their job."

She waited for him to precede her into the apartment. "They ought to give you a medal."

Jon rolled his shoulders as though he was trying to shrug off her words. "I didn't do much. I did the bare minimum."

"That's not true, Jon. You stepped up. Stopped that kid from getting another beating. You could have even saved his life."

They faced each other in her small entry hall.

"Don't make me out to be something that I'm not, Gabby." He said it quietly, firmly. With utter conviction.

Gabby watched him carefully. She didn't want to push—not tonight when he'd already been through so much—but she wasn't about to let this slip by.

"You did a good thing today, Jon."

"It was one thing, and it doesn't come even close to making up for all the times I did nothing."

Everything inside her went still at his words.

"I'm not sure I understand what that means," she said, but an idea was forming in her mind.

It was so simple and so sad that it made her want to howl for this man.

He walked into the living room, crossing to the

bookcase. He picked up the windup monkey, fiddled with him for a few seconds. She followed him into the room but resisted the urge to go to him. This was hard enough for him and she understood that he wasn't able to accept her comfort.

Yet.

"He used to hit us. When we were kids. Used to lay into us with his belt or whatever was on hand."

He was talking about his father, she knew.

He glanced at her quickly before concentrating again on the toy in his hand.

"One time he perforated Tyler's eardrum. Nearly knocked the teeth out of his head he hit him so hard. Another time he locked him out of the house even though it was the middle of winter." His hand closed tightly around the toy. "And I let him. I should have stepped in. But I didn't."

While a part of her reeled, a clear-sighted part noted that Jon had said his father hit both him and Tyler. Yet he hadn't mentioned any of his own injuries or punishments. It was all about Tyler. In Jon's mind, his own suffering was so unimportant, so negligible, it didn't even rate a mention.

Jon looked at her, his face tight with strain.

"That's what my dream was about last night. Me standing by while Dad beat Tyler." His lips curved into a parody of a smile. "Probably not what you wanted to hear. Not exactly noble hero stuff. But it's the truth. And if it changes things between us…I get it."

His words hit her like a blow to the solar plexus.

"Jon…"

She crossed the room and threw her arms around him, holding him to her so tightly that her joints ached with the intensity of the embrace.

"You were a kid," she said, her voice choked with emotion. "A little kid."

He stood stiffly within her embrace. Unable to accept her love. Her understanding.

"I was the eldest."

"You were a kid. Fourteen months older than Tyler. What chance did either of you have against a grown man?"

"I should have at least tried," he said doggedly.

She loosened her hold so she could look him in the face. "He was your father. He was the one who was supposed to protect you from the world. You were a victim. Just like Tyler. You were kids. *Both of you.*"

He stared at her. So much doubt in his eyes. So much guilt.

"You've been carrying this around for years, haven't you? My God."

She couldn't stop the tears from welling. Angry tears, sad tears. She ached to think of how much he had punished himself because of what he perceived to be his crimes.

His self-imposed distance from his brother. His exile to Canada. His refusal to let her—or, she suspected, anyone—close.

"Don't cry." He cradled her face, his thumb sweeping across her cheek to catch her tears.

"How can I not cry? You were a little boy, Jon. An innocent, defenseless little boy. You deserved love and protection. Instead you got violence and fear and you've been blaming yourself all these years, taking all that ugliness on yourself—" She gulped in a breath, everything in her wanting to make this right for him, to make him see. "That boy today. Campbell. If he has a brother at home, or a sister, would you blame him for not getting between them and his father? Would you think he was wrong or evil or weak?"

"It's different."

"Tell me how. Tell me how your situation was different."

Jon stared at her. She could see his mind working, could see him fighting to step back from beliefs he'd carried with him for a lifetime.

"Have you ever talked to Tyler about any of this?"

"No."

"Why not?"

Jon shrugged, but the answer was in his eyes.

"You're afraid he'll confirm it for you, aren't you? That he'll tell you it was your fault. That he blames you."

A muscle flickered in his jaw. She knew she was right.

"Talk to him. Ask him. Because I guarantee that he is going to say the exact same thing I did."

Jon started to say something, but his voice cracked. He cleared his throat and tried again. "You don't know that."

Gabby searched for the one, perfect thing to say that would take away his pain. Nothing came to her. She suddenly understood that this wasn't her battle to fight.

She couldn't do this for him. Nothing she could say would convince Jon that he deserved the same compassion and understanding that he'd offered Campbell Patterson today. He needed to unpack his own beliefs, sort through his own history. Reconfigure the past.

And there was only one person who could help him do that.

She spun away from him and grabbed her car keys. "Come on. We're going to talk to your brother."

For a long moment he didn't move. Then he put the toy on the bookshelf and walked past her to the door. It occurred to her as they pulled out of the underground garage that Tyler and Ally might not be home. She glanced at Jon. He was so tense and wound up she prayed that they were. He'd carried this burden for long enough. She wanted it gone tonight.

Even though she knew it would take years for him to truly let it go.

Her anxiety dropped a notch when she stopped in front of Ally and Tyler's house and saw Tyler's truck in the driveway. She glanced at Jon, noting how taut the tendons in his neck were. Again she wished she had the power to fix this for him.

But when had life ever been that simple or easy?

Jon had the car door open the moment she stopped the engine. Now that they had stepped onto this road, he wanted it done. To stare down the barrel and face whatever was coming.

Gabby caught up with him on the path. She reached for his hand and held it as they walked to the door. Everything that crossed her mind to say seemed trite or useless. She settled for squeezing his hand.

"I love you," she said simply.

His hand tightened around hers, but he didn't say anything. She had the feeling that maybe he couldn't, that maybe right now it was all he could do to prepare himself to face what he believed would be his brother's condemnation.

He raised his left hand and knocked.

JON'S HEART WAS RACING AS though he'd finished a sprint. He swallowed, trying to ease the tightness in his throat. Gabby slid her arm around him.

"Trust me," she said.

Her gaze was steady. Reassuring. He remembered what she'd said to him back at her apartment.

You were a little boy, Jon. An innocent, defenseless little boy.

Rationally he recognized her words made sense. He had been a child, just as Tyler had been. Just as Campbell was. Yet something in him couldn't release the guilt, the sense of responsibility. Tyler was his younger brother. It had been Jon's job to protect him. To save him. And he'd failed.

The door swung open. Tyler looked surprised to see them.

"Hey," he said, his questioning gaze going from Jon to Gabby and back again. "I thought you guys wanted time alone."

Jon swallowed again. "You got five minutes?"

Tyler frowned slightly before stepping back and swinging the door wide. "Sure, come on in."

Jon was aware of his brother's unspoken curiosity as Tyler led them to the living room. Ally was stretched out on the couch, a *Home Beautiful* magazine open in her lap.

"Hey," she said brightly. "Didn't think we'd see you two for a couple of days at least."

Jon tried to smile and failed. "I, ah, wanted to talk to Tyler."

Ally's expression immediately sobered. "Okay. Sure." The magazine slid from her lap as she sprang to her feet. "Gabby and I can go inspect the seedlings I planted in the yard. Can't we, Gabby?"

Gabby looked at Jon. He saw the question in her eyes. She'd stay with him if he wanted her to. She'd do whatever he needed. The unwavering, steadfast warmth in her gaze humbled him and gave him the faith he needed to raise their joined hands to his mouth and kiss her hand before letting it go.

She rested her fingertips on his arm—the smallest of acknowledgments and reassurances—before turning to Ally. “You know I know next to zip about gardening, right?”

“It’s easy. You buy the pretty pots from the nursery, you stick them in the ground. If they die, you buy more. If not, you brag like there’s no tomorrow.”

The two women chatted as they left the room, their voices echoing up the hallway as they headed for the door.

Jon stuck a hand in his back pocket and stared at the floor, trying to muster the courage to say what needed to be said. He could feel his brother waiting. Wondering. The sound of the door clicking shut echoed through the house and for a moment the world was silent.

“Grab a seat,” Tyler said after a beat.

Jon shook his head. No way could he do this sitting down. “I’m all right. You sit if you want.”

Tyler eyed him warily. “Mate, you’re starting to freak me out a little here. What’s going on?”

Jon took a deep breath. He felt sick. As though he was going to lose his lunch. “I need to talk to you about Dad.”

“Okay.”

“I need to tell you— I want to say—”

Jon swallowed bile. His heart was pounding, his stomach churning. Hands down, he’d never been so terrified in his life.

It was one thing to throw himself on Gabby’s mercy, but she hadn’t been there. She hadn’t suffered through his inaction. She loved him, for whatever misguided reason, and she wanted to believe the best of him.

But Tyler knew. He'd been there. He understood exactly how Jon had failed.

"I wanted you to know I'm sorry." Jon finally choked the words out. He forced himself to hold his brother's gaze. "I let you down. I should have done more, and I want you to know that there isn't a day that goes by that I don't think about it."

Tyler frowned. "Let me down? When have you ever let me down?"

A trickle of sweat ran down Jon's spine. "You don't have to keep up the happy families routine. I get that you want to forgive and forget, but that doesn't change anything. I should have stopped him. Should have protected you. But I didn't. And I'm sorry. More than you'll ever know."

For a moment Tyler seemed frozen. Then he swore, short and sharp, his face distorted by the strength of his emotion. "Unbelievable. This shit gets better and better. I think I've got a grip on it, that it's finally over, and something else comes up."

Tyler took a step to his right, then stopped. He lifted a hand to his face, dashed his knuckles across his eyes. When he looked at Jon his eyes were shiny with tears. "You know what I think about every day? Standing watching Dad beat the living crap out of you and feeling guilty because I was glad it wasn't me. Which is freaking great, isn't it, when you've been walking around feeling guilty about not protecting me all these years? Just freaking great."

Jon stared at his brother. "You have nothing to feel guilty about."

"But you do? What do you think he would have

done to you if you'd fought back, Jon? He would have pounded you into the ground. He would have annihilated you." Tyler stepped closer, his expression belligerent. "Is this why you went to Canada? Is this why you've been knocking back Ally's invitations, shutting me out? Because of some stupid misguided sense of responsibility?"

Jon was still stuck on the issue of his brother's guilt. Couldn't let go of it. Couldn't Tyler see that he'd only been surviving? That he'd been making the best of a lousy, terrifying situation, taking comfort wherever he could find it?

"You were just a kid."

Tyler surprised Jon by grabbing both his arms and shaking him, his fingers biting into his biceps.

"*So were you, Jon!* Don't you get it?"

Suddenly his brother's arms were around him and he was being crushed to Tyler's chest.

"All these years. What a freaking waste," Tyler said. "Both of us punishing ourselves. Bloody hell."

His brother's shoulders shuddered and Jon knew he was fighting tears.

"Shit," he said, but by then it was too late, the first tear was sliding down his cheek. He returned his brother's embrace tenfold, hanging on for dear life as years of grief welled up inside him.

"I came home because I wanted to make it up to you," he said brokenly, finally acknowledging the truth that had been sitting inside him for months. "I wanted to ask for your forgiveness."

Tyler hugged him tighter. "Well you can't have it, because you didn't do anything wrong. Neither of us did. We were both victims. Both of us."

Jon sniffed mightily, on the verge of totally losing it.

Tyler squeezed him for a brief second before loosening his grip and stepping back from their embrace. Neither of them looked at each other as they struggled to regain their composure. Jon used the hem of his T-shirt to wipe his face. When he looked up, Tyler was doing the same.

He smiled sheepishly. “Don’t tell Ally I did that. She’s been campaigning for me to start carrying a handkerchief.”

Jon raised his eyebrows. “What does she think you are, a Sunday school teacher?”

“That’s what I said.”

Jon smiled but it didn’t hold long. He felt as though his world had been tipped on its axis, all his beliefs overturned. He’d held on to his sense of responsibility for so long. Blamed himself. Punished himself. And all the while Tyler had been on the other side of the world, flagellating himself over the same issue.

“Why did they even have kids?” It was a question he’d asked himself over and over. There had been so little love and patience and so much anger and resentment.

“Ally and I have talked about that. I don’t think they knew any better. Back in those days, you got married, you had kids. End of story. Tough luck if you’d made bad choices or weren’t suited to it. Tough luck if you had no idea how to manage yourself and your own moods, let alone take charge of two little kids.”

He sat and Jon followed suit.

“It wasn’t just that. He hated us. When his blood was up, he really hated us,” Jon said.

The memory of his father in full fury still made him flinch.

“Well, according to Mom, we brought all that on ourselves.”

He made a rude noise. "Right. Leaving the back door open equals a backhander across the face."

"Sure. Just like leaving a wet towel in the bathroom equals a thrashing."

"She should have done something. She should have stopped him."

"Yeah. She should have," Tyler said.

Jon looked at his brother. Warmth flooded his eyes again but this time he didn't fight the tears. Talking about this stuff, airing it, somehow made it smaller. More manageable and less dirty and shameful. He felt…released. Lighter. And the tears were part of that, whether he liked it or not.

Tyler studied his hands, lost in his own thoughts. "Do you remember the time when he took us to the beach on holidays?"

Jon winced. "Yeah. I remember."

They talked for over an hour, exhuming old memories, sharing insights and observations, making connections. Hearing his brother's version of events that had lived large in his memory helped scale Jon's own demons down to size. And there were good memories among the bad. Moments of laughter that he hadn't consciously thought of for years. The time he and Tyler built a tree house in the backyard. The time they'd been given a bike each by a friendly neighbor who'd been clearing out his garage. Long afternoons by the river, flying out over the water on the tire swing while their Tarzan cries echoed in the trees.

At some point Jon registered that it was pitch-black outside.

"Gabby," he said, shooting to his feet.

She'd be worried. Wondering how this had all gone.

They found Gabby and Ally in the bedroom, leafing

through copies of Ally's extensive magazine collection. Gabby's head came up when he appeared in the doorway, her gaze scanning his face intently. He smiled faintly and held out his hand. Sliding off the bed, she crossed the room and wrapped her arms around him and lay her head on his chest.

Jon rested his cheek on the crown of her head.

One day he would find the words to thank her for pushing him to talk to his brother. Right now, he wanted to savor the feel of her in his arms.

Ally insisted on cooking pasta for them all, claiming that such a stressful day demanded some serious carb loading. And no one argued with her.

IT WAS AFTER TEN O'CLOCK BY THE TIME Gabby and Jon returned to her apartment.

She led him straight to the bedroom. Toeing off her shoes, she crawled to the head of the bed and patted the mattress beside her.

"Come here."

He sat on the edge of the bed to pull off his boots, then he joined her. He tried to take her in his arms, but she shook her head.

"No," she said, and she guided his head onto her breast and wrapped her arms around him. There was a lot of him and not quite so much of her, but it was the best she could do and it was what she needed to do to show him that she was there for him and that he was loved. She pressed a kiss to his temple and stroked his hair and breathed in the warm, manly smell of him.

She loved him. So very much.

"I think you should move in," she said eventually.

He turned his head slightly to kiss her chest.

"Is that a yes?" she asked, even though she knew.

"You know it is."

She bit her lip, then finally allowed herself to voice the question that had been top of her mind since Jon had appeared in the doorway of Ally and Tyler's bedroom.

"I don't need to know all the details of what you and Tyler talked about. I don't need to know any of the details, really. I just need to know that you don't blame yourself anymore."

"I don't want to have any secrets from you."

Precious, powerful words.

He sat up, crossing his legs so that he was sitting beside her. He picked up her hand, tracing the delicate bumps of her knuckles with his thumb.

"Tyler told me that he'd felt guilty for being relieved when Dad laid into me and not him."

Deep inside, Gabby flinched. That two of her favorite people in all the world had carried around such terrible burdens made her feel infinitely sad.

"And what did you say?"

"I told him that he was a kid. That none of it was his fault."

"And he told you that you were a kid, too, right? That you were both kids and that you didn't stand a chance against an adult?"

He smiled at her vehemence. "Yeah. That's what he told me."

She eyed him. "You believe him, don't you?"

"I'm thinking about it."

But there was a small smile at the corner of his mouth. Tyler had gotten through, as she'd hoped. Their shared experience had given Jon a new way of looking at the past.

"Thinking about it. I see." She pushed away from the headboard and closed the distance between them, climbing into his lap and wrapping her arms and legs around him. "Think about this, Jon Adamson. You are the most honorable man I know. Even when you didn't like me much you were worried about my personal safety. You tried to stop me from making a fool of myself, you drove me home and offered me good advice."

"The argument could be made that I was probably desperate to get you naked. Even if I wasn't ready to admit it at the time."

She ignored him.

"You don't do anything that you aren't one hundred percent committed to. You're extremely tough on yourself. You hassled Tyler into hiring an assistant for me, and today when I tried to quit, you offered to give up the partnership with Tyler because you wanted me to be happy." She laced her fingers behind his neck and looked deep into his gray eyes.

"Does that sound like the kind of man who would let people down? Ever?"

He smiled slightly. Almost shyly. But he didn't deny it or try to turn aside her words.

"I think the man I described might even be a bit of an overachiever in the taking responsibility area. He might even be a bit overbearing and overprotective sometimes," she said.

His smile broadened. She was glad to see light in his eyes. She knew there would be days ahead when they would talk about what had happened to him again—when and as he needed to—and she was going to do her damnedest to persuade him to talk to a professional. But right now he deserved a little lightness and a lot of love.

"This man we're talking about might even sometimes

verge on being patronizing when he thinks he knows better than others."

He kissed her, his tongue sweeping into her mouth. Then he flopped back on the bed so that she was sprawled on top of him. She'd barely caught her breath when he rolled to cover her, his weight pressing her into the mattress.

"Hey. I wasn't finished," she said. "I hadn't gotten to your really good qualities yet."

He ducked his head to bite her nipple through her top. She gasped, then made an approving noise when he soothed the bite with his tongue.

"I think you're finished," he said.

She reached to cup the side of his face, suddenly very serious. "I am, you know. You did me in. The moment I met you, my goose was cooked."

"You cooked mine first. Asking if I wanted a coffee while I was using your computer without permission. What kind of a hard-ass does that?"

"The kind who loves you with everything she's got," she said, tracing his cheekbone with her fingers, her eyes locked with his.

He turned his head to kiss the center of her palm. "Thank you for not giving up on me, Gabby."

"You're worth it. A million times over."

He trailed kisses down her belly. She smiled to herself, knowing where that trail ended.

She made a correction in her mental diary as he popped open the snap on her jeans. Last Saturday wasn't the best day ever. Today was. A tougher day, by many measures—especially if they counted the hard stuff that had happened in the early hours of the morning. But still a very, very good day because they were here in her bed and Jon loved her and at long last there were no secrets between them.

Jon pulled down her zipper and licked the skin he'd exposed. He glanced at her, a wicked glint in his eyes.

She settled against the pillows.

Of course, she was willing to revise the best day decision on a regular basis. Say, every day.

Because she had a feeling that they were all going to be pretty damned spectacular with this man by her side.

EPILOGUE

Seven months later

"IT'S REALLY QUIET IN THERE. Too quiet," Jon said, springing to his feet. He paced, striding from one end of the small waiting area to the other.

"Relax. Royal Margaret has the best maternity wing in Melbourne. Ally's got a gazillion specialists at her beck and call."

"She was calling out before. Why has she gone quiet all of a sudden?"

Jon ran an agitated hand through his hair. Gabby stood and stepped into his path.

"She was swearing like a trooper because she was in pain. But if she's not in pain anymore, that's probably a good sign, right?"

"I guess."

He looked so worried. She placed her hand over his heart.

"Everything's going to be all right," she said.

Her hand looked ridiculously small against the breadth of his chest but Jon lost the tight look around his eyes.

"I just want everything to be okay."

As always she was touched by the depth of his feeling. He had a big heart and she knew Tyler's happiness meant a great deal to him.

"Hey."

They both spun around to face the bedraggled, worse-for-wear figure standing in the doorway.

"Tyler. Is everything okay?" Jon asked, taking a step toward his brother.

"Yeah. We're all good." Tyler's face lit with a slightly dazed, beatific smile. "We had a little girl. She's so tiny. Ally wants you guys to meet her."

Jon didn't say a word, simply stepped forward and threw his arms around his brother. For a moment they held one another, fists thumping on each other's backs.

Gabby sniffed away the threatening tears. Maybe one day she would get over the fierce sense of satisfaction and rightness she felt whenever she saw these two men together, enjoying one another, loving and appreciating one another. But not yet.

The brothers parted and Gabby stepped forward to offer her congratulations. She could feel the damp fabric of Tyler's T-shirt as she hugged him.

"Hard work, huh?" she said.

"If you want to know what the definition of *useless* is, stand around while your wife gives birth. Come on."

He gestured for them to precede him to the birthing suite. Inside, Ally lay propped against a pile of pillows, one hand resting on the tiny pink and red body lying on her chest.

She looked exhausted, her hair matted to her forehead, dark circles beneath her eyes. She gave them both a weary smile.

"Hey. Come and meet our little girl—Alana Rose Adamson," she said.

"Oh, that's so beautiful," Gabby said.

"We think so," Ally said.

Tyler went to his wife's side, sliding his arm around her shoulders. Gabby and Jon approached tentatively.

"She doesn't bite," Ally said.

"We don't want to overwhelm her," Gabby said.

Her gaze was glued to the small figure curled on Ally's chest. The baby's face was creased, her eyes shut. Her hands were clenched into tiny fists, her legs pulled up tightly. A shock of dark hair covered her head.

"Hello, Alana Rose," Gabby said.

"She's so tiny," Jon said.

"No, she isn't, trust me," Ally said drily. "She has a head the size of a bowling ball."

"Can we touch her?" Gabby asked.

"Of course," Tyler said.

Gabby reached out and ran her finger ever so gently across the baby's shoulders. The baby moved in her sleep.

"She's beautiful," Jon said, so softly that Gabby almost didn't hear him.

He reached out and touched one of the baby's hands. The hand unfurled, tiny fingers wrapping themselves around Jon's much bigger index finger.

A bemused smile broke across his face. Gabby met his eyes and couldn't help but smile in return.

The past seven months hadn't been perfect. There had been highs and lows. Jon's court case where he'd been sentenced to a good behavior bond, as his lawyer had predicted. Teething pains when he'd moved into her apartment and she'd had to adjust to sharing her space with someone. And, much to her frustration, Jon was still resisting talking to a professional—although she hadn't given up hope on that one yet.

But through it all they'd kept talking and sharing,

and her respect and love for the man standing beside her had only grown deeper and more encompassing.

Her heart expanded yet again as she watched him gently caress his new niece.

Jon Adamson was a keeper. A gentle giant. A loving brother. A good friend.

And he was all hers.

Some girls really did have all the luck.

* * * * *

This little baby clearly belonged to Dev.

It explained exactly why his crooning and shushing and swaying had been so effective, earlier today. He'd had practice. Recent practice, and a lot of it.

"You'd better come in," he said. "I think she's going to sleep. You're not catching her at the best time. I wish you could see her smiling, the way she's been doing the past month."

"It's a girl?"

"Yes."

Dev had just mentioned she'd been smiling for the past month, and Jodie had enough nieces and nephews that she knew when smiling happened—six weeks or so. This baby had to be about ten weeks old.

Do the math, Jodie, do the math. Nine months plus two and a half equals almost a year. When you were busy "getting the old crush out of your system," last fall, the mother of Dev's baby must already have been pregnant…

But where was the mother now? *Who* was the mother?

Dear Reader,

As any writer will tell you, some books are harder to write than others. This was one of those times when it all came together so clearly. I found myself with a gutsy heroine facing enormous challenges and a miracle or two, a hero who does the right thing but hasn't yet learned what his heart really wants, and a loving family who sometimes make the wrong choices for the best of reasons, and there was the story.

Even so, there were some surprises as I wrote. Jodie's career as a teacher of riding became more important than I thought it would be. It draws on all the experience I'm gaining from being involved with my daughter's passion for horses. The night-time scene between Devlin and Jodie on their way back from an evening out wrote itself onto the page in a way I hadn't planned, but as soon as it was there I knew it was right.

I hope this book makes you laugh and cry, and that you're as eager for Jodie and Dev to find the path to their own happiness as I was.

Lilian Darcy

THE MUMMY MIRACLE

BY
LILIAN DARCY

MILLS & BOON

First published in Great Britain 2012
by Mills & Boon, an imprint of Harlequin (UK) Limited,
Eton House, 18-24 Paradise Road, Richmond, Surrey TW9 1SR

2in1 ISBN: 978 0 263 89423 3

23-0412

Harlequin (UK) policy is to use papers that are natural, renewable and recyclable products and made from wood grown in sustainable forests. The logging and manufacturing processes conform to the legal environmental regulations of the country of origin.

Printed and bound in Spain
by Blackprint CPI, Barcelona

Lilian Darcy has written nearly eighty books. Happily married, with four active children and a very patient cat, she enjoys keeping busy and could probably fill several more lifetimes with the things she likes to do—including cooking, gardening, quilting, drawing and travelling. She currently lives in Australia, but travels to the United States as often as possible to visit family. Lilian loves to hear from readers. You can write to her at PO Box 532, Jamison PO, Macquarie ACT 2614, Australia, or e-mail her at lilian@liliandarcy.com.

Chapter One

"I don't think she's ready yet." The words floated up through Jodie's open bedroom window from the back deck.

"Oh, I agree! She's not!"

No one in the Palmer family ever thought Jodie was ready. She sat on her bed, struggling to raise her left arm high enough to push her hand through the strap on her summery, sparkly, brand-new tank top. The hand wouldn't go, which meant she couldn't start the long journey down the stairs to join the Fourth of July family barbecue as the—not her idea—guest of honor.

She pushed again, the feeble muscle refusing to obey the muddy signal from her brain. It was noon; time for everyone to start arriving. "So I guess they're right. I'm not ready," she muttered, but she knew this wasn't what her sister Lisa's comment had meant.

It had meant Not Ready, capital *N,* capital *R,* and

during Jodie's twenty-nine years had covered everything from her learning the shocking truth about the Easter Bunny at the age of seven, to going out on her first date at fifteen. She vaguely remembered from last summer, about a hundred years ago, that Elin had even questioned her readiness to see Orlando Bloom's wedding photos in a magazine—and, admittedly, she had been a little envious of the bride.

What wasn't she ready for this time?

It could be anything. Going back to work?

Well, yes, she knew she wouldn't be doing that for a while, since she managed and taught at a riding barn for a living and spent hours in the saddle every week at Oakbank Stables.

Reading the police report on the accident scene? Might never be ready for that one. Fixing her own coffee? Wrong, sisters. She'd been practicing in rehab and, not to sound arrogant or anything, she was *dynamite* when it came to spooning the granules out of the jar.

"Guys?" she called out to her sisters. "Can I have some help up here?"

From down on the deck she heard an exclamation, voices, the scrape of chairs. Lisa and Elin both appeared half a minute later, flinging the bedroom door back on its hinges with a slam, wearing frightened looks to complement their red-white-and-blue patriotic earrings.

"It's okay," she told them. "You can put the defibrillator down and cancel the 911 call. I just can't get my arm into this top, that's all, and I know people will start arriving any second."

"Maddy and John just drove up," Lisa confirmed. "And Devlin was right behind them."

"Devlin's coming?" Jodie's heart bumped sideways against her ribs. Dev. Every time she saw Dev…

There was an odd little silence. Possibly there was. It ended so quickly that she wasn't even sure if it had happened.

"He's been so great, hasn't he?" Lisa said brightly. "How many times did he go in to see you, while you were in the hospital?"

"You tell me," Jodie joked. "I was unconscious for most of them."

"Do you remember anything from that time?" Elin asked, hesitant. At forty, she was the eldest of the four Palmer girls, and managed to be both the bossiest and the most nurturing at the same time. "The doctors said you might retain some memories, even from when you weren't responsive."

She and Lisa both stood there waiting for her reply, each almost holding their breath. Jodie fought a bad-tempered impulse to yell at them to stop the heck worrying about her so much!

Instead she said carefully, "I wouldn't call them memories...."

"No...?" prompted Lisa.

"But let's not talk about it now. Help me downstairs. I'm so slow. My brain sends the instructions but bits of my body don't respond. I'm thrilled I managed to get into the jeans."

Thirty-eight-year-old Lisa, sister number two, hugged Jodie suddenly with a warm, tight squeeze, and planted a smacking kiss on her cheek. Of the four Palmer girls, she and Jodie were physically the most alike, blonde and athletic, outdoorsy and lean. Lisa liked tennis and the beach and it had started to show in her tanned skin. She didn't take care of it the way she should. Hugging her back, Jodie decided she'd have to give Lisa a sisterly lecture about that, soon, because Palmer overprotectiveness could cut both ways.

The slight, strange tension in the room seemed to have gone, chased by the hug. "Honey, forget slow, we're just so happy you're okay," Lisa said. "Talking. Walking. Getting better every day. *Home.*"

"I know." Jodie blinked back sudden tears as they let each other go. "Me, too."

Devlin Browne was standing on the deck when she reached it, his dark hair showing reddish glints in the sun, his body tall and strong; there was no evidence of the accident that had injured the two of them in such different ways, nine months ago. He grinned at the sight of her, from behind his sunglasses. "Look at you!" She wished she could see the expression in his blue eyes. He ran his life with such quiet confidence and certainty. She loved that about him, wished right now that some of his qualities would rub off on her.

"Yeah," she drawled in reply, "all the grace of a ballerina."

With a walking frame for a dance partner. The doctors and therapists had promised that if she worked hard, she'd be rid of it soon. She planned to astonish them with her progress.

"Don't knock it," Dev said. "Compared to how you were even a week ago."

"I know. I'm not knocking it, believe me." She felt so self-conscious in his presence, so aware of the strong length of his body. Nine months and more since those three explosive nights of lovemaking, but to her they felt like yesterday. The way their bodies seemed to fit together so perfectly. The smell of him, warm and fresh and male. The words he'd whispered to her in the dark, naked and blunt and charged with sensual heat. Did he ever think about it?

Lisa helped her to sit down and took away the frame, while Elin handed her an ice-cold glass of tropical juice. The deck was dappled with sun and shade, and there was a breeze. It was a perfect day. Dev pulled up an Adirondack chair to sit beside her. He leaned against the wooden seat-back, casually stretched his arms. But his mood wasn't as casual as he wanted her to think. His gaze seemed intently focused behind those concealing sunglasses, and she didn't know if his sitting so close was significant.

Were they dating?

Could she ask?

Um, excuse me, Dev, I was in a coma for nearly eight months, and rehab since. Can you just catch me up on the current status of our relationship?

A thought struck her. That Not Ready comment of Lisa's a few minutes ago…

Not Ready to hear that Dev had moved on to someone else?

But she didn't have time to examine the cold pit that opened deep in her stomach at this idea. There shouldn't be a pit! He'd been up front with her nine months ago. "I have nothing to offer, Jodie," he'd said. "I'm only here until Dad is ready to go back to work. My career is in New York, it's pretty full-on, no room for commitment, and I'm not looking for it. I really like being with you, but if you're interested in something long-term, it's not with me."

How did a woman respond to something like that? She knew Dev had said it out of innate honesty and goodness of heart. He wasn't the kind of man who promised what he couldn't deliver, or tricked a woman into bed with sweet-talking lies. He called it how he saw it, and when he laid his cards on the table, he laid them straight.

Nine months ago he'd been all about the short term, about saying goodbye when it was over, with a big grin, warm wishes and no regrets for either of them, yet now he was sitting beside her, searching her face, examining the set of her shoulders as if he cared that she might not be coping.

Which she wasn't, fully.

Everything was happening too fast. Dev stood up to greet Lisa's husband. Mom and Dad came out from the kitchen, Dad in full male barbecue armor, with plastic apron and an impressive weaponry of implements. The front doorbell rang and Elin went to answer it.

And sister number three—Maddy—and her husband, John, were here, having at last managed to negotiate the trip from their car. They'd come around the side of the house and climbed the steps to the deck carrying two bulging diaper bags, some kind of squishy portable baby gym and a baby in a carrier.

Their baby. Their little girl. Tiny. Just a few weeks old. Jodie hadn't even known Maddy was pregnant. She'd only been told about baby Lucy after she was born—another questionable instance of Not Ready—and hadn't seen her yet, because Maddy and John lived in Cincinnati, two hours from Leighville, the Palmer family's Southern Ohio hometown.

"Oh, she's asleep!" Mom crooned. "Oh, what an angel! She already looks so much bigger than she did two weeks ago."

"Can we put her somewhere quiet?" Maddy asked.

But it was too late. The baby began to waken, stretching her little body in the cramped space of the car carrier and letting out a keening cry.

"Oh, she needs a feed," Maddy said. "Where shall I go?"

"Not here," Dad said. He was a traditional man, with a passion for woodworking and gadgetry. In his world, feeding and diaper changes didn't belong in the same space as a barbecue.

"You wouldn't believe how difficult it was just to get here, all the gear we had to bring. John, can you set up some pillows for me in…? Oh, where!"

"My room," Jodie said quickly. "There's a heap of pillows, and fresh flowers, and a rocking chair."

"Oops, I'm going to have to change her first…." But John had already gone to ready the room. Maddy held Lucy with the baby's legs awkwardly dangling and her little face screwed up as she screamed, and looked around for the diaper bag. "She's in a mess. Oh, I'm not good at any of this yet! Where's the monitor? We'll need it if she naps. I have no idea if she will. And when she cries like this… First baby at thirty-six, people do say it's harder."

"Here, don't worry, it's fine." Of all people, it was Dev who stepped forward and took the crying baby. He cradled her against his shoulder and commenced a kind of rocking sway and a rhythmic soothing sound. "Shh-sh, shh-sh, it's okay, Mommy's coming in a minute, shh-sh, shh-sh." Jodie felt a strange, unwanted tingling in her breasts and a familiar yearning in her heart. Why did he do this to her when she tried so hard to stay sensible? How could he possibly look so confident and so good, holding a poop-stained baby? Why was he still in Ohio, and not back in New York?

She had a vivid flashback, suddenly, to the first night

they'd made love. Bed on the first date. You weren't supposed to do that, if you were a female with a warm heart, but of course it hadn't felt like the first date. She'd known Dev since she was sixteen, and she'd responded to him with half a lifetime of pent-up feeling—to his hands so right on her body, to his voice so familiar in her ear.

"Thank you, Dev!" Maddy unzipped the diaper bag and rummaged around inside. She didn't seem surprised that Devlin had taken control, but Jodie was.

Not about the control, but about the thing he was in control *of.* If you were talking legal contracts or high finance or building plans, team sports, political wrangling, then, yes, Devlin Browne could take control in a heartbeat. Would always take control. But when it was a *baby?*

What did he know about babies?

He doesn't even want kids.

The thought came out of nowhere, one of the memories from before the accident that her brain threw out apparently at random. "Did I have amnesia?" Jodie had asked at one point.

"Not like in the movies," they—her doctors and therapists—had said. "But of course there are some gaps. Many of them you'll eventually fill in. Some you never will."

"Like the accident itself?"

"Yes, it's quite probable you'll never remember that."

But she remembered that Dev didn't want kids.

How did she remember that?

She searched her mind, watching him as he gently bounced the baby on his shoulder. He wore jeans and a gray polo shirt with black trim, filling the clothing with a body honed by running and wilderness sports. The fabric of the jeans pulled tightly across his thighs, and the sleeve-band of the polo shirt was tight, too. There was some impressive muscle mass there, and Jodie's fingers remembered it, even while she was trying to remember the other thing—the thing about him not wanting kids.

If he didn't want kids, how could he school all that male strength into the tender touch and soft rhythm needed to soothe a newborn baby? When Maddy was ready, he handed Lucy over to her, and casually warned, "Watch the wet patch on her back."

But he didn't want any of his own…

Okay, it was over dinner, she remembered. They'd been out together—and slept together, heaven help her—three times since his temporary return to Leighville. As far as Jodie's family were concerned, she and Dev had only been dipping their toes in the waters of the great big dating lake.

To her, though, it immediately felt deeper. She'd had a major crush on him at sixteen when he'd briefly dated one of her good friends before he—Dev—had left for college in Chicago a couple of months later. Turned out the crush had never really gone away.

She couldn't track back to how the subject of kids had come up that night. Maybe something to do with his restless lifestyle. He was based in New York these days, but his work in international law took him all over the world—three months in London, a summer in Prague. He'd only come home for a couple of months last fall to take over his father's small-town legal practice on a temporary basis while Mac Browne had heart surgery.

Okay, so she might possibly have asked Dev, over their meal, if he ever intended to settle down.

He'd probably said no, he didn't. The I-have-nothing-to-offer thing, again.

And then he'd definitely—twenty seconds or five minutes later—said that he didn't want kids. Fatherhood didn't fit with his plans.

Which was fine, she'd thought, because he was only in town for a short while, and she'd only gone into this dating thing so she could finally get a thirteen-year crush well and truly out of her system and then wave him goodbye. A big grin, and no regrets.

Or not.

If I sleep with him, he'll break my heart when he leaves, she'd thought back then. *And if I don't sleep with him, he'll* still *break my heart when he leaves....*

But that was last October, and he was still here. The accident would explain part of it. October eighth, the two of them driving home after dark from date number four, a fall hike in Hocking Hills followed by dinner, when a driver in an oncoming car had lost control around a bend. Devlin had broken his leg in three places and had a permanent metal plate in there, but he didn't even walk with a limp at this point, so shouldn't he be safely back in New York or in a hotel room in Geneva by now?

Instead he was standing here on her parents' summer deck sharing a joke with her dad, throwing up his head when he laughed, shirt fabric pulling across his broad shoulders when he raised a beer can to his lips, reminding her far too strongly that she hadn't remotely gotten the crush out of her system last fall, or during the nine months of coma and rehab since.

He'd come to visit her in the hospital five times since she'd woken up, seen her at her most vulnerable, in tears and struggling to move and speak, fighting her own uncooperative body. He'd been so supportive, but cautious at the same time, never talking about anything too personal, and she had no idea what it all meant. Her brain still felt scrambled, tired, and life was a jigsaw puzzle with too many pieces missing.

"Is she out here? How is she?" This was Jodie's Aunt Stephanie, following Elin out to the deck. Seemed as if *everyone* had been invited today. Jodie began to feel overwhelmed and more than a little tired. She'd been discharged from the nearby rehab unit yesterday, and would still be attending day therapy sessions there for a while. She'd spent just one night, so far, in her own precious bed.

"Jodie…!" Aunt Stephanie said, and leaned down to hug her.

Dad put hot dogs and burgers and steaks onto the barbecue grill. Lisa brought out bowls of salad. Lisa's husband, Chris, took a soccer ball onto the grass beyond the deck and began kicking it back and forth with a handful of kids. Everyone talked and laughed and caught up on family news.

Maddy came down with Lucy wide awake and contentedly milk-filled in her arms, and Jodie asked her on an impulse, "Can I have a hold? If you put a pillow under my left arm, so I don't have to use any muscle?"

She felt a strange yearning and a rush of emotion that she didn't remember feeling for her other nieces and nephews when they were newborn. Well, she'd only been in her early twenties then, not ready to think about babies. Lisa's youngest was seven years old.

"Do you want to, honey?" Mom asked, in a slightly odd voice. "Hold her?"

"Yes, didn't I just ask?"

"Quick, someone grab a pillow from the couch,"

Mom ordered urgently, as if baby Lucy were a grenade with the pin pulled and would explode if Jodie didn't have her nestled on a pillow in the next five seconds.

"John?" Maddy said, in the same tone.

"Coming right up." He ran so fast for the pillow Jodie expected him to come back breathless.

Sheesh, she thought, *I could probably ask for a metallic gold European sports car convertible with red leather seats right now, and there'd be one in the driveway by the end of the afternoon. You know, I should definitely go for that...*

Maddy stuffed the pillow between the arm of the chair and Jodie's elbow. "Now, just cradle her head here, Jodie. If you're not sure about this..."

"C'mon, Maddy, lighten up. I've held babies before. I've been holding them for years." Elin's eldest two were in their midteens.

"Yeah, but this is *my* baby," Maddy joked, in a slightly wobbly voice.

Okay, so it was a new-mother thing. Fair enough.

But there was that feeling in the air again, everyone seeming to hold their breath, everyone watching Jodie a little too closely. Mom, Lisa, Dev. Dev, especially, his body held so still he could have been made of bronze.

The accident. The coma. That was why.

When she was one hundred percent fit and well, would they finally stop?

"Shouldn't be such a fuss, should it?" Dad muttered from behind the barrier of the barbecue grill. No one took any notice.

Jodie held the baby, smelled the sweet, milky smell of her breath, the nutty scent of her pink baby scalp covered in a swirl of downy dark hair, and the hint of lavender in her stretchy cotton dress, from the special baby laundry detergent. Oh, she was so sweet, just adorable, and if everyone was staring at the two of them, well, that was fine and normal. It was one of the *rightest* sights in the world, a person tenderly holding a newborn child.

"Oh, you sweet, precious thing," she crooned. "Thank you for not crying for your auntie, little darling."

She bent forward and planted a kiss on the silky hair, and took in those sweet scents again, close to tears. As she straightened again, she could smell onions frying, too, the aroma unusually intense and satisfying, as if she'd never smelled frying onions before. Sometimes her brain reacted this way, since coming out of the coma. It was as if all her senses had been reborn.

And then suddenly they hit overload, like little Lucy hitting overload when she was due for her nap.

"Can you have her, Maddy? My arms are getting tired."

"You did great," Maddy said, and too many people echoed the praise. Dev growled it half under his breath.

But maybe they were right. She felt wiped. Dev leaned toward her. "Are you okay?"

"Need some lunch."

"Just that?"

"Well, tired…"

Baby Lucy yawned on her behalf, and Maddy murmured something about taking her upstairs.

"To Jodie's room," Mom said quickly. "Not in—"

"No, I know," Maddy answered, already halfway inside.

"But I definitely need lunch," Jodie admitted.

"Sit," Dev ordered. "I'll grab whatever you want." There was a tiny beat of hesitation. "You did great with the baby."

"So did you."

"Uh, yeah." A quick breath. "Hot dog with everything?"

"Please!" She managed the hot dog, covered in bright red ketchup and heaped with those delicious onions, managed replies to various questions from family members, and to a comment on the kids' soccer game from Dev, managed probably another half hour of sitting there—Maddy had come back downstairs with the baby monitor in her hand—and then she just couldn't hold it together, couldn't pretend anymore, guest of honor or not, and Dev said, "You need to rest. Right now."

Mom didn't quite get it. "Oh, but Devlin, it's her party! We've barely started!"

"Take a look at her."

Jodie tried to say, "I'm fine," but it came out on a croak.

"You're right, Devlin," Mom said. "Jodie, let's take you upstairs."

"But Lucy's asleep on her bed," Maddy said.

"Couch is okay," Jodie replied. "Nice to hear everyone talking." She joked, "I mean, it is my party."

"Here," said Dev, the way he'd said it to Maddy over an hour ago, about baby Lucy. He helped her up and she leaned on him, and he smelled to her baby-new nose like pine woods and warm grain and sizzling steak. He didn't pass her the walking frame, just said, "Don't worry, I've got you," and she found that he did. He was so much better than the frame, so much more solid and warm, with his chest shoring up her shoulder and his chin grazing her hair. Her heart wanted to stay this close to him for hours, but the rest of her body wouldn't cooperate.

They reached the couch and he plumped up the

silk-covered cushions, grabbed the unfinished hand-stitched quilt top her mother was working on, tucked it around her like a three-hundred thread-count cotton sheet and ordered, "Rest."

"I will."

"I'll leave your frame here within reach, if you need to get up."

"Thank you, Dev." She'd already closed her eyes, so she wasn't sure that he'd touched her. She thought he had, with the brush of his fingertips over her hair, but maybe it was just a drift of air from his movement. She didn't want to open her eyes to find out, or to discover he'd gone. Touch or air, she could feel it to her bones.

He must have gone. She hadn't heard his footsteps on the carpet, but now there was that sense of quiet.

Sleepy quiet.

In the kitchen, making coffee and cutting cake, Elin said, in a voice that wasn't nearly as soft as she thought, "I don't think she was ready for this many people so soon."

"It's just family," answered Lisa.

"It's a big family," Maddy pointed out.

"Mom wanted a celebration for her coming home." Lisa again.

"We should have waited a week or two for that." Elin.

"But by then…" Maddy.

"I know. I know." Elin sighed.

Jodie shut all of it out, the way she'd learned to shut out the noise and the interruptions in the hospital and rehab unit, and drifted into sleep. When she woke up again, her sisters were still in the kitchen.

No, she amended to herself, in the kitchen *again*.

They were cleaning up this time, and the way they were talking made it clear that most people had gone, including Maddy, Lucy and John. She must have slept for a couple of hours, and the house had grown hotter with windows and deck doors open. Was Dev still here? She could hear the vigorous, metallic sound of Dad cleaning off the barbecue out on the deck, and Elin and Chris's kids still playing in the yard, but no Dev.

She felt refreshed but stiff-limbed. Here was the walking frame within reach, just as Dev had promised. She twisted to a sitting position, inched forward on the couch and pulled herself up, automatically comparing her strength to yesterday, and a week ago, and a week before that.

Better.

I'm getting better.

Her therapists had told her it would come with work and so far today she hadn't done any work, just a few range of motion exercises for her hands and arms this morning.

Time for a walk.

She called out to her sisters in the kitchen, to tell them what she was doing, and Elin appeared. "You're sure?"

"I'm supposed to, now, as much as I feel like. I'll only go around the block."

"Need company?"

"No!" It came out a little more sharply than she'd intended.

The Not Ready stuff drove her crazy. It had been driving her crazy for years.

Not ready to go for a walk on her own, in her own street, at three-thirty in the afternoon on the Fourth of July? Come on!

She'd once said to her three big sisters, long ago, "I'm littler 'n you *now,* but watch out 'cause I'm getting bigger!" and somehow she was still insisting on that message, twenty-something years later, even though, thanks to a serious childhood illness at the age of five that had apparently scared the pants off of the entire family permanently, she never had caught up to them size-wise and was the smallest and shortest at size 4 and five foot three. But she didn't need the level of protectiveness they and her mother gave her. Why couldn't they see it?

Dad seemed to have an inkling, but he rarely interfered. She remembered just a handful of times. "Let her have horse-riding lessons, Barbara, for heck's sake!" he'd said to Mom when Jodie was seven. "It'll make her stronger." And then ten years later, "If she wants to work with horses as a career, then she should. She should follow her heart."

"No, thanks," she repeated to Elin more gently, because anger wasn't the way to go. "Send out a search party if I'm not back in forty-five minutes or so, okay? And I have my phone. You think anyone in Leighville is going to look the other way if they find someone collapsed on the sidewalk in front of their house?"

"You sure?"

"I'm sure, Elin. You can help me down the front steps, is all."

It felt so good, once Elin had gone back inside. To be on her own, but not alone in a hospital rehab bed. To be out in the warm, fresh day, with no one watching over her, or telling her, "Yes! You can do it!" with far too much encouragement and enthusiasm, every time she put one step in front of another.

I could walk for miles!

No, okay, not *miles*, let's be realistic, here.

But maybe more than just around the block. She had

the frame for support. It would be slow going, concentration still required for every step, and the afternoon heat had grown sticky, but she'd never been a quitter. There'd be a garden wall or park bench to sit on if she was tired. There were all those neighbors looking out for her, knowing about the accident and that she had just come home.

She could walk to Dev's.

Or rather, Dev's parents'. He'd mentioned today that he was living there for the time being, just a throwaway line that she hadn't thought about at the time because she'd been fighting the sense of fatigue and overload, but now it came back to her.

And it didn't make sense.

Why was Dev living at his parents' place, even as a temporary thing? Jodie was living with hers because of the accident, but that was different. Why was he still here in Leighville at all, when she had such a strong memory from nine months ago, of his insistence that he planned to return to New York as soon as he could?

It had something to do with her, with the accident, she was sure of it, and if her family had somehow roped him into the whole let's-protect-Jodie-till-she-can't-breathe-on-her-own scenario, then damn it, he had to be stopped. He had to be told.

I don't need it, Devlin. I don't want it. Not from you or from anyone else.

She was definitely walking to Dev's, and they were going to talk.

Chapter Two

"Shh-sh," Dev crooned, bouncing the baby gently against his shoulder. "Shh-sh."

It did no good. His rhythmic sway and soothing sounds had had more success with baby Lucy today than they were having now with his own child, in his own house. He'd heard her screaming as he came up the front path, and the sitter had met him at the door, looking harassed and more than ready to go home.

"I'm sorry, Mr. Browne, she just won't settle."

He'd taken the baby, paid the sitter, tried everything he knew in the hour since, but DJ was still crying. He knew from experience—over two months of it, since she'd come home from the hospital—that she would settle eventually, that it wasn't anything serious or horrible, just colic, but it wasn't fun to hear her crying and to feel so helpless.

Dev didn't *do* helpless.

He'd sent his parents off to their vacation condo in Florida three weeks ago with a sigh of relief. Both the Brownes and the Palmers were acting way too protective of everyone involved, since his and Jodie's accident nine months ago. He often suspected that the Palmers would take DJ from him completely, if they could. Maybe he should take them up on that, relinquish custody and go back to New York.

But his heart rebelled at this idea, the way it often rebelled at the suffocating level of Palmer helpfulness. Jodie's mother and her two sisters here in Leighville seized on his need for babysitting too eagerly, he felt, trading on their combined experience of child-raising and his own helplessness. His parents had been taking a hand at it, too, but seemed suspicious that he was somehow being exploited, that Jodie had trapped him into this situation.

Which was ridiculous, since she didn't even know about it.

Today, despite his misgivings about the attitudes of both Palmers and Brownes, he could have done with some family help, but it wasn't possible, the way things stood. He was supposed to keep the baby safely away from the Palmer house.

Keep her away until Tuesday, the day after tomorrow, when Jodie had her appointment with doctors and therapists and counselors.

Zero hour.

His stomach kicked.

How did you prepare for something like that? He and the Palmers had been politely fighting about it for several weeks. The Palmers thought she still wasn't ready, while Dev couldn't handle the covering up, the distortions, the silence, even though he often dreaded what might happen once Jodie knew.

Doctor-patient ethics had become more of a concern with every step forward in Jodie's difficult recovery. There was an insistence now that she had the right to be told, and that she was strong enough, so the moment of revelation had been fixed for ten o'clock Tuesday morning.

What would she want? Where would he fit? Would she understand how much he loved this baby girl, this surprise package in both their lives? He felt an increasing need to know how it would all pan out—he hated uncertainty, and not knowing where he stood—but there was a lot to get through first. For a start, how did you say it?

Jodie, you need to know at this point that while you were in the coma state...

DJ wailed and shuddered in his ear, but maybe it was easing now. Was she too hot? Dev preferred open windows and the chance of a breeze to the shut-in feeling of an air-conditioned cocoon, but what would be best for the baby? He rocked her a little harder and she seemed to relax into his shoulder, her sweet, milky breath soft on his neck.

He loved her more than he'd imagined possible, and he had no idea what this was going to mean, once Jodie was told.

"Stop crying, sweetheart. That's right. Settle down, it's okay. Is your tummy still hurting? Not so much now, hey? Not so much…"

How did this happen to me?

Nine months ago he'd been enjoying a hot fling, ground rules fully in place, with a warm, funny and surprisingly gutsy woman, who'd turned his temporary return to Southern Ohio from an act of duty into an unexpected pleasure.

Thanks to Jodie, he'd stopped seeing a slow-paced backwater town and started seeing the beauty of the changing landscape in the fall. Instead of feeling the suffocation of routine, he'd felt the sinewy strength of family ties. He'd rediscovered the pleasure of a good laugh, of collecting the morning newspaper from the front yard while the grass was wet with dew, of hearing rain or birdsong outside his window instead of city noise.

But it was just an interlude. They both knew it. He'd said it to her direct, because he didn't want the risk of her getting hurt.

Even after the accident, he'd at first only planned to stay until his leg was put back together and healed. Jodie had family here. She wouldn't be on her own, whether she stayed in a coma state or made a full recovery. He didn't belong at her bedside, keeping vigil, the way her parents and sisters had.

But then…

DJ went through another spasm of pain and stiffened and screamed harder in his arms. "Ah, sweetheart, ah, honey-girl, it'll stop soon." He rocked her and massaged her little gut with the pad of his thumb.

How did this happen to me?

And what would change, come Tuesday?

Everything.

"Everything, baby girl," he murmured. Hell, he was so scared about it!

The knock at his front door startled him a few minutes later, the brass rapper hitting the plate unevenly, a couple of strong, jerky taps and then a weaker one. With DJ still in his arms, her crying beginning to settle to a kind of shuddery grumble, he went to see who was there, and when he saw Jodie standing there, he knew he didn't have until ten o'clock Tuesday anymore.

Zero hour was now.

The baby wasn't Lucy.

Jodie worked that out in around forty seconds, as she and Dev both stood frozen on either side of the threshold.

The baby wasn't Lucy, because Lucy belonged to Maddy and John, and had gone home with them to Cincinnati, and was smaller and newer than this little thing.

This little thing clearly belonged to Dev, and explained exactly why his crooning and shushing and swaying on Mom and Dad's back deck had been so effective earlier today. He'd had practice. Recent practice, and a lot of it.

"You'd better come in," he said heavily, after standing there in what appeared to be a frozen moment of shock. Jodie was pretty shocked herself. "I think she's going to sleep," he added. "You're not catching her at the best time. I wish you could see her smiling, the way she's been doing the past month."

"It's a girl?"

"Yes."

"What's her name?"

"I…uh…I call her DJ."

"DJ," she echoed blankly. He *called* her DJ. But it wasn't her name?

"You look like you need to sit. Shoot, of course you need to sit."

"Yes. I do." She hadn't realized it herself until now, despite her shaky hand on the heavy door knocker, but, yes, her legs had turned pretty shaky, too, and the frame wasn't giving enough support. She had no idea what was happening, here.

Dev had a baby.

He absolutely, one hundred percent *had...a...baby.*

He had a cloth thrown over his shoulder to catch the spit-up, and a hand cradling the baby's little diaper-padded butt as if it grew there, and a puffy rectangle of baby quilt in the middle of the floor, with a baby gym arched over it, like the one Maddy and John had brought to Mom and Dad's today for Lucy, even though their three-week-old infant could hardly be expected to play with such a thing.

This baby was definitely older. Dev had just mentioned she'd been smiling for the past month, and Jodie had enough nieces and nephews, thanks to all of Elin and Lisa's kids, that she knew when smiling happened—six weeks or so. This baby, small though she was, had to be getting on for about ten weeks old.

Do the math, Jodie, do the math. Nine months plus two and a half equals almost a year. When you were busy "getting the old crush out of your system," last fall, the mother of Dev's baby must already have been pregnant....

But where was the mother now? *Who* was the mother?

"Here. Sit here," Dev said, after she'd made her way inside. It was a pretty house, but the décor was too frilly and fussy for a man like Dev, with lace and florals and porcelain knickknacks everywhere. His mother's taste. "I'll take the frame. Do you want coffee, or something?"

"No. I— No, I'm fine."

"Look, it's obvious we need to talk. Let me get you something."

"Is—? Who else is around?"

"No one. My parents are in Florida. They have a condo there. I made them go."

"You *made* them?"

"Don't you sometimes feel…haven't you felt, these past few weeks, as if sometimes there's just too much family?"

"Ohh, yeah!"

That she could relate to.

But the baby…

DJ had fallen asleep on Dev's shoulder. "Hang on a sec," he muttered, and picked up a roomy piece of cloth that turned out to be a baby sling. He draped it across his shoulder, tucked the baby inside and stood there, still swaying gently. "If I put her down now, she'll just wake up again," he explained. "She needs to go a little deeper before it's safe."

"You're very good at it."

"Yeah…not really. I'm getting there. I have a who-o-ole heap of help."

A heavy silence fell, during which the obvious reference to DJ's mother wasn't made.

Dev said nothing about her.

Jodie didn't want to ask.

"She's adorable," she said instead, feeling woolly and wooden about it, wondering if she should be angry. Or hurt. Or just cheerful. *Wow, you have a baby, congratulations. You said you didn't want kids, but whoever the mom is obviously didn't get the memo.*

Unless of course…

Well, accidents happened. Baby-producing accidents, as well as ones that break legs in three places and put people into comas and necessitate the removal of spleens. Dev and some unknown woman had had a contraceptive "oops" roughly eleven months ago, and here was a baby, and her mom had probably just run to the store for diapers and milk. She and Jodie would meet each other any minute now.

"I can't take this in," she blurted.

"I don't blame you. Jodie, this was all set up for Tuesday. Does your family know you're here? They couldn't!"

"Oh, my family… Didn't you just ask me if I felt there was too much family? Well, there is! I said I was going for a walk and I didn't need company. I just told them around the block, and that if I wasn't back in forty-five minutes, send a search party. Coming here was an impulse."

"I'd better call your folks." He rocked the baby in his arms instinctively.

"It hasn't been forty-five minutes."

"You're going to be here for a while." He'd already picked up the phone and hit speed dial, as if the matter was urgent.

He has my parents on speed dial, she registered. But she liked his directness, the decisive way he moved. It was reassuring, somehow. Dependable.

He spoke a moment later. "Hi, Barb?" Barb was Mom. "Just letting you know, Jodie's here.… Nope, not my idea… No choice, at this point… I can't argue it now, you have to trust me.… Of course I will… No. Just me. Please… Yep, okay, talk soon."

"What was that about, Dev?" She tried to stand up, but her legs wouldn't cooperate. The walk had tired her more than she wanted.

"We've both said it. Too much family."

"Right."

"First, tell me why you came. I mean, what made you

think—? What gave you the idea—?" He broke off and swore beneath his breath. "Just tell me what made you come."

His difficulty in finding the right words made her flounder a little, and struggle for words herself. "I wanted to ask you…or to thank you, too, for coming to see me in the hospital those times."

"Just that?" He sounded cautious, looked watchful, as if waiting for a heck of a lot more.

"Well, and for—I don't know if I'm even the reason for this, or even *part* of the reason, but…not going back to New York when you planned."

"Hell, of course I wasn't going back to New York!"

She looked at him blankly and he understood something—something that *she* didn't understand at all, but she could see the dawn of realization in his face, while her body stopped belonging to her and belonged…somewhere else, to someone else.

It was a familiar feeling. Just the accident and her slow recovery? Or something more?

He was muttering under his breath. Curse words, some of them. And coaching. He was coaching himself. He sat down suddenly, in the armchair just across from the couch, with the sling-wrapped baby cradled in his arms, as if his legs had drained of their strength just like Jodie's had.

"*Pretend* I've just been in a coma for nearly nine months, Devlin," she said slowly. "Tell me anything you think I might not know. *Pretend* my family has a habit of shielding me from the most pointless things. And from the serious things, too. And tell me even the things you think I already do know. What did you mean, *set up for Tuesday?* What did you mean, *no choice at this point?* And this might be totally off-topic, but how is there a baby? And where is her mom?"

Chapter Three

She doesn't know. She doesn't understand.

The realization kept cycling through Dev's head, paralyzing him. Hell, he hadn't wanted it to happen like this! He'd been so scared of the moment, sometimes—scared about what it would mean for his own bond with his baby girl. What if Jodie wanted the baby all to herself? What if he was suddenly shut out? He wasn't prepared to let that happen, but how tough would he be willing to get about custody and access, when Jodie's recovery was still so far from complete? What would be best for DJ?

He'd wanted to get the revelation over with, so that at least he would begin to know where he and DJ stood, but the timing had to be right. It had to be done in the right way.

With all the talk, the questions, the arguments back and forth between pretty much every member of the

Browne and Palmer families for weeks, the conjectures that maybe at some level she knew, and that some tiny thing might easily jog a memory, no one had considered that Jodie herself might be the one to determine when they broke the news.

Devlin had wanted her told sooner, and his parents had been on his side. The Palmers had wanted to wait, insisting she wasn't ready for such a massive revelation. The doctors, therapists and counselors wanted to respect the family's wishes, but had been growing more insistent with each stage in Jodie's improvement, after the setback of the serious infection she'd had just after DJ was born.

This was part of the problem. It had all happened in stages. It wasn't as if she'd just opened her eyes one day and said, "I'm back. Catch me up on what I've missed!"

All through the coma there had been signs of lightening awareness, giving hope for an eventual return to consciousness, but it had been so gradual. First, she followed movement around the room with her eyes, but couldn't speak. It seemed so strange that she could have her eyes open without real awareness, but apparently this was quite common, the doctors said.

Then her level of consciousness changed from "coma" to "minimally conscious state." She began to vocalize vague sounds, but had no words. She started to use words but not sentences. She began to move, but with no strength or control. For several days she cried a lot, asking repeatedly, "Where am I? What happened to me?"

Once she'd understood and accepted the accident and the need for therapy, she'd become utterly determined to make a full recovery and had worked incredibly hard. Every day, over and over, in her hospital room, in the occupational therapy room, or the rehab gym, they all heard, "Don't bother me with talking now, I'm working!"

Barbara Palmer began to say, about the baby, "Not until she's home," and her therapists cautiously agreed that, emotionally, this might be the right way to go. Let her focus on one thing at a time. Don't risk setting back her physical recovery with such a shock of news.

How did you say it?

How the hell was he going to say it now?

You were five weeks pregnant at the time of the accident, it turns out, although we're almost certain you didn't know. You gave birth, a normal delivery, at thirty-three weeks of gestation, when your state was still defined as coma, just a week after you first opened your eyes. This is your beautiful, healthy baby girl.

He said it.

Somehow.

Not anywhere near as fluently as it sounded in his head.

"Sh-she's yours…Jodie," he finally said, stumbling over every word. Yours? No! He wasn't going to sabotage his own involvement. "She's *ours,*" he corrected quickly. "I didn't know what to call her. I thought you'd want to decide. So she's been DJ till now, because those are our two initials. Is that okay? Are you okay? This was supposed to happen on Tuesday, at your appointment, with your doctors and therapists and people on hand to answer all your questions. To—to help you deal with it."

The words sounded stupid to his own ears. *Deal with it.* Doctors and counselors could help someone *deal with* a cancer diagnosis, but this was in a whole different league.

Her eyes were huge in her face. She couldn't speak. She was slightly built, which made a stark show of her current shock and vulnerability. He remembered thinking her funny and gawky and oddly impressive when she was sixteen and he was eighteen, and dating her friend. Impressive because she looked as if a breath of wind would blow her away, but, boy, did she get on your case if you treated her that way.

She'd been just the same in the hospital and during rehab, once she could speak and move. She'd insisted on her own strength and her own will, and proved with every step that she was as strong and determined as she claimed. She fought her family on it all the time, because she was seven years younger than her next sister and she'd had a serious brush with meningitis as a child, and the whole clan had babied her ever since.

Well, for once she wasn't fighting or insisting. She was too shocked. He'd half expected a protest or a denial. *You're messing with my head. It can't be true.* But she didn't say anything like that. She believed him at once, which made him wonder if there was a tiny, elusive part of her brain, or a lacing of chemicals—hormones—in her body that had known the truth.

Her conscious mind, though, and her sense of self, had been completely in the dark.

"I have a thousand questions," she blurted out.

"Of course. Ask them. I'll tell you everything as straight as I can."

"I can't."

"Ask them?"

"Do this." She tried to stand up, but her legs wouldn't carry her.

"Sit," he insisted. "You don't have to say anything. Or do anything. Let me talk, if you want."

"Okay."

So he talked, keeping it a little impersonal because that felt safe, and leaving out a few things, because he couldn't hit her with all of it at once.

He told her about the signs of labor, the quick delivery they'd all been praying for, to ease the stress on her body. Told her DJ's length and birth weight and head circumference. Told her proudly that the baby had Jodie's own strength. Despite her premature birth, DJ had been stepped down from the NICU into the lower-level special-care unit within a couple of days, and had come home from the hospital in less than two weeks.

"Home?" Jodie croaked.

"Here. And your parents' place. She spends a lot of time there." More than he was happy with, to be honest, but he hadn't wanted to fight them on that at a point when Jodie's full recovery had still been very much in doubt, and when his own future wasn't fully resolved. Would she ever be able to take care of a child? If she could, did that mean he'd go back to New York?

"Why are you here? In Leighville?"

She was asking the wrong questions, wasn't she? He took in a breath to suggest this to her, but then changed his mind.

Ah, hell, there was no script for this! She should ask whatever she wanted to, in whatever order it came. And if she didn't have an instant, overpowering need to hold DJ in her arms, he should be glad of the reprieve. He couldn't stand the idea of losing his daughter, not even with generous custody and access, when the bond between them had grown so strong.

"I'm still working at Dad's law practice," he explained, trying to stay practical and calm. "He's in no hurry to get back into harness. I expect he'll decide to retire. I'll head back to New York… Well, that's open-ended at the moment. All decisions on hold, I guess. My apartment is rented out. I have a conference coming up in Sweden in early October, followed by a couple of months consulting in London."

"You were supposed to be back in New York by last Christmas. Was it your dad's health that changed your plans?"

Shoot, didn't she understand?

"They found out you were pregnant before I even had the plates put in my leg."

"How?"

"Blood tests, part of assessing your condition. When they told me…" Again, how to say it?

"You knew you had no other choice," she supplied for him.

He couldn't argue. Not the words, anyway. Maybe the edge of—what?—bitterness, or anger, in her tone. He *hadn't* had any other choice. Not then. He wasn't going to abandon his child before it was even born. He wasn't going to deprive her of a father, when she might never have a mom. But it was different now. "I don't want another choice," he said. "This all needs time to work out, and that's okay."

"You said you didn't plan on ever having kids."

"You remember that?"

"Over dinner. You had steak with pepper sauce. I had strawberry mousse cake for dessert."

"Shoot, you do remember!"

"Yes. It's like yesterday, that mousse cake." The subtext of *explain yourself, Dev* was very clear. She wasn't really talking about dessert.

He said slowly, "What was it John Lennon once said?

'Life is what happens to you while you're busy making other plans.'"

"Or while you're in a coma," she drawled.

"Yeah, then, too."

Tentatively, they both smiled, and something kicked inside him. He had a couple of memories that were like yesterday to him, too. Her passion in bed, almost fierce, as if in lovemaking, too, she had to prove her own strength, had to fight against the wrong preconceptions. Her saucy grin when she undressed. And his ambivalence.

He really, seriously, hadn't known if it was a good idea to take her to bed that first time, even though she said she wanted it, and said she understood there was no long-term, and no promises, and that was fine. He'd told himself a couple of times their first night that he would stop kissing her soon, that he would reach out and still her hands if she went to pull off her clothes.

But then she'd done it. Crossed her arms over her chest and lifted her top to show a hot-pink bra and neat, tight breasts. Shimmied her way out of her skirt. Grinned at him.

And there'd been no question of stopping after that point. He'd used protection, but—not to get technical, or anything—maybe applied it just a little too late.

"But the dates don't fit," she said suddenly. "She's too old. She's smiling. Lucy isn't."

"Because DJ was premature," he explained again. "Healthy preemies learn to smile at the same age after birth as full-term babies, even if they're smaller and a little slower in other areas. DJ and Lucy would have been born within a week or two of each other, if DJ had come at the right time. The doctors say it's good that she didn't. It was easier on your body that she was little, and early. Would you like to hold her?"

He asked it before he thought. Blame Lucy for that. Jodie had looked so happy and comfortable holding her tiny niece today.

DJ was different. DJ had baggage.

Jodie stiffened and stammered. "No, she's—she's—N-not yet, when she's asleep. If I disturbed her and she cried…"

"It's fine. We'll transfer her in the sling. It'll be easy, I promise." Listen to him! Five minutes ago, he'd been scared about the strength of her maternal feelings and what they might do to his own connection with his child. Now he was trying to rush her into them. He didn't know what he wanted anymore.

Which was weird and unpleasant, because he *always* knew what he wanted.

Her weakened left hand made a claw shape on her thigh. "No. No, I can't. I just can't."

Jodie heard the note of panic in her own voice, but there was nothing she could do about it. The panic was there. She couldn't explain it to Dev. Couldn't even explain it to herself. But there was a huge, massive chasm of a difference between holding and clucking over Maddy's little Lucy and holding this baby.

My baby. Half an hour ago, I didn't know she existed. But she's mine.

It was overwhelming.

It should have been wonderful. A miracle.

Dev loves her. I can see it.

But it didn't feel wonderful, it felt terrifying.

Thank heaven Dev loves her, because I don't.

No. No! She had to love her own child! She did. Of course she did.

But why couldn't she feel it? Why wasn't it kicking in at once, the way it had with Elin and Lisa and Maddy and all the other normal mothers in the world, the very first moment they looked at their babies? Dev clearly expected it to, with his urging that DJ would be safe in her arms. It wasn't a question of safety. Why could she feel so tender toward Lucy today, and yet so distant and scared about this baby?

Scared? A surge of strength hit her. She wasn't in the habit of giving in to *scared.* She took in a breath to tell him that she would hold the baby after all. And she would have reached out her hands before the words came, except they were a little slow to respond to her brain's signal and she had to make an extra effort.

But before either the movement or the words could happen, Dev accepted her refusal, gave her an easy excuse. "You're tired," he said. He let out a breath that might have been partly relief, as if maybe he'd doubted the strength and coordination in her arms more than he'd let on. "We should wait a little."

She almost argued.

Almost.

But, oh, he was right, she was tired, and she'd tried so hard to stay on top of everything today. She let it go, and watched him tiptoe to the infant car carrier sitting in the corner of the living room and lay the baby down, easing his forearm out from beneath her little head with a movement so practiced and gentle it almost broke her heart.

"Very tired," she managed to respond. "I'm sorry."

I'm so sorry, DJ.

"Don't beat yourself up." The baby stirred a little, but didn't waken.

"I—I—" Did he know? Did he understand the extent of her panic?

"Let's take it slow. It's okay."

"Thanks. Yes."

She heard a car in the driveway, and footsteps and the voices of Elin and Mom. Dev lunged for the door before they could knock. He held it open and stood with the width of his body shielding the room from their view.

Mom said, "Is she still here?"

"Yes, but why are *you* here, Barb? I asked you very clearly to—"

"I'm sorry, we just couldn't— I'm sorry." This was Elin, clearly reading his anger. "We have a right to be involved in this, too, don't we? DJ is ours, too. We all care so much."

"You'd better come in."

"Thank you," said Mom, in a crisp voice.

"I really think it's best, Devlin." This was Elin, in a softer tone.

"We are as involved in all of this as you are." Mom again.

They dropped at once to sit on either side of Jodie on the couch, their voices running over her along with their hands, all of it a jumble that she heard at two steps removed, like recorded voices or lines from a half-remembered play. *Honey, are you okay? Obviously you know. Obviously there's so much to talk through. That's why we wanted to wait until you were ready. What has Dev said, so far?*

"You barely gave me time to say anything," he said.

"Listen, it's not as if any of us have had any experience with a situation like this, Devlin," Elin said.

"Shh...keep your voice down, can you?"

"Sorry…sorry." Elin glanced over at the baby and looked surprised. "You have her in the car carrier?"

"She seems to sleep better in there, during the day."

"Well, then, I guess…" *But I never did that with my babies,* was the implication.

"She's fine. She wouldn't sleep so peacefully if she was uncomfortable there."

"If you say so."

Both Devlin and Elin were holding it together with difficulty, and Mom looked trapped and unhappy, her mouth open as if she wanted to speak, although no words came.

Jodie slumped against the back of the couch. She'd started to shake. Could they feel it? She felt more tired than she'd ever felt in her life, and her lips had gone dry. She closed her eyes, willing this chaos of family and tension and questioning to…just…stop.

"Should we take her? Jodie, are you ready to go home?"

She opened her eyes. "Yes, take her."

I mean, who is she? How can she even exist?

"I—I don't know what I want to do," she blurted. "I think I need some space. Another nap." Her own bed seemed like the safest haven in the world.

There was a small silence, while Elin and Mom and Devlin all looked at each other, shrugged and raised eyebrows and gestured—body language that was beyond Jodie's ability to interpret right now.

"I guess that's an option," Dev said slowly to Elin and Mom. "For you to take her and Jodie to stay here."

"That's not—" *What I meant.* But the rest of it wouldn't come, and the first bit had come almost on a whisper, and they were too busy making plans to hear her.

"She should transfer to the car without waking," Dev said. "I have a couple of bottles made up in the fridge."

"We have bottles. We have diapers, clothes, everything. You know that. She's due for her bath."

"I'll drop Jodie home when she's ready. She's right. We need to talk. Have some space."

They'd worked it all out between the three of them, while Jodie was still struggling to lift an arm to brush a strand of damp hair from her eyes. She was staying here with Dev to talk. The baby was going back with Mom and Elin. Going back before she, the mother, had even touched her.

She wanted to argue the plan, but the words wouldn't come, so in the end she let it happen, and when the baby carrier was buckled into the car and Mom and Elin had driven away, she felt so relieved, and so ashamed of the relief, and so horribly, horribly tired. "I can't—" she said to Dev.

"I know you can't talk yet. Sleep first."

"Two naps a day. I'm like—" She stopped.

A baby.

My baby.

"Just rest."

"Why aren't you in New York? Tell me why. In simple words. Because it seems to me that you didn't have to still be here. Obviously DJ is being taken care of. Obviously she's loved. Obviously I have the support. So why?"

He looked at her steadily, with some of the anger he'd clearly felt toward Elin and Mom still simmering below the surface. He seemed to be thinking hard before he chose his words.

"Because she's my daughter." The last two words came out with a simmering intensity. "Because we're a family. You and me and DJ. Three of us. That's not negotiable. Three of us, not two."

"A family…" Jodie echoed foolishly, tasting the word and not feeling sure of how it felt in her mouth.

"Not a regular family, for sure."

"No…"

"But DJ needs a family of some kind…." He paused for a moment, and she filled in the words he didn't say, in her head. *And not necessarily a whole cluster of over-involved grandparents and aunts.* "I'm right here in the picture and I'm not going to go away. And we have a heck of a lot to do and talk and think about, to decide how that's going to work."

Chapter Four

Jodie woke to the smell of something delicious coming from Dev's kitchen. The daylight had begun to fade, which meant she must have slept a good three hours this time. She felt disoriented and not in full possession of either her body or her brain. It was just the way she'd felt coming out of the coma. It was like being in the eye of a hurricane—eerily quiet, with a sense of danger all around.

She gave herself a couple of minutes to regroup, then sat up and eventually stood, steadier on her feet than she would have expected. As before, Dev had left her walking frame within reach, and the quiet, considerate nature of this small gesture almost brought her to tears.

She could hear him in the kitchen, chopping something on a wooden board. The delicious aroma announced itself as beef sizzled in a pan. She'd had a crush on him thirteen years ago, she'd slept with him three times, and she'd had no idea until now that he could cook. It didn't surprise her, though. When Devlin Browne put his mind to something…

He heard her—the rubbery tap of the frame on the floor—as she reached the kitchen doorway, and he turned. "Hi. Better?"

"Think so. It's crazy. To need all that sleep."

"Your brain is still healing."

"So I've been told."

"I'm making brain food. A beef-and-vegetable stir-fry, full of iron and vitamins."

"It smells great."

"Ready in a couple of minutes. Sit down." He nodded at the wooden kitchen table, then moved to pull out a chair for her.

"No, don't," she said quickly, taking one hand off the frame to reach for the chair herself. "I'm fine. I hate—" *my family hovering over me* "—too much help."

"Duly noted." He turned back to the stove, tossed in slivers of onion and red bell pepper, sticks of carrot and celery, lengths of green bean. The pan hissed and made a cloud of aromatic steam, filling the silence made by their lack of conversation.

He seemed to understand instinctively that she didn't want to talk yet—or not about anything important, anyway—and to her surprise the interlude of silence between them felt easy and right. She didn't have that uncomfortable itch to break the quiet with a rush of words that people often experience in the company of someone new.

Not that Dev was new.

But this felt new.

Untested.

Three of us. We're a family, he'd said.

Anything but the usual kind.

She watched him. Just couldn't help it. The way his neat, jeans-clad butt moved as he tossed the contents of the pan. The way his elbow stuck out and his shoulder lifted. He added the cooked meat and leaned back a little as another cloud of hissing steam came up. There was rice in a steamer on the countertop, and a jug of orange juice clinking with a thick layer of cubed ice.

Nine months ago, he hadn't wanted a serious relationship, but now it was as if she'd simply blinked and woken up to find herself here, in his kitchen, and the mother of his child.

Connected.

Yet not.

Are we dating?

She felt they needed to talk about it—for *hours* surely—but had no idea what to say, what to suggest. He was the one who'd had time to think. The surge of chemistry she'd felt earlier at the family barbecue couldn't compete with her shock and disorientation. It hummed in the background of her awareness, but she didn't know what to do with it, just wished it would go away.

"Is there a schedule?" she blurted out.

"A schedule?"

"Of who takes care of—of DJ."

DJ. That's my baby's name. Well, it's not her name. It's what we're calling her in the interim.

A crazy litany of baby names began to scroll in her head, the ones she'd vaguely thought, over the years, that she liked. Caroline, Amanda, Genevieve, Laura, Jessica, Megan, Anna… The idea that it might be up to her to make a decision, replace temporary DJ with something different and permanent that would belong to the baby her whole life, was daunting. A huge, confusing responsibility that she didn't feel equipped to handle.

"Your family has her when I'm at work," Devlin answered. "Mainly your mom. She's set up Elin's room for a nursery."

"That's why Lucy had to sleep in my room today." An image flashed in her head of her sister's old room with the door firmly closed. Even if she had seen inside, she would have assumed it had been set up for Maddy's baby girl.

"But Elin and Lisa have her sometimes, too. And then I pick her up on my way home."

"The night shift."

"That's right. I expect she'll spend more nights at your parents' place now." *Now that you're home,* he meant.

"That's why you look tired." A rush of tenderness and guilt ran through her. Those creases around his eyes, and she hadn't been here to help. Crazy to feel that it was her fault, and yet at some level she did. What kind of a mother slept through her whole pregnancy and didn't even waken to give birth? What kind of a mother had an eleven-week-old baby that she'd never touched and held?

He made a wry face. "Yeah, she's not exactly sleeping through. Your sisters have been great with that. They've stayed over here three or four times to give me a good night. Your whole family has been—" He stopped, as if the word he'd originally intended to say was wrong. "Amazing. They have. I was a little short with them before, and I shouldn't have been. The boundaries—the roles—are complicated."

"It's okay. I know how you feel. Just be thankful they're not trying to cut up your food."

He laughed and she smiled at him and then her breath caught, and the question she'd been asking in her head even before she'd found out about DJ came blurting out, "Are we dating, Dev?"

He went still. She just knew he was going to say no. It was there in his body language so clearly, and she wondered why on earth she'd thought it necessary to ask. Well. She hadn't thought. Her brain didn't seem to control either her body or her words anymore.

Eventually answered in a slow, careful way, "That's a question, isn't it?"

"I mean, I'm not suggesting you have a thing for unconscious women." The humor didn't work. It was too dark for a moment like this. It didn't evaporate the tension, as intended. She apologized. Seemed as if she might be doing a lot of that. "I'm sorry. I was just—"

"It's okay. Lightening the mood. You had a right to ask. I talked about making a family, just now."

"When you came to see me in the hospital, I didn't know why you were there. Because I didn't know about DJ. And last fall we…"

"I know." He was still so uncomfortable. They both were.

"I don't think we're dating," she said, before he could say it. "It would be crazy. It's not what we need. It would just be a complication. We have enough of those."

He nodded, and looked relieved. "You're right. I guess that's what I've felt. First things first. Take care of DJ. Take care of you. Take all of it slow. You're not strong enough to do much with a baby right now. We want to find a way to share her and love her. There's no hostility or conflict. I want to keep it that way. We *have* to keep it that way. I want as much involvement as I can have."

"But she'll be with me most of the time." Was it a question, or a statement? She didn't even know.

"Once you know her," he said. "Once you can take care of her. You're her mother and most of the time the baby stays with the mom. I'm accepting that."

But am I?

She saw herself stranded with baby DJ in her parents' house for weeks at a stretch with barely a break. She imagined the winter days closing in, keeping her and the baby inside the house, when normally even in the cold weather she loved to be outdoors.

These weren't the pictures she wanted to have of herself and her baby, but they were the ones that came. She heard herself wrangling and bickering with Mom about when to introduce solid food and whether to dress her in pink.

Dress her in pink…

She tried to picture it, and couldn't. At all. With a stab of horror she realized, *I don't remember what she looks like.* All she had were two vague images of a little face distorted with crying and then peaceful in sleep. Would she recognize her, beyond the familiarity of Dev's arms, or Mom's? Could she pull her own daughter out of a lineup?

Another bizarre image came to her. Police station. One-way glass. "Now, Ms, Palmer, look carefully at the numbered cribs. Do you see your baby here? It's very important that you make a correct identification."

But she couldn't…

"Dinner's up," Dev said. "I think we're— I'm glad we said this."

She tried to stand, to go over to the bench and help

him dish out the food, but her feet caught and she almost fell. He was there just in time.

"He-e-ey. Who-o-oa." He caught her and folded his arms around her. "You didn't have to get up. I'm bringing it to you."

She felt his breath fanning her hair and his chin resting on her shoulder, and could have stayed like this forever. She loved the way they fit together despite their mismatched size. She loved the smell of him, the strength of him, the honor and humor and decisiveness and brains. She loved the fact that he could hug her like this so soon after they'd agreed—the only thing they *could* agree on, in this situation—that they weren't dating anymore.

It was just a hug, and yet if she just turned her face up, she was sure he would kiss her. The chemistry was still there, a deep pool of it, secret and still, magical and unspoken.

She wanted him to kiss her.

Desperately.

Just kiss me, Dev, so I don't have to think. Just kiss me, so I know that part is okay, even if everything else isn't.

I don't care what we decided.

I don't care about sensible.

Kiss me and say, "Let's get married, and I'll take care of whatever you need," so that we can play by the rules and be a normal mommy and daddy and then maybe I'll feel as if I belong in my own life, instead of being just a visitor.

"This is the most insane situation," he muttered. "I don't know what to tell you. Just take your time. That's all. We all need to give this time."

Kiss me. Say it.

Shoot!

This neediness, this wasn't *her! Jodie Palmer, don't you remember who you are? You've been fighting your whole life to show how strong you are, and now you're clinging to Dev as if he has all the answers and so you can just go with the flow?*

The familiar stubbornness kicked in. Maybe a little off-center, but at least it was there, and the feeling came as a huge relief. She pulled out of his arms and crisply said, "Thanks. You're right. We'll give it time. We'll work it out. Thank you. Mmm, that smells good!"

He steered her the few steps back to her seat then turned toward the stove, blinking as if he'd opened his eyes in bright light, and she was so happy that she'd held herself together. What if she had clung to him and expressed all that neediness?

He spooned rice into wide bowls and added a ladle of the hearty stir-fry, then placed the bowls on the table, and as they began to eat—it tasted so good!—she found something she wanted to ask him that didn't have the sense of dependency and need she so wanted to fight in herself. "The other driver, Dev. I—I haven't felt ready to ask until now. And you know my family wouldn't bring it up without direct questions."

"No, they wouldn't. We've had a couple of discussions about that, too."

"I bet you have!" She folded her mouth into an upside-down smile. "Who was it? Were they injured, too? He? She?"

"He."

"What happened?"

Dev put down his fork. "He wasn't badly hurt. You don't need to know anything about him."

"You don't sound too sympathetic. What went wrong?"

"He was driving over the limit."

"Speed or alcohol?"

"Both."

"Ah, okay. All bases covered, then. A fine upstanding citizen." She gave another twisted smile.

He shrugged and opened his palms. "Exactly."

"And where is he now?"

"Tried and convicted. All you need to know."

"It happened and it's over, and now we just live our lives. That's it, isn't it?"

"Is that what you really think?"

She paused with the fork halfway to her mouth. Most of the food fell off. She was still a little wobbly with her silverware control. "Yes. Don't you?"

"Yes, I do. I was a little concerned that you might feel differently."

"That I'd want a vendetta? Or that I'd brood and feel bitter?"

"Many people would." He was leaning toward her over the table, studying her the way he'd studied her several times today. She knew why. How was this going to work? How would baby DJ connect or divide them? What did they both want? Could they manage to keep this free of conflict and misunderstanding and hurt? Everything came back to that. Everything they said to each other gave a potential clue.

"Well, not me," she told him. "I just like to get back on the horse."

"Mmm," was all he said.

But she could see something in his face. Relief and approval. It was something they shared, this attitude to the accident and how to process it, and that was a plus.

In life, you have to play the hand you're dealt. She believed this, and so did he. You can't waste energy in "if only" and regret. You can't go looking for bitterness and revenge.

Especially when she had other things to think about.

Like a baby she didn't know she'd had.

Like a baby she wouldn't recognize in the street.

Too hard. Way too hard.

She felt a surge of restlessness and fight, a need for the physical movement that was still so challenging, and told him suddenly, "I seriously do want to get back on the horse."

"The real horse?" She'd caught his attention again. "You want to ride your horse again?" They were both making slow progress with their meal. "Your thoroughbred? He's leased out, since the accident, isn't he?"

"Leased out, to another rider, Bec, who's a good friend and who would give him back in a heartbeat. She lives out near Pictonville, on forty acres. I could go see him anytime. He's not sold."

She'd been so happy to discover this. Elin had told her, "Even though Mom's never been a fan of your riding, even in the darkest hours when we questioned how much you'd recover, she wouldn't hear of Irish being sold."

But now Dev said, "A spirited thoroughbred, Jodie? Twelve hundred pounds of muscle with a back higher than your shoulder?"

"Of course not yet," she said quickly. "Not him. I'd ride Snowy or Bess."

"Who are they? Are they quieter?"

"They're our hippotherapy horses, at Oakbank. They're trained for people like me, disabled riders and riders with special needs. You wouldn't believe how patient and understanding they are. They seem to know exactly what a rider is capable of, whether they have cerebral palsy or a missing limb or autism. I want to ride again. I need to ride. My life just can't change that much." She had to blink back tears, and was shocked at the way her emotions had shifted so fast. "Dev, I know this isn't what we should be talking about. We should be talking about…about DJ, but that's too big for me right now."

He reached across the table and covered her hand with his. "Nobody said we had to work everything out in one night."

"No. Okay. Good."

"Just eat. Talk about horses, if you want."

"I think I should go home after we eat."

"So I'll take you home."

"Thank you." She was tired of saying the words, but it seemed as if there were a thousand thank-yous she needed to give, and at least half of them belonged to Dev.

Jodie was quiet in the car, and Dev didn't push. It had been a huge day, for both of them.

Certain things stood out from the mess of conflicting emotions. First, the fact that she had never been given a real chance to hold DJ. He didn't know if that was his fault, if he should have made space for it—*forced* it—in the highly charged atmosphere between himself, Elin and Barb. Second, her wobbly little question about whether they were dating. Last fall seemed so long ago to him, but to her it must be so much fresher.

Those nights together. They were vivid and real for him if he thought about them, but too much had been overlaid since, and he didn't think about them often. He hadn't been in love with her last fall, and he couldn't have fallen in love with her during her long sleep. This wasn't Sleeping Beauty or Snow White.

There'd been desire in their relationship, yes…a ton of it. Care, even. But "in love" meant forever, and he couldn't see it, he wasn't open to it, not with anyone. It didn't fit with the way he saw himself and his life, and it never had.

He loved his parents. He admired them. They were good people. But marriage had made them so slow and staid. They never left their comfort zone. They never seemed to want newness or adventure or zest. His mother said it to him sometimes, with a combination of smugness and resignation. "You'll feel differently when you're married…. You won't care about those things when you're married with a family."

He'd seen it with most of his married friends, too. They began eating at the same restaurant every week. "They do such a good veal parmigiano." They didn't renew their passport when it expired. "We won't really travel until the kids are in college. Well, Orlando, of course, for the theme parks."

If marriage meant losing the capacity for curiosity and courage and adventure, he didn't want it. He'd decided this at twenty and nothing had yet happened to make him change his mind.

Not even DJ, because how would it be good for her, to submit to an institution he didn't want to belong to, purely for her sake?

All he wanted was to know that she was loved, so he could get his own life back on track and stop existing in this limbo of uncertainty.

He wondered what would be happening at the Palmer house. When he pulled into the driveway there was no visible light in DJ's room. The night-light would be too dim to show from the street. Was she down for the night? Should he take her home?

Jodie hadn't even touched her yet. Had he been wrong to let Barb and Elin whisk the baby back here? Should he have just ordered them to leave? He didn't want the conflict that came with their differing interpretations of what Jodie needed. He wanted to see the bond between Jodie and DJ, but he was scared of it, too.

Scared of its potential power.

He jumped out of the car and came around to open her door and help her out. For a moment, she looked as if she might protest, but she was clearly too tired to manage on her own. The doctors and therapists had said it would be like this. The difference between what she could manage when she was fresh and what she could manage when she was fatigued might be huge at first.

Sure enough, her body looked heartbreakingly awkward and frail in the passenger seat, and after several seconds of intense, futile effort, she told him, "I can't."

He bent down. Slid his arm beneath hers and around her shoulders. "Hold on."

But she couldn't do that, either.

"I'll carry you."

"Dev, no, I'm—"

"You're wiped."

He shifted position, one arm coming beneath her thighs. It was incredibly awkward, and if she hadn't been such a featherweight, he couldn't have managed it. Once he'd straightened, it was much easier. She laid her head against his shoulder, with her hip pressing into his stomach, and he felt this surge of tenderness and confusion and determination.

Somehow... *Somehow*...

Somehow, what?

What did he have the power to do? To make her get better? To make her come to the right decisions about her future? What were they?

"You can put me down now."

"I'm fine. You don't weigh much."

"Please." There was an insistence to it, the old stubbornness about her size and strength that had made him smile and piqued his interest at eighteen. How did such a small body house such a strong spirit?

Gently, he let her down, still holding her firmly until they both knew that her feet would carry her weight. They did, but there wasn't a whole lot of margin for error. "I'll need to lean," she said.

"Leaning is fine." Leaning was *too* fine, really. He liked touching her too much, felt too connected to the scent and softness of her skin. He had to fight to keep his awareness under control, with the slight weight of her breasts just above his hand and her silky fall of blond hair in kissing distance.

They'd agreed on this. They weren't dating. There was no place for this helpless attraction. Just imagine if they had a flaming purely-for-the-sex affair and then parted in conflict and anger. It happened all too often. Sex didn't solve anything. It had too much of an agenda of its own.

And where would that leave him? Shut out of DJ's life forever? Or limited to a hard-won weekend visit every three months, exchanging her back and forth in the parking lot of a service-plaza fast-food restaurant halfway between here and New York as if she were a packet of cocaine? Meeting her at the airport, once she was old enough, and discovering she'd become a school kid or an adolescent or an adult since they'd last met?

No. It wouldn't be enough. No!

He wasn't going to be forced back to New York by the sheer strength of Palmer will.

Barbara Palmer stood in the open doorway, having heard the car. She looked watchful and anxious, as if expecting them to have covered major mileage tonight in their talks about the future.

They hadn't.

They'd barely talked about DJ at all. More about horses, in fact. And no matter how much Dev told himself to go with what Jodie needed, to give her time and space, it worried him a little. He didn't want to lose his daughter to her mother, but he wanted her mother to love her. Anything else was unthinkable.

"Did you have a good evening, honey?" Barb said to Jodie.

She thumbed cheekily in his direction. "I never knew he could cook."

"Are you okay? You look—"

"Tired. Of course. But I'm fine." She managed the steps into the house. In some ways she was better on steps than on the flat ground. "I think I'll go up right away."

"She's asleep," Barb said.

But Jodie hadn't been talking about seeing DJ. From the side, Dev saw the little look of fright and reluctance on her face and said quickly, "We'll take a look at her, though, Barb." He still had his arm around Jodie's body and could feel her stiffen and flinch.

Barb had seen nothing, it seemed. She began, "You're not going to—?"

"No, I'll leave her here for the night," he reassured her, "if that's okay."

"Of course it is! Of course you shouldn't wake her and move her!"

"But we'll take a look, make sure she hasn't kicked off her covers." He pretended he couldn't tell that Jodie didn't want to.

Why didn't she?

Well, the hugeness of it. It made sense, maybe. She just needed that first bit of ice broken, that first sense of confidence in her new role, that was all. Maybe right now, if they just went into the baby's room together and watched her sleeping, something in her heart would open and settle.

He didn't give her a choice, just took her with him, helping her up the stairs, opening the door of Elin's old room, which was as familiar to him now as if it had once been his. Beside him, he heard Jodie's quick, shaky intake of breath, as if Elin's door was the gateway to a whole new kingdom.

Chapter Five

Mom had used Elin's room as a sewing den for years but hadn't redecorated since Elin moved out. In Jodie's memory, the walls were still painted a defiant, brooding purple and were covered in posters of Elin's teen heartthrobs—John Cusack, Michael J. Fox and Johnny Depp. Actually, Elin in her teens had had pretty good taste.

Now, though…

There was a ballerina night-light plugged into the socket low on the wall beside the crib, Jodie saw. It gave off a quiet, pinkish light, revealing a room utterly different to the one she'd always known. Gone were the purple and posters, to be replaced by walls of a soft golden yellow with a theme of ducks and daisies in the scattered groupings of toys and decorations. There was a crib made of blond wood, with linens of white *broderie anglaise* cotton, a white closet, chest of drawers and shelves, and in just a couple of places there were color accents in a light sage-green.

On the chest of drawers sat the baby monitor, its glowing light showing that it was switched on. But there was nothing to hear. Baby DJ was fast asleep.

Dev went across to her as if drawn like a magnet, his feet incredibly soft on the polished hardwood floor, a grin breaking onto his face in a way that told Jodie he didn't even know it was there. He had Jodie's hand trapped—not trapped, *held*—in his, so she had no choice but to go with him. He leaned over the crib and didn't say a word, just gazed, and Jodie's heart began to thump and her throat tightened, and the baby…the baby…

Didn't belong to her.

Was gorgeous, an angel, a sweetheart, a darling.

A stranger, when she should have been Jodie's whole world.

She knew this, because she'd seen it just today with Maddy and Lucy. Beyond the new-mother panic, or as a *part* of the new-mother panic, Maddy had been utterly mesmerized by Lucy, utterly in love with her. The way Elin had been with her firstborn, and her second and third. The way Lisa had been with hers.

Transformed.

Mothers to their bones.

The way Dev was already a father to his bones. A daddy. DJ's daddy. "Isn't she beautiful?" he whispered, as if he couldn't keep back the words.

"Yes. Yes, she is." She learned the baby's little face off by heart—the button of a nose, the plump cheeks—and thought, *at least I'll recognize her now...*

"I'm sure she won't wake up if you touch her."

"How? Where? I mean, I really don't want to wake her up."

"You won't. Anywhere."

Where would I touch her if she belonged to me?

Jodie didn't know. She reached out her hand, and felt Dev holding her tight as if he knew she might otherwise fall. She thought she might put her hand on DJ's head, to see if her hair felt as silky as Lucy's, but it didn't feel right. It felt…

Not her head.

She laid her palm on the baby's back, instead. She was sleeping on her side, propped in that position with two little baby quilts rolled up, so Jodie had to slip her fingers between the roll and the stretchy fabric of DJ's miniature pink sleep suit.

"She's breathing, I promise," Dev said.

"Oh, I wasn't— I was just—"

"It's okay. I didn't mean— It's okay. I check that she's breathing all the time."

But she didn't feel as if it was okay, and took her hand away. She wasn't strong enough to keep her arm in that position for long anyhow. It would start to disobey the signal from her brain pretty soon and just flop.

Flop onto DJ and wake her up.

Mom was hovering outside, peering around the door, which Dev had left ajar. "I thought about putting the monitor in your room, honey, but that's probably not a good idea just yet," she said in a kind of stage whisper as Jodie and Dev came out. "It would be hard for you to get out of bed quick enough to go to her."

Would I need to go to her that fast? Jodie wondered. Do all normal moms leap out of bed the second they hear the first tiny cry? What about in the dark, ancient days before baby monitors were invented? How fast did moms get to their babies back then?

She could argue the issue. She could insist on Mom letting her have the monitor.

Dev had gone watchful again, but she hid her panic, made it about common sense instead. "Yes, you'd better have it, Mom. I'd hate to…you know…" She indicated the common-sense issues with a flap of her fingers.

I'd hate to only reach her after that big spotty monster hiding under her crib had already drooled all over her. I'd hate no one to get there in time to catch her reciting Shakespeare in her sleep.

"I know. I think you're right. I'm sure that's the best decision," Mom said, as if it were momentous, like deciding on risky corrective surgery, or what college DJ would attend. "We can keep it that way as long as you want. Well, when she's sleeping here, of course."

Dev said nothing.

"I've done a spreadsheet," Barb announced when Dev arrived back at the Palmers' house the next morning.

"A spreadsheet?"

"I can do one every week. Here's a copy I printed out for you. The schedule has gotten more complicated now that Jodie is home, but see the color coding?"

Dev took the page. Yes, indeedy, he could see the color coding. Yellow for Jodie's hours at day rehab, blue for DJ's naps, even though she wasn't nearly as predictable in that department as the spreadsheet suggested. Green apparently meant DJ at Devlin's and he didn't like the scattered nature of those color blocks. So he was only having her two nights this week? Whose idea was that?

Barb had said to him some weeks ago, when Jodie's recovery began to unfold with such positive signs, "Now you'll be able to go back to New York," and he couldn't get those words out of his head. Did the Palmers want him to go? Did he?

Meanwhile, where was pink for Dev, Jodie and DJ go to the park? Or, better, lilac for Barb, Elin and Lisa get the hell out of town for a few hours so Jodie can make up her own mind about what she wants to do with the baby?

In fact, he couldn't see one color block or notation in the schedule that gave Jodie any time with DJ on her own.

"I mean, it's just a draft, obviously," Barb said, reading the disapproval in his face.

He said in apology, "I'm not a huge fan of spreadsheets, to be honest."

"But you must use them all the time, in your work."

"People put them together on my behalf. And I file them in the cylindrical file." He mimed balling a sheet of paper and tossing it in the trash.

"You throw them *out?*"

"Spreadsheets can make you feel like you're organized when really you're not, don't you think? Like bullet-point presentations. I'm not a fan of bullet points, either." He dropped the flippant tone and spoke gently, because despite everything, he was becoming fond of his daughter's grandmother. He knew she meant well. "You know DJ won't nap to a schedule, Barb, so why pretend about it on paper? We don't know how much time Jodie's going to be spending with her at this stage. Can't we keep it flexible?"

Barbara pressed her fingertips to her temples. "I'm just trying to manage this situation."

"I know. And I appreciate it. But I don't think a spreadsheet is the answer. Where are they, anyhow?"

"DJ is in her bassinet on the deck. I just gave her a bottle. Elin was helping Jodie in the shower, but I think they're done."

"So Jodie's upstairs?"

"Let me call her. I'm sure she hasn't come down."

He hesitated. It bothered him that Jodie wasn't with the baby, and yet why should it? What did he expect? He'd been so afraid of the opposite happening, of the love kicking in too fiercely and possessively and shutting him out, and now he'd done a full turn-around and wanted to push the other way.

It wasn't logical. *He* wasn't logical. He was a mess of conflicting wants—to go back to his real career in international law, yet keep the strongest possible bond with DJ, to see Jodie discover her love, yet for that love to be generous when it came to his own needs.

Jodie had huge needs of her own. She still struggled to manage dressing and showering and the most ordinary day-to-day things. She was so brave about it. Brave and funny and stubborn. She couldn't have taken over all of DJ's care even if she wanted to.

Did she want to? This was the crunch, the big question. Was she holding back from DJ in order to work harder on her own recovery, or because she couldn't cope with suddenly being a mom?

"I'll go up," he told Barb.

"I'll be in the kitchen, if you need me," she said. "You'll…say the right things, won't you?" Her face twisted with worry and he felt his frustration build. What did Barb want from him? It would help so much if she could just relax a little.

He found Jodie in her room doing some range-of-motion exercises for her arms and legs. She wore calf-length black leggings and a strappy white tank, little more than a scrap of stretch fabric and lace. The swell of her breasts peeked above the neckline of the tank, and the leggings made her tight, round butt seem even tighter and rounder. Dev had trouble keeping his gaze where it belonged.

But there was a serious point to the stretchy clothing. She was working hard. There was a sheen of sweat across her forehead and her collarbone, and she lifted her top away from her stomach to let in some air. "Nothing's working this morning," she said, slightly breathless. "Starting to come back a little."

"How about doing them on the deck?" He didn't like the way she was shut in her room like this, with DJ out of sight and out of mind.

"I guess that would be okay."

She managed the stairs on her own, while he went a few steps ahead of her, ready to brace her if she fell. When they reached the deck and she saw the bassinet with its lacy white canopy, she froze for a moment. She hadn't known until now that DJ was out here. "Oh, right," she murmured, then began to grab the air with her hand as if seeking something solid for support. Dev helped her get comfortable on the built-in wooden bench that ran along the railing and went to peek at his daughter.

She'd woken up. The wicker of the bassinet creaked a little as she tensed her body and let out a whimpering cry. She writhed, as if her digestion was bothering her, but then her gut settled and she blinked a few times and looked up at the view. Dappled leaves. Dev had learned that small babies, when awake, just lo-o-ove to look at dappled leaves with a background of sky.

Ooh, and here's something else they love to look at—their daddy. She caught sight of him and her face broke into the darlingest smile in the world. "That's right, sweetheart," he whispered, and smiled back. He was pitifully in love with her, and "in love" meant forever, and he didn't even care.

Jodie was watching him, he could see, distracted from the exercises she'd been so dedicated about up in her room. He felt a thud of sudden vulnerability—all that fear of the unknown where DJ's future was concerned.

He had to bite the bullet.

They both did.

Jodie had to have her first hold.

He didn't give her a choice today, just picked DJ up—she was wearing a stretch-cotton smock dress with tiny blue flowers on a white background, and matching bloomers—and brought her across. "Here, why don't you take her for a bit?"

"I—I— Now?" Jodie stammered.

"Yes, but you need a couple of cushions, right?"

"I think so."

"I'll grab some." He was more than capable of managing a baby and two cushions at once. He'd recently managed a baby, a poopy diaper and a handful of wipes with a phone pressed to his ear at the same time, talking international law. He settled the cushions on either side of her.

"Can you…? I'm leaning, I think."

She was right. Her body had slipped a little on the bench. He sat down beside her and nudged her bare, pale shoulder with his.

"I hate this," she said.

"*Hate* it?"

"No… No!" she corrected quickly. "Not the baby! Not her. My body. The fact that sometimes I'm not co-ordinated enough to sit straight, by myself."

"Right. You'll get there."

"I know. But it's frustrating." She sounded wobbly. Scared. Maybe she didn't hate the idea of holding the baby, but she definitely had issues with it. Because she didn't trust her body?

"I would never let her fall," he said, and lifted the baby across.

This is my baby. To Jodie it still didn't seem real. *This is my baby, in my arms.*

DJ didn't seem to consider this event to be miraculous in any way. She looked up at Jodie, fixing her gaze just below her hairline. She didn't smile. Her eyes were a dark, swimmy blue and she had translucent blisters on her lips from sucking on her bottle. The neckline of her tiny dress was still a little damp from where some of the formula had leaked from the corners of her mouth. She felt heavy.

No, it wasn't the weight, it was the tension in Jodie's muscles. "I didn't feel this tired, holding Lucy yesterday," she said.

Dev had risen and moved away. He stood on the far side of the deck, beneath the thickest shade from the black-cherry tree, watching her to check that she was all right. "You were in a chair with armrests for that," he said. "And Lucy's a little lighter than DJ. Can you not manage it? Let me know if—"

"No, I want to." Something kicked inside her, a stirring of tenderness and love. But it wasn't strong enough. It wasn't the overwhelming certainty Jodie wanted it to be.

I love her, she said inside her head.

No, that wasn't quite right.

She tried again. *I love you!*

It was true. She knew it was. But she couldn't *feel* it. She looked down at the baby, smiled at her and learned by heart every crease in her little arms, every strand of her hair, but she couldn't *feel* her love.

Those swimmy blue eyes looked up at her, so serious and unsmiling and somehow so wise and *old.*

She'll see it. She'll feel it. She'll know.

She still wasn't smiling. Jodie tried to coax it out of her by showing her how. She stretched her lips, crinkled her eyes. *This is your mommy smiling at you, DJ.* But it didn't work. DJ didn't smile back, and Jodie knew why.

You couldn't tell lies with your own body. You couldn't fake love coming out of every pore of your skin. Lying here in her arms, DJ would soon know that this person, this mommy person who was supposed to have such a total skin-to-skin bond and connection, didn't yet love her in the right way, and she absolutely *must not* be allowed to know that.

Jodie broke into a sweat. "Can you take her, Dev?"

"Or I could give your arm some more support."

"No, take her. I don't think more support would be enough."

"Here…" he said, and sat down beside her again, twisting around so that his left arm cradled hers and his chest shored up her shoulder. His strength and warmth and clean male smell slammed into her, seeming far more *right* than the feel of a baby in her arms. More real. Stronger. Could he feel it, too? She thought so. His breathing had changed, growing shallower.

She felt weak and shaky and tingling with need, all at the same time. Her body was far better at remembering familiar things than learning new ones, it seemed. Every cell and all her senses remembered last year so vividly. The way his touch and his laughter had set her alight, the way she'd felt strong and alive yet safe in his arms. The feel of his mouth making a hot trail from her neck to her breasts. The sureness in the way he caressed her, slipping his hand between her thighs, curving his palms over her butt.

Last year, he would have pressed his lips to her neck and teased her and set her on fire. She would have turned her face toward him and kissed him back, brushing her mouth against his and sliding it away, making him go after her and coax her lips into parting and drinking him in, and it would have lasted for minutes on end. She would have gloried in the feel of those hard muscles covered in satiny skin.

Their physical connection was magic and wonderful and made her dizzy.

Still.

But the new thing, the magic and wonder and dizziness of being a mother, her body couldn't learn. She couldn't even *fake* a smile now. No wonder DJ wasn't smiling back.

"I really think you need to take her now, Dev," she said shakily.

Mom appeared in the doorway to the deck. She was wearing a flour-spattered apron, and was brushing her hands against it, as if dusting them off in readiness to be of help. She must have heard the note of panic in Jodie's voice, the panic that Dev had ignored.

"No, see?" he said quietly. "You're fine."

"I—I think I'm not. I think I need a break. Can you please take her?"

He still wouldn't. Instead, he pressed his body more

tightly against her, curved his other arm over her shoulder to support her on the opposite side. Her back wasn't touching the bench at all now, it was only touching him, and she began to take calming breaths, giving in to his insistence and certainty.

Maybe she could do it, after all. Maybe with him here, loving his baby girl so much, the love would filter into Jodie as well, filter through her into DJ so that wise DJ wouldn't guess who it really came from. She could smell the mingled scents of both of them, Dev and DJ. Baby powder and milkiness and aftershave and warm male skin.

Mom stepped forward. "Dev, she says she's tired. Don't push it, please, until after we've talked to her doctors and therapists on Tuesday."

"Does that make a difference?" He slid his hand around the bundle of baby.

"Well, yes, doesn't it? They may have very specific guidelines about how much she's allowed to do."

"How much baby holding?"

"How much child care. How much of anything. She has a heap of exercises to get through every day. Just brushing her teeth..." She bent down, and Jodie could smell that, too—flour and vanilla and peaches. Mom must be making a pie.

She picked up the baby, cradling DJ's head against her shoulder. Dev loosened his supporting grip and she saw him rake his lower teeth across his top lip in a gesture of unspoken frustration. There were so many pairs of arms in this little baby's life, reaching out to her.

"Let's bring her bassinet inside," Mom said. "It's getting too hot out here now. Maybe she could lie on her blanket on the lounge-room floor and have a kick. She loves that. I'll get her baby gym, too. She was really hitting those rattles the other day."

"Thank you, Mom," Jodie said.

Just as had happened last night, Dev didn't say a word.

Chapter Six

"Is there anything more you want to talk about at this stage, Jodie?" asked Dr. Reuben on Tuesday morning.

Everyone waited for her response. Mom, Dad, Elin, Jodie's physical and occupational therapists, the neurologist and the obstetrician who'd delivered DJ nearly twelve weeks ago.

And Dev.

DJ herself was at home with Lisa. She and Elin were both schoolteachers, with the summer off, which Mom had pronounced to be a blessing. Jodie wasn't so sure. Dev seemed restless about the baby's absence, moving as if his empty arms needed filling, although Jodie herself had agreed there was no point in bringing the baby in for this meeting.

"No, I think I'm fine. For now," she said brightly. "I mean, you've all said I can call, talk to anyone about anything at any time. You've said—" she turned to the obstetrician, Dr. Forbes "—that my body recovered very well from the birth itself, and that there's no reason why I shouldn't conceive again in the future."

She bit her lip. Why parrot this back to him, this reassurance about her future fertility, when she hadn't even begun to deal with the baby she already had? She couldn't think of the right things to say. She couldn't think of *anything* to say.

"You're doing very well indeed," the man said.

He was older and a little distant, somehow exactly the kind of man you would expect to have delivered a baby you'd had no knowledge of until two days ago. The kind of man who would have looked after Jodie's physical well-being perfectly and professionally during and after the birth, but who would be rather glad that her emotional adjustment now was an issue for other professionals, such as Dr. Reuben, to deal with.

She felt stubborn and protective and private about it, suddenly. She didn't want professionals helping her to learn to love and take care of her baby, she wanted to do it, like a three-year-old, All By Herself.

Even though she'd already proved to herself that she didn't know where to start.

Trish and Lesley, the therapists, began to speak, stressing the importance of keeping her rehab on track in other areas. It couldn't all be about the baby. Jodie would have to put her own needs first. "It's what they say on airplanes," Trish said. "First, fit your own oxygen mask, then assist your child. If you're not taking care of yourself, how are you going to look after a baby?"

They all seemed to feel that this was a huge risk, that Jodie's own therapy would be derailed by her tiring herself out with her child, attempting one hundred and ten percent.

"I have plenty of help," she managed to say. "I think I'm going to be sensible about it. I know how much love DJ already has, even without me."

Trish and Lesley seemed to approve. Then Trish repeated, "But is there anything more you need? Anything you want?"

Anything I want? Anything I need? I want to love my baby. I want to be the one who knows when she's hungry or tired or hurting. I want to be the one who can soothe her to sleep. I want her to know in her bones that I'm her mom, but she doesn't know it and I don't know how to teach her. She responds to Dev and Lisa and Elin and Mom but not to me, and I'm scared about that.

So scared, she couldn't begin to express it, especially not with all these eyes fixed on her face—the professional gaze of the therapist, the more personal ones belonging to Dev and Mom, trying to hide their concern but without success. Her whole life felt wrong and mixed-up, compared to last fall, before the accident. She remembered one of her last horseback rides, a trail ride through the woods belonging to Oakbank Stables with some intermediate riding students, the hooves of the horses soft on the carpets of newly fallen leaves.

That day, everything had seemed right with the world. The sweet secret of Dev and their plans to see each other that night. The fresh, peaty smell of the woods. The clink of stirrups and bridles in time to the rhythmic movements of the horses.

"I need to see my horses," she said.

It wasn't what Trish or Lesley had expected. Dev and Mom, maybe, but even they didn't understand, she could tell. They thought she had her priorities all wrong. Horses, when she had so much work to do on her body? Horses, when she had a baby to learn to love and care for?

Dad shifted in his seat, and made a gruff sound, but said nothing. He could take her side sometimes, but when he stayed silent, she never knew what he was keeping back. Approval? Or the reverse?

So she backpedalled, ashamed and guilty and scared. "Not yet, of course. I mean, I know that. It's not a priority. But when it happens, it'll do me a world of good, I know it."

"We'll certainly work toward it," Trish promised. "Hippotherapy is a definite possibility for you, given your background." She looked at Dev and Mom, who both nodded. "But that's not what we're here to talk about today."

Jodie understood that she'd gone off-topic, that her therapists and doctors were focused on her adjustment to the baby and the fact that she'd given birth. "I—I really can't think of anything else for now," she told them lamely.

Dr. Reuben and Dr. Forbes both shifted in their seats just the way Dad had, busy schedules dictating that they make a move to the next patients on their lists.

"Thank you," Jodie said to them, and everyone stood up.

Thank you was incredibly useful, she'd begun to discover. You could make it mean so many different things. You could fob people off with it and they never guessed. She thanked Mom for the spreadsheet she'd printed out, even though they weren't sticking to it. She thanked Lisa for her words of experience regarding diaper rash, even though she—Jodie—hadn't done a diaper change yet. You could use it as a piece of very effective camouflage against revealing what you really felt.

The fear.

The doubt.

The distance.

The shame.

She said it again, just to make sure. “Thank you.” And everyone nodded and smiled and murmured and told her she was doing incredibly well.

For the next three weeks and more, *thank you* worked like a charm.

She said it to Dev when he picked her up and took her to the park with DJ and did all the carrying in the baby swing and the strapping in and out of the stroller so that Jodie barely needed to touch the baby—or Dev himself—at all. She said it to Mom and Lisa and Elin when one of them took her to rehab while another took care of DJ at home. She said it to Dad when he carried DJ in her car seat or filled her little plastic bath.

Maddy called from Cincinnati to suggest coming up with Lucy for a mommies-and-babies play date, and Jodie said that rehab didn’t leave enough space in the schedule right now, but thank you for thinking of it, it was a great idea for sometime down the track. Trish said that Jodie could have the baby at rehab sometimes and they could work on some strategies for taking care of her safely within Jodie’s current limitations. Again Jodie hid behind “thank you” and “down the track.”

If anyone noticed that she’d only actually held DJ in her arms twice since that first time on the deck, they didn’t comment. DJ commented, in her own way. She didn’t smile. If anyone noticed that both those smileless times Jodie had to fight an overwhelming feeling of distance and inadequacy and panic, they didn’t comment on this, either.

Or not to her face, anyhow.

Three weeks and four days after her discharge from the hospital, a Wednesday, she caught them commenting behind her back. She'd been taking a nap—this napping business was getting old fast—after a tiring but encouraging day at rehab, when she heard the front door open and the voices of Dev, Lisa and Mom. Moving with the necessary slow precision across her bedroom rug and into the carpeted corridor, she was too quiet and they didn't hear her. She'd only been asleep half an hour, a shorter time than usual. They wouldn't expect her to surface for another hour.

It was the same old line, from Lisa. "I just don't think she's ready, that's all."

"But what's going to make her ready, Lisa?" Dev's voice, low and intense, an emotional, threatening growl that did something to Jodie's insides every time she heard it. "Do you think I was ready, when DJ was newborn? I'd never held a baby in my life. Isn't it only doing it, doing the hands-on with no one to step in the moment you have the slightest episode of not coping, that makes you ready as a parent? You do it, you have to do it and you learn. You live it, you can't imagine life without it and the love kicks in."

"The love?" This was Mom. "She loves DJ! Of course she does! You can't be seriously suggesting she doesn't love her own baby, Devlin!"

"I'm not sure that you're letting her love her, Barb."

"That's not true!"

"I appreciate that she mustn't be overloaded, but do you ever let her feed DJ? Or hold her in the bath?"

"That's not the point!"

Jodie stood with her hands on the stair rail for support, hearing it all. She wanted to tell Dev that it wasn't

Mom's fault. She wanted to say, "Hey, I'm here! Let's discuss this face-to-face, not when you think I'm asleep because you think I can't handle it."

But maybe they were right. She couldn't handle it. She wasn't handling it. The love hadn't kicked in.

"She's working too hard on her rehab, for one thing," Lisa said. "You know what she's like. One of her riding instructors, when she was about twelve, said she had more guts than a slaughterhouse."

"Oh, Lisa!" Barb wailed.

"Yeah, graphic image, but I'll never forget that and it's true. She's an incredibly brave person, and she's exhausting herself with work on her exercises."

"Because she wants to be strong enough to take care of DJ," Mom argued. "Which she isn't, right now. She's told me. She's afraid of letting her fall."

"She's too tired to take care of DJ." Lisa again. "She needs a break, just some time out. From everything."

"I think you're right," said Mom. "Time out. How can we do this?"

"Dev, leave the baby here and just take her out tonight, or something," Lisa said. "Take her to dinner. Take the pressure off. You want her to take more of the load off your hands—"

"It's not about the load," he interrupted. "Do you think that's what this is about? That I want to be able to hand DJ over to her and get the hell out? Shoot, that's the opposite of what I want!"

"I'm not saying that." Lisa stopped, then added in an abrupt tone, "Well. I don't know. You're going back to New York, aren't you?"

"Look, that's a decision I can't make yet."

"You had made it, I thought."

"When we weren't certain she'd ever come out of

the coma. When she was so sick. Of course I wasn't going back to New York if I had a daughter to raise on my own. The situation's changed now, hasn't it? Everything's negotiable. All I know is, I'm not going to be shut out."

"Okay, but I'm assuming—" She cut herself off again. "I don't want to pressure you about the status of your relationship when it's none of my business."

Dad passed through the hall at that moment, and offered, "You got that right!" before he kept right on going, on his way out to mow the lawn.

"It is our business!" Mom said. "It's about DJ's future, and Jodie's well-being. Is there a relationship, Dev?"

"Of course there is. We're the parents of a child."

"You know that's not what I mean."

"Yes, I know it, but that's the only answer I can give you right now."

"We're going around in circles." Lisa gave a sigh that traveled all the way up the stairs to Jodie on the top landing.

"We are," Dev said. "But taking her to dinner is a good idea, and I'm happy to do it."

Lisa kicked into action at once. "I'll make a reservation. How far are you willing to drive? There's that gorgeous new French place in Fairfield—La Brasserie. If you cut across through the back roads, it's not too far."

"And I'll run DJ's bath," Mom said. "By the time Jodie wakes up, she can have the bathroom to herself to take a shower and get ready. It's still early. If you make the reservation for seven, Lisa. That way Jodie's not out too late."

"Isn't La Brasserie a little too—?"

But they didn't let Dev finish. "Make it special,"

Lisa insisted. "Make it a milestone. A new start. She's off the walking frame. She's already so much stronger and better than she was a few weeks ago. She knows we're here for her. And she's always fought so hard to be independent and to achieve her goals. If she's not fighting us for more hands-on with DJ, it's because she doesn't feel it would be safe. When she's ready, I know my baby sister, she'll say so! She'll absolutely insist!"

Thank you, Lisa.

Was it true, though? It would have been true, before the accident, Jodie knew. Now, though… Would she absolutely insist?

"You're right," Mom decreed. "She will."

Jodie started carefully down the stairs. "Are you guys making plans for me?"

Mom looked up at her. "Oh, you're awake already?"

"Just now. It's great, isn't it? Down to one nap, most days, and it's getting shorter."

"We're sending you and Dev out to dinner," Lisa said. "DJ's staying here."

"Can I help with her bath?" She caught the covert, meaningful looks Mom and Lisa exchanged that seemed to say, "See? Jodie's absolutely insisting."

"Of course, honey," Mom said.

But they didn't let her, not really. Dev went home to shower and change. Lisa made the restaurant reservation. "La Brasserie, Jodie, it's gorgeous. You wouldn't have been there, since it's new." Mom ran the water, testing it expertly with her elbow to make sure it wasn't too hot.

"Let me get her undressed," she said, "because that's tricky."

Jodie stood back and watched as the little wriggly arms came out of the stretch cotton dress, looking so fragile and small and wobbly it seemed as if one wrong move from Mom's expert hands and the arms might break.

Jodie hissed in a horrified breath at the mental image and Mom turned to her with a question in her face.

"It's okay," Jodie said quickly. "Just glad you're doing this bit."

But then Mom did the next bit as well, sliding DJ into the bath and scooping the warm water over her perfect, satiny, slippery skin.

"Doesn't she ever smile in the bath?"

"Ooh, no, bath is way too serious for that," Mom cooed, gazing down at DJ, her own smile as gooey as a marshmallow. "She used to shriek, at first, but she likes it now. Don't you, sweetheart precious?"

"H-how can you tell, without her smiling?"

"Look at her splashing her little arms and wriggling around." Mom was still beaming, her hair damp around her face, a damp patch on the front of her blouse and two pink spots on her cheeks. She looked as happy as a young girl, but she also looked deeply tired. She was sixty-five years old, with forty years as a parent and seventeen years as a grandmother already under her belt. How much longer could she keep this up?

I have to start learning.

"Could I shampoo her hair?"

"Of course." Mom took a step to the side. She kept hold of DJ, while Jodie pooled a tiny amount of baby shampoo onto the round head with its water-slicked hair. She massaged it in, her coordination still jerky. Mom cradled the little head in her cupped palm to keep it steady.

"I don't think I'd better rinse it off," Jodie decided. "I might get shampoo in her eyes."

So Mom did that part, also, then picked her up and wrapped DJ in a towel and sent Jodie for a clean outfit and a fresh diaper. "Just one of her little playsuits, in the second drawer. This is what Maddy used to do for you when you were newborn and she was seven, choose your outfits after your bath."

Great, Jodie thought. *My child-care capabilities are those of a seven-year-old. I'm so proud.*

But it wasn't funny. It hurt. It shook her up. And she couldn't talk about it because that would only shake her up more.

Dev appeared at six-thirty, because Fairfield was a half-hour drive away. Jodie had spent nearly an hour getting ready, and in this area there was genuinely something to celebrate because she didn't need help with any of it now. She could get her arms into both sleeves. She could manage the whole shower. Lipstick and mascara were another story, but this was easily solved. Her face was cleansed, exfoliated and moisturized, but makeup-free.

She met him at the front door and his expression seemed to approve the swirly print dress and tiered jacket, which she had teamed with flat shoes in basic black because managing killer heels at this stage would have made managing lipstick seem easy. He looked so good himself, in dark pants and a lightly patterned button-down shirt, freshly shaven and his hair still a little damp around his neck from the shower.

They'd both dressed as if it were a date, she realized. Was it a date?

But no, they'd answered that one already.

"How's DJ?" was the first thing he said to her.

"Oh, great. Asleep. I gave her her bath. Well, helped."

"Did you?" She could tell he was pleased, and felt

guilty that she'd overstated her involvement. What was that really about? Wanting to make him happy? Or hiding her own distance and fear?

He put his arm around her back as they walked to the car. To an outsider they would have looked like a standard pair of new parents, taking a well-earned break for couple time while Grandma babysat. It was such a long way from the truth. Such a long, long way.

Dev had a glass of red wine with his meal but Jodie kept to plain water. "I'm not putting anything into my body that's going to interfere with my control."

It made sense, yet still he told her, "You can let go a little, can't you?"

The idea of this evening had been to relax her, but so far it hadn't worked. He could see her intense concentration on managing the meal, to the point of twisting the pepper grinder over her chicken all by herself when the waiter was eager to do it for her.

He could see her making the right kind of conversation, too, refusing to rehash today's milestones in rehab and instead dragging in current events and politics and celebrity gossip as if this were a neurological examination. Could she remember the name of Scarlett Johansson's latest film? Could she keep track of this summer's star players in baseball and golf?

"I want to progress," she answered.

"You won't, if you push too hard. You'll get overloaded and go backward. Was this dinner a mistake?"

"No, it's great." She squeezed out a smile.

"It's not what you need," he said on her behalf, because he could suddenly see this, and knew she wouldn't say it herself.

"No, you're right, it's not." Her face fell. "I thought maybe it was, but—"

"I'm sorry. It was Lisa's idea, and I know how much she cares about you and wants you to get strong."

"They all care about me. It seems to blind them, sometimes. It's always been this way, and it's so hard to fight it when I'm fighting with everything I have just to use a damned fork without messing up!"

She blinked back tears of anger and frustration and all he could think was *Hell! Hell!* Out loud he said, "But that's them. Your family. This is me. You can tell *me* what you really want and need, can't you?"

There was a pause and he could see her struggling, pushing things back deep inside. A familiar fear surged inside him. What might she say? What would he do if she wanted him out of her life completely?

She had no right to insist on it, since he was DJ's father, but how much of a battle did he want, with his innocent daughter as the winner's prize? Would he take her to family court over it? Hell, he dreaded anything like that. He knew that the law could make custody issues worse as well as solving them, especially when the matter crossed state lines.

She pressed her lips together and he knew she'd decided to keep something back, and yet when she spoke, he could see it was going to be important and honest, even if it wasn't the whole truth. "I want to go to Oakbank. I want to see the horses. And ride. People are acting as if that's something trivial, something to think about down the track, but it's not, it's something I want now. It was so much a part of my life. Way more a part of my life than—" She stopped, flooded with color and pressed her lips together again.

He understood and said it for her. “Than being a mom. Because you weren’t one.”

“I l-love her.”

“I know you do. Of course you do.” How could she not? He loved her to pieces.

“I want to take care of her, but I’m scared, and Mom and my sisters… They’re so experienced with babies. I need to go back to something I used to do well. Even if I can’t do it well anymore, I just need to…be a tiny bit of that person again, for a while, or else I can’t learn—I won’t learn to be the new— This doesn’t make any sense.”

Oh, but it did. Shoot, it did. Dev felt he’d been blind, and fallen into the same trap as her family. Not really listening. Not seeing her real needs. “I’ll take you tomorrow,” he said.

“It doesn’t have to be—”

“Tomorrow,” he insisted. “We can spend the whole day there, if you want.”

“Rehab—”

“Rehab can wait. This is rehab. I’ll call Trish and tell her what’s happening. I’ll call my office and have Marcia cancel my appointments for the whole morning. No arguments, okay, Jodie?”

But she wasn’t planning to argue. Her face had lit up. Her eyes were shining. “Thank you, Dev. Thank you so much for not being like my mother and my sisters.” She had some color back in her cheeks now that she’d been able to spend a little time outside and the contrast of that smile and that skin and that blond hair took his breath away.

He remembered the way she’d felt leaning against him a few weeks ago, the first time she’d held their baby, so warm, so focused, yet shaky and uncertain, bringing out a kind of tenderness in him he'd barely known could exist. If he could have cut off his own leg to have her fully healed and complete and strong the way she used to be, he would have done it.

"You're welcome," he said, and she must have heard the huskiness in his voice.

Chapter Seven

Driving to the restaurant, the summer evening had still been bright and hot, but now it was dark, a kind of misty blue darkness with a big yellow moon rising in the east. The last time she'd been out driving with Dev in open country in the dark, Jodie realized, was the night of the accident. Oddly, she wasn't scared about it. Maybe because she had no memory of the accident or the drive.

They came around a swoopy bend, the same kind of bend they must have come around that night, with forest on both sides. An oncoming car swept past them, going fast. She heard Dev swear beneath his breath. He was thinking of that night, also.

"Do you remember it?" she asked him. "I mean the—"

"I know what you mean. Yes, I remember it. I was conscious the whole time. Let's not talk about it."

"You were thinking about it."

"Can't help it, sometimes."

"Like now, when someone speeds past the other way."

"Yes." Gritted teeth.

Oh, Dev. It shocked her to think of how much he'd been through. She hadn't thought of it this way before—that her long sleep had been a protection, in many ways, while Dev had suffered through the accident, suffered the agony in his leg echoing the agony of uncertainty, not just for that one terrible night, but for months afterward. Would there be a healthy baby? Would the baby's mom ever wake up?

She put her hand on his arm. Ole Lefty, which wasn't always fully responsible for its actions. She pressed and gripped too hard, and he took his eyes off the road to look at her, and slowed the car. She could see the suffering in his face, the surge of memory. His hands were clenched and shaking on the wheel.

A turning appeared just ahead, a side road with a sign that shone brightly when the car headlights hit it. *Deer Pond Park.* He took it without a word and slowed even more, taking his foot off the gas pedal as if he didn't trust himself with the vehicle's power.

The parking area was deserted. The car rolled to a stop in the farthest corner, with Dev's arms slumped over the wheel. The engine died. "I'm sorry," he said, his voice thick as if he was fighting nausea. "It just...hit me. Hell, I'm shaking. And when that car just now— It wasn't even really speeding. It was a family minivan, for heck's sake."

"I shouldn't have talked about it."

"It wasn't your fault. I was thinking about it already. It's the first time I've driven on a dark country road."

"In so long?"

"Couldn't drive at all for the first few months, because of my leg. Since then, I've been pretty busy sticking close to town." Taking care of a baby. Watching her mom wake up.

"I'm an idiot."

"No." He shook his head, ran a still-unsteady hand down his face as if to wipe the emotion away.

"I am. 'It's not always about you, Jodie,'" she said out loud, with bitterness, mocking herself.

Dev opened the car door. "I need some air. For a minute. But this is not your fault. Let's not do that to each other."

He slid out into the fresh night air, walking away from the vehicle, lacing his fingers behind his head so that his elbows stuck out. She heard him breathing, big whooshes of air blown out through rounded lips. He circled back and leaned his thighs against the hood of the car, looking out over the moonlit pond just yards away, still blowing those careful breaths.

She scrambled out of the vehicle and went to him. "Dev..."

"You were lying there," he said, the words torn from him as if by a force he couldn't control. "I could barely reach you to touch. Just my fingertips. Couldn't do anything for you. I could see blood in the dark. I could hear the other driver yelling and moaning. Crying on the phone when he got himself together enough to call 911. I didn't know... I thought you were breathing but I wasn't sure. And my leg was trapped. And shattered. They had to cut us out. It took three hours."

"Oh, Dev..."

"I'm sorry." He pressed his fingers into his eyes. "Your family didn't want me to tell you all that."

"No. They wouldn't."

"I'm sorry."

"Don't do that to me, Dev, don't treat me like a child, the way they do. I'm not. I'm a grown woman. A strong woman. And I'm— I'm—" She didn't know how to finish.

In your debt, forever.

Here for you, forever.

Words weren't strong enough.

Touch just might be.

She reached for him, running her stronger right hand—the one that she might actually be able to control—up his arm. She rested it on his shoulder, beside his warm neck, and leaned her body close. "You're amazing," she said. "You've carried this load of memory all on your own, while I've been free."

"I guess I did need to talk about it." He was still shaking a little, not from weakness, she guessed, but from the effort of holding everything in. She didn't want him to hold it in. Such tightness and control would surely kill him.

Let go, Dev, let go.

Not fully aware of what she was doing, she began to soothe his muscles with her touch, the way her own muscles had been massaged back into life with physical therapy. She knew all those movements so well, by now.

That's better. That's good. Let go, Dev.

He let out another shuddering sigh and wrapped his arms around her. She felt the warmth of the car hood from the hot engine, and heard it begin to tick as it cooled.

"When the paramedics arrived and confirmed you were alive, this rush of relief, I can't describe..." His voice rumbled against her chest, his breath making a heated caress in her ear. "And then they gave me drugs for the pain and I had this hallucination. I thought we were in a shipwreck, floating in a lifeboat with sharks circling in the water, the only two people left in the whole world. All I could reach was your hair. I held on to it...."

He showed her, taking a soft handful in his fist. She could feel his thumb resting, light and warm, on the back of her neck. He moved a little, bringing his cheek against hers. It was a little rough, so familiar, so good. She turned her head and pressed her lips there, because she couldn't stop herself. He sighed and she felt his mouth against hers, kind of soft and absentminded as if he weren't really here. He was still back in that horrible night.

"That was all I could reach," he repeated. "And then they cut you free and took you away. And it was just me and the sharks." He laughed.

"Wasn't funny at the time," she whispered.

"Nope."

"Wish I'd been there."

"I'm glad you weren't."

"Well, I'm here now." She took his face in her hands, and her hands did what they were told as if they wanted this, too. She pressed her lips to his forehead and then—because she couldn't help it, she was so overwhelmed with feeling for him, with a sense of all the power that connected them—to his mouth.

Oh, Dev. Oh, Dev.

He kissed her back, hungry about it, desperate. His mouth was almost too hard against hers, and he crushed the breath out of her lungs, leaning into her. She had to ease him away, but, oh, not too far.

Yes, Dev, if kissing you helps to let go...

I'll kiss you for whatever reason you want, for every reason there is.

Their two mouths melted together once more, sweet with the chocolate that had finished off their meal. He let go of her hair and moved his hands down to cradle her backside and pull her closer, the swirly skirt of her dress falling against his legs.

She could feel his arousal and he didn't try to hide it. He wanted her to know what was happening, and he couldn't be in any doubt, himself, about what this was doing to her. Her body came alive, her senses reborn. Even the texture of his shirt seemed magical. The woodsy male smell of him. The dark fan of lashes against his cheek that she glimpsed when her eyes drifted open.

She touched him, her hands not fully controlled so that sometimes her grip wouldn't let go or her hand would land in the wrong place. There weren't any wrong places, really. Everywhere felt right. His hip, the top of his thigh, his shoulder blade.

And then it got serious.

He slid his hands beneath her top to touch her bare skin and she wanted those hands on her breasts. He must have known. He dragged his mouth away from hers and trailed it down, pulled her summery jacket from her shoulders and traced the neckline beneath it with his lips. The straps of her top and cream lace bra fell against her upper arms.

He lifted her breast in his cupped palm and breathed a warm breath against her peaked nipple, ran his tongue around it and sucked, released, kissed, sucked again. A fire of pleasure and need stabbed down into her groin, and her body told him *keep going, we are so good at this, both of us.*

She reached for the fastening of his pants, but couldn't make her fingers work. They scrambled helplessly and in the end she just left them there, curled against his stomach, while she kissed her way down his chest then pushed her forehead into the hard, flat place between his hips. Through the textured fabric of his pants, she felt the push of his erection against her mouth.

"No..." he groaned, pulling her up. "I want you closer."

"That's not close?"

"I want you like this...." He pressed himself into her, kissed her mouth again.

"Yes, oh, yes." She tried his fly again and did better this time. The button came through the hole, the zipper eased down.

"We can't do this," he muttered, but he didn't mean it.

"I want to." She always did, when it was Dev. Always. Something about him. No explanation. Just chemistry. "Do you?"

"Hell, do I? How can you ask?" He straightened from his lean against the car hood and flipped her around in one twirl of a movement so that she was the one leaning. The engine was still warm. He cupped her bottom again and lifted her higher until she sat on the smooth metal. "It's not going to be pretty."

"I don't care."

"Good. Neither do I."

Maybe it wasn't pretty, but it was beautiful—dark and moonlit and beautiful. He grew patient, as if there were no hurry in the world now that they'd agreed on what they wanted, and just kissed her for a long, long time. Her mouth. Her shoulders. Her breasts. Touching her everywhere. Teasing her deliberately until she was almost whimpering, wanting him so badly, swollen with it, more than ready.

Of his own readiness, there was no doubt. His erection nudged at the apex of her spread thighs, hard and hot. She wrapped her legs around him and he slid her skirt until it bunched at her waist, then pushed aside the triangle of fabric at her crotch. They were doing this fully clothed, and that was just fine.

Fully clothed.

He had his wallet in his back pocket and it carried protection. She held him while he rolled it in place, running her fingers over the taut skin across his lower stomach, brushing the small, tight buds of his nipples through his shirt.

When he entered her, she was as smooth as silk around him, tight with her own need and he filled her so completely that she gasped at the first thrust. Oh, Dev. Oh, Dev. Yes. She clung to him, legs and arms shaking with effort, and he guessed it would have to be quick or not at all.

The car rocked and Jodie sobbed. He pinned her with his hands, stroked her with his hardness until the night exploded. She was a little ahead of him and took him with her, shuddering with gut-deep sound.

Yes. Oh, yes.

They were both breathless. He laughed and held her hard, and maybe she should say something. *That was amazing.* But it seemed trite and so obvious. Hell, yes, it was amazing. When had it not been amazing with Dev? So she just laughed with him and kissed him clumsily. He was just as clumsy, kissing her back.

"You can make a man forget, can't you?" he said.

"That wasn't the reason for it."

"No, I know, but it helped. It was good, Jodie."

"Good?"

"Amazing."

He sounded humble, which was how she felt, too. Humble because she didn't know what happened next. Didn't know how to ask. Didn't know *what* to ask.

Are we dating?

They weren't. They'd agreed.

And yet there was this. Stronger than ever.

He'd gone very quiet, very still.

"I'm not allowed to drive yet," she said, even though he knew this perfectly well.

"Are you asking if I'm okay to drive?"

"Don't particularly want to have to call one of my sisters to come with her husband and ferry us home."

"We won't have to do that. Just give me a minute."

"Have lots of them. As many as you like."

"Not too many, or we'll get a phone call asking where we are."

"Mmm, true, and Deer Pond Park probably wouldn't be a good answer."

"No."

They giggled like teenagers, and she thought, just as she'd thought last year, *don't spoil this, Jodie, don't try to nail exactly what he thinks and feels. Life is so precious. You almost had it taken away. Don't spoil this, when it's been…*

Amazing.

Dev made it back to the Palmer home without cracking up at the wheel. His whole body tightened and went on high alert, heart racing and sweat breaking out, every time a car went past, but he made it, breathing out a sigh of gratitude when they left the dark country road and came beneath Leighville's street lighting. He sighed again when he turned into Barb and Bill's driveway.

Jodie fell against him a little as he helped her out of the car. She often did. It was nothing new, something she couldn't help because of that weakened left side of her body. This time, though, he pulled her against him and kissed her sweetly, because he didn't want her to think he'd just closed the book after one quickie on the car hood in a deserted nighttime parking lot.

It wasn't supposed to be a long kiss, but he couldn't help himself. Lied to himself about it, in fact. Told himself it would be just one more moment of sensing her sweetness and grace, just one more moment of smelling her clean skin, tasting her peachy mouth. He didn't intended it to last long. Just one more sweet touch, that was all it would be.

But he couldn't stop. He tried. Took his mouth away in a brushing movement that only made him want to go back again, and go deeper this time.

Oh, so much deeper, the way he had twenty minutes ago in Deer Pond Park.

He ran his hands over her neat, sweet backside, made into the perfect rounded shape from her years of riding. He brushed the undersides of her breasts with his fingers. He slid his thigh between her legs and felt the silky swish of her dress fold around him in a way that mimicked the much more intimate kind of folding he'd so recently known.

It seemed incredible that his need could mount again so fast.

And she kissed him back. There was no doubt in the world about that. She lifted her face, parted her lips, shaped her body to fit against his so perfectly that she could be in no doubt about what his was doing to him. Again.

"One thing my body can still do," she whispered.

"Yes, oh, yes," he whispered back, his voice raspy with need. "You hadn't been scared about that before tonight, had you? Scared that it couldn't?"

"I hadn't thought. I hadn't considered—"

"Of course you hadn't." He brushed her mouth again, teased her lips with his tongue, cupped her head in his hands.

But the moment had changed. The whole Palmer family was inside the house, and Jodie had remembered the fact. She hadn't asked Dev what it all meant, back at the park, and he was glad about that because he wouldn't have known what to tell her.

"This isn't a good idea right now," she said.

"I'm sorry."

"It wasn't just you."

"I started it."

"I let you."

"You're not really strong enough yet to push me away."

"Oh, you think?" She did it with a cheeky smile, a nice shove to his chest—a little clumsy but very well-directed—and began to steer herself firmly toward the house, the shoe sole on her weaker side brushing the paving with a light rasping sound.

The front door opened, and Barbara appeared. For a moment, Dev wondered if she might have seen that steaming kiss. Lord, he shouldn't have let himself! It should never have happened! It hadn't *needed* to happen when he'd kissed her so thoroughly—and done so much more—in the moonlit park.

But Barb's face seemed untroubled, and he had no

doubt that she would have looked and behaved differently if she'd been watching them from the window. "Elin said you were home. You're a little later than we expected. How did it go, honey?"

"Major victory with the pepper grinder. Slightly challenging drive home in the dark, on the country roads. That's why we're home late. We took it slow."

Some of it they took slow, Dev amended to himself, fighting back his awareness of everything she hadn't said. Some of it they took at magical, erotic speed.

"And I'm cutting class tomorrow," Jodie finished.

"Cutting class?"

"Dev's taking me—" She stopped and corrected herself. "Dev's taking *us* to Oakbank."

"Us?"

"Me and DJ." Her voice wobbled a little at the end, and there was a little note of triumph in it, too. Dev heard it, and was so happy she wanted to bring the baby, too.

Barb looked at him. "Dev?"

"I think it's a great idea," he said firmly. But he knew from Barb's face that she wasn't going to let him off the hook that easily.

Chapter Eight

Elin appeared at Dev's front door just as he was about to head upstairs to bed, after some mindless TV to wind himself down. For the first three seconds, he thought it was about DJ and the strength drained from his legs. It was after eleven at night. His little daughter had been fast asleep an hour ago when he'd left the Palmers, just a few blocks away.

But this was anger on Elin's face, not panic. "We need to talk," she said.

She was a strong woman, a good six inches taller than Jodie and more heavily built, with the weight of her three children starting to gather around her hips. She had Jodie's blue eyes, blond hair and wide smile and Dev liked her a lot, but he didn't particularly want her here on his doorstep with such a hostile look on her face, and arms folded in a way that said she meant business.

"Come in." What else could he say?

She launched in before she'd even crossed the threshold. "I heard your car in the driveway. I was in DJ's room picking up a load of laundry. I looked out the window to see how Jodie was managing the climb from the car. And I saw what happened." The accusation was crystal clear.

"Right," he answered. What would she say if she knew what had happened half an hour before that? He shuddered to think. "Would you like coffee, or something?"

"No, I wouldn't. I'd like to know what the hell you think you're doing with my sister."

Pretty obvious, wasn't it?

Unfortunately, however, Elin was right. He knew it as he'd known it all along. He hadn't absorbed a second of the TV murder mystery he'd just watched, because he'd been thinking about tonight instead. He should never have kissed her, let alone sat her on the hood of his car, pushed her pretty skirt up to her hips and—

Yeah.

Had that shattering episode of flashback to the accident done so much to destroy his good sense? Or was that only an excuse?

He sighed between his teeth. "Okay, you don't have to tell me."

But Elin told him anyhow. "She is so vulnerable right now! She has so much to deal with and to work out."

"Don't I get a share in that?"

"A share in what?"

"The vulnerability, the stuff to deal with."

"All the more reason I shouldn't have to say this, Dev. You have no right to add any kind of complication whatsoever, and especially not that kind. Can you honestly tell me she's in the same place she was in last year—or that you're in the same place—when it was okay for both of you to have a no-strings-attached relationship with a use-by date of three months? Can you honestly tell me DJ doesn't make a massive difference to the equation?"

"No, I can't. You're right."

"Are you going back to New York?"

"You'd like me to, wouldn't you?"

"What makes you say that? Is that an accusation?"

"I guess it is, Elin. I think you and Barb would sometimes be only too happy to have me out of the picture, now that Jodie's recovering, because it would simplify everything, wouldn't it?"

"It would, if you're going to start messing with my sister's emotions. I'm not having that, Dev, I'm just not. Are you in love with her?"

"Don't ask me that."

"I'm her sister and I care about her."

"It's not fair. You're right, we shouldn't have kissed. And yes, I'm phrasing it that way because you must have seen that she kissed me back." *And if you could have seen her in the park, gasping when I suckled her breast, arching her back, clinging to me and moaning...*

"She's vulnerable."

"I know. It won't happen again."

It couldn't. It was too big a risk.

That pang he'd felt just now when he thought DJ might be ill… Imagine if Jodie tried to shut him out because he'd slept with her and messed with her emotions and she couldn't forgive. Imagine if he lost his daughter because of one piece of very male loss of control. His whole body ignited in Jodie's arms, but his head and his heart had to rule right now. His body didn't get a vote.

"So you're not in love with her?"

"I don't even know what that means, Elin."

"Sure you do."

"I care about her." Otherwise why the heck would he be busting his gut to help her bond with her baby, when it could so easily backfire on him? It didn't make sense.

"You'd damn well better!"

"We have DJ. I don't want conflict. I want whatever we decide, long-term, to be the best outcome we can find for DJ."

She snorted, part pacified, part bristling and protective. "If I think you're going to hurt her…"

"I would never hurt my daughter."

"My sister. I know you wouldn't hurt DJ. That's the only thing that's stopping me from hitting you right now." She bracketed her hands on her hips. "But if you hurt my sister…"

She didn't finish, and he didn't dare to make a promise he might not be able to keep. Sometimes it just wasn't in one person's power to stop the other person from getting hurt. The idea of hurting Jodie… Well, it hurt *him*, it made his chest go tight and his breath catch. But that didn't mean he had the power to prevent it.

"I hear you, Elin," he said wearily. "You've said the right things. I won't forget. I'm glad you came."

The weather was perfect, with a breeze from the northwest making a rare break in the summer's humidity and heat. Jodie couldn't have wished for a better day. Mom and Elin had both said they wished they could come to Oakbank with her, but they had errands to run this morning and Jodie wasn't sorry. The idea of being alone with Dev and DJ frightened her the way it always did—two very different reasons, there—but it was still less daunting than the prospect of her mother and sister watching her like a hawk the whole morning.

DJ was awake and happy when Dev arrived to collect them, to Jodie's relief. It meant he focused on the baby, on cooing at her and picking her up. It gave both of them a distraction and a way to keep their distance from each other after everything that had happened last night.

The unsuspected vulnerability he'd shown over his memories of the accident. The bone-deep need she'd felt to soothe his fear away. The explosive power of their lovemaking. On the hood of the car, for crying out loud, with both of them climaxing within seconds of each other, not caring that they were right in the open air, not caring about the previous agreement they'd made.

He regretted it.

Every word he spoke and every movement he made telegraphed the fact.

Minimal eye contact.

No touching at all.

When his body softened and his voice went tender, it was because of DJ. When he smiled, he smiled at his daughter, and she smiled back. It was the right thing, Jodie knew, the only thing. She should be grateful for it. Instead, she had to fight not to feel shut out. Still, DJ hadn't yet once smiled for her.

Mom and Dev had a little back-and-forth over whether he'd packed enough diapers, and whether she'd be sheltered enough from the sun. "She's too young for sunscreen," Mom said.

"I have a hat for her," Dev promised, "and the stroller's canopy shades her when she's in that."

"Wipes?"

"Right here."

"Pacifier."

"She doesn't like it."

"You mean you don't like it. You don't believe in them. But I raised all four of mine and they were never too attached—"

"I have a pacifier, Barb," he said patiently, "but she just spits it out again whenever I try it."

"It's not important, is it?" Jodie said, and they both looked at her, their frustration with each other spilling in her direction.

"Ready?" Dev asked.

"More than."

DJ was getting on for four months old now, and growing every day, her periods of alert wakefulness getting longer and her body strengthening as fast as Jodie's. You would scarcely know that she'd been born seven weeks premature. Dev strapped her into the car seat and they were away in just a few minutes, after those first awkward moments, heading west out of town to the rolling green hills where Oakbank's twenty horses grazed.

Their route covered part of the same road they'd taken on the way back from the restaurant last night, but it seemed so different in the daylight, none of the menace and memory, and they turned onto a different road before reaching the sign and turnoff leading to Deer Pond Park.

Oh, Oakbank was so familiar and so well-loved and she'd forgotten so much of it, but it all came flooding back, every fresh sight and sound. The gravel of the long driveway entrance popping beneath the tires, the lush shade of the summer-clothed trees, the white-painted fences, the loom of the big red barn as they turned into the parking area.

Behind the barn, beyond a screen of greenery, was the manager's cottage she'd been living in at the time of the accident. Katrina and her boyfriend had it now, although they hoped to buy their own place soon, apparently. Jodie's family had moved all her things back to Mom and Dad's after the accident because no one had known if she'd ever be able to return to her little home. She'd recovered so much better than they'd all feared, but still it might be a while before she could live independently.

Independently…

On her own?

Her and DJ?

She couldn't picture it, tried to imagine herself and a baby in the manager's cottage, but it was such a scary idea. Her fine motor control would have to improve a heck of a lot before she could even think about it. The thought came with a flood of both relief and guilt.

So don't think about it, Jodie, think about just being here right now instead.

She saw a string of kids on horseback heading out on a trail ride with members of the summer staff at the head and tail of the group, and realized they must be a batch of vacation day-campers. There was another group doing a beginner lesson in the outdoor arena, where morning shadow still stretched across the sand from a line of cool oaks.

Anna and Katrina, the two full-time riding instructors, knew she was coming. Dev had phoned this morning from his place. They came hurrying out as soon as they saw her climb from the car, and she had to blink back tears as she hugged them both.

"Oh, it's so good to see you!"

"We wanted to visit more...."

"We're so glad you're here."

They'd each come to visit her once in the hospital, but hadn't seemed to know what to say. She'd been a little hurt at the time. They couldn't have come more often? They couldn't have stayed longer, and talked more?

Now, of course, she understood how hard it must have been. They'd known about the baby, but couldn't talk about it because of the medical decision that Jodie herself wasn't yet recovered enough to know. She felt their apology about all those unsaid things in the warmth of their greeting, and something inside her eased a little.

"And I'm so glad I've come," she said. "It's the best thing. Do—do you want to see DJ?"

Dev was unstrapping her carrier from the back of the car. She'd gone to sleep, lulled by the journey. "Can we bring her inside first?" he said. "The sun's so bright." He draped a soft flannel blanket over the top of the carrier handle to shade her.

Anna and Katrina led the way, and Jodie almost kept up with them, she felt so strong and energized just by being here.

The barn was cool and quiet, its wide end doors flung open to catch the fresh breeze. Clean sawdust covered the arena, horses poked their heads over the half doors of their stalls and there was Bess, saddled and working, walking patiently down one long side with a child holding the reins and a therapist by her side.

Dev put DJ's car carrier on one of the bleachers that overlooked the arena and took off the flannel blanket. Anna and Katrina both bent over the carrier, clucking and cooing at the sight of the sleeping baby. "It's incredible, Jodie," Anna said.

"I guess it seems so right and natural to you now," Katrina said. "But we're still in shock. She is beautiful."

"And you are amazing."

That word again. Dev had said it last night.

"I don't feel amazing." And if they knew that it didn't feel right and natural at all with DJ, if they knew she still hadn't smiled at her…

"No, you never do," Katrina said, "but trust me, you are."

"Tell me that once I'm in the saddle!"

"You really want to ride?"

"Katrina, have you ever known me to *not* want to ride?"

"Holly's about to finish her session," Anna said. "You're next."

"Oh, that's Holly?" Jodie looked at the girl in the saddle. "Wow, she's grown since I last saw her!"

Holly had cerebral palsy, and had been coming to Oakbank for hippotherapy since she was six years old. She adored her riding lessons, and had shown significant improvement in muscle tone and coordination over the past four years. As always, she slid down from Bess's back wearing a huge smile, put her arms around the horse's neck and kissed her. "I love you, Bess."

Jodie hung back a little, not knowing if Holly would recognize her after ten months of absence and so much change. Her hair was shorter. Her body moved so differently. She was thinner and so much of her athlete's muscle tone had disappeared. Jodie didn't think that she looked actively *scary,* or anything, but still…

"Say hi, Jodie," Dev prompted. "I don't think she's seen you."

"I— Yes, okay. Of course I'm going to say hi. She's a great kid."

But the moment had gone. With the therapist at her side, Holly had started toward the arena's opposite exit where her mother was waiting, already full of news about her ride. "Did you see me trot, Mommy? I was on the correct diagonal the whole time."

Oh, well, there'd be another time. Jodie walked up to the patiently standing horse. "Hi, Bess," she said softly.

Bess turned a big brown eye toward her, and gave a satiny little prod with her nose. Recognition? Probably. Horses had good memories. Jodie rubbed the horsey face gently, fighting to keep her coordination so that it felt good on Bess's shaggy cheek. "There? Is that okay? Is that how you like it, Bessie-girl?"

Katrina brought a mounting block, something Jodie had never needed before. Then, remembering, she proclaimed, "My helmet!"

"Here," said Anna. She'd crossed the soft sawdust with barely a sound. "It's been hanging on the hook behind the office door this whole time."

"Need help?" Dev offered.

"I'm fine." But it was tricky, and in the end she couldn't manage the helmet's plastic catch and had to accept his offer. His fingers brushed her jawline and the tender skin beneath her chin as he fastened the clasp and she closed her eyes, thinking of last night. Was Katrina watching? Could she see…?

See that I'm thinking about kissing him, about feeling him inside me.

It had kept her awake for far too long. The need and wanting. The powerful body memories. The regret. Why had she let it happen? Why had his vulnerability caught so strongly at her heart? Why hadn't she found a different way to respond? How could her awareness of him surge so fast when she had so much else to deal with? It didn't make sense. She didn't want it.

And she didn't want one simple brush of his fingers to take her back to last night with such immediacy and power. The clasp snapped into place and she stepped back, unsteady but very relieved.

"Ready?" Katrina asked.

"Not sure how we do this."

"You've helped other riders a thousand times, Jodie." Kat's voice was an odd mix of deference and encouragement. She was five years younger than Jodie, and had begun working here part-time at seventeen, when Jodie was twenty-two and already a well-qualified riding instructor. Their relationship of mentor and student had changed, too, because of the accident. "You were the one who taught me how to assist a rider with special needs, remember?"

"Different when it's me. Different when my legs don't work right. Can we talk it through?"

"Of course." Katrina talked her through each movement, where each hand and foot went, when she would give a boost.

It felt wrong, and then as soon as she arrived in the saddle, she was at home. "Oh, Bessie, you good girl!"

The horse's broad back was alive and warm beneath the saddle, her mane shaggy in front. Jodie reached forward and ran her fingers awkwardly through it, while the familiar horsey smell rose to her nostrils. "Are you going to lead me, Kat?"

"Yep, if you want."

"I haven't been led on a horse since I was seven years old!"

"Well, I could set up a show-jumping course for you,

with twelve fences and five-foot-high rails, but you'll have to give me a few minutes for that."

"Okay, just for you, we'll save that for the next ride," Jodie said.

It was so weird and at the same time so good. Katrina led Bess at a walk, and the horse's rocking rhythm was more even and steady than Jodie could yet manage on her own legs. This was one of the benefits of therapeutic riding. It gave people a sense of the natural rhythm of movement that they might never have experienced on their own.

Soon she was smiling broadly. Her family had never understood her passion for horses. Where had it come from? No one knew. No one else shared it. No cowboys or rodeo riders in the family history, that they knew of. But somehow it was just there, growing in her bones from when she was seven years old and had taken her first pony ride on the woolly back of a chubby Shetland pony.

Sitting on Bess now, she felt like *herself* for the first time since the slow slide out of her coma, and it was so wonderful to discover that the old Jodie still existed somewhere inside her, even if her body couldn't show it yet.

I'm me. I'm still me.

And I'm a mother. I have a baby girl.

"Could DJ come up here with me?" She didn't even think about it, just said it.

The baby was awake now, Jodie knew, because she could hear the start of some little fussing sounds coming from the car carrier. Dev had turned a couple of times to check on her. She was getting bored, all the way over there on the bleachers. Maybe she couldn't see her mommy riding, from so far away, and wanted to take a closer look.

Katrina asked Bess to halt. "Could she? I think it's up to you, Jodie. You know better than me that Bess is the safest horse in the world, and she's not depending on your cues with the reins. You want to sit DJ up there and hold her?"

"Is it okay with you, Dev?" It felt strange to be looking down on him. He stood there, watching her intently, head a little tilted to one side, eyes narrowed. She must have shocked him with the idea of having DJ up on a horse at less than four months old, but not a bad shock, apparently. He was thinking about it, not rejecting it.

Jodie held her breath. *Please agree. Please. Just say yes. Don't question it.*

If he wanted to know why it was so important, she knew couldn't explain in words.

"She does seem to be getting a little bored over there." He'd echoed her own thought. "You think she's going to be a pony gal, like her mom?"

"Hope so!"

He gave a brief nod, didn't say anything out loud, then began walking in DJ's direction. A minute later he'd unstrapped her and brought her over. She was wriggling, sitting up in his arms. She was reaching the same kinds of milestones as Jodie herself. Growing stronger. Becoming more alert.

"How is this going to work?" Dev asked.

"Could you hand her up to me? And then keep ahold of her, just in case? I'll sit her here at the front of the saddle so she's leaning against my stomach. If you just put a hand on her front…"

"Should work," he agreed.

DJ seemed to like the idea. She was waving her arms,

taking happy little breaths and making sounds. Katrina stood beside Bess's head, stroking her nose and cheek and telling her, "You're getting another passenger, but she doesn't weigh a whole lot. Is this a first for you? I think so."

Dev lifted DJ up and settled her against Jodie's front. Jodie wrapped a hand around her middle and found Dev's hand there already, as she'd asked. Their fingers touched and laced together because there was no room for them to do anything else, and the downy back of DJ's little head bumped gently against Jodie's stomach.

With Dev's other arm behind her on the saddle, she felt so close to him. Closer, in some ways, than she'd felt last night with his hands and mouth on her breasts. He could have pillowed his head against her thigh by moving just an inch or two. She remembered what he'd said that first evening at his place, when she'd learned the truth about DJ's birth. *We're a family.* For the first time, with Bess's warm, living strength beneath her, and DJ and Dev both so close, she actually believed it might be true.

"She seems real excited about this," Katrina commented.

"Is she smiling, Kat?"

"No, not smiling, but so alert. Are we standing still, or walking?"

"Walking," Jodie answered. "Ready when you are, Kat. Dev, are you? Will you be able to keep pace in that position?"

"I'm fine. She is really happy, look at her, she's bouncing."

"Still not smiling? I can't see."

"Serious, still, but so eager. You're not missing anything by not seeing her face. It's her body doing the talking."

"Oh, it is, I can feel it. Oh, DJ, you're so happy, aren't you?"

Not smiling, but maybe just as good.

Katrina clicked her tongue and told Bess to walk, and the wonderful rocking motion of the horse began again. Her hooves barely made a sound on the soft sawdust, and when they passed the big open doors where the sun came streaming in, her brown coat gleamed. DJ bounced and made her cooing and gurgling sounds. Dev muttered, "Just managing to keep up, here" beneath his breath, and then, a little louder, said, "She's loving it. Isn't she?"

All Jodie could say was, "Oh! Oh!" Her face hurt from smiling, and her vision blurred with tears.

I'm holding her and it feels right. We're on a horse together and she loves it. She feels like my daughter. My very own daughter. For the first time. I can feel it. I can feel what Dev feels about her. If only I could see her face! That's the only way this could be any better. I never understood. I never knew this was how it could feel.

Oh. Oh.

There were just no words.

I must not let her see how scared I am, Dev thought.

It was perfectly safe. He knew it with his head. His heart couldn't feel it. DJ? His precious baby girl? Fifteen weeks old and on a horse, five long feet from the ground?

But he could see what it was doing for Jodie and that made the fear unimportant. It was such a beautiful sight. Jodie's smile. DJ's excited bouncing, her little mouth open but serious, her hands batting in the air. The horse so slow and steady and patient.

He had to walk almost leaning against the warm equine body in order to keep one hand in place against DJ's stomach. The other hand he rested on the back of the saddle, an inch from Jodie's rounded backside. She'd worn stretchy jodhpurs, sand-colored, because that was what she always wore for riding, and man those things looked good on a woman's body!

His half-side-on position gave him a perfect view of the rhythmic rock of her hips in the saddle, and the only thing that stopped him looking too long and hard and thinking all sorts of forbidden thoughts about last night and those rocking hips on the warm hood of the car was the better view he got from looking higher up, where the big, teary-eyed, dazzling grin on her face just wouldn't go away, and the slight crookedness and lack of control in her arms and shoulders didn't seem to matter at all.

"Oh!" she kept saying. *"Ohh!"* And kind of laughing and crying at the same time, while DJ sat pressed up against her and all that Jodie body language of reluctance about holding and touching her baby had miraculously gone.

He wanted to wrap his arms around her and plant exuberant smooches of congratulation all over her face. *You're amazing!* He wanted to soften those same arms and give her kisses that were tender and wondering and soft on her mouth. *You're amazing.*

This was what he'd been drawn to at eighteen, even though he'd never acknowledged or acted on it back then. This was what still drew him—the combination of fragility and strength, the petite body that had a warrior's fight in it, the determination and perseverance along with a huge, dazzling, sexy smile.

If this was his old life, in New York, he knew what his next move would be. Whisk her away somewhere so that this fizzing need inside him could find a happy release. Ten days in Paris, a three-day weekend in the Bahamas. It had worked for him, in the past.

He always picked the right kind of woman, sophisticated and high maintenance and impossibly well-groomed. Always had a great time, while in the back of his mind—and the woman's—the clock ticked and the objections mounted up.

He couldn't have spent his life with a woman whose grooming rituals took up two hours of every single day. She—a series of them, over the years—couldn't have spent hers with someone who read the international section of the newspaper every day like he was prepping for an exam and then actually wanted to *talk* about it. He couldn't have seriously fallen for someone who paid that much attention to shoes and whose voice went whiny and childlike the moment she didn't get her own way. A few weeks together, though…great.

He'd been smug about it, he now realized. He'd been far too certain and confident about his choices. The right kind of relationship, with the right kind of woman. He'd had it all sewn up, all his bases covered.

Jodie wasn't the right kind of woman.

But she was the mother of his child.

And he'd be stepping back from the whole situation as soon as she was able to take care of DJ herself, as soon as he trusted that they had the right arrangement in place. It was the only thing that made sense. It was—even though they never said it straight out—what her family wanted.

But hell, she looked fabulous up there, grinning from ear to ear, with DJ nestled against her front. He didn't want it to end.

His first inkling of the new arrivals was the sound of Barbara Palmer's voice. "Oh, sweet jeepers, and she has the baby up there, too!"

Before Katrina, Jodie or Dev himself could react, Barb and Lisa came hurrying across the arena. He couldn't see them fully, as Bess's body masked his view, but there could be no doubt about their attitude. Katrina told Bess to halt, which she obediently did, while Jodie had stiffened in the saddle and tightened her arm around the baby.

Dev tightened his own fingers, so that their two hands were knotted tightly together. He felt Jodie squeezing, and squeezed her back. *It's okay, they seemed to be saying to each other. We're in this together, and we're not going to apologize for any of it.* He came so close to laying his cheek against her thigh.

You're amazing....

"It's fine, Mom," she said. "Katrina has the horse, Dev has DJ, nothing bad is going to happen."

"It's not fine! How can you be so irresponsible with your own daughter? How can you even put this as a priority, coming here, at this point in your rehab? Getting on a *horse?* When walking and showering and brushing your hair are still so much of a challenge? How can you?"

"I thought you had errands this morning."

"Lisa called, and I told her you were coming here, and she wanted to take a look. I decided the errands could wait."

"Honey," Lisa said to her sister, "Mom's right, don't you think?"

She was already reaching up, standing on Bess's other side. Dev would have had to fight her for the baby, snatch the little body from Jodie's front with a rough movement, to keep her under his own control. He didn't do it.

"Never mind yourself," Lisa went on, "although that's bad enough. But to put a fifteen-week-old preemie baby on horseback?" She had DJ safely in her arms in a couple of seconds, and began to stroke her silky little head, kiss and hug DJ against her sun-darkened collarbone. She loved her baby niece, no doubt about that. She seemed genuinely shaken by the idea that DJ had been all the way up there on scary Bess's back.

"She liked it," Jodie said.

"Liked it? How could you? Project that onto her? I mean, seriously!"

"We could tell. It was clear."

"You are *projecting,* Jodie. I'm actually pretty angry about this! After we've been so careful, so worried—"

"Lisa, I promise you—"

"Honey, Lisa doesn't mean to sound so—" Barb began, cutting in.

Lisa shook her head back and forth. "Yes. Okay. I'm sorry. Not angry. Just questioning your judgment, okay? And your priorities. Sure, I mean, I guess it sounds great." She mimicked, "'Wow, I was back in the saddle four weeks after I came home from the hospital. My daughter started riding when she was less than four months old.' But it shouldn't be about your ego, should it?"

"It's not about my ego." Jodie's voice had grown strained and tense. The happy grin had gone. And the tears. She was frowning, dry-lipped. "Is that what you think?"

"It's what I thought when you tried to give my Izzy riding lessons when she was three years old. You wanted to turn her into a superstar in a few months, winning ribbons in show-riding competitions and heaven knew what else."

Dev felt his tension level climb as the argument grew more heated. He knew about siblings. He had an older brother in California, a criminal defense attorney, who could still push his buttons when they met up at family gatherings. *Just keep DJ out of it,* he wanted to say, but managed to press his mouth shut.

"That was ten years ago," Jodie was saying, "and I was only just starting out instructing. Izzy didn't like it and so we let it go."

"After she almost fell."

"She didn't *almost*. I had the pony by the bridle and he settled down in about five seconds. I had no idea you were still upset about that, after so long. And it was never about winning ribbons."

"I'm not still upset. I'm not." Lisa shook her head frantically again. "Just seeing you there with DJ reminded me, makes me question what it's really about. Photos for the Oakbank website?" She gestured behind her.

"Photos?" Jodie and Dev both looked where she was pointing, over at the bleachers nearest the office, and discovered Anna there with a camera.

Anna began to walk toward them, her movement a little graceless and awkward as if in apology for the tension she sensed in the air. "I'm sorry, did I do the wrong thing? I didn't want to interrupt and get you to pose, but you looked so great, I just couldn't resist grabbing the camera."

"Great?" Barb exclaimed.

"I didn't know Anna had the camera," Jodie said tightly, then turned to her friend and spoke in a bright tone. "But it's fine. Did you get some? I'd love to see them."

"So they're not for the website?" Lisa persisted.

Dev answered her. "Of course they're not for the damned website! And if they were…"

Had they not seen how Jodie had looked relaxed and happy and *herself* for the first damned time since she'd woken up, how she'd held DJ like a mother for the first damned time since she'd learned the truth about her pregnancy? Had they not even taken a moment to notice any of that before barging in? Would it be such a terrible thing to have a picture of Jodie and her baby girl on the Oakbank website, when she loved the place so much?

"I'm tired," Jodie suddenly announced. "My legs are starting to shake. I think I'd better call it quits for today."

"For today?" Barb wailed.

"Yes, I want to keep doing this. Get better at it. Move on from Bess to Snowy, and see how I go."

"You can't mean you're going to try to ride again the way you used to?"

"You said you hadn't sold Irish."

"Because I knew you'd want to see him. Not *ride* him. You'll never ride him, Jodie."

There was a sharp, painful silence. Dev could have shoved his daughter's grandmother facefirst into the sawdust floor, he was so angry with her. Nobody yet knew whether Jodie's recovery would be complete enough to allow her to ride the way she used to. How could Barb preempt the worst-case scenario like that? How could she shatter Jodie's hopes?

Jodie's jaw set hard and stubborn at her mother's words. "Then DJ will ride him instead. He's only nine years old. She can start on him when she's ten. She'll be a strong rider by then, and he'll be mellow as a lamb at nineteen."

"This is ridiculous," Lisa muttered.

"You got that right," Dev said, his own jaw painfully tight.

It was ridiculous that they'd come. Insane that they were creating conflict out of something that had been so joyful until five minutes ago. Ridiculous and insane and just plain insensitive.

He managed not to say any of this out loud. But he pulled DJ out of Lisa's arms. "I think she needs a diaper change."

"Kat, can you get us back to the mounting block?" Jodie asked in a strained voice.

"Sure, of course. You okay to get that far?"

"I'm fine. As long as Dev has DJ."

"I have her." He turned his back on Lisa and Barb, not certain which of them owned the greater share of his anger. He'd thought of Lisa as an ally, until now. Out of all of the Palmer women, she was the one who was least inclined to underestimate Jodie or overprotect her, the one who might understand that Jodie's bonding with DJ was incomplete and that they might need to try some pretty imaginative strategies to get things on track.

Like putting the two of them up on a horse.

But now he felt betrayed. She was the one who'd gotten Barb's blood up this morning. So Lisa had "wanted to take a look"? Wanted to sabotage the whole event, more like. He didn't doubt that her motives were good. Pristine and pure. She loved her baby sister. Maybe that long-ago episode with Izzy and the riding lessons really did still scare her, even if at heart she knew it wasn't Jodie's fault. The whole family loved her. But boy could love be blind sometimes!

He wanted to tell both women, "You have ruined the best moment Jodie has had since the accident." Even better than last night, because it was right, while last night, in hindsight, probably wasn't. He wanted to say, "You have set her back weeks with DJ. Maybe even months."

And there would be no second chances on those months. They would be the months when DJ would learn to laugh and sit up and look at picture books and maybe even crawl. They would be the months when her sounds would start to mean something to her, and when she would start to distinguish between the faces that looked at her with love and the ones that didn't.

If Jodie lost that little spark of love and rightness that had ignited in her today, when the two of them had sat on Bess together… If it didn't fan into a bright, life-long flame because Barb and frigging Lisa had come along and put it out…

Freaking hell, he would find that hard to forgive.

Chapter Nine

Maybe a real mother, a good mother, wouldn't have done it. Maybe it was the last thing a normal, good mother would have done, asking to have her tiny baby up there with her in the saddle.

Jodie thought about it all day, through the drive home with DJ and Dev, through the tense lunch of chicken salad rolls that her mother made for the two of them after DJ had had her bottle and Dev had gone.

She and Dev had barely spoken to each other in the car, so different from the mood last night when he'd revealed so much and she'd felt so much care. "Are you angry?" she'd asked him.

"Of course I am. Not with you."

She'd wanted him to say more, but he hadn't and she hadn't felt able to push. Angry with Mom and Lisa for interrupting? Angry with them for being right? Angry with himself? He drove less smoothly than usual, those strong hands sliding around the steering wheel, foot stabbing at the brake, eyes unreadable behind his sunglasses.

The powerful body language made her intensely aware of him, the way she'd been up on Bess, with their fingers twined together and his head so close to her thigh. She had to fight not to steal sideways glances the whole time, and itched to touch him, too, to place her hand on his shoulder or his thigh, in an attempt to connect. It wasn't a very obedient hand, though, Ole Lefty. It tended to crab into a tight claw, or twist its fingers at the wrong time. Even if she had dared to touch him, the touch would have turned out all wrong.

He wasn't just angry, but absent. Somewhere else. His thoughts ticked furiously—she could almost hear them—but she didn't know what they were about. They'd almost reached home when she ventured to say, "I guess we'll wait a bit before we try this again."

"Mmm?" Her words had pulled him back from a faraway place, it seemed.

"Before we go back to Oakbank," she explained.

"Look, I don't want to create a rift between you and your family."

"I know. I hate being at odds. They care about me. And they care about DJ."

"Yeah, Oakbank…" He was still deep in his thoughts. Oakbank apparently fit someplace in there, but she didn't know where.

"Well, here we are.…" she told him. Unnecessarily, as he was already turning into the driveway.

And now lunch with Mom, and DJ's spreadsheet-dictated schedule, and a quiet afternoon, when Jodie had half hoped to be at Oakbank most of the day, watching the day campers and group lessons, visiting her favorite horses in their stalls. The whole morning had left a sour taste, far more so than what had happened between her and Dev last night, and she questioned everything about it.

Lisa called in that evening, saying, "I'm sorry," before she'd even entered the house, and they sat in the kitchen together and drank glasses of iced tea. Mom had DJ out on the porch swing at the front of the house, and Jodie could hear the sound of lullaby singing.

"I think I came on too strong this morning," Lisa said. "I know I did. I was just so scared, that's all, when I saw you there, and with the baby."

"I was perfectly safe, Lise. I had Dev and Katrina right by me. Bess has been a fully trained hippotherapy horse for ten years, and she is incredibly well looked after so she doesn't get tired and sour. She is wise and perceptive and calm as a pond. I would trust her with my life."

"We're just a little worried about your priorities, that's all."

"I want to get as strong as I can. I want to put the accident behind me and start being normal again. And riding has always been so much a part of normal for me."

"I just question—" Lisa stopped, huffed out a breath. "Look, I'll just put it out there. How often are you going to blow off your rehab to go to Oakbank?"

"Don't say it that way. I didn't blow it off. Dev called Trish and she thought it was a great idea, as long as I was careful."

"We're just concerned. We care about you."

"I know. Just don't smother me, okay? I hate it."

"Is she fussing tonight? Is that why she's out on the porch swing with Mom?"

"Um, I think she's fine."

Mom had kept DJ to herself all afternoon, telling Jodie that she needed to rest "after that whole mess this morning." And it was true that she'd felt extra tired, emotional and not as capable as she wanted to be. She'd spent too much time trying to recapture the morning's wonderful, heart-melting sense of certainty about DJ and her own role, but she couldn't. Was it because the mood had been bruised so abruptly? Or was it her own fault?

She didn't want the baby to pick up on all her self-questioning. Horses had such an uncanny instinct about human emotions that they were practically psychic, so why shouldn't babies be the same? It meant something that DJ hadn't yet smiled at her. It hurt her and scared her and she didn't want to make things any worse. So she stayed away, and DJ seemed to have a contented, peaceful afternoon.

Dev hadn't called. The spreadsheet said he was supposed to have DJ overnight today, but the spreadsheet hadn't seen what had happened at Oakbank this morning, so it was even more out of the loop than usual.

"Anyway, I'm sorry," Lisa said again, repeating it and explaining her motives until this, too, felt like a form of smothering.

Mom came into the kitchen with DJ propped on her hip. She rubbed at the small of her back with her free hand as if it were aching, and every pore of her skin looked tired.

"Mom, give her to me," Jodie said, too concerned about that aching back and tired skin to remember her own fears and doubts until after the words were spoken.

Mom shook her head. "It's fine."

"Are you sure?" But, so help her, she felt relieved.

"She'll be ready to go down as soon as she's had her bottle, I think. Dev hasn't called, and he's usually here earlier than this. Is he coming, I wonder? Well, I'm not going to call him. If he wants her, he needs to say so, and if she's down for the night and he shows up, I'm not disturbing her."

"We're all tired," Lisa announced, as if it solved everything.

Dev arrived at the Palmers' twenty minutes too late.

"She's down," Barb told him at the front door. "She went down at seven. Why didn't you call?"

"Because it was already settled that I was having her tonight." He tried to sound patient and pleasant about it, but knew he wasn't succeeding. He gentled his tone further, but still couldn't keep the frustration at bay. "Was she that tired you couldn't have kept her up? It's not like she's asleep at the exact same minute every night."

"You're usually here by six."

"I was…caught up." He'd had a crazy afternoon, getting back to the office to encounter an unexpected crisis with a longtime client of his father's, and then a long call from New York about the international legal case he was supposed to be working on in London in the fall.

The call pulled him back into his work, reminded him how much he enjoyed it. For the first time since DJ was born, he almost forgot her existence, and then he remembered with a flood of conflicting emotion… all that love, all that uncertainty.

He'd spent hours on the phone and at the computer, dealing with the client's problems and the London case while at the same time trying to put a plan in place that he had no intention of sharing with Barbara at this stage.

He just might share it with Jodie's dad, Bill, because occasionally the quiet man gave an inkling that he was more on the ball about Jodie's needs than he let on.

He'd grabbed coffee and a sandwich on the run, had twice been about to send a text to Barb or Jodie to tell them he was running late, but then something else had come up and the text never happened. In the back of his mind, because of Barb's own spreadsheet, he hadn't thought it mattered that much. Now, she'd used a poor excuse yet again to keep DJ under her own roof.

If this was so that Jodie could spend more time with the baby, then he wouldn't have a problem with it, but that wasn't happening. None of the Palmer women seemed to have any thought that Jodie needed help, not with baby-care but with bonding. They were in a state of massive denial, and if he didn't take drastic action soon, then his relationship with the entire family would descend into open conflict.

He couldn't let it happen, because if they or Jodie somehow managed to shut him out of DJ's life… His scalp tightened with dread at the very thought.

"You're not going to wake her?" Barb asked, telegraphing her disapproval very clearly.

"No, I won't wake her. Is Bill around, though?"

"In the basement. Shall I call him?"

"No, I'll go down."

Ignoring Barb's visible curiosity about why he might be seeking out her husband, Dev found him at his workshop bench, planing a curved piece of oak with an old-fashioned handheld plane. Dev couldn't work out what the piece of oak was for, and said so.

"It's the main," answered Bill.

"The main what?"

Bill chuckled. "No, m-a-n-e. I'm making a rocking horse. For DJ."

"Oh. Oh, wow."

They both stood there in a manly silence for several moments, while Dev took in the other pieces of the rocking horse. He began to see how it would all fit together. It was going to be a beautiful piece of workmanship. "I'm not good at the fussy stuff," Bill said eventually.

"This doesn't look fussy at all. It looks…like a piece of art. Incredible."

"I mean the fussy stuff with diapers and bottles."

"Right. You must have done your share."

"When I had to." He chuckled again. "But I like to be involved in my own way. Things like this."

"She'll love it."

"Her first Christmas, I thought. She'll be able to sit on it by then, with help."

"It's going to be really wonderful."

"Going to paint it like Jodie's Irish, dapple gray." He fell silent again, and his laconic manner transmitted itself to Dev, who couldn't find a way to say what he wanted to say. He wasn't even quite sure what he was trying for. In the end it was Bill who helped him out. "I love my wife and my girls," he said, "but it's not going right, is it?"

"No…"

"With DJ, I mean, and Jodie."

"No, I don't think it is."

"Right now, she's everybody's baby, the way Jodie was when she was little, especially after she was ill. She fought it. The horses were the best thing that ever happened to her, although Barb still can't see it. I don't want to watch Jodie hanging back with DJ, not knowing where she fits, not trusting herself with the baby. My wife and my daughters are trying to help, but they're doing it wrong. You can see it, can't you?"

"Yes, I can."

There was another silence. Bill picked up his plane. "Should we get involved?"

"I think we have to."

"Any ideas?"

"That's what I wanted to talk to you about," Dev said.

"And…score!" Trish said.

"Yay, it went in the tub." Jodie clumsily clapped her hands. "That's three times, now."

"Wow, Jodie!" Elin said. She'd dropped in as she occasionally did, to play cheerleader to Jodie's efforts.

Trish moved to retrieve the tennis ball from the big pink plastic bucket, which was about three feet in diameter, six feet away and hard to miss. But the close proximity hadn't stopped Jodie from missing it with the ball about nine times before her first hit. "I'll get it," she said quickly.

"Sure?"

"You and Elin keep scrambling up, and it's good for me to do it, right? Makes the whole exercise more complex and useful." She stood up, walked over, bent down, put in an intense mental effort and got her fingers to close around the ball. Back in her seat, she threw it again—*let go, crazy fingers!*—and there came another rubbery plop as it landed in the bottom of the tub. "Yeah, all right!"

"You're getting much better at this," Trish said.

"Wanna move the tub farther away?" Jodie asked.

"Not today. Practice a little more on your own, if you

want, before we break for lunch. I need to go check on Alice." Trish gestured across to another rehab patient working on a puzzle on the far side of the room.

"Of course I want," Jodie said, and went once again to pick up the ball—before Elin could do it for her.

She threw it, let go at the wrong time and missed by a mile.

She went to retrieve the ball from under the occupational therapy unit craft table—before Elin could do it for her—but someone else had gotten there first.

Dev.

He had a fabric baby pouch strapped over his shoulders, with DJ cradled against his chest.

She went hot and flustered at the sight of them, since Mom's spreadsheet hadn't breathed a word to suggest they were coming. Dev looked somehow formidable today, despite the softening accessory of a baby dressed head-to-toe in pink, right down to a tiny bucket-shaped pink sun hat. His jaw was set, and there was an electricity of intent humming inside him. It flustered her even more, as soon as she picked up on it. "Hi," she said, and asked—before Elin could do it for her—"What are you doing here?"

"It's all okayed with Trish and Lesley."

"It is? What is?" She looked in Trish's direction and received a smile and a thumbs-up in reply.

"Yes, Dev," said Elin, who hadn't been looking at Trish. "What are we talking about?"

"Um, Elin, if you don't mind this is between me and Jodie."

"Well, it isn't, really." She frowned at him. "If you recall our talk the other night."

"Talk?" Jodie came in. "What talk?"

They ignored her. "This has nothing to do with what

we talked about the other night," Dev said to Elin. "I've already agreed you were right about that. So would you mind please—?"

"Butting out? You're telling me to butt out? Mom told me what happened yesterday at Oakbank."

"I told you, too, Elin," Jodie said. "I told you it was great."

Again, they ignored her, glaring at each other, then Dev very deliberately turned in her direction. "I'm a little early, Jodie, because DJ woke up earlier than usual and it seemed best to show up now, before she gets fussy. Ready to go?"

"If you tell me where."

"Can't do that." He picked up her purse.

"Devlin!" Elin said.

"I am not dealing with you right now, Elin. I am not justifying myself to you, or to Lisa, or to your mom. Talk to Trish about it, if you want, but I need to get going before DJ falls apart. Jodie?"

He began to walk toward the door, his stride so long and assured and angry that Jodie had this dizzy, illogical panic that she would never see DJ again if she didn't follow him, so of course she did.

It was as if he had a gun pressed to DJ's head. Or to her own. It was a hostage situation or a kidnapping, he was that cool and controlled and ruthless about it. Elin seemed rooted to the spot. Trish was watching carefully from the far side of the room. When Elin took a pace forward, she called her quickly, and Elin went over to her, chin defiantly raised but ready to listen. A moment later they were in a very female huddle, with Elin nodding and frowning, and Trish persuasively arguing… something.

In a summery skirt and white lacy top, Jodie wasn't

dressed for a kidnapping. In fresh blue jeans and a designer polo shirt, neither was Dev. Where was the no-brand jacket and pulled-down baseball cap? The baggy clothing where he could hide the gun? "Dev, you have to explain."

"When we're in the car."

"Okay. I mean, I'm pretty hungry, so if it's lunch…"

It couldn't be lunch. You didn't kidnap someone to take them to lunch.

"Lunch is included."

"Good." She managed a skipping step to keep up with him, and almost fell.

He stopped. "Sorry, I'm going too fast."

"A little. Some people might say it's me going too slow."

He kind of gathered her against him, running his arm beneath hers and around her back, reaching up to settle her uncooperative left hand on his shoulder. Her whole body began to blur. That was how it felt. Blurry and fuzzy and soft. Happy. Her mind was racing but her body was happy, where it belonged.

His hip pressed into her side and DJ in the front carrier was right there with her little leg flapping against Jodie's stomach. Her hat was about to fall off. Jodie made an ineffective reaching movement with her right hand, and Dev saw what was happening and flipped the darling little pink-flowered bucket back into place.

"Let's not go slow, if we can help it," Dev said, in the corridor, and she could feel the vibration of his voice against her ribs. "Elin's probably sending out an APB, as we speak."

"So I'm right." She'd gone breathless, could he hear? "You are kidnapping me?"

"Yep, me and DJ."

"Oh, she's in on it?"

"Joint criminal masterminds, the two of us."

"That's a relief. I was scared she might be the hostage."

He turned serious suddenly. "Never, Jodie. I promise you that. I'll never try to use her as any kind of weapon or leverage or— But I think we really need to do this."

"I—I think so, too. Whatever it is."

"Thank you." He lost a little of the gun-to-the-hostage's-head feeling, and they walked together, in step, with DJ making sounds against his front and it just went on feeling way too nice, a complication Jodie didn't need when there was so much else to work out.

"Can I ask what it is?" she managed to ask.

"We're not telling you till we're on the road, are we, little pink person?"

"DJ, you'll tell me, won't you?" she said to the baby.

But DJ wouldn't spill.

Dev's car was parked in the visitor spaces out front. The day was bright and sunny and hot, and the effect of the air-conditioning had worn off during the time it had taken him to come into the rehab facility and collect her, so he opened all the doors to vent the hot air before strapping DJ back into her car carrier.

Jodie stood waiting and watching. She couldn't do that yet, the bending with DJ in her arms, the adjustment of the little body in the carrier, the fiddly, fine-motor-control-requiring snap together of the safety straps. He straightened and closed the car door. "Need some help getting in?"

But this she could manage on her own.

He went around to the driver's side, started the engine and the air-conditioning and they swung out of the parking lot and into the street.

"Now explain," she said. "You're not taking me to Oakbank behind my family's back?"

"Would that be terrible?"

"I— They're driving me crazy, if you want the truth, but they're doing so much to help. I hated that Mom and Lisa just showed up like that yesterday. It ruined the moment—"

"You got that right."

"—but it's because they care."

"Starting to wish they cared a little less. Or thought a little more."

"So we're not going to Oakbank?"

"Nope, although we can go visit horses at some point, if you want."

"At some point? What is this, Dev? Trish approves, I could see that. She was arguing with Elin back there and going blue in the face about it. Do Mom and Dad and my sisters know?"

"Your dad does. I talked to him last night. He packed your bag for you."

"Mmm, that might be interesting…"

"I gave him a list. He said he hadn't had any trouble with it."

"That might be even more interesting."

"Your mom and Lisa must know by now, because Elin would have told them the second Trish finished explaining. But your dad agreed it was best to keep quiet till we swung into action. Of course you can tell them, as soon as you want. Call them," he suggested, "once we're fully on the road."

It wouldn't be long. The car swooped between the traffic lights, made a tidy right and a wide left. Another two minutes and they'd be out of town. Jodie felt a surge of exhilaration and freedom that she hadn't had since before the accident. It was such a familiar feeling, yet distant somehow, because she hadn't had it for a long time. It was like urging Irish into a gallop across a wide green field, scary and wild and wonderful. Free, yet not alone. In control of something stronger than you were yourself.

"Yesterday was— I am not having that happen again," Dev said. "And even to find Elin there with you this morning. I appreciate she wants to support your therapy, but yet again, it turned everything into a big deal when it shouldn't be. That's why you need this. We both do. DJ does."

"You mean it really is a kidnapping?" She began to laugh. "You're not giving me back? There's not even a ransom note?"

"Not for at least a week. We need some time on our own, the three of us—I've found a cabin, made a reservation—and this is the only way it's going to happen."

"So you haven't even given them an address?"

"When I talked to Trish about it, she could see how important it was, and she's happy to have you take a break from rehab for a week or so, since you're tiring yourself out trying to make progress. She has the address."

"But she'll only hand it over once there's five million dollars in unmarked bills deposited in a locker at the bus station."

"You're really getting into this kidnapping idea."

"Yep."

He thought for a moment, then laughed. "Me, too."

They hit the highway and he sped up. DJ lay quiet in her seat. Jodie turned to look at her and found her kicking her feet in her tiny pink cotton shoes as if she were getting into the kidnapping idea, too. She smiled at the baby. *Hello, sweetheart.* But the smile was self-conscious and she wasn't surprised when DJ didn't smile back.

You can't make it happen, Jodie. Just give it time.

"Can I be the one to fire the gun from the car window to blow out Elin's tires when she comes after us?"

"Sure, since you've decided you're in on this, too."

"What should it be? A rifle? A sawed-off shotgun? I'm not real clued in on weaponry."

"Me, neither. But let's go for total overkill and make it an AK-47. You'll find it on the backseat next to your daughter."

She laughed again, then thought…daughter…mom. "What's my mother going to think? She's not going to let it rest with Dad."

"Your dad sees and knows more than he lets on. And he's strong-minded, when he wants to be."

"Oh, you noticed that, too?"

"He'll handle her."

"He will." Once more, she laughed. "He sure will!"

Dev pulled off the road at a shaded picnic area where there were wooden tables with bench seats and playground equipment and a picturesque pond with a viewing platform for spotting turtles and water birds. He'd brought a simple lunch of sub-style sandwiches and cartons of juice, and DJ watched them eat it from a commanding position in her car carrier, resting on top of the table. Dev cooed at her and she batted her hands for him and broke into the most dazzling smile.

So I do get to see her smile, even if it's not smiling for me, Jodie thought. "It's so quiet," she said out loud, because the smiling thought was painful despite how sensible she tried to be. "I love the quiet."

"Yeah, no phone calls, so far."

"They're probably running hot, back in town."

He packed up the picnic things, strapped DJ back in the car and they set off again, zoomed along in their bubble of air-conditioning, changed from highway to county road and the bends beckoned like a movie's happy ending, and DJ, without a care in the world, fell sound asleep.

Chapter Ten

Dev buzzed with victory and optimism the whole drive. To tweak Jodie's kidnapping comparison a little, he felt as if he were driving the getaway car after a billion-dollar heist. Yes, he had the precious cargo right here with him, and there was no one on his tail and he owned the world.

Almost four weeks ago, he'd told Jodie that the three of them were a family. Now at last they might have a chance at working out what that meant, the way he'd wanted from the beginning. He was a lawyer. He liked to know where he stood. He liked the ground rules in place.

Most importantly, he had a deep-seated need to see Jodie being a mother. Something would have to fall into place then, wouldn't it? She would find out what she wanted. She'd talk about it. They would come up with their own much simpler version of Barb's ridiculous spreadsheets, and if they could present a united front, then the three Palmer women would surely step back and give them some space.

He accepted that he wouldn't get to have DJ under his own roof, long-term, as much as his heart wanted, but he thought—or told himself—that he could deal with this as long as everything was amicable and settled. He'd *have* to deal with it.

It might even be pretty nice, down the track. He pictured a tomboy of an eight-year-old girl arriving at his place for regular visits with a purple backpack full of stuff. He saw himself on the phone with Jodie, negotiating in a friendly, casual way over what each of them would give DJ for her birthday and which of them would get to have her for Thanksgiving and Christmas. He saw himself returning from consultancy work in Asia or Europe with exotic trinkets for his daughter and her mom.

Braking to a halt in front of the cabin, it struck him that this picture was a little too simplified and idyllic to be plausible. DJ would probably acquire a stepfather at some point, for example. Jodie was too amazing to spend her life without a loving partner, if she wanted one.

And would Dev always buy those exotic trinkets himself, or would there be another woman in the picture with him, tolerating his absorption in his growing daughter, for the sake of a short-term sizzling affair?

New York was ten-hour's drive from Leighville. London and Hong Kong were a heck of lot farther. Right now, twenty-four hours without seeing DJ seemed like too long. What made him think it was going to get easier? What would happen if Jodie's bond with DJ became so strong that his own role ceased to matter?

The sense of victory ebbed like water out of a bath, but he pushed the doubts and questions aside. He'd been told the keys to the cabin would be waiting for them, beneath a flowerpot containing a red geranium beside the front door, and he could see the geranium from here.

Jodie stirred herself beside him. She hadn't been sleeping but she'd been very quiet, almost dreamy, and had now been roused by the dying of the engine. "So this is it?"

"Take your time. DJ's asleep. I'll bring in our stuff."

"Okay. Might grab a drink of water." She stretched in the passenger seat and found the water bottle he'd given her earlier.

Dev hit the trunk catch and brought out his bags and the cooler and boxes he'd packed with food. Jodie had opened the car door and pivoted to stretch her legs down to the ground. She was sipping on the water, looking around, apparently liking what she saw. She stood up and pushed all the car doors wide to give DJ plenty of fresh air while she slept. With the car parked right in front of the house in the shade and the whole place quiet and secluded, it would be perfectly safe to keep her there until she woke up on her own. Jodie bent to brush her cheek with one soft finger, then began to walk toward the cabin, a soft smile on her face as she took in the peaceful setting.

I've done the right thing, Dev decided. The only thing.

The place was beautiful, more like a log home than a cabin, larger than they really needed, only a few months old and built by the people who farmed this land to rent out for family vacations. It was also adjacent to a state park. He'd found it on the internet, looked at the photos and the map, liked the high ceilings and huge stretches of double-glazed window, the loft bedroom upstairs that he could use, and the master bedroom downstairs for Jodie, so that she wouldn't have to climb up and down.

Behind the cabin was a huge stretch of forested state park, with walking trails and a lake for boating, while the view through those enormous windows took in rolling green farmland and a wide bowl of sky. Outside, there was a garden and a deck, a swing set and a barbecue, while inside he liked the huge open-plan kitchen and living area, with its big squishy tan leather sofas and clean-cut décor. There was even a bookshelf crammed with vacation reading, ranging from crime fiction to teen vampire novels to romance.

The only downside, made apparent before Jodie had even made it through the front door, was the cell phone reception.

It was wa-a-ay too good.

When Dev came out for a second load of gear, Jodie had her phone pressed to her ear and was seated on the wooden steps that led up to the deck. She hadn't even made it inside. "It's beautiful.… No, she's asleep.… Plenty of space, it looks huge… Do? Does it matter what we do…? No, please don't call that often, Mom, you'll only get frustrated.… Why? Because I'm switching it off!"

She slid the phone shut with a click, stuffed it into her bag, looked up at Dev and gave him an upside-down smile, which he read like a book and reflected right back to her.

Families.

It's so great to be here.

Oh, you understand? Perfect.

They should be looking away from each other at this point. It had gone on for too long, and it was dangerous, after the massive flare of heat between them two nights ago. But he couldn't do anything about it, he just kept looking.

She leaned her head against one of the sturdy verticals of the deck railing, while Dev had stopped with his hand holding the door. His breath caught in his chest at the sight of that amazing, contradictory Jodie package. The strong will. The petite body. The forgiveness toward her family. The stubborn, triumphant action with the phone. The failed bond with her baby that his head understood the reasons for, while his heart just couldn't get at all.

Then she raised her arms in the air and deliberately broke the moment with a goofy grin and an exuberant yell, that echoed into the forest. "Woo-hoo!"

How was he going to keep from touching her? He'd promised Elin and himself that he wouldn't, but how? How was he going to make this week work the way it needed to?

He had to tough it out, that was all, pure and simple, keep his focus and his priorities, and he thought that Jodie did, too.

She'd yelled too loud, Jodie soon realized. She'd woken the baby.

Which was probably a good thing.

Because if she and Dev were going to look at each other like that again anytime soon, she might just conclude that way too much interference from her mother and sisters was exactly what they both needed. She had so little willpower where Devlin Browne was concerned.

DJ began with a whimper and a snuffle, progressed to a short riff on her current favorite sound—

"eeaaaah"—and then began to cry, building to full volume in around forty-five seconds.

Dev just stood there.

Jodie looked at him, heart sinking, head a mess. Her sense of peace had vanished so fast.

By now, at home, there would already have been at least two pairs of feet hurrying across the grass, two voices cooing and two pairs of hands reaching out, neither of them hers. She would have seen DJ safe in someone's loving arms being soothed and settled, and possibly changed and fed and made to smile, before she'd even pretended to herself that she was getting up and going over, before she'd begun to wrestle with the frightening, horrible reality that she didn't want to.

But Dev just stood there. Daring her. Waiting her out.

Judging her how much? Seeing how much?

Seeing *everything.*

She could see the muscles bunched at his jaw and his fingers tightening against his palms. He wanted to go to DJ. But he wanted Jodie to go more. And he understood exactly how much she struggled with it. It shocked her that he knew what was in her heart. She felt naked and guilty and defiant and just miserable. Why had she thought going away, just the three of them, would be a good idea?

"Don't make it into a big deal," she blurted out.

"You're the one who's doing that."

"No, I—" She stopped. "Am I?"

"I can't stand to hear her cry, by the way."

"Are you angry?"

"Not at all. Can you stand it? Listen to her."

"Please, please don't make it into a big deal."

"I'm not."

It was true. He wasn't *making* it into a big deal, because it already was one, all on its own. Dev didn't need to do a thing. The problem was her.

"I'm afraid I'll let her fall."

"I won't let that happen." He moved a little closer, treading down the front steps to ground level as if to reassure her that he'd be close behind.

"I'm afraid she'll cry worse if I pick her up, because I'm not the one who's familiar and I want her to love me and I'm scared of what she can see and feel. She's never yet once— Dev, she's never—"

"Come on." He reached out and pulled her up, and she decided not to make the horrible confession. *She's never smiled at me.*

Oh, DJ was a mess already! No question of smiling now. Her face was red and screwed up and even though Dev had parked in the shade and they'd left all the doors open her fuzzy, dark little hairline was slicked down with sweat from the effort of her crying.

Jodie fumbled with the clips of the car carrier, hating the fact that her fingers were still so wrong. They gripped when they should be loosening, they wouldn't obey her at all. Dev had to step in. He had the straps undone and loosened and out of the way in a couple of economical movements, intending to help but only underlining Jodie's inadequacy in the process. How could she take care of a baby safely?

She slid her hands behind DJ's back and managed to lift her. "I'm sorry I'm so bad at this, sweetheart…"

Sweet.

Heart.

She is, but I'm not feeling it. All I'm feeling is the fear. All I'm hearing is the sound of her cry, and it's so loud and piercing and desperate, and makes me feel so helpless because I don't know how to make it stop.

She couldn't even feel Dev, although she knew he was right beside her. He was a pillar of rock, hard and blind. She straightened with DJ in her arms, and the baby was so wriggly and heavy. Jodie's disobedient left hand made a claw on the little pink-clad back. "Are my fingers digging in? Am I hurting her?" she asked in a panic.

"No, you're fine. Your hand's a bit tense, but it's okay." He covered her hand with his, eased the claw position into softness. "Can you carry her into the house? Let me know the second you think you're losing it. She's due for her bottle. She wasn't ready for it when we had our lunch but now she's probably crying from hunger, so let's just head right for the couch."

"Can I get that far?"

"If you can't, I'm here. Try."

And she knew he was asking for much more than simply making it to the couch.

So she tried.

This is my baby. I love her. She's precious and tiny and such a massive bundle of potential. Dev and I made her. She's the two of us in combination, but she's unique. She's dynamite. She might be president, someday. An Olympic champion, a world-famous musician, a beloved wife. Beautiful and clever and kind and brave.

Who are you, DJ? When will you stop crying? When will you smile at me?

They climbed the steps. The cabin was cool inside, shaded by the nearby woods, its screened windows thrown open so that the breeze came right through. The place was so new it still smelled like cedar and pine.

Jodie reached the couch and sank into its softness.

Dev slid a pillow beneath her arm for DJ's head. She wasn't so frantic now, but still she was crying. The sound and movement of it consumed her whole body and she didn't even seem to know that she was cradled in someone's arms.

Her mother's arms.

"I have a bottle made up for her," Dev said. "It's in the diaper bag. She'll need it warmed up, but that'll only take a minute or two."

They seemed endless, those minutes. DJ's eyes were screwed tight with crying. Jodie tried smiling down at her. Babies smiled when they saw someone smiling at them. So far it hadn't worked for her and it wasn't going to work today. "I love you, precious girl," she said, wondering what punishment life had in store for a woman who lied to her own baby.

"Here," Dev finally said, handing her the cylinder of plastic, warmed to blood heat.

Jodie shoved it into DJ's mouth. Oh, she didn't mean to do that, but her muscles weren't cooperating and it just happened. The plastic circle that kept the rubber teat in place bumped hard against DJ's gums and the baby shrieked.

"Oh, no… Oh, no…" Jodie said.

"It's okay. Did you slip?"

"Yes."

"It's okay."

"I hurt her."

"She's forgotten about it already."

And she had. Her little pink mouth had closed around the teat and she knew exactly what to do. She sucked it and the bottle began to make a singing sound as it emptied. "Will she get gas?"

"Give her a break. Lift her onto your shoulder and pat her back. Can you do that?"

"I think so." Clumsy, but still. DJ gave a burp and then a big wobble. Jodie half expected her to start crying again but she didn't, and with Dev's help she was soon in that lovely cradle position again, crooked in Jodie's left arm, beneath her breast, ready to finish her liquid meal.

She slowed toward the end of it. She was getting sleepy again. Jodie thought about enlisting Dev's help to put her down in the bassinet he'd brought, but decided there was no hurry. Okay, so DJ hadn't smiled yet, but she wasn't crying. Okay, so there was no overwhelming wave of love like the one Jodie had caught such a short, lovely glimpse of in her own heart at Oakbank, but still, this felt… It felt…

Peaceful.

Unhurried.

Unpressured.

Worthwhile.

Maybe I'll close my eyes for a little, too...

She woke up when Dev took DJ gently from her arms. "How long was I—?"

"Half an hour or so."

"And you've been sitting there the whole time in case I let her fall."

"Not the whole time. I took out some insurance." He gestured to a big, soft nest of pillows laid out on the floor in front of the couch. "She wouldn't have gone far. So I did some unpacking, set up the kitchen. It's beautiful outside. Hot, but there's a breeze, and the woods are shady. Want to explore?"

DJ did. She was wide-awake, bouncing in her daddy's arms, a pink frenzy of energy. With a dexterity borne of experience, Dev strapped her into her little front pouch carrier, facing forward so she could see everything that was going on.

"I'd love to explore," Jodie told him. "Let me change out of this skirt, though."

Dev screwed up his face and said slowly, "Yeah, about that..."

She gave him a questioning look.

"Remember in the car when you questioned your dad's capabilities in the packing department?"

"Uh, yes, I do."

"Well, you'll see for yourself."

"You're scaring me now." She stood up and made her way to the bedroom at the back of the cabin that looked out onto the woods. It was a lovely room, spacious and clean-lined, with the greenery outside giving it a cool light.

Dev and DJ followed her into the room and she saw that he'd opened the suitcase Dad had packed for her, but had left it on the bed with the top flipped back and everything still in place inside. "Just so you don't check the contents and decide I sabotaged them," he said. "This is exactly the way he had it."

She looked at the tangle of garments in the crammed piece of luggage. "This is it? This is what he packed?"

"I gave him a list, remember? He told me he'd followed it."

She looked some more, dipped her hands into the tangle and pulled out a pair of scarlet pantyhose she'd once worn as a Moulin Rouge dancer to a fancy dress ball. "Can I ask what was on the list?"

"Underwear and socks, a swimsuit, something warm in case the nights chill down, a couple of outfits for going out, daywear, et cetera."

She rummaged a little more. "Well, okay, I guess it's all there."

She set everything out on the bed, while Dev and DJ watched. DJ seemed to love the color and movement.

Item one—what looked to be the entire contents of her underwear and sock drawer, and she'd had "tidy underwear drawer" on her to-do list for a good six months before the accident. She thought about apologizing for the number of bras, since Dev had been the one to lug the suitcase inside, but didn't want to call attention to it.

For some reason, he seemed to be smiling.

"Did, um, my family toss any of my stuff when they moved it out of the cottage at Oakbank?"

"You tell me. You seem to own forty pairs of socks now. How many did you own before?"

"What can I say? Horse people need a lot of socks." She turned back to the suitcase.

Item two—a chocolate-brown halter-neck bikini she hadn't worn in five years, because on vacation in Florida where she'd bought it, it hadn't seemed too skimpy, but in Ohio it definitely did. Well, at least it didn't weigh much.

No comment from Dev.

But he was still smiling. Or had it progressed to a grin at this point?

Item three—the huge, vibrantly colored and fringed silk-and-wool gypsy shawl was warm, for sure, and finely woven and beautiful, but she kept it hanging in her room more as a decoration than something to wear.

"Where'd that come from?" Dev asked.

"Lisa bought it for me when they went to Europe."

"I think DJ likes it." Facing out at his chest height,

she was kicking her legs and flapping her arms. Not smiling, but close.

Item four—the bridesmaid dresses from Maddy's and Lisa's weddings. Maddy had gone for a sophisticated look, and her bridesmaids had worn strapless gold-and-silver sheaths. Lisa had wanted a Victorian feel with a hint of burlesque, which for some reason added up to sage-green satin overlaid with black lace. DJ liked both of those, too.

Item five—a single summer top, one pair of shorts and some hiking boots. "Those will team great with the shawl once the sun goes down," Dev said.

"Well, as long as I color-coordinate the socks…" She'd reached the bottom of the suitcase. "There's no pajamas or shoes."

"Huh. Sorry. My bad." He spread his hands, but they were grinning at each other, because how could you not? The whole bed was a mess of fabric and balled socks.

"Or toothbrush or makeup."

"Those were meant to be covered by the et cetera."

"Not as far as Dad was concerned, apparently."

"I should have checked."

"Or brush or comb or shampoo." She looked helplessly at the mess and thought of Dad, Dev's coconspirator, his intentions so good and the result so…*not*. "It's too funny, Dev. I love it!"

"You do?" DJ jiggled her little legs some more, against his front.

"It's so Dad. It's— Mom and Elin would have packed perfectly and sensibly and used up three suitcases. Dad just wanted us to make a clean getaway and didn't think it through."

"The clean-getaway part was pretty important."

"Yep."

"So…shop first and then explore the place, or the other way around?"

"The other way around. I didn't come all this way to buy a toothbrush. Even the hospital gift shop had those."

"And dinner out tonight, I'm thinking. Some low-key kind of place where they won't hate us for bringing a baby."

"Is there any other kind of place in Southern Ohio? Not sure I'll be wearing either of those dresses, though."

They took an easy ramble around the cabin, finding the start of the trail through the woods, a bench for sitting and looking at the view over the rolling woods and farmlands, a stone birdbath, and a newly planted stretch of garden that would look fabulous in a few years, especially in spring when the dogwood trees came into their extravagant white and pink colors.

With the baby right in the thick of things against Dev's front, Jodie expected him to push her a little, the way he had earlier when she'd been crying in the car, but he didn't and she was thankful for that. She needed breathing space. She couldn't bear to rush, or push herself.

In case DJ felt her tension and doubt.

In case Dev guessed just how blocked and lost she was, and despised her for it.

"It's so peaceful here," she said, aware of him watching her too closely, as he sometimes did. Did he see as much as DJ? She mustn't let him see. "So beautiful."

Look at the beauty, Dev, don't look at me.

Beyond a field of tall corn, they could see the farmhouse belonging to this piece of land. Jodie wondered if they'd meet the owners during their stay. She'd like to thank them for this place. "We'll definitely be back," she would want to tell them, but she didn't know if that would be possible. Who was "we"? Herself and DJ? All three of them?

"Like it, then?" Dev asked.

"Very much."

"DJ seems pretty happy, too." Okay, that was a push from him. The baby dangled against his front, completely at home in that position.

Because Dev expected it—and because she knew he was right—Jodie said to her, as brightly as she could, "Are you happy, DJ? Are you having fun?" And DJ gazed back at her with those big, wise eyes and didn't smile.

Chapter Eleven

That night, as planned, they went to a family-style place where no one minded that DJ lay in her stroller right beside the table and sat on Dev's lap for her bottle, and where there was a change table in a space of its own adjacent to the bathroom. The place quickly filled up with groups of all sizes, parents and grandparents and kids, couples with toddlers, dads with daughters, moms with sons.

An older couple came past on the way to their table, while Dev and Jodie waited for their entrées, and paused when they saw the baby, back in her stroller and growing sleepy. "Oh, she's beautiful!" the woman said.

"I'm sorry," the woman's husband apologized, standing back a little. "She never can resist a baby."

"It's fine," Dev said. "We think she's pretty hard to resist, too."

Jodie smiled and nodded and felt so exposed.

"How old is she?" The woman turned instinctively to Jodie.

Because I'm the mom.

"I— She's—" Her mind went blank and she didn't have the right answer. Did she say four months? DJ looked too small for that. So did she explain right away that the baby was born early?

"Almost four months," Dev answered easily, before Jodie had solved the dilemma in her head. He'd met these kinds of questions before.

"She's tiny!"

He'd met this reaction before, also. His answer was as easy and cheerful as before. "Getting bigger as fast as she knows how."

"What's her name?"

"We call her DJ."

"Oh, but that's short for something, right? My niece is CJ, short for Caroline Jean."

"We haven't decided yet, so for the moment it's just DJ."

"You haven't decided? And she's four months old? Well, if that don't beat all!" The woman laughed, not unkindly but definitely in surprise, as if today's new parents were a mystery to her, in a cute sort of way.

Jodie said quickly, "I like DJ. I can't imagine calling her anything else."

"Well, she is adorable."

"You make a beautiful family," her husband said, and the couple moved on.

"You like DJ?" Dev echoed quietly, once they were out of earshot. He leaned a little closer across the table and she felt their complicated connection like honey melting over her.

"I do. It belongs to her now." She remembered that

shocking day four weeks ago when she'd found Dev at his front door with his crying daughter in his arms. "It's…how we were introduced."

He sat back again. "I'm sorry, it just worked out that way."

"You don't have to apologize."

"We do need to find something, though, or she'll get that woman's reaction about her initials for the rest of her life."

"Dani Jane," Jodie blurted out, because suddenly it seemed important for DJ to have a proper name, one that came from her mom, one that was chosen with joy, even if no one used it very often.

"Yeah?" The intent look came again, coupled with a spark deep in his eyes. "You want it to be Dani Jane?"

"I don't know where it came from. But I just had a feeling. It's kind of sassy and strong, as well as being feminine. It's not too big a step away from DJ. When she's older, it gives her some choices about what she calls herself."

"I like it. What do you think, baby girl?"

But DJ had fallen asleep and couldn't give an opinion. Their meal arrived, in the form of two steaming plates of home-style meat and vegetables—one meat loaf, one sirloin tips. The other adult diners were tucking into similarly hearty fare, while kids mostly had plates of nuggets and fries or spaghetti with meatballs. There were at least four high chairs in use, and lots of messy kid faces streaked in ketchup or sporting milk moustaches.

"We fit right in," Jodie said.

"Weird, huh?" He frowned, suddenly.

"Not so weird."

"Different, then."

"You don't like it?" All Jodie wanted right now was to fit in, to be a normal mom.

"Let's just say, I'm a little suspicious when I fit in too well."

"You're an outlaw at heart?"

"I like a little adventure, for sure."

"This gravy is an adventure, as far as I'm concerned. What is that?" She speared a dark blob.

"Mushroom, I'm pretty sure."

"Okay, not such an adventure. Well, but it is, actually. Just being here. When a few months ago I was… nowhere. Something strange happened at first, Dev, although it's ebbing now. Sometimes when I smelled or tasted or touched something, the sensation was so strong and new. The day of the barbecue, when Dad was cooking those onions. It was as if no one in the world had ever smelled fried onions before, and the ketchup, too. It was like discovering gravity or gold."

"I've had that feeling sometimes with DJ," he answered slowly. "I hadn't thought of it that way, but you're right. As if I'm the first person in the world ever to take care of a baby. Just the smell of her hair…"

"Adventures and experiences don't have to be big and splashy, do they? The tiniest moments can be precious, and so fresh they sparkle."

"That's true…" His eyes had gone smoky and thoughtful.

I just wish I could find those moments with our baby, she wanted to tell him. *I wish the smell of her hair would make me feel as if the whole world was new. I wish I could see her smile for me.*

Should she say it?

But she left it too long and the moment passed and she was too scared. It was good being here with Dev.

She couldn't bear to spoil it, couldn't stand the idea of seeing his face change if she said too much about what was and wasn't in her heart.

DJ stayed asleep for the whole of their meal but wakened and grew fussy as they drove back to the cabin. Dev could tell that Jodie was tired, she knew, and he gave her the kind of easy way out she'd come to expect from her mother and sisters, not from him.

"You need a good night's sleep. Find something to read from that shelf of books to lull you off, and I'll take care of DJ. She can sleep in my room upstairs, and that way we won't disturb you if we're up in the night."

She should have argued. A normal mom would. A normal mom would never have reached the point where her baby was four months old and she'd never yet wakened in the night to handle a feed or a diaper change. But she didn't want to argue. What if she did wake for DJ and couldn't get the baby to settle again? What if she ended up calling for Dev because nothing was working, including her left hand as she attempted a solo diaper change?

To hide her feelings, she teased, "I must have worked pretty hard today to get that kind of a break."

But he was very serious when he answered. "You did great today, Jodie. You named her."

"I—I guess I did. Must have really taken it out of me, because I'm wiped." Don't cry, Jodie. Don't let him see. Step back so he doesn't feel how close you are to the edge. "Thank you," she said, falling back on those very useful words, not even knowing what she was thanking him for, right now. "In that case, I'll see you in the morning."

For nearly an hour she lay in bed listening to the

sounds he made as he took care of DJ, settled her in her bassinet, then relaxed in the living area with music playing.

Aching for him.

Aching for herself and what she was missing.

Aching for DJ, who had the best dad in the world.

The baby had a good night, Dev said. They ate breakfast out on the deck, just cereal and fruit and coffee. Since it would be kind of useful to have a toothbrush and more than one pair of pants, they drove half an hour to a major store and picked up a few essentials. Jodie would have bought more, but DJ began to signal that she thought shopping was way overrated, so the one extra pair of shorts and a strappy tank would have to do.

After lunch and naps for both mom and baby, Dev suggested exploring the trail through the woods, and that sounded safe. A family thing to do. A time when the dad carried the baby in that little front pouch.

"Time to break out the new shorts, you mean?" she said, so that he wouldn't guess what she was thinking.

"Sounds like a plan."

He left her alone to change. She was getting faster at it, but Ole Lefty still made some of the movements a challenge at times. In ten minutes or so, she met him back in the living area and they left the cabin, found the start of the marked trail leading into the woods and lost themselves in the cool greenery.

They walked slowly, because that was all she could do, but the pace didn't matter. Side by side, Jodie could hold on to Dev when she needed to, and he seemed to have an instinct about that, turning a little whenever the terrain grew too uneven. There were simple wooden benches at intervals, really just two tree stumps with a plank nailed across the top, but they gave her the chance to sit and regroup, and meant that they could go farther.

There was a stream gurgling just out of sight, tantalizing them with its delicious sounds. There were cardinals and warblers, and they saw a greenish-brown salamander flick itself beneath a rock. The air had a fresh, peaty smell and it was so peaceful and quiet, just the sounds of water and leaves, their footfalls on the mushy earth, and Dev talking to DJ about the things they saw.

"See the cardinal? It's red. Look at it flashing through the trees, baby girl."

Jodie felt shut out of his ease with the baby, even though she was right by his side. How could he talk to her like that, so unselfconscious about it, when DJ couldn't possibly understand? Red? Cardinal? How old would she have to be to learn colors and birds? She looked so happy there against his front in her pink outfit, with his voice so familiar in her ears.

I'm jealous....

Jodie felt the painful, complicated twist of it and hated herself. How could she ruin such a perfect afternoon with her own messed-up feelings? She'd thought a walk in the woods would be so safe, but instead she felt as if she'd walked into an ambush.

"She's a little young for the nature talk, isn't she, Dev?" The sour twist of shame and disappointment came out in her tone, despite her best efforts.

"I hate when I hear parents talking to kids as if they're not really people," he answered easily, as if he hadn't heard the tone. He must have.

"But you coo at her." Her throat was tight. She'd cooed at DJ, too, but it felt as if she were acting a role that she'd been cast in by mistake. Faking it. And badly.

Like last night, when she hadn't been able to answer a simple question about DJ's age.

"I coo at her," Dev said. "I talk to her, I sing to her, I even confess things to her, sometimes."

"Confess things?" What did Dev have to confess? He had become the most amazing father in such a short time. He was doing everything right, the way he always did, without making a big deal out of it in any way.

He mimicked himself. "Man, honey, I'm not so keen on this diaper change stuff. I'm hoping you'll potty train real early."

She gave an upside-down laugh, disappointed. "Oh, that kind of confession." She blinked fast, feeling the wash of tears.

"Why, what did you think?" He leaned a little, his shoulder giving a gentle, playful push against hers. He couldn't have seen the tears. She'd blinked them away. He mimicked again. "DJ, don't tell the cops, I wrapped the gun in a rag and buried it in the backyard under the red rose bush."

But she couldn't laugh about it. "Thank you for kidnapping me," she said, her voice even tighter, unsteady now.

"We're back to that?" He put his arm around her.

"I need this. I'm not getting it right yet. You're being...so patient. But I need it so much." She stopped and pressed her lips together. Could she tell him? A part of her wanted to hold it back. Because what would he think if he knew? But then the words just came. "I'm afraid I'll never get it right."

"Get it right?"

"The love. Loving her. Being her mom." She was crying now. "It was a bad start. But that shouldn't matter. Other mothers have bad starts. A difficult birth, or a baby in the NICU so they don't get to hold her right away. I don't know why it matters for me, what's gone wrong, why I can't feel it. Don't tell me I need professional help. I have a ton of that with the rehab, and it's great, Trish and Lesley are both amazing, but I don't need any more of it. I just couldn't bear to have a therapist teach me how to be a mom, no matter how sensitive and skilful and well-meant."

"Hey… Hey…" He half turned her to him and she buried her face against his shoulder so he wouldn't see just how much she was crying.

Oh, who was she kidding? He didn't need to see. He could feel.

Her shoulders were shaking and she couldn't make them stop. For a long time she just let herself cry about everything in the whole world. About the accident and Dev's suffering that night and the birth. About the struggle with her body and brain. About Mom and Dad and Elin and Lisa and Maddy caring so much but understanding so little. About Dev putting his high-flying career in New York on hold, whether temporary or permanent, so he could be DJ's dad.

Oh, and why not just throw in war and the environment and a few natural disasters at the same time, and cry about those, too? She couldn't remember when she'd cried this hard.

Finally she spoke again. "I love her." DJ made the third side of their triangle. She'd gone quiet now, against Dev's chest. "I must. I do." Those little legs had stopped jiggling. "But I can't feel it. That's the most awful thing, Dev, such a terrible thing." Of course Dev talked to DJ like a grown-up, because those big, swimmy eyes of hers seemed to be taking in every horrible word Jodie spoke, every sobbing gasp of breath. "You must hate me right now."

Both of you.

He said gently, "What, you think I didn't guess from the beginning that you were having problems?"

"I—I— Mom and Elin and Lisa keep telling me it's because of the rehab, because I get too tired."

He made an impatient sound.

"But you don't buy that idea…."

"Maybe they really think that," he said. "Or maybe they're in denial. Or maybe they want to go easy on you for the best reasons in the world."

"That's pretty pointless, when I can't go easy on myself."

"You have felt it, the love. You felt it on Thursday at Oakbank, when you had her sitting up in front of you."

"I—I did. It was so wonderful. Such a relief. But it didn't survive Mom and Lisa showing up, and yesterday I struggled so hard, and that's crazy, for it to be so fragile."

"So it's fragile, for now. Dressing yourself was fragile a few weeks ago. Before that, talking was fragile. Your brain and body got stronger."

"It's not my brain. It's my heart."

"Don't worry about your heart."

"How can you say that, when for you it's so easy."

He gave a snort of laughter. "Easy?"

"It is easy. You change her and feed her and bathe her and carry her around and all the time you just love her without even trying."

It was true.

So help them both, it was true.

Dev fought to find an answer, a reassurance that wouldn't be glib and wrong, but he couldn't find one.

Jodie was right. Against everything he would have predicted about himself a year ago, he found it so easy to love DJ, and he couldn't just tell her mom how to do it, step-by-step, not when she was crying and crying like this, when the difficult words she spoke were just temporary lulls in the storm of sobbing and tears. He thought that the crying was vital and necessary, and it had been a long time coming, he guessed.

Tell her how to do it?

First, kiss her darling forehead and blow a raspberry on her tummy....

No. They were both out of their depth. Everything seemed like a platitude.

Relax. It will happen.

The only thing he could think of, the only thing that seemed to make sense at the moment, was to give love and reassurance to Jodie, and hope she'd be able to pass it on. Love worked that way, didn't it? The more you gave, the more there was. DJ had taught him that, just as Jodie had taught him that adventures could happen in the tiniest sparkling moments. He was still thinking about that.

"So maybe you shouldn't try, either," he finally said. "Maybe you should let go, and forgive yourself, and have some trust."

"Mmm." She sniffed and he clapped a hand to the back pocket of his pants in search of the wad of clean tissues he kept in there for DJ's needs. Jodie mopped at her face and he led her back to the last bench they'd passed, about fifty yards along the track, and they sat.

Just sat.

Shoulders pressed together, bodies like magnets, hearts in tune.

She needed this.

"I think you've always worked for what you wanted, haven't you?" he said, after a while. "I remember when you were sixteen when we put on that play and you wanted to do the lighting. You didn't know anything about theater lighting, but you promised you'd learn, and you did. You worked so hard at it. You've worked so hard at your riding, worked to gain the management skills so you could run the whole stable."

"You remember the lighting?"

"I wanted a red spotlight for my big speech and you wouldn't give me one because you thought it was melodramatic. You argued with the director—I've forgotten her name—until she saw your point."

"And you've hated me for it ever since. I'm amazed you remember this."

"Haven't hated you. Got over my ego, discovered you were right and admired you for fighting. But I don't think you can fight and work in that same way to learn love. Love just…happens."

"How did it happen for you?"

"With DJ?"

"Yes. Tell me about it, Dev. You've told me about the birth and how much she weighed and how much oxygen she had to have and all of that. Tell me about you. Because you were there. And I wasn't."

So he told her. Because she was right, she wasn't there, and *of course* he needed to tell her, and he should have realized it weeks ago. Just like her family, he'd protected her too much. While he spoke, DJ sat in her little pouch against his chest and listened to the sound of his voice coming through his shirt until she fell asleep.

"Well, after the first shock of the blood test showing you were pregnant, it was a while before anything happened," he said. "They focused on getting you stable, and I was pretty busy with getting the plates in my leg. Then they did an ultrasound and I saw her. Saw the beating of her heart."

"Oh, wow."

"I'm so stupid, they gave me pictures and I put them away and there was too much else to think about and I haven't shown them to you."

"It's okay. I'm picturing it now. I can see the real pictures later. I want to."

"They did another ultrasound at twenty weeks and I was so scared they'd find something was wrong with her because of the accident, but everything was normal and we could see she was a girl."

"So you knew she was a girl three months before she was born."

"And you weren't there to talk about names with me. And I didn't want to give her a name you turned out to hate. So she has the two initials on her birth certificate. We're allowed to change it officially later. The more I think about Dani Jane, the more I like it."

"Thank you."

"No, thank you. You gave her her name. That's important. Maybe if—"

"You're skipping ahead. Don't. Please."

"I am. Sorry. The next thing that happened was seeing her move, watching your tummy rippling and kicking up. It was…hard…amazing. But hard."

"Hard, why?"

"For your mom and dad and sisters. They laid their hands on your stomach and felt her kick, while you weren't moving at all and we didn't know if you ever would."

"Oh."

"It was… Yeah, the doctors weren't saying much

about your recovery at that point. Some encouraging signs with your scans and tests, but a long way to go."

"And did you, too?"

"Did I, what?"

"Put your hand on my stomach."

"Once. It seemed— I wasn't sure that I had the right to. But your mom wanted me to."

They both sat and thought about this for a moment. Dev remembered it so vividly, but couldn't put it into words. Jodie with her eyes closed, never moving, with those high-tech mechanical guardians around her, the monitors and alarms and tubing. The cool weave of the white hospital sheet. It had grown warm to his touch. He'd thought the baby had stopped moving for the moment and that he was going to miss out. He couldn't feel anything. She was as still as her mom. But then…

A twitch. A flutter. And then an actual kick, two or three of them, hard little bumps against his hand.

And he believed that day, as they all did, that if the baby could move so vigorously then Jodie had to be functioning in there somewhere. She had to be making progress.

"Were Mom and Dad angry that I was pregnant?" she asked.

"Angry? Jodie, it was just about the only thing that got them through it. Something to hope for. A sign that your body was still working enough to grow a healthy new life. None of us ever once thought about the fact that it hadn't been planned. It felt as if it *was* planned, by something greater than ourselves."

"And what happened next?"

"Well, you opened your eyes." Could she hear the scratch in his voice? Could she see him blinking too much? "That was pretty exciting. We'd been talking to you all along. We did tell you about the accident and the baby, but you don't remember."

"Not at all. Not even an inkling."

"We stopped talking about the baby at some point, because the doctors thought it might be too confusing for you, too stressful, if you kind of half understood in the coma but couldn't speak or react."

"I don't remember opening my eyes."

"No, well, it didn't last long, the first few times. That was hard for your mom. She expected too much, too quickly. She kind of nagged you about it and got very frustrated and upset and had to back off."

"I can imagine."

"Then DJ put on a growth spurt and they didn't like the fact that you couldn't move. They were afraid the blood supply would be compromised. They started talking about inducing labor early, but it happened on its own. Your mom was sitting with you and she could see the contractions, the tightening. You grimaced when they happened, and we all got pretty excited about that, too."

"Were you there at the birth?"

"Yes, right there the whole time. It was a quick labor, only a few hours, I think I told you that. Dr. Forbes had me cut the cord. They had to get her stable, but within a few hours I was able to hold her. They had us skin-to-skin."

"Skin—? Both of you? You and DJ? You mean you had your shirt off?"

"Yes, and she was just in a diaper. They do it a lot, now. It helps the baby's breathing and heart rate. They've done studies. Preemie babies gain weight faster if they can have skin-to-skin contact with their mom or dad."

She was quiet for a little while, thinking about this, and then she asked, "Did I have her skin-to-skin with me?"

He had to clear his throat. "Yes, a couple of times, the first few days."

"Oh. Oh, wow. I think— I think— No, for a moment I thought I could remember it. But no. I don't think it's a memory, I think it's just— Why didn't they keep doing it?"

"You got an infection and you were very sick for a while, and it wasn't safe for DJ to be with you. She went home, and that was when you started to wake up, and you were so confused."

"Confused... Maybe I remember that, a little. I didn't like it."

"You moaned a lot and seemed very distressed for several days. They didn't know at that point if you had permanent brain damage, and they decided it would be best to keep the baby away."

"Oh, I wish that hadn't happened."

"We just didn't know at that point, you see, if you'd ever be able to take care of her, or even take in that she was yours. It's been a miracle, really. It's so amazing to see you now, walking in the woods, talking and laughing, when a few months ago... Don't beat yourself up, Jodie. About anything. You're amazing."

You're amazing....

Pull back, Dev. This is too strong. This isn't what she needs, or what you need, either.

They both knew it. Jodie eased away from the shoulder-to-shoulder contact, pressing her lips together, visibly fighting to steady her breath. "Thank you," she said. "I've said that about five thousand times since I came home. But this is the biggest. Thank you. I needed to hear all of that. It's hard. This dramatic life story that I don't remember. But it helps. It will help, I think."

She stood up and walked to the nearest tree. Her movement was unsteady and lopsided and Dev wanted to jump up and give her his arm but he held himself in place, tried to watch her without it being too obvious that he was concerned. They both needed some space.

She leaned on the tree, her good hand running up and down the smooth trunk, then pressed her forehead against it as if it could infuse her with strength. She was thinking about something, wrestling with it, trying to decide what to say. He could see it, didn't know whether to prompt her.

"Need to head back?" he asked.

"We'd better."

He checked his watch and found it was already five o'clock. DJ would be wanting another bottle soon, or a nap first if she wasn't hungry yet. Later they could give her a bath and put a blanket on the floor so she could have a kick and a play. He outlined the plan to Jodie. Would she leave it all to him? Maybe he shouldn't have responded so much to her fatigue last night.

She stood straight, and there were two bright spots of color in her cheeks. "I want to take care of her tonight," she said. "By myself."

Yes-ss!

But there was more, and it was important, he could see. The color flamed even higher and there was a glitter of courage and determination and stubbornness in her blue eyes, the same glitter he'd seen yesterday when she'd told Barb and Lisa that if she could never ride Irish again, then DJ would.

"Dev, I want to have her skin-to-skin, the way I did in the hospital but don't even remember. Could we do that?

There's a spa bath in the master bedroom. We could go in it together. I'd want you nearby in case I slipped. But when you said I'd had her against my bare stomach in the coma when I don't remember… I want to have that happen. Then maybe she'll— Maybe at last I'll get her to—" She stopped and took another shuddery breath. "I want to know how it feels."

Chapter Twelve

"Of course we can do that." His voice came out on a husky rasp. "Absolutely, we can do that. We'll put you both in the spa bath."

"That would be perfect. I—I'd love it."

Forget giving Jodie space, he couldn't help himself, he had to touch her. Because of the color in her cheeks and the brightness in her eyes. Because of the emotional roller coaster that was still taking her on the ride of both their lives. How could he not touch her?

Hand on her hair, brush of his mouth across her lips to say, *I'm proud of you, I know how hard all of this is, you're amazing.*

She responded briefly to his kiss and the magnetism between them would have kicked in as strongly as ever, if there hadn't been this one thing that was even more important.

"Help me get back to the cabin?" Her left hand had

gone into its crab shape on his arm. He was coming to love Ole Lefty, as she often called it, because it tried so hard and was so brave when it failed, clawing and unable to let go, as if a victim of its own determination. Like Jodie herself. "I've done too much walking, Dev. Too much of everything." She laughed. "Crying. Living."

He put his arm around her waist and she leaned against him and they didn't need to speak anymore. It was a slow journey. He could have kept reassuring her, she could have kept apologizing, but they didn't. They didn't need to. The apologies and reassurances were understood between them without words. If he hadn't had the baby against his front, he would have offered to carry her, even though he knew she would have refused.

"So, did I win? Where's my gold medal?" she said as they came up the steps. "What, last place? Oh, well…"

"Last place? Of course you won," he told her.

DJ had gone to sleep. He laid her in her bassinet in the living area, over near the kitchen area, with the curtains and slatted blinds pulled across to darken the room, and she didn't waken, just sighed and snuffled and went quiet. They both stood and watched her in the new dimness, her parents, tangled together by her very existence, helpless about it.

Suddenly, Jodie was crying again, apologizing for it. "I'm sorry. I don't know why."

"It's okay. It's okay." Dev felt a rush of very male inadequacy, coupled with an equally male need to make things okay.

Right now.

In one move.

But he'd already said everything he knew to say. Did she want words? What else was there?

Well, holding her. They were standing so close it would be very easy.

It *was* very easy. Just his arms and her shoulders, the bump of their hips, stillness as she sighed against him. It happened before he planned it, a familiar phenomenon where she was concerned.

And then it changed.

He couldn't have her in his arms like this without wanting her, no matter what his head told him about Elin's warning a few days ago and his own understanding of the emotional risk.

Risk? Wasn't everything already at risk? Would fighting this heat really help?

He couldn't see it, couldn't remember Elin's arguments, or his own. All he could think of was Jodie's sweet, fierce little body pressed against him, proving her womanhood. All he wanted to do was quiet those shaking shoulders with the touch of his mouth on hers.

He did it and her mouth was right there, seeking his, wanting it just as much. It began as a kiss, but they both knew it wouldn't stop there. He could feel her bare legs against his, sliding their warmth across the muscles of his thighs. Her collarbone was bare, too, and he kissed the little hollows above it, making her gasp.

They sank to the cool brown leather of the couch and she stretched her body out, her spine and shoulders against the couch back, her legs half beneath his. He tried to lift her top and she sat up again and peeled it off, her breasts pert and round in a coral-pink satin bra. "Can't manage the catch," she said. "I always twist it around...."

But he'd already reached behind her and flicked the

hooks. You just needed the right angle, and the right movement with your thumb. The straps dropped from her shoulders, he tossed the bra out of the way, and there were those breasts he loved. He buried his face between them, lifted their tender weight with his hands and heard her breathing change. She'd forgotten about her tears.

I'll make you forget everything, sweetheart.

It seemed so simple. He forgot why he'd ever thought it wasn't.

It seemed like an adventure, a sparkling jewel of a moment, and those moments were the best adventures of all.

"Stand up," he whispered.

"Can't. Remember that marathon I just ran?"

So he helped her, popped the fastening on her shorts, shimmied them down and then the scrap of cotton and lace beneath. He loved her hips, loved the way they rocked so neatly. He bracketed his hands at her waist, amazed by the shape of her, the curves and lines, that butt so soft and silky against his palms.

She tried to lift his shirt. "This is where it all comes apart, sadly. Ole Lefty doesn't want to do this."

"Ole Lefty can have plenty of help. Don't even have to ask." He pulled off his shirt and she sank her fingers into his chest, rougher than she'd intended, probably, but he didn't mind. Hell, he totally didn't mind. The roughness heightened the beautiful chaos of everything, the sense that he didn't know quite what would happen next, where she would touch him next, whether it would be light or hard, what her breathing might do.

He ripped at his jeans, took his briefs down with them and stepped out, his hardness blatantly apparent. She reached down and touched him there, cradled his weight and he ached, just ached, and the ache radiated outward, up to his hairline and down to his toes.

"I never understand this," she said. "Why it's so magical."

"Just is."

"For you, too?"

"Yes."

How? Why?

Wanting her at eighteen but letting it go because he thought there must be a million women out there he'd want in the same way. Which had never really happened. There'd always been something missing. He'd put it down to his own naïveté. He didn't believe that anymore.

Discovering her last year, and then the accident cutting it all short, never letting him reach the usual moment with a woman where he began to think about how it should end. A final dinner out? Jewelry? A phone call? It could never have ended like that with Jodie.

Discovering her again three nights ago and finding that nothing had changed. If anything, had only grown stronger because of the complexity of what bound them together and pushed them apart.

He'd never known anything like this.

She pushed him onto the couch and sank on top of him, looking down into his face, those neat breasts grazing his chest and pushing higher, the softness at the apex of her thighs making a warm, perfect nest for his throbbing arousal. "You have to understand that this might not be pretty," she said, echoing what he'd said to her the other night as they stood against the front of the car. She was more serious than he'd been with the words, shy and fierce at the same time. "You might have to—"

"I don't care what I have to do," he interrupted. "Hold you, or guide myself. Start over. Shift. Anything. We managed fine the other night."

"You had protection right there in your wallet, the other night."

"Have it right there in my wallet now."

"On the floor?"

"Let me get it."

"I have it." She stretched down, giving him the perfect opportunity to take in the shape of her butt, the delicious curvy paleness of it in the dim room. A minute—quite a long minute—later she slid higher on his body, wearing a triumphant grin, clutching a square packet.

"You do have it."

"You have no idea. A wallet? Wasn't easy."

"Proud of you."

"Are you?"

"You're amazing."

"You always say that…."

"Yeah, I do. Because it's true. But let's quit talking now…."

Oh, yeah, let's definitely quit talking. There's way too much else to do.

She was right, there were a couple of times when it wasn't pretty, but hell, as always it was beautiful, more beautiful than ever. She laughed when her body wouldn't cooperate, gasped and shuddered and sighed when it did. He held her, rolled her, eased her thighs apart, caressed the whole length of her as he heard the build and raggedness of her breathing.

Inside her, he almost let go within seconds, had to school himself back, let her catch up, and when she did she took him over the edge so fast he lost all sense of time and space, could only feel and cry out and breathe.

They went into a bit of role reversal after this. She was the one who fell asleep within seconds, while he lay there in her arms wondering how to make the universe stop right here in this moment forever. Wishing she would wake up so they could talk and kiss. Glad that she didn't, because it meant he could watch her sleeping with his hand resting across her breasts. Wondering what would happen next.

He was scared of how important this felt, of what an adventure it might be, scared of this strange, vulnerable feeling that he couldn't really find a name for, didn't know what to do about it.

DJ was waking up. He heard the creak of her bassinet, the sound of a snuffle and the beginning of a cry. If she woke Jodie…

He eased himself away from her and she didn't stir. In the bedroom, some of Bill's chaotic wardrobe decisions littered the bed after Jodie's attempts to find something to wear this morning. He swept them aside, back into the suitcase, folded the sheet and quilt aside, then went and gathered Jodie up from the couch.

She was so warm and relaxed. Would she stay asleep? She wanted to have her bath with DJ, her session of skin-to-skin, but she was too tired for that right now. She needed to stay asleep until her energy rebounded.

He caught this tiny moment in himself of wanting her to change her mind about the skin-to-skin idea. How much would it achieve, really? She'd seemed so hopeful about it, what if it ended up a huge disappointment? What if Jodie couldn't manage to hold the baby? What if DJ cried?

We can deal with all that, he thought. *I'm making an issue out of nothing. What's wrong with me?*

She murmured something and he told her, "Just carrying you to the bed."

"Mmm."

He tucked her beneath the sheet like a child, laid the gypsy shawl on top because the quilt would be too warm, then went to get DJ before she began to cry in earnest.

Jodie woke some time later to find Dev treading softly out of the bedroom. He turned when he heard her move. "Damn, I woke you up, coming to check on you."

"You didn't. I was ready. How long did I sleep?" She felt a little self-conscious about it, and about what had led up to it. Her fierceness. His acceptance. The fact that it had happened at all. The fact that it had happened *again*.

Are we dating, Dev?

"A good hour," he said. "DJ's had her bottle and she's raring to go." He was silent for a moment, then said, "Shall I run the bath now? Do you still want—?"

"That would be great. Of course I still want." Beneath the sheet she began some stretches and range of motion exercises to shake off the heavy blanket of sleep, while Dev made preparations. She could see him through the open bedroom door, adding a generous squirt of bath foam and a sachet of scented salts.

The spa bath sat in the corner of the master bathroom, directly beside the two huge windows. They were made of clear glass and looked onto a thick screen of greenery with a barely visible lattice screen beyond, so that in complete privacy and warmth you would nevertheless feel as if you were bathing in the open forest.

When the water had been running in for several minutes, she levered herself off the bed, took the gypsy shawl he'd spread over her, wrapped it around her body, and went to the doorway. "How are we going to do this?"

"Can you get in by yourself?" He looked at her in the shawl, his gaze running down and up again, hard to read. "Do you need help?"

"It shouldn't be a problem."

"It could be slippery," he warned.

"There are steps and handholds."

"So once you're in, I'll give her to you. I'll stay right close by."

"That's safest, I think."

He seemed relieved. "It'll only be lukewarm, so she doesn't overheat or burn. Might feel a little cool to you."

"It's a warm day. Cool is good." Funny, for a change she was the one reassuring him.

And yet they were both nervous. Or not so much nervous, but keyed up. Was that it?

It was a bath, she told herself. Just a bath. But it was important. Too important even to talk about, so they talked about the tiny practicalities. Did they have enough towels? Was there a diaper and a clean outfit ready for DJ when she came out? Did Jodie need a robe? *Were* there any robes? Ah, yes, thick luxurious ones made of white towelling, two of them, folded in a small closet tucked behind the bathroom door.

She still felt churned up over what they'd said to each other out in the woods. Her painful confession about the state of her love for DJ. His stories about the pregnancy and birth. Now, on top of their lovemaking, it was like the aftermath of a storm, with a renewed sense of calm and a ton of work to do to deal with the litter of damage.

No, *damage* was wrong.

This wasn't about damage anymore, it was about healing.

Did Dev think so? "I'll give you a minute," he said.

For her to let the gypsy shawl drop, he meant, and climb into the water.

She felt crazily self-conscious when he left the bathroom and closed the door, as self-conscious as if he'd just stood there watching. She'd put on some weight in the weeks since leaving the hospital. Her breasts and hips were a little rounder, which was good, as the enhanced curves masked movements that were clumsier and less gracefully athletic than they used to be.

An hour ago when they'd made love, she'd warned him seriously that it might not be pretty. It couldn't have been, with this body. How much had he taken in? Why did the idea of being naked in front of him now seem so much scarier than it had the other night, or just now? It shouldn't have been any different.

She'd just begun the climb into the tub when he called to her, "How's it going?" She heard a creak and a movement, as if he were about to come through the door.

Naked, she froze in place. She didn't want him to see her. The reaction didn't make sense but existed anyway. "Not breaking any world records on the timing," she called to him. "Just climbing in now."

"Tell me when you're ready."

She sank into the water, wondering if the thick, mounded expanse of white foam was deliberate on his part. If it was, she was grateful for it. Beneath the waterline, you couldn't see a thing. "Okay, I'm good."

He opened the door. "Comfortable?"

"It's perfect." She looked up at him. His expression was serious. Worried, even. Reluctant. Out of his depth. He didn't need to be. Not as far as her safety was concerned, anyhow, or DJ's. "There's this sloping section on the side that I can lean against, and a kind of step to prop my feet so I don't slip too far down in the water. I'll be able to hold her. It's so lovely and deep, I'm almost floating."

He had his hand on the door handle, motionless, and for some reason the whole world seemed to echo his attitude. Everything went still and quiet. Beneath the water, her body tingled. "Uh, nice bathroom," he said, pulling the words out of nowhere. "I mean, it's just right for this."

"I know." She tried not to notice his awkward attitude. "The big tub is perfect. It would have been difficult in a smaller one. Where is she?"

"In her bassinet, to give me a chance to set up."

"What's she doing? She's not asleep? Please say she's not. I—I want this to happen, Dev. I'm not feeling patient, right now."

"It's fine. Composing a sonata for creaking wicker and plastic rattle, I'm pretty sure. I'll go get her."

A minute later he was back with DJ, who was wide-awake and happy, gurgling and cooing. He gave her a big squeeze and a fierce kiss on her tummy, then laid her on the bed and took off her clothing and diaper. "What a kick you got there, baby girl," he crooned. "Daddy's little athlete, aren't you, sweet thing?" He picked her up and came into the bathroom, knelt on the tiled step, cleared his throat. "Ready?"

Jodie lifted her arms. "Ready," she whispered.

Ohh.

DJ wriggled as she touched the water. Dev still held her firmly. She was tiny and soft and slippery, and she half floated as her little arms and chin came to rest on Jodie's front. She had no bottom whatsoever, just a series of creases and folds. "Got her?" he said.

"Yes. But stay."

"Of course I'm staying." Right there, he meant. He didn't move from beside the tub, just rested his forearms on the cold white porcelain and watched.

Watched, and belonged.

Ohh.

There were no words for it. DJ's little body. The warmth. The soft lapping of the water. The slipperiness. The tenderness. The way the water helped with Jodie's imperfect coordination and control.

"Can I…play with her, Dev?"

"Play with her?"

"Bob her around, float her from side to side. I mean, she's never been in a tub this big, has she?"

"Of course play with her." He was still watching closely, his hair getting damp with steam from the tub, his shirt wet from the splash of the baby's legs. "As long as the water doesn't get into her mouth."

So they bobbed around and floated from side to side, her little legs making trails in the foam. The foam began to melt away, which was good because then Jodie didn't worry so much about it getting in the baby's mouth and eyes, as Dev had warned.

"Oh, you're beautiful," she crooned. "You're so beautiful."

And something shifted and changed inside her. She let go of the doubt and fear and questions because the moment was too huge and didn't leave any room for those things. She slid DJ a little higher and those pink starfish hands grabbed at Jodie's skin and suddenly it came.

A smile.

A big, sweet, soft-lipped, toothless, beaming baby smile.

"Ohh," she crooned. "You're smiling. Oh, you darling girl! Why are you smiling? Mom says you never smile in the bath."

"Because you're right in there with her," Dev said, "and you're smiling right at her."

"But I've tried that before and it's never worked. She's never ever smiled at me till now. Oh, baby girl!" She just couldn't take her eyes away.

"Tried it." He slid closer, along the side of the tub. "That was the difference. Now you're not trying, you're not thinking about it, you're just smiling."

"Oh. Oh."

No words. Just kisses. On DJ's tender shoulders, her forehead, her wet baby hair, her chubby cheeks. Jodie cradled her against her shoulder and almost swam with her, floating around the generous-size spa tub, bobbing and bouncing DJ through the water.

The sense of rightness coursed through her with as much warmth and vitality as the blood in her veins. *Oh, my baby girl, oh, my sweet precious angel.* It was a part of her, this new feeling. It wasn't like the short-lived flicker of feeling that had come two days ago at Oakbank. That had only been a glimpse. This was real and powerful and bone-deep, an utter, beloved certainty.

The water was getting too cool. Dev turned on the faucet and a blast of warmth jetted in, bringing the temperature back up. They stayed in there until Jodie and DJ were both wrinkle-skinned and even then, as she lifted the baby to pass her to Dev, she didn't want to let her go.

"You can have her for now," she warned him, making it a tease so that she didn't cry instead. "But watch out, because I want her back as soon as I'm out of here." It had been so precious and wonderful. She felt as if she'd recaptured something she hadn't known until today had been lost.

And it would last, this time. She believed it. Knew it. Knew that the overwhelming sensation of love had been real and true and deep enough not to ebb or fade. It was what Dev had. It changed everything.

"Careful, she's so slippery," she told Dev, and there was a wet, drippy tangle of arms and movements as he bent down to take her.

"I've got her," he said gruffly. "I know she's slippery. It's fine." He captured her in the big, fluffy towel and dressed her in a fresh outfit—lilac, this time—right there on the glass vanity while Jodie lolled in the water and watched him with their daughter. When she was dressed, he stepped into the next room and laid her on the bed. Jodie heard the sound of pillows being plumped and settled to keep her safely in place. "That's the way," he sang to her. "Not going anywhere like that, are you, sweetheart angel?"

DJ cooed at him.

"Now let me pass you a towel," he said, back in the bathroom. "Do you need help getting up?"

"No, there's enough to hold on to." But she slipped at her first try and slid back into the tub, her feet squeaking across the porcelain. The water churned. She gritted her teeth. Why was it so hard? How did such a clumsy episode follow so quickly from some of the most precious moments of her life?

I won't let the clumsiness spoil what I feel, she vowed, and made another effort, pulling herself from the water and into the towel Dev had waiting for her. *I couldn't let it spoil that, because it was too strong.*

"Everything okay?" he said.

"Like a miracle. Oh, Dev, I can't tell you…I can't describe it. I can't even think about the difference it's already made."

"Good. Good. I'm so glad."

She thought he was going to kiss her. She was sure of it, after the way they'd made love so recently, after the emotion unleashed by her holding DJ in the bath. His eyes had pooled with glinting darkness, half-shielded by a sweep of lashes, his mouth was so soft, his lips had parted and he was looking at her. She swayed closer, and her hands loosened on the towel. It would drop to the floor in another moment, and she didn't care.

As long as Dev kissed her.

But it didn't happen.

He took a long, harsh breath and stepped back, pressing his lips together, turning his head. "Better not leave DJ on the bed for long," he said. "I'll put her on the floor, with her baby gym. Time to think about dinner, too. It's been a big day."

"A great day."

"Yes." He left, picking up the baby on his way out.

Wrapped in the towel in the steaming bathroom, Jodie felt abandoned and hated the ebbing of that glorious feeling of love and relief that had made her so complete and so happy just moments ago.

The change in his mood was as stark and apparent as the sun vanishing behind a dark cloud. The air felt colder. The light seemed different. It no longer streamed like gold through the thick greenery as it had when she'd first climbed into the bath. The sun had almost set, and the bath water had taken on a greenish tinge from the sachet of bath salts Dev had poured in.

There was no more foam, Jodie realized. She and DJ had stayed in the bath for so long that it had gradually disappeared, and she'd been so absorbed in the baby that she hadn't noticed.

Dev would have seen everything. Not just the shape of her body lying there, but the awkwardness of it in movement, and somehow this left her more naked and vulnerable than she'd been the other night when they'd made love, or just now on the couch, because both those times it had been dark, or at least dim, and their need for each other had wrapped both of them in a kind of protective blanket. She'd felt a lot of things, but she hadn't felt exposed.

Now, she did, because Dev's mood had changed so suddenly, it seemed, and this had to be the reason why.

Jodie took a long time to reappear. DJ had grown bored on her blanket, even with the baby gym positioned above her. There was only so much rattle-whacking a four-month-old could tolerate, apparently. Dev picked her up and propped her on his hip while he attempted to put oven fries on a baking tray, toss a salad and grill steaks with one hand.

He'd cooked that way before.

"Wouldn't put you in your bassinet even if I thought you'd stay happy there, would I, baby girl?" he murmured to her, heart lurching in his chest at the stark thought of losing her.

Not losing her.

He couldn't lose her.

Jodie wasn't like that. No matter how strongly her bond with the baby kicked in, today and in the future, she wouldn't punish him with it, would she?

Not deliberately. She surely wasn't like that.

But the punishment could happen anyway, because he wanted too much. He'd been kidding himself so stupidly right up until tonight, thinking through all these plans about shared custody and generous access, about making it work even when he was in New York or Europe, not understanding that the bond he had with DJ was so much stronger because the baby hadn't had the chance to build a bond with her mom.

Just now, in the bath, when they'd smiled at each other, gotten lost in each other for minutes on end, forgotten about him so completely, both of them, and then Jodie had seemed so glowing and different after she stepped out of the tub, so much freer and more full of life, he'd seen it in the look on her face, felt it in the way her body moved.

The shutting out.

Like the slamming of a prison door, with himself on one side and Jodie and DJ on the other.

He felt sick at himself, a miserable wreck of selfishness and blindness and jealousy. Did he *want* to see Jodie go on floundering the way she had been, purely so that she would leave the best of the parenting to him? That was horrible. He was appalled about it.

But he felt it anyway, this sense that he was shut out and that it was a conspiracy coming from both of them.

He didn't understand why it had such a grip on him or what it meant.

Couldn't do a damned thing about it.

Here she was, at last. She was wearing a pair of

stretchy cream long johns and a flowery camisole top—amongst the more useful contents of her underwear drawer, he guessed—and she was wrapped in the gypsy shawl her sister had given her, that he'd laid on the bed. Strangely enough, the outfit almost worked. "Cold?" he asked, pushing his dark, unwanted feelings aside.

"From the bath."

"Right. DJ felt cool, too. You'll both warm up soon."

"Mmm."

"Dinner's nearly on the table."

"Thank you."

"DJ won't last much longer. We can eat, then I'll put her in her sleep suit and give her her last bottle and she'll go down. Can usually count on a good eight hours after that. With luck it'll be getting light before she wakes up. That's mostly how it works with her now." He sounded as if he were giving a lecture, and knew it came from his need to assert his own role.

I'm the one who took her home from the hospital. I'm the one who saw the sonogram and felt her move in your belly, when you knew nothing about it.

He'd told Jodie all that stuff himself, just a few hours ago, and it had changed everything, along with DJ's smile and Jodie's tearful smile back, and now he wanted Jodie's glow to fade? He was despicable.

Despicable, and lost.

The steaks were almost done. She helped him serve up and they ate without saying a lot. He talked about what they might do tomorrow—go visit the nearby lake, go back to the store to fill more of those gaps in her dad's packing—but it was all on the surface and they both knew something was wrong.

"May I feed her and put her to bed?" Jodie asked, after she'd finished eating. "Would you mind?"

"Mind? You're the mom," he said stiffly. "And you've missed out on a lot. You don't have to ask."

"No. Right. I guess I don't. Thank you."

"Don't say that."

"Sorry, I didn't mean—"

"We can't go on thanking each other for the most mundane childcare tasks. How's that going to work?"

"It's not, I guess, but— Yeah, okay, I won't keep thanking you."

"Let me know if you need any help."

"I will."

He was worse than Elin and Barb. He left the rest of the dinner mess in the kitchen and hovered around in the open-plan living area, ears almost aching from the effort of listening. He could hear her talking to DJ as she changed the baby's diaper, not the same way that he talked to her, but *right,* all the same, not forced or self-conscious, and the thick knot of incomprehensible jealousy tightened inside him.

Chapter Thirteen

"Yes, I'm fine," Jodie said into her cell phone. "I keep telling you, Mom… No, I'm not going to keep it switched on, from now on. I'll call you once a day to tell you I'm fine, and that's it."

She stood out on the deck, with her left hand pressed awkwardly against her ear to block out distracting sounds, and she had her back to Dev, even though he could hear her quite clearly. Was she trying to block him out, also?

She listened some more, then said to her mother, "Well, we've been out to dinner, we've explored the woods, we've been shopping to replace all the things Dad forgot to pack for me, we've been to the lake and had a picnic, soaked up the sun, cooked a barbecue here on the deck…" She listened again. "Coming home? Dev told them a week when he made the reservation." She turned and looked at him. "We've only been here three nights."

Was that a question in her face? Did she want to leave sooner?

His gut twisted. Maybe for her, the purpose had been achieved, there was no more point to this, and she wanted to go home. He wouldn't blame her. He hadn't been the best company since that magical session between Jodie and DJ in the bath. Hell, he was trying!

But he was trying to protect himself at the same time. He was floundering and she had to know something was wrong. "It's up to you," he murmured. "If you want to leave sooner…"

"Only if you do," she answered quietly, with her hand over the phone. Her eyes had narrowed, intent on his response.

"I don't."

"Good." She turned her attention once more to her mother. "I'll call again tomorrow." She listened. "Mom, you don't need to know the exact details on how many exercises I'm doing, okay?" Another pause. "Listen, I'm ending the call now. I'm not hanging up on you or anything, but there's nothing more we need to say." She thumbed the phone off and put it down on the outdoor table.

"Only if you do," she repeated deliberately, fixing Dev with those blue eyes.

"I don't," he repeated back.

"So what's wrong?" She crossed the space between them and tried to touch him, but he eased away, as he'd been doing since Saturday night. He didn't trust himself, close to her, and there was this massive sense of risk and vulnerability crashing through him that he didn't understand.

"Nothing," he said. "Just giving us both some space."

Her expression turned fierce and she stuck out her jaw. "Was that a one-off, on the couch, then? A two-off, I guess I should say, counting the other night in Deer Pond Park coming home from the restaurant. Be honest. Tell me up front."

"Up front..."

"It's not so hard, is it? You were pretty good at it, last year, the up-front stuff. You said straight out that you weren't in the market for anything long-term and I appreciated your honesty."

Maybe if I knew the answer, it wouldn't be hard. Out loud, he told her, "Just...not a good idea."

"Yeah, you keep saying that."

"Twice. I've said it twice."

"Once for each time. If we go for a third, I'll let you say it again." She put a hand on her hip, jutted her chin in a defiant grin and struck a sassy pose that he knew ran only skin-deep.

"Stop..." he almost begged.

Stop being so brave. Stop asking for answers I don't have.

"Oh, me? *I* should stop?" She glared at him.

"No, okay, you're right. That's not fair. It's just... This—coming here—is about you and DJ, isn't it, not about you and me? I don't want anything to get in the way of that. What you're finding together. It's so great. It's beautiful to see."

"Yes, it is." A smile lit up her face, a new kind of smile. "Thank you for making it happen."

"That's her now, waking up."

"Oh, it is? Yes, I can hear her. Yes."

Three days ago, he would have had to urge her, *blackmail* her, almost, into going to her baby. Now she was already on the way, eager and awkward, calling out as she went. “I hear you, baby girl. I’m coming.”

It was exactly what he wanted, better than he could have hoped, and she wasn’t using it to hurt him, she was still giving him all the time he could want with his baby girl, so why was it killing him like this? What was he so afraid of?

He needed action and answers, not this pointless self-questioning.

Jodie had left her cell phone on the table. His was in his pocket, switched off just as hers had been. He took it out. It felt cool and compact in his hand, a familiar symbol of certainty and control.

Touching the screen, he had his office in New York on the line within seconds, knowing he was kidding himself about what this would achieve, even while he heard his assistant’s voice. “Catch me up, Angie,” he told her. “Has there been any news from London on the consultancy?”

“Can you believe I changed your diaper and your outfit all by myself?” Jodie cooed to DJ. “Your daddy will be so proud.”

I’m lying to her. Again.

He wouldn’t be proud, he would be uncomfortable and reluctant, and if she told him, “I changed her all by myself,” he would say all the right things, but underneath there would be this distance. “Space” he’d called it, just now.

It wasn’t space.

It was withdrawal, shutting down.

And she got it.

Yeah, don’t worry, she got it completely, even though he hadn’t spelled it out.

Mission accomplished, as far as he was concerned. He'd taken her and DJ away from Mom and Lisa and Elin in order to strengthen their bond and deepen her love, and it had worked better than either of them could have hoped. She loved her baby girl, her Dani Jane, in a way she hadn't imagined possible just a few days ago, with none of that thick, ugly layer of self-doubt and fear and unfamiliarity that had held her back.

Which meant that now Dev was free.

He loved his daughter, and he never would have abandoned her to the distance of her mother and the overinvolvement of her Palmer grandmother and aunts, but now that Jodie had her bonding in place, he was free. He could put this "family" thing he talked about onto the same footing as so many other kids had—live with the mom, see the dad occasionally for visits and weekends, while the parents maintained a cordial relationship if the kid was lucky.

Visits, where? Would he go back to New York? Jodie's family always seemed to assume so. Her heart lurched and sank at the idea. It felt so wrong to think of them at such a distance from each other, all the complicated arrangements they would have to make to keep DJ in his life.

She didn't want arrangements. She wanted him.

It was pretty simple, really.

She loved him.

She'd known last fall that he would break her heart when he left, whether they slept together or didn't. He would break her heart when he left now, and little DJ, who knew nothing about any of this, was powerless to help, because there was no way in the world that Jodie would ever use her as leverage or a weapon.

"Look at you, sweetheart," Jodie whispered to her.

"How can I keep you happy and safe? How can I keep you from guessing how much I'm hurting? I can't let him guess, either."

She picked the baby up, put her in her stroller because that was the safest way to move a baby when you weren't sure of the strength of your own arms, and wheeled her back out to the deck, hearing Dev on the phone as she approached.

"Yeah, very glad I called," he was saying. "Sorry I had it switched off. I was trying for some space, but I'll keep it on now in case anything else comes up. It's going to be a mess if we don't straighten it out.… Yes, please, make the reservation.…" He was so absorbed in the conversation, he hadn't seen her. He was staring out at the woods, not seeing them, either. "Yes, for Wednesday, if you can, so I'm there for meetings Thursday and Friday… I can fly out of Columbus to Chicago and then over the Pole, or through New York if that connects better. Just let me know the schedule when you have it.… Okay, talk soon."

He flipped the phone into his pocket, turned and saw her with the stroller wheels resting against the threshold between the living area and the deck. "Something's come up," she said, so that he didn't have to say it. "And you need to get to London before the end of the week."

"Yes. If my assistant can get the right flights, I'll have to leave here tomorrow and I won't be back before Tuesday."

"Tuesday," she echoed.

"I can't leave you here on your own."

She took a deep breath, let go of the instant, aching sense of loss, tried to hold on to what she had, the wonderful new sense of motherhood and love. She didn't have Dev's love, but she had DJ's. "I don't have to be on my own. We have the cabin till Friday. Mom could come out, I expect, or Lisa and the kids. Keep me company. Help pack."

"That's a good idea," he said slowly. "It would be great if you and DJ could stay for the full week. The timing on this is—"

Tough.

And yet he seemed relieved, too, which she understood. He didn't want to be here anymore, and this gave him the perfect excuse.

"What time tomorrow?" she asked, as if everything was fine.

"Depends on the flights."

"She'll get back to you today?"

"Within an hour, I hope. I hate not knowing what's happening."

He didn't have to hate it for long. His assistant got back to him as promised, with details on confirmed flights. By eleven o'clock tomorrow morning, he would be gone.

Jodie called home and spoke to Mom, fighting her way through the usual overanxious questions about her well-being and the baby's until she could get to the point. "Something's come up, Mom, and Dev has to go to London."

"London?"

"For work."

"Well, I gathered that. For how long? When?"

"He's leaving tomorrow."

"So you're coming back?" Mom sounded relieved.

"Well, I'm hoping I don't have to. It's been wonderful here. That's really why I'm calling."

"You can't possibly stay there on your own. You're

not driving yet. There's so much you can't manage. You're not saying that Dev's taking the baby?"

"Mom, if you'd let me get a word in edgewise, I'm not saying I'd stay here on my own, I'm wondering if someone can come out and keep me company. You or Dad or—"

"Of course we can." She sounded eager, now that she'd grasped the situation. "Yes, we absolutely can, one of us at least. You don't have to say another word. We'll work it out. What time do we need to be there?"

"He has to leave by eleven."

"I'll get right on it. We'll work something out. Just leave your cell phone switched on."

"Nope, not doing that."

"Jodie…"

"Because you'll call me every five minutes to update. Send a text, if there's anything important."

"Jodie, honey…"

But she stayed stubborn, gave Mom the directions to the cabin, ended the call and switched off her phone.

Again, Dev seemed relieved. "Last dinner out?" he suggested.

"Sounds great."

Sounded so final.

Chapter Fourteen

Jodie was in the bathroom when she heard the sound of a car arriving at the cabin at ten-thirty the next morning. Dev had almost finished packing. DJ was asleep in her bassinet. She hurried out and almost tripped on one of the rugs in the living area. There was a flash of red, parked out front.

Elin.

Her heart sank. Elin was the bossy sister, the one most likely to lecture, the one bluntest when she disapproved. And Jodie was quite sure she'd find something to disapprove of today.

But they had a big hug anyhow, because they were sisters, and in the end bossiness and lectures and bluntness took second place.

"I was sure Mom would be the one to come," Jodie said, while Elin took her overnight bag from the trunk of the car.

"She would have, if I'd let her. We had a great fight about it, her and Lisa and me. I won."

"So I gather."

Elin put her hands on her hips in a pose that said she wanted answers. "What's gone wrong, honey?"

"Nothing." *Make it bright, Jodie, make it casual.* "It's just business. Dev has to be in London. Only for a week. Less, really. Six days."

"Right." If there was one thing Elin was good at, it was communicating that she had a lot more to say, by means of saying nothing at all.

They went inside and met Dev with his luggage, ready to go.

"So fill me in," Elin ordered both of them.

"Well, she has a proper name," Dev said.

"Oh, she does?"

"Dani Jane."

"Your idea?"

"Jodie's."

"Really, honey?" Elin turned to her, face suddenly lit up. "I like it. I love it."

"It feels good," Jodie said. "Although I can't imagine calling her anything but DJ most of the time."

Nobody spoke. The brief moment of harmony and happiness had gone.

Dev studied his watch as if the hands and numbers had all turned back to front. "I should get going." He snapped his mouth shut, then opened it again and growled, "I wish she wasn't asleep."

"She won't wake up if you kiss her," Jodie told him. For some reason, she needed his goodbye to DJ to be a good one.

Only a week, she kept telling herself. Only a week. Less.

But it felt so much more final than that.

Dev was treating it that way. He'd been silent and distant this morning, as if in spirit he was already on the flight, sitting in his business-class seat and opening his laptop, eager to get to work.

He'd said to her from the beginning that the three of them were a family—himself, her and DJ—but it didn't feel that way, right now. This felt like the breakup she'd dreaded last year, the no-strings, no-regrets goodbye she would have said to him—pretended to really mean—when he went back to New York, if the accident and the baby had never happened.

"Please keep your phone switched on," he said to her, as they stood together beside DJ's bassinet.

"Oh, you want Mom to bug me every five minutes?"

"No. So I can call. To see how things are going."

"You can trust me with her, Dev."

"Of course I can."

It was horrible. There was nothing she could safely say. He tossed his laptop in its carrier case onto the front seat and she realized she hadn't seen it when he unpacked on arriving here. Then, he'd had it in his suitcase, out of sight and out of mind. Now, it occupied Jodie's passenger seat, the prime position.

Replacing her.

Making his priorities clear.

He didn't even hug her in farewell, just let his arm trail briefly across her shoulders. "Take care." Gruff, not looking in her direction.

He drove off, she couldn't help watching him with helpless, miserable longing until the car disappeared behind a patch of thick green summer foliage, and then she had Elin to contend with.

"What was that about?" She was still watching down

the road, where every now and then a flash of color or light from his car would reappear.

"I— What?"

"Did you have a fight? Help me, here, Jodie!" She wheeled around, stepped closer, put her hands back on her hips in what was a classic Elin-wants-answers pose. "I can't work out if it's killing him to leave, or if he can't wait. Whichever, I should be mad as hell at him, right? Shoot, I am mad! I could kill him!"

"We didn't have a fight."

"Then what the heck is his problem? What is yours?"

"Elin, I can't take this right now." She closed her eyes, knowing the tears would squeeze through her lashes anyway, and Elin would see them. She waited for the onslaught of critical big-sister words, but they didn't come.

Until finally, quietly, "You're in love with him, aren't you?"

"Only took you a year to work it out, sis."

"A year?"

"Okay, twelve years. Since high school. Not that I've been pining that long, I only thought about him if I happened to see his parents, or in the holidays wondering if he was back for a visit and I might see him. I saw his brother once, and thought for a second, from the back, that it was him."

"Yeah, you haven't been pining at all."

Jodie ignored this. "But last year, when he came back to town, I knew then, and it went bone-deep in a heartbeat, and—"

"And because of the accident, last year seems like yesterday," Elin said, understanding. "And now you have a baby together, and you don't know if that's the best or the worst thing that could have happened. Ah, honey…"

Elin *understood!*

"Real clever strategy on my part, wasn't it?" Jodie said wearily. "Get pregnant, spend eight months in a coma. Ten points for imaginative variation on the shotgun wedding."

"You didn't get pregnant on purpose."

"No. Which is a plus, really. Since it clearly hasn't worked."

"Hasn't worked?"

"He left. Did you notice?"

"For a week. Less."

"Not just a week. His whole heart left. He left, in spirit, a good thirty-six hours ago. The trick with the departing car just now was only an illusion."

"What happened, honey? What changed?"

"Dani Jane smiled at me. For the first time." Even thinking about it, in the midst of her turmoil about Dev, brought a smile to her face. "And I suddenly discovered how to love her. Which I hadn't known before. Did you—? You must have seen. Or suspected."

"We were worried. We thought maybe you just needed more time with your therapy."

"It was more than that."

"We thought a whole lot of things. Jodie, I realize we've behaved like interfering witches, the whole family, but we didn't know. If you would ever wake up. If Dev would want DJ all to himself and we'd never have that part of you, that legacy. And then when you found out about her and it seemed you weren't bonding with her the way you should, we didn't want to make a big deal of it, in case that made things worse."

"Well, it turns out that was what he was waiting for.

The love. The bonding. So he could pull back, get on with his real life, and know DJ was safe and happy."

"Bull. *Bull!*" Elin challenged.

"What?"

"That's *not* what I saw in his face!" she almost shouted. "That's not what that weird, distant goodbye meant, just now, Jodie. He wouldn't do it like that, if you're right about his reasons and his feelings."

"How do you know, Elin?"

"Because I've seen him, remember?" Her voice softened. "I've seen the way he sat by your bed while you were in the coma. I've seen how he bonded with DJ from the moment she was born, how he did everything he needed to do for her without question or complaint, how he fought with Mom—and, yes, with me—over who should be her primary carer and when you should be told about what had happened."

"So…"

"I can't tell you exactly why he went off like that. I really can't. But I can tell you it's not because he's just been waiting all this time to dump the baby on you and get out. I've accused him of that. Lisa has. We…we had a talk after you came here, Jodie, and we both realized we've let our emotions and our fears dictate the pace too much. But we were wrong to say that to him, or to think it, that he wanted to dump her. He loves her. And whatever else is going on—there's something, there's more—I think you need to find out."

"Find out…"

"Call him." It wasn't a request, it was an order. She pulled out her cell phone, made one press and his number was right there. She pushed it into Jodie's hand and pushed the hand to the ear in time for Jodie to hear a recorded message. Switched off, or out of range.

"So we'll go after him," said the bossiest sister in the Palmer family.

"DJ is—"

"Asleep. So we'll wake her up. It's only the first baby whose sleep schedule is the most sacred thing in the family timetable, honey. Once you get to number two and three… She'll live."

"Wh-what exactly are we doing? Saying to him?"

The hands went back on the hips. "Well, have you *told* him? That you love him?"

"No."

"So we're telling him that."

Easy-peasy, Elin.

Elin had a baby carrier strapped in her backseat. Jodie realized just how much the whole family had stepped in to help with DJ, because Elin's own kids hadn't needed special car seats for years. It was frustrating as hell to have so much family interference, and she loved Elin for it this morning with her whole heart.

Elin flirted with the speed limit out as far as the county road and for several miles beyond. There was no sign of the back of Dev's car. He'd had too much of a head start.

Too much of a head start, but what was this dark blue vehicle coming toward them? Elin screamed to a halt on the shoulder, and the blue car halted also, on the other side.

Dev.

Elin's window slid smoothly down. "What did you forget, Dev?" Her hands weren't on her hips this time, but only because they were on the window and the wheel.

"Couple of things." He opened the car door.

Elin climbed out, also. "One big thing, I hope." She

met him in the middle of the road, both of them ignoring the possibility of traffic.

"Yeah, you could say that." He cleared his throat.

Jodie sank into the passenger seat. She wasn't a fearful sort of person, but she was scared right now.

Scared?

Okay, a person was allowed to be scared.

Giving in to it?

No, she *hated* when she let herself do that.

She began the awkward process of going to join them. Maybe the white line in the middle of a county road was the right place for family treaty negotiations, after all.

Elin seemed to have a pretty clear idea of what was going on. She reached out, pulled Jodie closer, sent her in Dev's direction with a commanding nudge. "She's in love with you, Dev," she announced. "And I damn well hope you feel the same. Talk to her. Work it out. I'll be back at the cabin with Dani Jane."

And then she left, screeching through a turn that curved across both sides of the shoulder and made Jodie glad about the regulations on safety for infants in cars.

"Sometimes I'm glad your family is so keen on babysitting," Dev said. He moved to the side of the road, where a line of young sycamore trees gave shade against the summer heat.

She followed him, found a tree trunk to put her hand against, because she wasn't convinced she could stand without support for much longer. "Helps when there are things to work out," she agreed carefully.

He had his gaze fixed on her face, as the sound of Elin's car receded. "What your sister said..." He broke off, swore beneath his breath. He looked like a soldier ready for hand-to-hand combat and she couldn't look away. "Shoot, it almost doesn't matter."

"Doesn't matter?"

"Doesn't make a difference," he explained, frustrated and impatient and bristling with things she couldn't read. "To me."

"Oh."

"Because even if she's wrong about what you feel, I'm stuck with this. I love you, Jodie. Love you. I'm sick at myself, it's killing me."

"Loving me is so…h-horrible?"

"Loving you is horrible when it makes me so scared there isn't any room for me in the mix. When I see you and DJ together and I think my role disappeared, evaporated, the second your bond with her kicked in. I have this horrible jealousy…"

"Of me?"

"No. Of her. I'm jealous of *her*." He stepped closer, close enough to touch, but then he didn't touch her. "Of my own baby. For earning your smile, for earning that soft look on your face that says you have all the answers and everything that matters. For having your arms around her and owning your whole heart." Finally, he touched her, ran his hands around her back, looked into her eyes with his mouth just a few inches from hers. "Jodie, I need you to look like that at me," he whispered. "I need you to feel like that about me. That I'm your world. Not instead of DJ, but as well as her. Both of us. Your world. If Elin's right… Is she right? Can you look like that at me?"

"Aren't I looking at you like that already?" she whispered. "Right now?" She brushed her mouth against his. "You are my world, Dev, you and DJ, and when you left just now and I thought you didn't want that… You always said it and I always believed you. You weren't looking for anything long-term. How could I trust that any of that had suddenly changed? I was so scared. I hate being scared. I always fight it."

"You don't need to be scared about this. You're the bravest person I know. You've showed me that love can be the best adventure in the world, if two people want it to be. It doesn't have to be safe and boring and a massive compromise. And if you'll marry me, we'll make a family for DJ and she'll be part of the adventure, too, and neither of us will be scared of losing her or fighting over her or any of that." He dropped his voice still lower. "Will you, Jodie?"

"Yes, oh, yes." Her body decided to have a say in things at this point, and her legs suddenly wouldn't hold her up. She fell against him and he laughed and it was the best thing that could have happened, because what choice did he have now but to kiss her?

A car went past.

And then another one.

And then two more.

"I guess you could call it brave and adventurous to say yes to a marriage proposal on the shoulder of a well-used road," Jodie teased him.

"Brave and adventurous to *make* a marriage proposal in that situation. Some might say foolish. You deserve roses and candles and champagne and a whole heap of romantic planning, and here I am doing it in the exact opposite way, with no planning at all, and maybe I deserve, 'Do it better and you might get a yes,' but it… just didn't pan out like that."

"What was it John Lennon said? You told me, Dev. 'Life is what happens to you when you're busy making other plans.' I love that it happened like this. Of course

I said yes. We seem to have a history of doing things in the wrong way."

"In our own way. The adventurous way. A family."

"Let's go back. I'm missing her already. And I want to tell Elin."

"Wish the cell phone reception wasn't so good. The whole family will know in about five minutes and it won't be our sweet secret."

"Cell phone…" The outside world intruded, as she thought about it. "You'll miss your flight."

"They can wait a day, in London. I'll be away five days instead of six. It'll still seem like five times too long."

"Oh, it will…"

"But for now, I'm spending the day with family. And the night with my future bride."

Chapter Fifteen

The day Jodie and Dev got married was one of the best days of her life. "Let's not wait," they'd said to each other, and so it happened on a sunny fall day when DJ was still only just learning to sit up, and when Jodie's progress down the aisle of the Palmer and Browne family church was still a little uneven and slow.

The day, Christmas Day, when she and Dev sat DJ on the rocking horse Dad had made for her, was heart-warming and amazing and wonderful.

The day the following spring when she rode Irish for the first time since the accident was pretty good, too. Her friend Bec had kept him in training and given him an hour's workout before the ride, so by the time Jodie climbed into the saddle in the indoor arena at Oakbank, he wasn't in the mood to mistake any of her awkward leg aids as the instruction to go into a full gallop. He nuzzled her after the ride as if to say, "I'm glad to have you back," and if a good part of his appreciation was because of the carrots she gave him, well, that was okay.

The day DJ said her first word—"hot"—the day she took her first steps, the day Dev and Jodie finally tore themselves away from their baby and flew off for a delayed honeymoon in Aruba, were mighty fine days, all of them.

But if you backed her against a brick wall and pointed a water pistol at her head and made her choose the number-one day, the very top, most memorable, wonderful, important day, after eighteen months of wedded bliss, would have to be the one where Jodie discovered that she couldn't stand the smell of ketchup anymore, when it had smelled so good during her rehab.

It was in spring, and DJ had celebrated her second birthday the previous week. She was energetic, happy and talking a mile a minute, even though only her mom and dad could work out what she was saying half the time.

She loved children's music DVDs and playing in the sandbox and petting the ponies at Oakbank. She loved story time and bath time and Daddy coming home. She loved spaghetti and ice cream and strawberries, but her favorite food of all—this month, anyhow—was hot dogs.

Which was where the ketchup came in.

Dani Jane liked ketchup on her hot dogs.

A lot.

"Mo-ore, Momm-eee."

"There's already a big squeeze on it, DJ, honey."

"More, plee-eease?"

"Okay, one more squirt."

They were in the kitchen of their brand-new, log-cabin–style house on their brand-new twenty acres of land adjacent to Oakbank Stables, and Dev was due back from an overnight trip to New York that afternoon.

I can't wait, Jodie was thinking as she squeezed the ketchup bottle, and then she caught the smell of it full in her nostrils and almost threw up and she just knew.

It was a Palmer thing. Mom remembered it. Elin and Lisa had both complained of it. Maddy swore it was nonsense, and then had called Mom from Cincinnati in tears one day to say, "I put ketchup on my fries and then I couldn't even look at them let alone eat them, and I didn't dare hope after we'd been trying so long, but John went to the drugstore and bought a test and *I'm pregnant!*"

I'm pregnant.

DJ ate her hot dog with her mommy being somewhat less patient than usual about how long it took and how much mess there was to clean up. Her nap time should have followed her lunch and she seemed a little surprised when Mommy bundled her into the car and zoomed off down the road to the nearest drugstore.

Dev arrived home at four, when DJ was still sleeping thanks to the late start to her nap, and when Jodie hadn't been expecting him for another two hours. She heard his car and met him at the door. He pulled her into his arms before she could speak and kissed her, hungry and happy and so familiar. "Finished early," he said. "Raced to the airport and took an earlier flight. Glad I've put the international stuff on hold for another year or two. Couldn't wait to see you."

"Me, too. I've been trying to call you. You had your cell phone switched off, I thought you must still be in meetings… Dev, guess what?"

She told him.

He kissed her again, and she found that his face was

wet with tears. She pulled back a little, looked at his wet lashes and narrowed eyes and mouth pressed tight to contain what he felt, and melted at the sight of such a strong man in such a tender state. She took some of the moisture onto her fingertip and showed him. "Wh-why, Dev?"

"Do you have to ask?" he whispered. "Because you're *here,* this time."

"Here?"

"With DJ, you weren't. You weren't present at all, and we both missed out on so much because of it. To have you here, and healthy, and my beautiful wife... Don't you want to cry?"

"I cried the whole afternoon." And she was crying again, laughing and sniffing and feeling crazy happy and emotional at the same time. "I went back and smelled that ketchup bottle three more times just because I could."

He laughed. "There you go."

"Because you're right, and it's just how I felt, too. I wasn't here, for DJ. This time, I'm having two pregnancies in one, and no one is going to stop me."

It was truer than either of them knew. Better than either of them knew. Three weeks later, a routine scan in the dark and quiet of the obstetrician's office showed that in roughly seven months, she and Dev would become the proud and happy parents of twins.

* * * * *